"How are you feel̶ ̶ ̶ ̶ ̶ ̶ ̶ ̶ ̶ ̶ ̶ ̶ ̶ ̶ ̶ ̶ ̶ ̶ ̶ She was all business, addressing him formally, although there was an edge of softness to her tone that only Chris could discern. He'd heard that same softness when her naked body had pressed against his.

"Let's get this over with." He slid back into the bed and yanked the covers roughly over his bare chest, more as a shield than for any particular modesty, and out of respect for the job she was here to do.

To have to talk about this, time and time again, was hard enough. To have to share every last vulnerability in front of Jamie made every primal instinct in him scream.

It's not Jamie—it's Special Agent Michaels standing there watching you.

He rubbed his cheek, bruised and tender from where he landed after the embassy exploded in front of him, remembered cracking his nose back into place on his way to the helo.

She remained standing, nearer to the window than to him. She had a pad on the sill, pen in hand, and she kept her eyes focused on his. "Can you confirm that your team could not save the UN peacekeepers?"

Chris's hands fisted the sheets tightly. "Do you think you'd be here asking me these questions if the mission had gone well?"

"Are you going to answer the question?"

"You don't want to fuck with me now—if you're not going to ask real questions, get out."

"I'm trying to make this easy on you, Chief Petty Officer."

"Well, thank you for that, Agent Michaels. I sure as shit appreciate it." His voice was guttural and Saint shot him a warning look. But he ignored it, too busy watching Jamie.

She didn't react, didn't blink. He wanted to see something from her, but she had her game face on.

HOLD ON TIGHT

STEPHANIE TYLER

A DELL BOOK
NEW YORK

Hold on Tight is a work of fiction. Names, characters, places, and incidents are the products of the author's imagination or are used fictitiously. Any resemblance to actual events, locales, or persons, living or dead, is entirely coincidental.

A Dell Mass Market Original

Copyright © 2010 by Stephanie Tyler

Published in the United States by Dell, an imprint of The Random House Publishing Group, a division of Random House, Inc., New York.

DELL is a registered trademark of Random House, Inc., and the colophon is a trademark of Random House, Inc.

ISBN 978-0-440-24436-3

Cover design: Lynn Andreozzi
Cover illustration: © Alan Ayers

Printed in the United States of America

www.bantamdell.com

2 4 6 8 9 7 5 3 1

Again, for Zoo and Lily—

and for Gus,

who is a wonderful writing companion.

ACKNOWLEDGMENTS

Writing a book is never a solitary process and I have many people to thank for their enthusiasm and unyielding faith in me.

First and foremost, a special thanks to my editor, Shauna Summers, for her wonderful insights and guidance through this entire process.

Thanks to everyone at Bantam Dell who helped make this the best book possible, cover to cover—from Jessica Sebor, who always goes above and beyond to help; to the art department, who rock my world with their awesome covers; and to Pam Feinstein, for being such an amazing copy editor.

Special thanks to Boone Medlock, Bryan Estell, Doug Simmons, and J.D.—all of their military insights and personal stories were invaluable.

Thanks to authors Lynn Viehl, aka PBW, and Holly Lisle, for giving so much of their time to mentor and share their own experiences with so many writers via their blogs. I can't tell you how much this helped me.

Finally, last but never least, thanks to my fellow authors whom I'm proud to call friends, Lara Adrian, Maya Banks, Jaci Burton, Alison Kent, Amy Knupp, and especially Larissa Ione, for all their support in ways too numerous to list.

CHAPTER

1

So I may be tainted in my truth
When I claim I'm bullet-proof
But every half-assed assault
Has been a death by default
—Abby Ahmad, "Tri-Me"

Chief Petty Officer Chris Waldron knew he looked like hell and he felt a hell of a lot worse.

He didn't know how long he'd spent strapped to a bed staring up at a plaster ceiling in some kind of drug-induced haze while his body healed and his mind remained numb.

He floated in and out of consciousness, mainly because the doctors kept waking him up, which was really starting to get on his last fucking nerve.

He'd been a SEAL for eight years, long enough to know that complaining never did anyone much good. But inside his head—man, he was bitching up a storm and a half.

Someone had shoved his iPod earbuds in, and until the

battery died he'd been slightly contented listening to AC/DC's *Back in Black* album in a continuous loop.

He woke himself up singing the chorus of Creedence's "Green River" out loud. The nurse was staring at him as if he was crazy and normally he'd be all *Oh honey, I could give you some of this crazy if you'd just lay yourself down here*.

But not today.

Because even though she was pretty, with a kind face, he realized on some level that his mind could take longer to heal than his body if he didn't start dealing with what had happened. Sex wasn't the answer.

Still, the nurse was so intent on staring at his eyes—the two different colors tended to do that to people—that she'd forgotten about the needle she was supposed to inject into his IV tubing. Now the drug that had kept him foggy hovered in his periphery.

He was slower than normal, but still pretty damned fast. The nurse called for the doctor, but it was too late. He'd yanked the needle out and held the IV pole like a weapon, since they'd confiscated all of his.

"Son, it's all right—you're on a U.S. military base infirmary in Djibouti. The nurse was trying to give you your pain meds but we can talk about it first." The doctor spoke slowly while Chris stared at him, willing himself to believe that, but his body was still reacting—his hand held tight to the IV pole in a fight-or-flight response, and since flight wasn't an option, he was going to bash whoever came near him with the damn pole.

"Chris, come on, man—put that down before you fuck someone up."

It was his CO's drawl, heavy like thick syrup, which meant Saint was as tired as Chris felt.

"No more drugs," Chris told the doctor while he continued to retain possession of the *I won't take any more drugs* pole.

The doctor looked at Saint, who said, "If he needs them, he'll ask."

The doc relented, motioned to Chris for his arm, which was bleeding all over the place, and Chris reluctantly let go of the metal pole.

"Sorry, ma'am," he told the nurse as she put a bandage on his arm.

"You've got a great voice, Chief," she said with a smile. Saint rolled his eyes because normally one comment like that could make Chris a one-man concert. But even though the music was still playing in his head, all he did this time was say, "Thanks."

He remained seated at the edge of the bed once he and Saint were left alone, struggling to get his equilibrium back. He stared down at his bare feet and felt a sudden urge to rip the hospital gown off his body. Which he did promptly, throwing it on the ground while asking, "How long have I been here?"

"Twenty-four hours. You made it to the helo on your own steam."

He didn't remember that fully. The memories were there, but the edges blurred, bleeding into the bigger, slow-moving picture like he was attempting to see clearly underwater.

Cam. His teammate's face was the last thing he remembered seeing before he surrendered to the safety of unconsciousness. "Where's Cam?"

"Already in Germany—he stopped by to see you before he left."

"I remember, thought I was hallucinating."

"You're getting transported there yourself at 0500 for evaluation before they'll take you home."

Chris took stock of the various bruises and contusions on his body—a few stitches here and there, but nothing major. His head, however, was a different story. There was a definite aching throb behind what was left of the narcotics. "Concussion?"

Saint nodded. "No fractures. You're pretty banged up, but you should've been hurt a hell of a lot worse. They held you here so they could run some tests."

Chris closed his eyes for a second and said a silent prayer to his momma, who he was sure was responsible for this one. "Do Jake and Nick know about this?"

"It's been all I could do to hold them back. They're calling every hour on the hour. They weren't going to tell your father but—"

"He knows." His dad always knew when things went wrong—it was next to impossible to hide anything from a parent with second sight. His brothers would've found out by the more traditional routes and were, no doubt, freaking. Not that he would've been any different had one of them been in his position.

"Are you awake enough to answer some questions for me?" Saint asked.

It wasn't really a question, since Saint had already pulled up a chair. His CO had remarkable patience, but Chris could tell it was wearing thin.

He didn't relish this conversation one bit, thought

about Jake and Nick and wished his brothers were here with him now.

He wondered if he'd make it through this without throwing up.

It wasn't every day that you had to tell a man how his best friend died. Their team was close, for sure, with so much history tying all of them together. This was the first tear in the fabric. "Yeah, I'm awake enough."

"What's the last thing you remember about what happened with Mark—what did he say?" Saint stared at him steadily, searching for some kind of answer before Chris even began speaking.

"He told me he was going in, against Josiah's orders. He told me to stay put. I tried to talk him out of it, but he pulled rank. And I don't remember him going in, Saint. I remember every other fucking thing . . . but all I remember is Mark's hand on my shoulder and then . . ."

And *then* Josiah, the FBI member of the Joint Task Force Team and the man in charge of the Op, was arguing with them, angry that Mark had gone in against Josiah's direct order to stand down. Chris and Cam insisted on going into the embassy—which was already taking heavy fire—but they were at least fifteen minutes behind Mark for the hostages. Inside was chaos; they both heard Mark yelling down the hall but they couldn't get that far without leaving the ambassador in greater jeopardy.

"We made a decision to get the ambassador and his wife out and then go back in for Mark," Chris said. "Everything was happening at once and we had a split second."

"Don't second-guess it."

Chris nodded, swallowed hard. "I was just outside the

building, Cam was maybe twenty feet ahead of me, with the ambassador and his wife and their kids close behind. I was backing him up."

"Were you alone?"

Chris thought hard. "No. Josiah was with me."

Chris and Josiah were providing cover, with Chris ready to go back in for Mark, when the explosion rocked the building. He'd been thrown hard, woke up maybe half an hour later, ears ringing and still looking for Josiah and then for Mark.

"And then they killed him," Saint spoke quietly, his voice tight with anger. "The rebels killed Mark and took him away from there so they could have an American trophy rather than leave him in the building to die in the explosion. There are already reports that have the rebels claiming they killed a U.S. Navy SEAL after they'd gotten him to give them some classified information about antiterrorism initiatives."

"There's no way Mark would've given intel." The rebel soldiers might have killed him in the most inhumane way imaginable, but they'd never broken him. Chris was sure of that.

"His body still hasn't been found." Saint spoke quietly, stared at the white wall of the hospital room, a tinge of disbelief in his voice that this was really happening. His jungle greens were fresh, his blond hair damp, as if he'd just showered, but there were circles under his normally bright blue eyes, his mouth pulled into a tight, grim line.

Saint and Mark had come up through BUD/S together, had served in Coronado and had come to Virginia to take charge of Team Twelve.

To leave Mark behind in this country left a knot in Chris's stomach that no amount of IV drugs could take care of. No body meant no closure, signified a failure. "I'm sorry, Saint."

"Don't give me that sorry bullshit, Chris. Mark died doing what he loved. You did everything you could, so fuck the guilt. He'd kill you for it." Saint's words were more than ironic, and more than true, and still Chris knew it would be a long time before he was able to let any of this go.

"They'll keep looking?"

"If they don't, I will. I already told the admiral that." Saint stood, looked toward the small open window, jaw clenched for a second before getting back to business. "You should get some clothes on. There's an FBI agent who needs to hear what you've got to say in more detail."

FBI. *Jamie.*

And he didn't bother to ask Saint if it was her coming to question him, because he could sense her, in the hall, maybe right outside the door.

He caught himself rubbing the fingertips of his left hand together lightly.

"Yeah, it's her," Saint said, catching the familiar, pensive sign that meant Chris was processing something important.

For as far back as Chris could remember, he'd been different, stood apart from everyone but his momma and dad, because he knew things.

Over the years, he'd attempted to convince himself that he was only dealing with a sharper, more refined intuition, that he'd merely honed an ability others never took the trouble to do. His brothers called it *psychic Cajun bullshit* even though they knew, the way Chris himself did, that there was much more to it than that. More than he wanted to think about right now, and so he forced his palm flat against the sheet as Saint asked, "Are you ready?"

Chris wondered how long Jamie had been here, if she'd questioned Cam before he left. She hadn't come in to see him before this—he'd have to be dead not to remember that. "You can let her in."

The Joint Task Force Chris had been a part of on this mission had consisted of himself and Mark; Josiah Miller, a hostage negotiator for the FBI; a Force Recon Marine named Rocco Martin, whose specialty was languages; and a Delta operative named Cameron Moore who had extensive knowledge of the kidnappers as well as the area.

It was a relatively straightforward mission—rescue the four kidnapped UN peacekeepers, the American ambassador and his movie-star wife, who worked as a Goodwill Ambassador and visited many war-torn countries, and their two adopted children. Africa was her newest project—hence, the massive publicity when she and the ambassador arrived in the Sudan.

That was never a good thing in a country like this.

As of today, the ambassador and his family were safe, the UN peacekeepers had been assassinated and all of the men on the Joint Task Force were dead except for Chris and Cam.

Chris reluctantly pulled on a pair of sweats that Saint had brought him, the pain coming on stronger now. But the pain was good—he needed to feel that after days and days of numbness. The burning hot grief was as fresh as if time had stood still while he was out cold.

Nothing was ever going to be the same, especially not after Special Agent Jamie Michaels walked into his hospital room. Her stride was confident, more than necessary, as if trying to hide her hesitancy in seeing him again.

He couldn't blame her—he'd walked away from her two months ago in the DRC and hadn't gotten in touch with her since.

To be fair, she hadn't exactly been knocking down his door either.

"You know Agent Michaels," Saint said, acknowledging the elephant in the room as he pulled his own chair closer to Chris in a show of support.

"How are you feeling, Chief Petty Officer Waldron?" She was all business, addressing him formally, although there was an edge of softness to her tone that only Chris could discern. He'd heard that same softness when her naked body had pressed against his.

"Let's get this over with." He slid back into the bed and yanked the covers roughly over his bare chest, more as a shield than for any particular modesty, and out of respect for the job she was here to do.

To have to talk about this, time and time again, was hard enough. To have to share every last vulnerability in front of Jamie made every primal instinct in him scream.

It's not Jamie—it's Special Agent Michaels standing there watching you.

He rubbed his cheek, bruised and tender from where he landed after the embassy exploded in front of him, remembered cracking his nose back into place on his way to the helo.

She remained standing, nearer to the window than to

him. She had a pad on the sill, pen in hand, and she kept her eyes focused on his. "Can you confirm that your team could not save the UN peacekeepers?"

Chris's hands fisted the sheets tightly. "Do you think you'd be here asking me these questions if the mission had gone well?"

"Are you going to answer the question?"

"You don't want to fuck with me now—if you're not going to ask real questions, get out."

"I'm trying to make this easy on you, Chief Petty Officer."

"Well, thank you for that, Agent Michaels. I sure as shit appreciate it." His voice was guttural and Saint shot him a warning look. But he ignored it, too busy watching Jamie.

She didn't react, didn't blink. He wanted to see something from her, but she had her game face on.

It was time for him to put his on as well. If nothing else, he owed calm and collected to Mark Kendall.

It was Mark's own words that came to mind now, a speech he'd given to the new BUD/S recruits during their first E&E session.

Mark, who'd been captured twice before and escaped, had used his own experiences to pound the recruits under his charge. *Capture comes when you least expect it. Sometimes it's because you lost focus momentarily. Sometimes it's because you let your guard down when you shouldn't have.*

In real life, letting your guard down happens. In combat, it never should.

When anyone would ask Mark if he felt like he had nine lives, he would always answer, *No one's that lucky.*

"I'm going to cut the title crap, call everyone by their first names. I know that's not how you like to operate..."

"I can live with that," she told him, and at least she was focusing on him and not Saint. Progress.

He fought an urge to drop his head into his hands and rub his temples. "You know the mission was to rescue a group of UN peacekeepers who'd been kidnapped outside Khartoum along the road to the British Embassy. They were with an American ambassador and his wife, traveling to a meeting with the Sudanese government because they're trying to adopt a child from the country."

"And they had their own children with them," she added.

"Yes." Losing an American ambassador would be bad enough—losing an internationally beloved movie star and her two small children would've put an international spotlight on both the kidnapping and the failure of the United States to protect their own. It would lead to copycat kidnappings and a breakdown in communications at a time when Homeland Security needed to gain much more cooperation from the Sudanese government. "That trip was a nightmare from the beginning—way too much publicity and not nearly enough protection. They didn't even bring a bodyguard with them to the embassy—a show of good faith."

"I guess they thought that the publicity would protect them," Jamie mused. "That and the peacekeepers."

He didn't answer that, still couldn't get over what the ambassador had done in leaving his family wide open like that.

Jamie pressed on. "From what I've read, your instructions were specific—you were given an exact time and place to meet the rebel soldiers and make the trade."

Except there wasn't going to be a trade. The United States didn't play that way. The trade was supposed to have been a surprise takeout of the rebels. Nothing Chris and his team hadn't done before. Working with the Joint Task Force was new, but all of the men were more than qualified to pull the mission off.

"We arrived hours earlier than the meeting," he explained. "We were on the ground waiting by 0200 and we knew something was off." In fact, all of them had gotten an instant sense of goatfuck.

That was the problem with covert missions—they were so classified, so secret that sometimes getting help to the correct areas was difficult if not near impossible.

"But you didn't leave, didn't radio anyone for clarification, correct?" she asked.

"No, we didn't. We made the decision as a group to move forward. We had the cover of night on our side."

"And by going in early, weren't you afraid of compromising the lives of the peacekeepers?"

He forced his voice to be dispassionate. "Those men had been dead for a long time, probably since the night they'd been kidnapped."

The mud-and-brick makeshift structure where the trade was to have taken place was still hot from the warmth of the day, the stench of death overpowering from the second they'd opened the door. Without even closing his eyes, he could still see the faces of the four men who'd been hanged, the blood pulled from their faces. It had taken him several long moments before he'd been able to force himself to look away.

Jamie paused for a second, the rat-tat-tat of muffled machine-gun fire echoing around the building—a near constant, most familiar sound in this part of the world. "The ambassador and his wife weren't among the dead."

"No. There wasn't anyone else there—I searched the area myself, with Cam. Mark, Rocco and Josiah cut the bodies down and prepared to carry them back down to the beach to the LZ."

But the blast of mortar fire rocked the structure, already precariously built into the mountainside, and the men scattered, looking for cover.

"Rocco was killed instantly," he said bluntly. "The firefight cut off comms on our end. When we got the bodies to the beach, we were given intel that the ambassador and his family were being held at the Sudanese embassy, which was surrounded by Darfur rebels."

"Were you wounded?" she interrupted.

"Most of my injuries occurred after the explosion."

By the time they'd arrived at the embassy—close to dawn—the place was getting rocked. There was as close to a riot as Chris had ever seen, and he and his remaining team members waited quietly by the back wall, assessing the situation.

The carnage was everywhere, victims splayed all along the main area—men, women and children indiscriminately murdered.

But there were signs of life . . . signs that none of them wanted to see or hear. More rebel soldiers than their group of four could effectively deal with.

Of course, that didn't matter—each of them was more than willing to go in, despite their injuries from the earlier skirmish.

But Josiah refused that plan. "We're not going in. It's suicide."

Mark hadn't argued at the time, but Cam had, the pain in his face evident.

Seven hours later, even as Cam and Chris escorted the ambassador and his wife onto the helo, that pain was still there, as if etched forever in the man's features.

It was the screams that had gotten to them, had most likely been what forced Mark into the building against Josiah's orders. Chris had always thought he could get lost inside his own mind, the way he did during capture-training exercises. But nothing could've prepared him for the gut-wrenching cries of the ambassador's wife.

"So Mark Kendall disobeyed a direct order from Josiah."

"Mark sacrificed himself so we could get the ambassador and his family out of there," Chris shot back.

"Did everyone agree with his decision?"

"I was the only one he told, until Josiah realized he'd gone. At that point, the three of us took a vote—Josiah still said no to going in but Cam and I disagreed. Josiah wasn't happy about that, he advised we stay put and refused to come into the embassy with Cam and me. But when I came out the back door, Josiah was there, waiting for me. Ready to give cover."

"How did things escalate from the rescue to the explosion to what happened afterward?"

What happened afterward. What a nice way to put it.

Made it sound like he sat down and had tea after the entire embassy exploded instead of waking up facedown in the dirt, head pounding and ears ringing.

Even now, he still smelled the burning fire, the aftermath of the explosion, as if it was embedded in his senses. "I saw the rebel soldiers carrying Mark's body out of the embassy. The next thing I knew, the building exploded. When I woke up, most of it was down—I couldn't find any of my team members. I circled what was left of the building, looking for signs of life. Still saw none of my team and ascertained that my best course of action was heading to the LZ for backup.

"Who was at the helo when you arrived?"

"Cam."

"So he'd left everyone behind."

He let his gaze flick over her coolly for a few seconds, wondering if he could make her squirm at all.

Nothing. Fuck. "His job was to get the ambassador and his wife and children to safety. That was his charge—his order from Josiah."

"And what's the last thing you remember about Josiah, the last order he gave you?"

"One minute he was next to me. The next, there was no sign of him." Chris heard the small break in his own voice, blamed the dizzying combination of exhaustion, pain and grief.

"What is the last order you received from Josiah?" she persisted.

He practically shot up in bed, which startled her. "There was none, Jamie. At that point, there were no more orders."

"I think we're done here for now." Saint stood and prepared to escort Jamie out, whether she wanted to go or not.

Chris definitely had mixed feelings about that, but Jamie didn't protest.

"Yes, we're done for now. Thank you for your candor, Chief Petty Officer Waldron," she said, her voice tight as she left the room with Saint in tow.

He buried his face in the pillow and mumbled, "Call me Chris. For fuck's sake, Jamie, just call me Chris."

Jamie hadn't seen Chris in two months. Two months, four days, and if she thought hard enough, she could probably figure out the hours and minutes as well.

Pathetic. Completely and utterly pathetic.

Not that she'd thought about him exclusively. No, she'd worked her ass off to forget about the way his body had pressed hers against the floor of the downed plane in Africa.

The way he'd left her standing in the middle of a dirt road in Kisangani when he'd told her, *I can't compete with a ghost, Jamie* . . .

And still, the way he *looked*—and the way he'd looked at her just now . . . he was the one seeing ghosts on this day.

It had been all she could do not to crawl into the hospital bed with him and hug him.

Soft. She was soft and stupid. It was more than obvious Chris couldn't wait for her to leave the room.

He'd looked good—tired, heavily bruised but good. Alive.

"Agent Michaels." Captain St. James came up behind

her, his drawl more pronounced than Chris's was. Chris's CO was handsome, but he wasn't happy.

"Obviously, I'm going to need to speak with Waldron again," she said.

"Interrogate him, you mean."

"I'm sorry about the loss of your teammate, but the FBI lost a man on that mission as well. I'd think you'd want to learn all you can about what happened out there."

St. James's face went hard. "I know all I need to know. And you will not question him any more today—nor will you do so without me there."

"I wouldn't dream of it, Captain."

He nodded curtly in agreement and walked down the hall, away from Chris's room and her, his bearing stiff. She would've bet that, before this, it was as easy as Chris's own gait had been, and she understood.

She hadn't known Josiah, but it didn't matter—he was one of her own as well. The *leave no man behind* creed didn't just apply to the military.

Her stomach lurched, the way it had for the past few days, ever since she'd learned of the failed mission. It had taken three days before she'd been able to ascertain that there were survivors on the Joint Task Force, a day longer to find out that Chris had been one of the lucky ones.

She hated the way Chris's getting hurt affected her, brought her back to that terrible place she'd been last year when she'd been shot and Mike had been killed, when she'd lost her partner and the man who was supposed to be the love of her life all in the same second.

When she met Chris, she'd been in mourning for what felt like forever. Her body ached in strange places it never had before, as if Mike's death opened up a void inside of her that she'd never even known existed.

Chris had immediately responded to her needs, saw her as a female rather than a straight-and-narrow FBI agent and she liked it. It wasn't disrespectful—no, he got it, knew what her job entailed and how she'd worked her ass off to get where she was.

He knew it so well he was able to help her leave her work and her worries behind, if only for a short time.

We're just men and women underneath it all, he'd told her that night as they lay, naked bodies inside the crashed Cessna, waiting for the rain to subside. A life-or-death experience, followed by intense sex—and no, she couldn't blame the danger. The attraction had been electric from the second she'd met him.

The attraction was still there, underneath the tension and the thinly veiled hatred at the job she needed to perform.

That wouldn't be a problem. Practicality was her strong suit—she had always been incredibly logical, while her older sister, Sophie, was the impulsive one.

In Jamie's profession, her traits had never been a liability, nor had they been in her relationship with Mike. But lately, she felt caged in by herself—there were limits to be stretched, and she wasn't sure if it was Sophie's influence or Chris Waldron's, but something inside of her had changed.

Now she just needed to figure out if that change was for the better.

God, this past year of her life had been the longest ever—the hardest probably since her parents had been killed. First she'd lost Mike, and then Sophie hadn't come back home after Jamie had gone to Africa to rescue her—two types of loss, but the sting was equally painful.

Jamie had risked her own life and career to save her sister, only to have Sophie tell her she didn't need or want any help.

Sophie was out there somewhere—alive. And Jamie was never sure if the FBI would ever fully trust her again thanks to the role she'd played in outing the group of government mercenaries who'd stolen her sister from her.

For now, Jamie had been reinstated. But there was always an on-edge feeling following her, a disturbance to her own privacy, which she'd always treasured.

Chris had been there when she'd searched for Sophie in Africa—she'd been forced to tell him that she and her sister had been part of the witness protection program for a long time, since they were both little. But the hows and whys she'd kept to herself, and he'd never pressed.

She didn't like that someone she was investigating knew that part of her past, knew parts of her she hadn't even known existed. And still, she'd known she could trust him with that information.

He'd been right to walk away from her. She hadn't been ready for him. Now she was and he was lying in a hospital bed, expression remote, and she couldn't get a read on him.

She stared at the closed door again and then pushed it open firmly, without knocking. When she thought about Chris, she just *wanted* with an immediacy that both frightened and fascinated her.

He was gone—bed vacated. The sheets were rumpled and there was the subtle scent of cypress left behind. She'd loved the way he smelled and now she resisted the stupidest urge to sniff his pillow.

She wasn't about to screw up her job . . . which was exactly what she was doing by being in Chris's room right now.

There was water running in the bathroom. Of course—he wouldn't simply leave the hospital. She turned to leave quietly, when Chris's voice rose up from behind her.

"How's PJ?" he asked. She froze, her hand already on the doorknob, surprised by the intimacy of the question.

She turned to him—he looked more like his old self now, six feet six inches of cocky arrogance, complete with crazy eyes and a wide smile. Half Cajun, part gypsy and who knew what else combined to make him the most down-to-earth man she'd ever met in her life and also the most mystical.

Water ran down his body—all lean, tan muscle on display—and he stood there, dripping on the floor without bothering to reach for a towel.

"My sister's name is Sophie. And I wouldn't know. She hasn't gotten back in touch."

"I'm sure she's worried about you too."

"Yeah, I've been hearing that one my entire life. Everyone seems to forget I'm more than capable of taking care of myself." Coming back in here alone had been a mistake, and so she turned and left the room, closing the door like a shield between them. And still, she had to hold on to the wall for a moment to get herself back under control.

She'd been deep in thought, hadn't realized Chris had opened the door and was standing watching her, leaning on the door frame for dear life. He was in pain—physical, emotional, it probably didn't matter. Right now he was suffering in every way possible.

"Would you have come here to see me if you weren't assigned this case?" he asked.

Tell him no. He walked away from you. "I don't know." The words tumbled out before she could stop them.

He smiled then—a small one but it still tugged the corners of his mouth. "So you're going to run away from me again?"

"I wasn't the one who ran last time."

"I might have been the one who took the walk, but you were the one running from our relationship. Make no mistake about that, Jamie," he told her before he went back inside the room and shut the door behind him.

The power went out a second later.

Her first instinct was to look for an escape route, because that's what she'd been trained to do.

But Chris's door opened again. "Stay away from the stairwell." His voice was calm even as he tugged her arm gently to pull her back into his room. She conceded, let him shut the door behind them once she was inside.

"What's going on?"

"Power's out."

"Thanks for that update. The hospital has to have a generator." As she spoke, the lights flickered back on and then off again, and then they came on dim, like they were running at less than half power. "Well, that's something, at least."

"Yeah, something," Chris said as the floor beneath their feet began to shake and the window cracked from mortar fire.

The base, which really consisted of a couple of administrative buildings, a bunker for troops and this two-story hospital clinic, was getting rocked. Chris had suspected it wouldn't take much for that to happen and this live fire experience was making his already pounding head not very happy.

Over the loudspeakers, a general announcement blared. "Patients, please remain in your rooms and stay away from windows if at all possible."

"Let's get into the bathroom to wait this thing out—no windows in there," he said, just as the window close to his bed shook and then shattered, glass spraying everywhere.

And then Jamie was yanking him into the safety of the smaller room. He went off balance for a second, grabbed for the wall and nearly fell onto her. He was more fucked up from the pain meds than the actual pain and he hated that.

Seconds later the lights went out again.

"It's okay, I've got you," she was telling him as she eased him down to the floor. And as much as he liked hearing that, helplessness was something he did not do, at least not well. He jerked his body from hers, painfully aware that all he'd wanted earlier was for her to touch him and he blamed his irrationality on the past days' events. On grief and stress and pain.

She pulled away and for a moment they sat in the dark, listening to the rumblings just outside the door, before she spoke again. "Look, about before . . . I was just—"

"Doing your job. I know the drill, Jamie." He rubbed his forehead as the floor continued to shake, the vibrations going straight through his skull more effectively than a jackhammer. He wanted to close his eyes, to try to block it all out, but that wouldn't happen. The second his eyes closed, he'd see the entire scene of what had transpired twenty-four hours before. "Fuck, I don't want to be here."

"I'm really sorry." Her hand settled on his knee and he let it stay there.

"You were sorry the last time we were together in Africa too."

She shifted in the dark so she was closer. "I'm sorry about what happened to you and your team. About what happened in Africa. God, I was so worried when I heard about this..."

"I've been worried about you too. I guess neither of us acted that way earlier." No blame to his voice, not now, when she was seated close to him.

"Answering all my questions is for your own good, Chris. If I can dismiss this investigation as quickly as possible, you can get back to work."

Back to work. That seemed like a long way down the list, after mourning Mark and the failed mission. "I've told you everything I know. It was mass confusion. Always is, no matter how hard you try to control the situation."

"But you're trained to see above the confusion."

"You can't see shit when you're in it." He shook his head. "I'm human, Jamie, even though my ability to snipe might make it seem otherwise."

An explosion made the door rattle behind him, jogging his memory. "The door..."

"It's all right."

"No, not this door—that night I tried to get behind a door at the embassy. Josiah and I both did. It was locked."

He rested his head against the wall. "Whatever was behind that door was what blew that building sky high."

"You're sure?"

"Shit like that doesn't happen from RPGs."

"Hand grenades?"

"Wouldn't level an old stone, highly secured building. It took down a bomb-proof wall. No, there were explosives in that building already . . . like they'd planned it. Only they wanted us inside."

Another explosion shook the hospital in short order—went on for much longer than any of the previous ones and made Jamie nearly hit the ceiling. Chris hadn't fared much better, but her hand squeezed his biceps and hung on for dear life.

He brought his hand up to cover hers. "You okay?"

"I could never get used to this," she breathed.

"My life stopped flashing before my eyes a long time ago," he admitted.

"Wish I could say the same. And don't give me any of that *fear is good* psychobabble."

"I didn't say I didn't have fears." He winced when another large boom shook the floor and the walls, rattling his teeth.

"They're getting closer." She peered out the door before turning back to him. "Maybe we should try to get downstairs."

"Maybe not." His hand trailed her cheek. She'd missed that touch, found her head tilting toward his and then—

"Chris, what the fuck?" Saint had burst through the bathroom door holding a flashlight and Jamie jumped again.

"Nice entrance, Rambo," Chris drawled.

"Fuck off, Waldron. Agent Michaels, I thought we had an agreement."

"I didn't plan the assault so I could question him further."

"Could we not talk about me like I'm not here?" Chris asked. He sounded tired, even to his own ears.

As soon as Jamie rose from the floor, he missed the contact of her body near his.

"You're not allowed to leave the hospital until the shelling's over and the base is secured," Saint told her. "But you're sure as hell not staying here with him. There's a safe room set up down the hall for visitors."

Chris wanted to argue, but knew it was no use. Instead, he pulled himself to standing in time to see the door slam. Jamie was gone. Again.

CHAPTER
2

After finally escaping the war zone of the hospital six hours after she'd left Chris, Jamie planned to spend the rest of her evening holed up in the hotel outside the military base, trying her best not to think about Chris Waldron as anything other than a case.

Impossible, of course. Even as she rustled through her bag to find the candy bars she'd packed, she knew fooling herself wasn't an option any longer. But still, she finished transcribing her report and e-mailed it to her supervisor. Case closed, she hoped. She'd fly stateside tomorrow morning.

A knock on the door—quiet and firm—had her on her feet in seconds. She peered through the peephole, gun in hand, as was her habit when traveling alone on an investigation, and saw Chris. He'd stepped away from the door so she could actually see his face rather than just an eyeful of camouflage.

She threw the safety on the gun and flung the door open.

"What are you doing out of the hospital?"

"Running after you."

"No one asked you to."

"I've only got an hour."

"That's not my concern. Especially if you're out against medical advice," she told him, knowing full well none of this would make him leave.

Those eyes—one blue and one green, their colors made more vivid by the bruises that surrounded them—bore into her with an intensity that rocked her to the core. "What is your concern, Jamie? Because whatever it is, I want it to be me. Me on you—in you. I've missed hearing your moans in my ear, missed coming inside you."

Her mouth dropped. Without thinking, without wanting to think, she grabbed the front of his shirt and yanked him close, tipped her face up to meet his kiss.

He groaned, and she knew that was at least part pain, but he wasn't pulling back, practically had her naked before she could close the door to the room.

Chris wouldn't mind rolling around the hallway naked—rolling anywhere naked. The fact that he wanted to do so with her only made the ache between her legs intensify, until he put his hand there, stroked her quickly with two fingers until she stiffened, mouth opened to moan through an orgasm that took over her body. The intense spiral of pleasure made her knees buckle, and still she pushed her hips forward against his hand for more.

"So fast, Jamie... were you waiting for me all this time, wanting me?" His drawl was more pronounced now, a slow, easy slide down her body. The way he talked to her while she was naked in his arms gave her nearly as much pleasure as his hands; his tongue; his long, thick arousal he rubbed against her belly.

Her shiver gave him the answer he looked for. He chuckled lightly, his fingers still strumming her. Her nipples tingled and she resisted the urge to play with them herself.

She pulled her face away from where she'd buried it in his shoulder, realized they were still standing—she was holding him for dear life and he was pressed against the wall by the door. "You knew I was, or else you wouldn't be here."

"Don't be so sure about that. I can be pretty persuasive either way." He leaned his head back and closed his eyes momentarily.

"You're still in pain." She stroked his cheek lightly, her bare breasts seeking relief in brushing the hard rub of his fatigues.

"Little bit."

"Then maybe you should let me do all the work," she murmured. He didn't argue, not when she unzipped his fatigues and stroked him, just sucked in a hard breath and smiled—and oh, that smile...

His hands wandered over her breasts—finally—fingers playing with her taut nipples as she continued to caress his cock in her palm.

"Hurry, Jamie," he said suddenly, his hands grabbing at her hips, urging her against him again. His arousal brushed her wet sex and yes, she was more than willing to hurry.

But this time, they weren't on a downed plane in Africa, away from most forms of civilization, and her mind was clearer. Somewhat. "Protection. We need—"

He was staring at her, head cocked to the side while she spoke. And then he shook his head like he was clearing it and pulled a condom out of his pocket, rolled it on quickly. "I remembered this time."

It was her turn to tell him, "Hurry." She pushed his pants down over his hips, freeing him.

Despite his injuries, he had her back against the wall, legs around his waist. He entered her in one excruciatingly slow stroke and they stayed that way for a moment, both speechless, eyes locked.

When he moved again, her eyes went wide and a gasp escaped her throat. He braced himself with his hands, palms flat on the wall behind her as he began to rock his hips harder and faster.

"First time since Africa?" he asked.

She nodded, because she was damned near incoherent as he pressed into her, long strokes that filled her to the hilt, his cock throbbing inside of her.

"We always . . . end up . . . like this," he panted, his breath warm in her ear. "Want a chance to take . . . my . . . time . . . Fuck, Jamie."

She came first, he was right behind, struggling to stay on his feet as she clung to him, not caring about anything but the way he made her feel.

She groaned when he pulled out, eased her legs down, and once her feet were on the floor she finally let go of him.

He remained close, his forehead pressed to the wall above her head, his breath quick.

"Are you okay?"

"Fucking-A right I'm okay," he muttered, his hand warm on her belly, as if to keep her in place near him. "Just need a minute."

She started to reach up to stroke his hair and stopped herself, pulling back the way she had months earlier. This time, it was for far different reasons. "About today…"

"Let's not go there again," he said. And she didn't push it further. Granted, she'd just gone way out of bounds, but the case itself was simple. Unfortunately straightforward, with a horrible toll. Heartbreaking for him and seemingly over for her.

"Seriously, why did they let you out? I didn't think the hospital gave out passes."

"Yeah, they kind of don't." He shrugged. "They don't exactly know I'm gone. Well, no, that's not true, two people know. I promised I'd be back before midnight."

"You shouldn't have done that—you're hurt."

"I needed to," he said simply. "I couldn't sit staring at those walls anymore. Couldn't relive it for another second. At least this way, I've gotten an hour of peace."

He pulled away from her and began to straighten his clothes. She did the same, attempted to button her shirt back up until she realized most of the buttons had gotten torn off. She opted for a T-shirt instead, and then walked him to the elevator—out of concern for his health, she told herself. Nothing at all to do with the fact that he'd wound his hand into hers and tugged her along like they were teenagers on a date.

She and Mike had never done PDA, not so much out of concern for their jobs, but because that wasn't who they were. With Chris, his touching her seemed as natural as breathing.

"I want to see you again, after we get home," he told her when the elevator doors opened.

"I don't know if what we've got between us is anything more than sex and danger." She pulled her hand from his. "When I'm with you, I want to be reckless. And I don't think that's good for me."

He nodded, slowly. "You may be able to lie to yourself pretty well, but don't bother trying to lie to me." He remained facing her as he backed into the elevator. "You should never turn your back on a second chance."

She didn't move until the doors closed completely and then she turned away reluctantly and headed to her room alone.

Second chances. She'd had more than her share over the years. Whether or not she was open to another remained to be seen.

Her cell phone, which had been tossed aside earlier, was ringing when she returned to the room. After a second of fumbling under the bed, she fished it out of her jacket pocket and answered. "Michaels."

It was her supervisor, Lou Carter. "Michaels, I've read your report. We've gotten further intel that makes it necessary for you to revisit the case. You're going with Chris Waldron on the transport to get him back to the States."

"What's going on?"

"Waldron's under investigation, along with Cameron Moore. You'll take both men's statements again."

"What are they under investigation for?"

"Josiah Miller was killed before the explosion. Single bullet to the head."

"Why does that implicate Chris Waldron and Cameron Moore?"

"According to what I'm seeing in your report, Josiah Miller gave the order that no one was to go into the embassy. Mark went in against Josiah's orders."

"Once Mark went into the embassy, the remaining three men took a vote—Cam and Chris decided to go in and Chris said Josiah joined them in the end at the embassy," she explained, the way Chris had told it to her.

"Then why was Josiah Miller killed by a single sniper shot, right between the eyes? Why was his body found nowhere near the explosion sight, with no signs of being taken down by the blast?"

Her breath caught for a second. "I don't know, sir."

"Well, you're going to find out. ASAP."

There were two things Chris knew well: his rifle and a woman's body. With either, he could spend hours studying their intricacies, their individual quirks and hot spots... their flaws.

He knew when either one was going to jam up and let him down or settle in to give him the shot of his life. Rifles and women—he loved them both, and not necessarily in that order.

His fingertips had itched from the second he'd touched

Jamie's bare skin, from when he'd pressed his lips to the pulse point on her neck and smoothed his palm across her belly.

For fuck's sake, Jamie was pregnant.

Chris let that news settle into his post-orgasm, still half-sedated brain as he caught a ride back to the base hospital. He would've walked, because he needed air, but midnight and Africa, weapon or no weapon, didn't mix well.

The baby was his—had to be.

Jamie didn't even know herself. He couldn't explain how *he* knew, except for the fact that he came from a long line of gypsies and midwives, had been raised around women in labor until it became the most natural thing in the world to him. He'd delivered so many impromptu babies himself it had become a running joke not to let any woman past her eighth month come into contact with him. Add to that the fact that both his momma and his dad were honest-to-goodness psychics, evidenced by the fact that neither he nor his brothers could ever get away with shit growing up, and yeah, he was always right about things like that.

She wasn't quite glowing yet—no, she looked tired, worn out. Probably didn't know why she'd been feeling like crap lately.

She still looked fucking beautiful to him. Tough and regal all rolled into one long, lean package. And at that moment he didn't give a shit that she'd come there to investigate him—her admission outside his door that afternoon told him what he needed to know.

The way she'd let him hold her hand on the way to the elevator told him even more.

Sneaking back into the hospital was easy enough. After

he'd stripped down and shoved on the stupid hospital gown so as not to draw any more attention to himself, he thanked the guy who'd lent him the gun and the cammies.

His bag, which had been brought in from the helo, contained only dirty clothing. His weapons were with Saint, who would bring him fresh fatigues in a few hours for the trip, so for now he pulled the hospital garb off, shoved his sweats back on and powered up his cell phone to call his brother.

Jake answered on the first ring. "You're all right."

"Yeah, I'm all right." He paused, throat tight. "But Mark..."

"Fuck, Chris. Just fuck." Jake's voice was hoarse.

"Yeah" was the only thing he could say in response, the only thing he needed to say. And for a few minutes there was silence over the line as the two men shared their grief together.

Jake spoke first. "Saint said the FBI came by to see you."

"I'm sure he said more than that."

"She still hot?"

"She's all right." Chris smiled to himself as he lay against the pillow. His window hadn't been repaired but someone had taken out the remaining jagged glass, so the sounds of soldiers on night watch on the base floated through, gave him comfort that a civilian hospital wouldn't.

He'd see Jamie tomorrow. Maybe, when they landed, he could spend some more time with her, figure things out.

Christopher wasn't speaking to him. It was the second time in twenty-seven years his son had done this—it had cut Kenny to the quick the first time and was much worse now.

It didn't matter that he understood his son's struggle, probably more than Chris did himself. But sitting here in a stadium in Texas, clutching his cell phone in his hand so he wouldn't miss a call and surrounded by blaring music and the thousands of fans there to watch the first leg of his band's big comeback tour—a success, to be sure—Kenny hated every second of the non-contact.

Nick had called to reassure him that physically Chris was fine, as did Jake, multiple times, even though neither of his other sons had seen Chris in person yet. And their *He's all right* rang hollow on both ends, because they all knew Chris was far from all right. None of them were.

His sons had suffered losses, had seen and faced death multiple times, but Mark Kendall's death, his sacrifice, was something they'd be struggling with for a long time.

"Great comeback, Kenny." One of the record execs clapped an enthusiastic hand on his shoulder and he nearly jumped out of his skin. "We didn't think they'd be alive this long, never mind performing."

Yes, Kenny had brought this particular band back from the dead, so to speak—got them through rehab and divorces and kept them hidden from the paparazzi until they were ready for public consumption.

Now the band was all about the music. The members thanked Kenny over and over again for helping them find their way back to where they'd started—back to the beginning.

"They're good kids" was all Kenny told the exec before excusing himself. He pushed his way through the front-row crowds, toward backstage, where it was no less loud and chaotic, and finally found a small, empty dressing room to rest and think about his boys.

"It doesn't make sense, Kenny," his young wife had whispered twenty-seven years earlier on that snowy Christmas Day morning. "They told me I'd have three boys."

"I don't know, Mags." He'd been lying on her hospital bed, where she'd been rushed after the home birth had gone wrong. He'd almost lost both the small baby they'd named Nicolas Christopher and his wife. The doctors and nurses looked at both of them as if they were too young to have tried any of this; to be sure, he and Maggie had married young—they'd only been seventeen, and she'd gotten pregnant the first month of their marriage, but none of that mattered, none of that had been the cause of this.

"She can't have any more children," the doctor told Kenny bluntly, as if Maggie wasn't in the room, as if she couldn't hear what he was saying. Kenny didn't bother to tell the man that Maggie had known the diagnosis from the second she'd given birth—maybe even sooner. Being of gypsy blood, Maggie had been born with the gift of second sight in the same way Kenny had, although her gift was stronger.

Both knew they wouldn't have an easy path in life because of it; despite often being called a gift, psychic power could easily become a burden, a drain on the soul.

"A reason for everything," Maggie murmured as she brushed the top of their baby boy's head. "You'll explain it, right, Chris?"

And so, in spite of his birth name, their son had always been called Chris, because Maggie deemed that calling their boy Nicolas hadn't felt right.

Of course, years later, when both Nick and Jake came into Chris's life—with a literal bang when Nick threw a chair at Chris in the principal's office and all three boys had gotten suspended—it made perfect sense. Maggie had smiled and brought all three boys back home; together they'd discovered that Jake was being abused by his step-father, and that Nick was being neglected by his own family. Their decision to take the boys with them to Virginia came right after Jake's stepfather tried to kill him and, in the process, died himself. Maggie knew the New York foster care system wouldn't miss having another case to manage.

Nick's situation was slightly more difficult, but solved when his very wealthy and politically connected family agreed to let Kenny and Maggie take him in exchange for Nick forfeiting any rights to the family fortune. And so, Jake and Nick remained in their lives as their sons and Maggie's prediction was complete.

Maggie's death nine months later had been a surprise to everyone but Christopher.

Later, looking back, both Kenny and Chris realized that his momma's hadn't been the first death he'd predicted. No, he'd forced his thoughts about his grandparents, an aunt and a neighbor out of his mind efficiently.

Kenny had tried to tell Chris that was normal, but could barely get the words out before Chris was stomping away from him in some kind of teenage haze of angst and rebellion.

Before Maggie died, there had been nothing to rebel against. They'd never set boundaries for the boys, and all three had been content with the new living situation. But after . . . he'd wanted to rein all three of them in after practically disappearing for months.

None of it had sat well with his boys.

Chris had been described as having clairsentience, or clear-knowing, had told himself after his momma's death that he'd refuse it if it ever happened again, read extensively on how it happened so he could block it.

He'd never been able to, never would be. And all of it was about to play another role in his life, or had already. Kenny was helpless to do anything—and like all three of his boys, he didn't do helpless well.

He could almost hear Maggie whispering in his ear, her heavy accent telling him, *It's Chris's mountain,* cher. *He has to climb it alone because there's no way to get around it.*

He sighed and punched the numbers on his phone so he could hear Jake and Nick's voices again.

Five A.M. came much too fast. The military medevac was waiting on the tarmac to transport Chris to Germany and then back home to the States.

Jamie slung her bag across her body and walked out to meet the pilot, who looked over her ID and granted her clearance.

Within minutes, Chris and Saint walked out together, an orderly attempting to corral Chris into a wheelchair.

Chris spotted her immediately—his wide smile nearly breaking her. She forced herself to stay strong, even as his long strides brought him face-to-face with her in seconds.

"You didn't need to meet me here. It's early," he murmured. "But I'm glad you did."

"I did have to meet you here," she said, but Saint cut her off before she could say anything more.

"Agent Michaels, to what do we owe this pleasure?"

"Chief Petty Officer Waldron, I need to speak with you again," she said, and his face hardened instantly. He took a step back and waited. "The FBI has decided to continue the investigation."

His mouth opened and then closed and then opened again. "You're still investigating me?"

"Yes."

"Saint, I need to speak with Agent Michaels alone."

Saint shook his head, as if he didn't like that idea, but he walked away.

Chris took her by the elbow and led her back toward the building. "Did you know about this last night?"

"Not until after you left."

"What the hell is it all about?"

"Josiah was killed."

"I know that, I was there."

"There's evidence that he was killed before he ever had a chance to hold cover with you at the embassy."

"He was a member of my team. What's my motive, Agent Michaels?"

"That's what I'm investigating."

"You think I killed Josiah during the mission?"

"I don't know what's true right now, that's why I need to dig further into exactly what happened that night—step by step. I'm hoping I have your full cooperation."

He snorted at her. "So what, am I under some kind of surveillance? Am I being arrested?" he asked angrily.

"I need to escort you back home to Virginia. And then you'll be turned over to the Navy's jurisdiction."

"What about Cam?"

"He's been questioned. His story corroborates yours."

"So you're going to keep us separated and see what you can do to change that, right?"

She didn't comment. Couldn't, mainly because her throat had tightened, mouth dried. He could have easily turned her in for last night, because even though he'd been the one to approach her, she hadn't stopped him.

"So much for second chances, Jamie." He brushed past his CO and headed onto the plane alone.

She had no choice but to follow.

CHAPTER
3

"You can't just keep breaking up with him and coming back like this, Jules." Chris's adopted brother Nick was barely able to keep the anger out of his voice.

He only did so out of respect for Chris, and for her brother, Glen, who was one of their childhood friends as well. Jules Sinclair knew that if she pushed it, though, she'd feel his wrath.

But something he said snapped her away from thinking about his temper. "What are you talking about, me breaking up with him?" she demanded as she stood in the kitchen of Chris's childhood home, the place he still lived now, with Nick and their other brother, Jake.

Jake sighed loudly and gave her an *Are you fucking*

kidding me? look—that hadn't changed from high school—and then spoke to her as if she was a small child. "You keep breaking up with him, the way you broke up with him back in January."

She stared between Nick and Jake, the exhaustion she'd felt earlier quickly fading with the sharp sting of their accusations. "I don't know what your brother's been telling you, but you're wrong. Chris is the one who broke up with me."

Jake opened his mouth and then closed it, while Nick merely stared at her, and yes, neither of them had an answer for that one.

She crossed her arms and waited for the inevitable response. Because although they could say many things about her, they knew she wasn't a liar.

"Having her here is not a good idea," was all Jake could say.

"I'm not leaving until I see him." Chris's dad, Kenny, had called to let her know that Chris had been hurt and she'd gotten a private jet in the middle of the night to take her from L.A. to Virginia, back to where she'd grown up. Where she'd fallen in love with Chris Waldron, where she'd left him to pursue first a modeling and then an acting career.

She was twenty-nine years old, rapidly on her way to becoming one of the highest paid actresses—she had her pick of movie roles and of men, and she still couldn't shake Chris from her mind. "I'm very sorry about your teammate."

"Thanks, Jules," Nick said, and Jake just nodded in her direction.

"I have to be here. You don't understand, when I heard . . ."

She didn't say anything further. They did understand.

Whether she and Chris were together or not, he was—they all were—too big a part of her life to ever forget.

And being here in this house again, forgetting was next to impossible. It was different inside now though, Maggie's touch fading through the years as new furniture replaced old, dark paneling a startling contrast to the lighter paint, the leather furniture, pictures of Chris and his brothers from younger days littering the walls.

This was a home for men, not boys, and yet when she'd walked through the front door, she was sixteen years old again on a hot summer night, her skin warm and tan from a day at the beach, her lips bruised from kissing Chris in the backseat of his car.

Even then, his hands held magic. He'd never really been a boy, and he'd been the best thing to walk into the high school cafeteria.

"Jules . . ."

Nick's rough voice broke through her reverie. She'd been tracing a picture of Chris and Maggie with her finger a black-and-white photo, hastily snapped and slightly off center, with a four-year-old Chris running half-naked through the bayou, Maggie standing in the background, watching and smiling. "Please, Nick, I just need to see him."

"Tomorrow. Give him a day. There's a lot coming down on him."

Nick's green eyes were so serious, had always been so even when he'd been young and carefree. But that had been her own illusion—none of these men had ever been truly carefree. "Please tell him I'm here. For him."

————

After nearly sixty hours of straight traveling, Jamie was tired and grimy and tense, her shoulders aching from holding herself so tightly together. There'd been tension ten feet deep on the plane even though Chris had slept—or pretended to—for the majority of the flight time, in between checking out fine in Germany and proceeding onward back home.

She'd stayed with Chris and Saint until the military transport landed in Virginia just after five P.M., and then he was officially turned over to the Navy's custody. And she'd left him there, watched him get into his CO's car and drive away before she'd wearily climbed into her own black SUV and driven home.

She'd go to the office in the morning. Now she needed a shower, needed to regroup and figure out if she should bow out of this investigation based on the fact that she'd slept with the witness.

But when she pulled in her driveway, she stopped the car dead, jerked it hard into park and sat staring at her front steps.

Sophie was sitting there in the early spring chill. She wore some kind of shawl and ripped-up jeans, looked like a cross between a rock star and a model. At thirty-four, she was prettier than she'd been when she was younger. Haughtier too.

She'd chopped off all her hair, so it fell in a gaminelike fringe around her face, the dark color a strong contrast to her smooth ivory skin and big brown eyes, which looked dark and haunted, even from Jamie's view through her windshield.

"I was going to call," Sophie told her as soon as Jamie forced herself out of the car, but Jamie stopped her.

"I can't do this—not now, Sophie. I'm tired. And you can't walk back in, just like that, after the way you pushed me out of your life."

Typical Sophie, didn't offer an explanation, merely shrugged, stood and picked up the large duffel sitting next to her. She swung it over her shoulder and prepared to leave.

"I didn't say you needed to leave; you can stay here. I just . . . I just need some time tonight." Jamie leaned tiredly on the railing.

"You're still really angry with me."

"How long did it take you to figure that out, Sophie?"

"I'd prefer it if you called me PJ."

Jamie's head began to throb. "I'm not calling you by that name."

"You're upset that I didn't fall all over you for saving me."

"You really think that's what I'm upset about? Fine, *PJ*, if you're coming in, come in. If not . . ."

But Sophie was already walking away from the house, down the driveway.

"No wonder I'm so good at running," she muttered as she watched her sister's retreating back.

For a few minutes, she thought about going after Sophie, apologizing. But then her stubborn streak kicked in and she went inside instead, too tired to argue with anyone anymore.

She flipped on the lights and stood uncertainly in the foyer, because sometimes when she walked in after being away for a bit, it hit her.

She lived alone.

She'd never been alone before Mike's death—she'd moved from her foster father's house to college. After that, she roomed with another FBI trainee and then she'd moved into Mike's house, first as his roommate while looking for her own place and then later as his lover.

But she'd been on her own now for ten months, refused Kevin, her foster father's invite to stay with him and his wife, Grace, who'd reluctantly helped raise Jamie and her sister. No, this was her time to grow up. To fly, at twenty-eight years old.

She couldn't seem to do either correctly. Plus, she still slept with the gun under her pillow. Cliché, but true, because there was no alarm system in place. With Mike, it hadn't felt necessary and since his death she couldn't bring herself to have one installed. To admit failure. It would prove that she couldn't get over her past.

Instead, she was up most nights, waiting to hear from Sophie and wondering if things would get better.

When Jamie had returned from Africa two months ago, things seemed better. Now she wasn't so sure. She'd certainly screwed things up with Sophie just now—so wasn't sure if she was angrier at herself or her sister.

What a mess.

She dropped her bag by the door, locked it behind her securely and kicked off her shoes on her way through the living room. And then she stopped short.

Things had been moved.

She was meticulous in everything she did and her house was no exception. Nothing seemed to be missing, just... moved. Her living room furniture was rearranged a bit—

the chairs neatly placed across from the couch instead of one under the window and the other next to the couch, the way she'd left them.

A walk into the kitchen showed that the four-person table had been moved as well. Dishes were all in the cabinets but they'd been rearranged too—not everything, but enough to trip the alarm bells in her mind. She'd done this for too long not to react.

Cold. She was cold, and with her gun pulled she went to the bedroom and grabbed a sweatshirt. Nothing in here had been touched—clothing still in the same place, both in the drawers and in the closet. Had she come home too soon, foiled someone's plans?

Or did they intend to come back?

She should call someone. The police. Kevin. Her supervisor. But she didn't call any of them, just sat on the floor and forced herself to breathe.

And that's when she saw the small vase full of fresh flowers, sitting on her dresser—the same way it always was after Wanda had been there.

Wanda was here while I was gone. Dammit. She put a palm to her forehead and remembered the housekeeper she and Mike had hired years ago to come in twice a month. Wanda had a key.

Typically, the woman didn't rearrange things but she was always on Jamie to change things up. Jamie had grown tired of explaining that she liked things the same and made sure she worked late on the days Wanda was here. She always came home to a vase of flowers, fresh from Wanda's garden.

Jamie had *definitely* done this for too long—twenty-two

years of being in hiding with witness protection, even though the first two were relatively uneventful, did not get easier over time.

Heart beating too fast, she put the safety on the gun and left it on the table next to the bed. She sank into the mattress and shook her head, glad no one else had been around to see her overreact.

Her head began the familiar throb—by morning, she'd have a full-blown migraine if she didn't take medicine. But she hated the meds; they made her feel loopy and not like herself. Kind of the way she was around Chris.

She didn't want to like Chris Waldron. Didn't want to get involved with him, sleep with him or find herself fascinated by him. Didn't want him to know the things he did about her past. She'd exorcized him from her life two months ago. The only place she'd been unable to rid herself of him was in her dreams. At night, in the dark, her hands would trail over her body the way Chris's had in that dark, downed plane, and she could hear the rain strumming the roof as she touched herself.

The sensation was never the same, left her with a big, empty ache that forced her to curl into a ball until morning light. And when morning did come, she was that cool, confident woman again. She was capable.

No, she hadn't told Chris Waldron everything. And she never would.

CHAPTER

4

The JAG lawyer was waiting for Chris and Saint in the admiral's office. The admiral himself was long gone, but insisted that Chris meet with the lawyer that night, *Before more of this shit comes down on Chris's head,* he'd said irritably.

Saint and the lawyer spoke, while Chris focused on the large TV screen in the corner of the room, displaying CNN.

"Five went in, two came out. It was a dangerous mission. They're all dangerous. But when major world figures go to Africa and bring massive publicity with them, there's going to be trouble," Saint was saying, even as an interview of the ambassador and his wife was displayed in living, breathing Technicolor across the screen.

They'd been on every major news media outlet since their escape, praising the military for the action it took. However, the actress mourned the loss of African lives, as well as those of the peacekeepers. All Chris could hear when he watched her speak were her cries.

She still bore bruises on her cheek and arms, although she swore she hadn't been raped. She'd told Cam that the men who'd kidnapped them had threatened her, scared her—that she'd been screaming because she heard them torturing an American in the next room.

Hearing that spoken out loud made Chris wince.

In retrospect, it probably hadn't been the best idea to meet tonight with the lawyer defending him.

"I'm advising you not to speak to Cam," the lawyer, whose name was Bob or Todd or something, told him.

Chris nodded in agreement, knowing full well he had every intention of not following that advice. Cam was driving in to see him tomorrow—the two men planned on hashing out what had happened, the way they hadn't been able to before.

"I'm serious, Chief," Bob-Todd continued. "You don't want to be set up to take the fall. The FBI's got some serious allegations and some damned good evidence. The agent assigned to investigate you hasn't pulled any punches—she wants a meeting for tomorrow. According to the ME's initial report, they're doing an autopsy to see if ballistics indicates a match grade M25. Only you and Mark carried that particular weapon."

"And rebel soldiers as well." Saint slammed his fist down. "Do you have anything helpful to tell us?"

The lawyer shifted and Chris knew the man hadn't ever

seen combat. Not that he couldn't be excellent at his job, but for this...well, he'd have a tough time understanding. "Chris needs to get his story straight. It sounds...confused."

"Because he is confused. He was trying to keep the whereabouts of the men straight in the middle of a rebel coup and an explosion. I'd worry more if he knew, point by point, what happened. That would tell me he was lying." Saint's eyes blazed.

Chris watched Saint arguing with the lawyer with a strong sense of disinterest, as if they were talking about another person entirely, as if he didn't witness Mark being dragged off in order to be killed. "I can't do this now." He stood and walked away from the table and out the door, toward his motorcycle. He'd parked it here two nights before he boarded the plane to Africa—they'd had only forty-eight hours of prep, for going through every possible scenario of what could happen.

He paused for a few seconds—out of respect for his CO, waited to see if Saint would walk out the door after him. Reprimand him. But no one came out and so Chris started the bike and took off, the wind buffeting him hard as he tried to pretend that the events leading to Mark's death hadn't ever happened, and fuck, he'd never had to regret anything about his career up until this point.

He guessed he'd been lucky as shit and that was the only luck he'd concede to in this entire fucking disaster.

It was well past midnight when he arrived at Jamie's house, thanks to Max's contacts at the DMV. Max was a captain in Naval Intelligence, the man who brought the teams home and did them more favors than they could ever hope to repay. Chris had never been to Jamie's place before, but her car was in the driveway and all the lights in the house blazed behind heavy curtains.

He slammed down the kickstand on his bike and eased his battered body off it and then headed toward her front door. It was time to tell her about a few things, to see if he could explain his gift to her . . . it was time to tell her she was pregnant.

The door contained no glass and when he knocked, he noted it was made of heavy reinforced steel. Odd for an old house like this, but for an FBI agent, maybe not so odd. For a woman who'd grown up in witness protection, probably perfectly normal.

He'd been haunted by what she'd revealed to him about her past, wondered what she'd lived through as a young girl.

After two more quick raps, he heard her feet on the other side of the door. He stood back slightly from the peephole, the way he'd done in Africa so Jamie could see him. In seconds, she was opening the door, her gun in her hand, even though it was down at her side and not pointed at him.

She was unapologetic. Dressed in a gray sweatshirt and dark blue FBI shorts, she looked young. Her hair was out of its usual ponytail, loose around her bare face. Her toenails were polished a bright blue and that made him smile. For a second.

"What are you doing here?" she demanded, but he ignored the start of the tirade and pushed past her. She only offered the slightest resistance and he ended up in the middle of her living room, his boots probably ruining the white shag rug. Everything in the place was white—her couches, the chairs. The walls. There was a touch of color, thanks to some throw pillows, and shit, he never did understand much about design, but he'd be scared to touch anything in here.

Well, anything but her, and he was pretty sure he'd get over worrying about messing something up once that happened.

He wanted to tell her that he was here to see her, to take her to bed, to wake up with her in the morning, but fuck, none of that was an option. Not with the investigation hanging between them. "I can't believe you think I'd kill Josiah."

With great reluctance, she closed the front door— locked it too but didn't let go of the gun. "The evidence points to you. Even Cam doesn't have that kind of sniper experience, nor did he have that kind of rifle with him."

He motioned to her own weapon now. "You feel the need to defend yourself against me now, Jamie? Are we back to that?"

"We're not back to anything. You're being investigated in the murder of an FBI agent—"

"And you slept with me. During your investigation," he pointed out.

"I thought the case was closed. Based on what you'd told me, I didn't see anything out of the ordinary. Just a tragedy."

"And then someone at the FBI told you what to think."

"Forensic evidence dictates where my investigation leads. We take care of our own, just like you, right?"

Yes, she was right—his own were fighting their asses off

to clear him. "I didn't come here to fight with you. I have something to tell you. Something else about that night."

"You shouldn't be here, telling me things. You should tell your lawyer. I'm not on your side."

He wanted to tell her that was bullshit, but he didn't. Instead, he concentrated on why he'd come here in the first place.

"What I'm going to tell you, I'm not telling anyone else. Not my lawyer. And I know you're not going to use it, I know that. But I thought maybe, if I told you..." He trailed off, realizing he sounded ridiculous. Pathetic. *Fuck.* "I saw what the soldiers had already done to Mark. He wasn't conscious when they carried him out. He'd been stripped, beaten. Whipped. Burned. Missing fingers."

Jamie stared at him from across the room but he refused to back down now. "How did you know he was still alive?"

"I just...know."

"That answer's not good enough."

"It's going to have to be."

"I don't understand—do you want to go to jail?"

"I knew he wasn't dead then because I knew he was about to die." He paused. "I didn't think. I'd hoped I wouldn't be able to sense death again. This was the first time in nearly thirteen years it had happened."

"You know when people are going to die?"

He shook his head. "No, not everyone. Just when it's someone close to me. Really close. I can see that they're going to go right before it happens."

"So you think you're psychic or something? God, I can't believe that you're using this crap now, as a defense."

"It's not a defense, Jamie. It has nothing to do with

Josiah—I have no idea what happened to him. I wouldn't. I barely knew the guy." He didn't take his eyes from her, wanted to see her gut reaction. But she had a really good poker face and she wasn't letting him inside this time. "You don't believe me."

"I don't know what the hell to believe, Chris. You come here and tell me some crazy story that you're a fortune-teller."

He sighed and stared up at the ceiling. "I'm not a fortune-teller. My skills are . . . different." And something he'd never wanted.

You couldn't tell we'd be arrested? Nick had bitched at him years earlier while the two of them sat overnight in the jail cell, right before they'd enlisted, and yeah, Chris had known it was a distinct possibility, felt the danger in his gut. He'd attempted to beat the odds and his own instincts and he'd lost, big-fucking-time.

Since then, he hadn't tried to outrun his instincts or change an outcome. Sometimes he was able to ignore them successfully. More often than not, he wasn't—something he ignored as well as he could.

The sight is what made him a superior sniper—used to living his life on complete instinct, he just knew the right time to fire.

"Why are you telling me this now?" she asked.

He couldn't reveal that to her, not yet. Maybe not ever. "I just needed to tell you. I didn't when we first met. You shared a lot with me and I didn't tell you."

"None of this helps your case."

"I didn't say it would. Shit, after I saw that, I can't be

sure of much else beyond the explosion. I was just so focused on getting to Mark."

As soon as the words came out of his mouth, he understood why Jamie was looking at him oddly. She took a deep breath, spoke the words they'd both been thinking, albeit reluctantly. "And if Josiah got in your way when you were trying to save Mark, if he held you back or ordered you to stand down..."

"I would've punched him, not shot him."

"Did Josiah pull a weapon on you? Threaten you?" she persisted. "Everyone knows how quick you are, Chris. Even if he threatened you with a weapon first, you would've won that battle. Was that it, was it self-defense?"

"I didn't shoot him." He did move toward her now, close, so close that he could smell the shampoo she used—something with coconuts, reminded him of the beach. Of Africa. Of bad times made good because he'd been with her. "You have to know that too."

"I don't know anything—don't you understand that? You turned my life upside down when we first met and now you're back, doing it again."

"But when I do come back, you don't exactly turn me away," he pointed out. "You didn't at the hotel."

She tucked some of the hair that brushed her cheek behind her ears impatiently. "We have chemistry, yes."

He pulled her body close to his—slight resistance but not enough to deter him. "Lots of it. It's more than just sex and danger."

"You didn't try to get in touch with me." Her voice was practically a whisper. "Not once."

"I couldn't push you. Not then."

"But now . . ."

"But now," he agreed.

"Why didn't you tell me about this psychic thing before, back at the hospital?"

"I don't like talking about it, don't like having it. Can't you see how it gets in the way, how it can cloud everything for other people?" He fisted his hands in frustration, his gaze cutting to her kitchen, where the counters held stacks of cups and plates. She was doing some major reorganizing. "You're worried about something."

"I'm busy. You need to leave, Chris. I'm sorry— about everything, about your teammate and the other night."

"That's not what's bothering you now." He reached out to touch her shoulder, her cheek, but she pulled back.

"I thought you were psychic. So why don't you tell me what's wrong."

"You're pregnant," he said bluntly, and yeah, so fucking *not* the way he'd wanted to break the news to her.

"What are you talking about?" she asked, even as her hand went to her belly unconsciously, and she knew—just knew—that he was right.

Knew that he was the father too, although he'd bet she'd try her damndest to deny that too. "When we were together, the first time in Africa, you got pregnant."

"How would you know that?"

"I can tell, Jamie. The changes are subtle, but they're there." He stuffed his hands in his pockets to keep himself from reaching out to touch her, because right now, she looked like a woman who didn't want to be touched at all. She looked more like she wanted to throw something at him, and since she still held the Glock in her hand, he didn't want to risk anything.

"You're just saying this to get me to resign from the investigation. Goddamn you, Chris. I didn't think you'd sink this low, but I guess you're really worried. And from what you just told me, you've got good reason to be."

Yeah, this wasn't going well. Nowhere near what he had planned. He was handing her ammunition. And yet, somewhere deep in his heart, he didn't give a shit. Mainly because Jamie and the baby were more fucking important than his job—he'd always valued relationships over career. "What I'm telling you about the baby—"

"There is no baby."

"—has nothing to do with the case."

"You tell me you're psychic and then you tell me I'm pregnant. If you know that, then you know why I was put into witness protection, right? And you know exactly what happened with Mike. You'd know so much. So why don't you tell me what else you know."

"I know you're pregnant, but that's all. I can't see inside to your deepest, darkest secrets. I just know that you have them."

"Get out of my house."

"Not until you promise to take a pregnancy test and start taking care of yourself."

"I take care of myself just fine. You don't get to walk back into my life and tell me what to do."

"This isn't just about you anymore."

"I'm investigating you. What aren't you getting about this, Chris? I'm trying to find out the truth."

"And you know, deep down in your heart—the one

you're trying to pretend is cold as ice—that I'm innocent. One hundred percent."

"I don't know anything but the fact that you shouldn't be here."

"Take the test, Jamie. Take the damned test."

It took all he had not to slam the door after him on the way out.

Jamie's hand was still on her belly when Chris closed the door. As she reached the lock and twisted it securely into place, the rumble of Chris's motorcycle was already growing faint. She would not give him the satisfaction of taking any kind of pregnancy test. She'd been on the pill when they were in Africa together. There was no way this was happening.

God, the man really was crazy. She'd seen hints of it in Africa...okay, more than hints. He'd delivered a baby. Sung to her. Made love to her on a downed plane and then rescued her from it before it slid into a ravine.

Awareness pervaded her body—that sharp jolt of feeling from belly to groin that reminded her she was a woman with needs, ones Chris had fulfilled well.

She headed to the bathroom to get a look in the full-length mirror. She pulled her shirt up to just below her breasts and held it there while she turned sideways and ran her hand over her exposed belly and abdomen.

This was impossible.

She'd actually lost weight over the past couple months. She'd been tired and she'd felt sick some days, but she'd attributed it to stress. To missing Sophie. To missing Chr—

She dropped her shirt and slammed the lights off on the way out of the bathroom, away from the mirror.

Chris was levelheaded. Calm taken to the extreme when he worked. He'd been to hell and back on many missions when his team had been threatened.

He'd bared his soul to her about what happened during that mission and she'd taken the information, twisted it and thrown it back in his face.

It wasn't that she couldn't believe he had some level of psychic awareness. In fact, the FBI utilized psychics with varying degrees of success. But she'd always stayed away from those people just in case they could actually sense something about her past. Mike had always believed, though. Had used a psychic's tip to hunt down Gary Handler, the man who'd ended up killing him.

What Chris had admitted to her tonight gave him motive. In the heat of the moment, he could've killed Josiah if the agent had gotten in Chris's way.

In the heat of the moment, if someone had gotten in your way of finding Sophie in Africa, what would you have done?

It was a question she couldn't answer. At least not out loud. Because the answer, *Anything*, might be exactly what Chris had done.

Saint hadn't allowed anything to break his exterior of calm control, not until he'd let himself into his house in the late evening and closed the door behind him. He turned off his phone and beeper, locked away his weapons, took off his tags and stared out the sliding glass door overlooking the beach, willing himself not to sob.

Like he told Chris, Mark would fucking kill him if he did that. But Mark wasn't here, and Saint didn't give a fuck anymore. He hated the anger he felt today—the loss, the fact that if Mark hadn't made it through . . .

He grabbed the first thing he could—some military manual—and flung it hard against the wall. It left a satisfying hole, and he didn't have to finish the thought that had been running over and over in his mind.

And then he went out the door to the back deck, into the cold air, stripped down and headed across the beach toward the water.

The man was sitting by himself in the middle of the surf, the foam coming up over his bare body. The temperature outside had to be under fifty—the water was at least twenty degrees colder, if not more.

When PJ had come up behind him, he'd been sobbing. Deep, heart-wrenching sounds she distinguished even above the roaring surf, his legs pulled to his chest, face buried in his knees.

But he was silent now.

She should've expected the tackle, but bracing for it would've made it harder on her body. As it was, he knocked the wind out of her as he laid her flat on the hard-packed sand.

If she'd wanted, she could've fought him off—she'd had plenty of training, and even though he had more than a hundred pounds on her, she'd learned how to fight dirty thanks to the CIA, and even dirtier thanks to her recent stint in Africa.

She no longer had any job now—she was an outcast, swimming by herself. And so she lay there, under this man, unafraid.

He was hurting more than she was, and anyone hurting that much couldn't be all bad.

"You shouldn't go sneaking up on people, little girl."

"Were you trying to kill yourself?" she asked calmly, her breath coming in short gasps. He was big. Handsome, from what she could make out of his face in the dark.

He rolled off her suddenly, lay on his back in the sand and stared up at the sky. "I was just going for a swim. Why don't you fuck off?"

That did it. In a flash, she was on him, straddling his prone body, knife blade at his throat.

"I wouldn't flash anything you're not planning on using," he told her, his drawl deeper than it had been just a minute earlier.

"Who said I'm not planning on using it?" she asked, the anger reaching a near boil far too quickly. Shit. She thought she left this back in the DRC. And in that brief second of hesitation, the man easily took control, the knife flying out of her hand.

He towered over her while she lay on her back in the sand. "Look, honey, I've had a really bad week. I don't know what your game is, but if you're looking to rob me, you picked the wrong guy." He pointed to his body—he wore only a pair of black boxer briefs that clung to him.

When he spoke again, his voice was quieter, like his mind was far away. "If you need some money for a place to stay tonight, I'll see what I can do."

"I don't need money."

"All right, then." He turned to walk away. When her eyes followed him, she saw a house about thirty feet up from the beach, lights on, sliding doors open. His house.

"I'm sorry about the knife," she said. "I really thought, when I came up on you . . ."

"Who are you?"

Who was she? Jamie still wanted her to be Sophie, but she was far more comfortable these days as PJ. Although that wasn't saying much—most of the time, she felt ready to jump out of her skin.

"Is that a hard question?" he asked.

"I'm PJ. I'm not from here. I was supposed to be staying with my sister, but that didn't work out."

"You're military?"

"I was, a long time ago." A whole lifetime ago. "Are you sure you weren't trying to kill yourself?"

"No, ma'am. I'm Navy. We enjoy cold water."

"SEAL?" All the ones she'd known had always hated being cold and wet, but she didn't call him on that, even when he didn't answer her question but rather asked one of his own. "What happened with your sister? Did you pull a knife on her too?"

In a way, she had—if he asked Jamie, she'd claim there was one buried in her back. "She's angry." She looked around. "Maybe I'll hang out here for a while, if you don't mind."

"Too cold."

"Says the man who just came from a swim in the ocean."

He stood. "Come on inside."

"And what, you'll be the perfect gentleman?"

"Not likely."

"I'll take my chances with the elements. I don't even know your name."

He rubbed his palms together, looked up at the sky. "It's Saint. And my best friend was killed five days ago. Normally, I wouldn't take no for an answer, but I'm damned tired. Do whatever the hell you want." He gave a single, definitive good-bye nod in her direction before he walked slowly up to the house.

She turned back toward the ocean and wondered if she'd ever feel right again.

Chris's brothers were waiting up for him. Truth be told, Nick barely slept anyway and Jake only slightly more than that, but still, this pre-dawn powwow was all about him.

And when he walked into the living room where both men were, he stopped cold. Looked around as if the three of them weren't the only ones there, mainly because he'd know Jules's perfume anywhere. The scent was faint, but she'd been there recently.

"I told you he'd know," Nick said without moving his lips.

"I wasn't the one who told her to get out of here," Jake answered him in the same fashion.

"I can hear everything the two of you are saying." Chris sank into the leather chair in the den and rubbed his head, which still ached like a mother. "Where is she?"

"At the Hilton. Penthouse suite. We told Jules to take herself and the reporters who are bound to follow her the hell out of here," Jake said.

"Only we said it nicer than that," Nick added.

"Not much," Jake muttered, and Chris sighed.

"What does she want?"

"You," Jake deadpanned.

"Ah, fuck."

"Yeah, that too."

Chris went to throw something at his brother, then decided it wasn't worth the trouble. Because yeah, if he and Jules weren't fighting, they were fucking, and that wasn't the kind of relationship he wanted.

He also didn't throw anything because Jake was hurting. Nick too, but Jake had known Mark the longest. Mark had been the one to help his brother through BUD/S when Jake was only fifteen and still having nightmares about his stepfather.

Neither brother asked where he'd been, why he'd come home so late, why he was on his own. Instead, Nick made him the coffee he liked and Jake had already filled the prescriptions he needed and he wondered if they'd continue to hover over him like two mother hens for much longer.

He just wanted back to normal. Craved it. And yet, that wasn't going to happen for a long time. "Saint said Mark's memorial is planned for next week."

Jake nodded. "No body."

"No body. Saint said he's going back—leaving in the morning," Chris told them.

Nick leaned against the back of Jake's chair. "He can't go back there on his own."

"You try telling him that." Chris rubbed a hand over his side—it had started to ache on the ride to Jamie's. On the way home, it had turned into full-blown pain.

He popped, dry, two of the pills Jake handed him. "I told Saint to stay there—he insisted on escorting me home. If it's too late to find Mark now..."

He trailed off.

"I'll go with him." Jake stared past Chris, toward the sliding glass doors behind him. Those doors led to the deck, and with the curtains open, dawn was starting to peek through.

Wordlessly, the three men headed outside. Barefoot, they stood on the deck waiting for the sun to rise. Watching it come up over the horizon, peeking through the woods behind the house.

It was a tradition that Jake had started himself when he was a young boy—now, seeing the dawn held significance for all three of them. It was something they rarely missed, whether or not they were together.

A reminder that they were alive, no matter where the hell in the world they were. Survivors.

This morning, with Mark's death hanging over them, the silence stretched out long after the sun had risen.

"He saved my life on our first mission," Chris said finally, and Nick nodded, because he'd been there too. They all knew the story, but somehow telling it now seemed important.

It was a night Chris had a permanent reminder of. The bite that ran along the right side of his chest and back was due, in part, to an impromptu water escape in the shark-infested waters off the Ivory Coast.

The shark had grabbed him, but its grip on Chris had been thankfully awkward. Chris had slammed the thing hard on the nose with the O_2 tank, and by the fucking grace of God, he'd been dropped, and then dragged by Mark to the safety of the waiting boat.

Today, the set of scars from the tiger shark's teeth looked like tiny white pearls that ran along his right side, both chest and back. The story had become something of a folklore among the new recruits, with the shark getting bigger and Chris getting stronger with each telling.

He didn't have the heart to explain that it was luck, pure and fucking simple. That, at the time, he'd been pretty sure Mark had saved his ass from the rebel soldiers so he could die in the warm waters in Africa.

"When I was going through BUD/S, Mark found me outside—I'd catch my rack time on the beach instead of in the bunk with everyone else so if I woke up with a nightmare, no one would hear me," Jake recalled. "He could've ridden me so hard for that. I know the master chief would've too, if he'd known. But Mark never said anything about it, to me or to the master chief. Didn't ask me why until Hell Week was over."

"He was good like that," Nick said.

"He was," Chris agreed. Nick and Mark were probably the most similar, background-wise, both from wealthy, fucked-up families. Chris wasn't sure if the two men ever talked about their pasts, but they were probably as close as Saint and Mark were.

"Is Jamie Michaels really investigating you?" Nick asked finally. He leaned against the deck's railing, his broad back turned away from the sun.

Chris nodded. He'd been attempting to be angry with

her—and not succeeding, because he kept picturing his hand on her belly.

"I went to see her," Chris told them, heard the defensiveness in his own voice. "Tonight—that's where I was."

"Great idea to hang out with the woman who's trying to hang you," Jake pointed out.

Nick, who'd been in Africa with him and Jamie, didn't say anything for a long second, and then, "You fucked up, didn't you?"

"Yeah."

Jake immediately leaned forward to take his brother's hand. "We'll fix it. Whatever you did—"

"I told her. About the thing... the psychic Cajun bull-shit."

"Okay, so she thinks you're nuts. But she probably thought that before," Nick reasoned.

"She's pregnant." Jesus, that was the second time he'd blurted out that information.

"She told you that?" Jake asked.

"I told her."

Nick and Jake shot each other looks. When Jake spoke again, his voice was low and soothing. "Come on, you've been to hell and back. Let's get you settled in so you can sleep some of this off."

Chris shook his head. He wanted nothing more than to settle in and relax, but the thought of being on the fourth floor all by himself wasn't something he could handle. "It's already morning."

But Nick motioned to him and he followed Nick into his own bedroom, which was on the first floor. He didn't argue, crawled under the covers even as Jake plopped down next to him and Nick took a chair by the side of the bed.

"We're here," Jake told him. "Sleep now."

"I haven't spoken with Dad," he mumbled when his head hit the pillow. His brothers knew that, didn't say anything, didn't tell him what he had to do. They never really did.

Right now, he appreciated that more than anything.

CHAPTER
5

P J was on his deck, curled on one of the cushionless wooden chairs with an all-weather sleeping bag wrapped around her. It was unseasonably cold, and judging by her slightly mottled skin tone, she'd been out there all night.

Dammit.

Saint slid the door open roughly. "You're going to freeze to death."

"And you don't want the trouble of calling the coroner?" she asked sleepily. "I may not be Navy, but I can handle the weather. Besides, it's spring."

All right, then. Far be it from him to argue. Again. He slammed the door shut, locked it, just to make a point, and tried to figure out what the hell to do now.

Mark's memorial service wasn't for another week. Still no body, and Saint couldn't get the uncomfortable absence of closure from his mind.

What if he's still out there?

Mark's face—beaten and bruised—had followed him in his dreams all night, made him toss and turn, until he'd woken up half-dazed, sweating as though fevered, everything on the nightstand pushed to the floor.

"Fuck." He'd knocked over the glass of juice he'd been attempting to pour; it shattered, flying everywhere. And she was there, watching through the door that went straight across from the den to the far side of the kitchen, making for a spectacular view of the ocean—and of him, walking through glass and leaving a nice trail of bloody footprints because he didn't give a shit.

He sat heavily in one of the kitchen chairs and looked at the ceiling, wondered when the hell any of this would get easier.

When he brought his gaze down, she was kneeling in front of him.

He didn't bother to ask how she'd gotten inside as she gently inspected his sole.

"I'm going to have to pull this piece of glass out—it's going to hurt," she told him. He snorted and she yanked.

He cursed as she held the dish towel she'd grabbed from the counter near the stove to staunch the bleeding. "You'll need a stitch."

"I can do it," he said roughly.

"So can I."

His cell phone began to ring—without thinking, he grabbed and answered it. "St. James."

"It's Admiral Tucker, returning your message."

Saint instinctively sat straighter, all business, as he spoke. "Thanks for getting back to me so soon, sir. I'm hoping you'll allow—"

The admiral didn't even let him finish his sentence. "The answer's no."

"Admiral, please . . ."

"St. James, I get it. But I'm not losing you in that riot. Once it settles down . . ."

"Once it settles down, there won't be anything left." He hated pleading, hated more so that he had to do it with his superior.

"There are Marines in that area, our own boys. They're holding this in the highest priority."

They might be, but it wasn't the same. Yet he said, "I understand. Thank you for calling, sir."

He hung up without knowing what the admiral said next, wasn't sure how long he sat there, staring into space with the cell phone held loosely in his hand. He hadn't noticed that PJ was still there and had begun to work on his foot.

She'd grabbed a stool, sat on it and placed his foot in her lap. She'd cleaned it and was just starting to make the first stitch. It was obvious that she had done this type of thing before. Her face was serious, and he watched for a second.

And then, "They won't let me go look for his body." He didn't know why the hell he was telling her this . . . or letting her stitch up his foot.

She sat back, raised her eyes to meet his. "Are you going anyway?"

"I don't have the leave. Or the clearance. I'd basically be giving up my career to do it."

"And your friend wouldn't want that."

He sighed, ran his hands through his hair.

"Where did it happen?"

"Africa. Sudan." Classified, but he didn't give a shit— the mission was all over the news. Not that PJ had seen any of that, sleeping out on his deck. "Thanks...for the first aid."

She'd finished with his foot and he took it from her lap and began to bandage the stitches himself. Then he stood, walked toward the door.

"I'm going to try to make up with my sister." She didn't look as if she relished doing so, not at all. But he couldn't give her a reason to stay. Admitting he didn't want to be alone wasn't something he ever did, and he had to go to base and make sure Chris kept his meetings with the JAG and the doc.

"You can use the shower...and you can come back," was all he said, gruffly. He didn't pick his head up from sifting through his mail on the front table, where his neighbor had dropped it for him. "Spare key's under the side mat."

There was a long pause, and then a short, "Thanks."

He didn't stick around to see if she'd take him up on the offer.

Jamie hadn't checked in with Kevin, her foster father, since before leaving for Africa. Having her movements tracked by him wasn't her favorite thing, but it had become as familiar to her as breathing, a quick e-mail or phone message and he felt better.

It was something PJ ignored and Kevin never pushed it with her.

Now Jamie sent Kevin a text and checked her e-mails. Her supervisor had cleared her of all cases except Josiah's.

The department's counting on you to get to the bottom of this, he'd told her earlier that morning as she'd poured coffee into her mug in her office's kitchen. She'd poured it out of habit, and a moment later dumped it in the sink. Until she could assure herself that what Chris told her about the pregnancy was wrong, she'd stick with water.

The reassignments meant that her current witness protection case had been shifted. She was relieved, and upset with herself for feeling that way ... but that was one more thing she didn't need to relive.

She was still *living it* on a daily basis.

As she sifted through her messages, she saw that Cam's lawyer had blocked the day's planned interview, as had Chris's. And so she spent time rereading her notes of both accounts of the story, plus reviewing her typed recollection of sitting with Chris when the hospital was under fire; she went over them until she knew them by heart and her eyes saw only blurred words on the page, running together into one long, tragic story of a failed mission.

Then she turned back to the 3D diagrams of the area in Africa. Daniel, an FBI programmer extraordinaire had helped her plug in the team's members and given her the ability to play out a number of different scenarios, including the one that Chris and Cam asserted.

But nothing she'd come up with seemed right. The pieces didn't fit together.

All she wanted to do was *not* think about Chris, and yet her entire day consisted of thinking about him, imagining his thought process . . . his fears.

She thumbed through his file right before she'd left for the day—all classified intel and nothing that surprised her. Most of his previous missions had been blacked out, leaving at her fingertips only the barest bones of his life as a Navy SEAL.

His earliest records showed the government had signed off on the judge's orders for him to stay in the Navy for six years or spend the rest of that probationary period in jail.

Chris had gone Navy and never looked back, but unlike his brothers, he hadn't bothered with Officer Candidate School and the like. Instead, he'd moved up the ranks of the enlisted, his status as something of a sniper extraordinaire happening very early in his career.

The FBI and the CIA had both tried to recruit him multiple times, even before his six-year commitment was up. The most recent was another FBI attempt, in March. Right before she'd met him.

Now she sat in the driveway in her car, listening to a song on the radio that Chris had sung to her in Africa when she'd been scared and in pain.

She'd never been big on signs, but lately there were far too many for her to ignore.

She grabbed the drugstore bag—she'd gone to the store early that morning but had chickened out of taking the pregnancy test before work—got out of the car and headed for the house. Gun drawn, she opened the front door and inspected the living room. Last night, she'd spent a couple of hours rearranging the furniture and dishes back to where she liked them. Now, with the lights blazing, she saw that the furniture remained exactly as she'd left it.

Breathing a sigh of relief, she closed the front door behind her and locked it. It had most definitely been Wanda who'd moved things around—Jamie had thought about calling her last night or today to ask, but she'd felt foolish. Now she was glad she hadn't.

She went straight to the bathroom and peed on the stick. She'd leave it for the requisite few minutes and go to the bedroom to change and calm her nerves.

She wasn't two steps in when her breath caught. No, she'd been wrong, all was not as she'd left it, not in there.

The bed was moved, much more haphazardly than the furniture had been yesterday. All her drawers were open, her clothing spilling out. The closet doors were both open as well. All her clothing had been yanked off the hangers and tossed to the floor. Mike's closet was empty, but she'd done that herself a month ago.

At least it was obvious no one was hiding in it.

But he could still be in the house. Waiting.

A chill ran over her skin. Forcing herself to breathe calmly and quietly, even though what she wanted to do was hyperventilate, she palmed her pistol and swept the room. Closet, clear. Shower, clear. Under the bed, clear.

She crept toward the doorway, but a tapping noise froze her mid-step. For a horrible moment, she thought she'd missed something. She whirled, aimed at the window... where the knock of a tree branch against the glass made her heart leap again, and dammit, she had to get a grip.

She eased down the hall, her steps light and silent, leading the way with her weapon. Adrenaline rushed through her veins, but she kept the gun steady. Sweeps of each room turned up nothing. Whoever the asshole was, he'd left. She double-checked the locks on the windows and doors, the sense of violation growing by the minute. She tamped it down with ruthless effort. She could freak out later.

Still, she didn't want to be inside the house, where someone had broken into her life and torn through her things.

Snatching up her keys, she headed for the door. She passed by the bathroom, where the little pregnancy stick lay on the sink. For a moment, she hesitated, her heart beating wildly.

"What the hell," she breathed, and snatched it up. Two clear, pink lines.

Oh, God. Pregnant. And it was most definitely Chris's baby.

Numbly, she flung the test into the garbage. Funny how when she was searching the house for some maniac intruder, her hands had been perfectly steady, but now they shook as she collected the garbage bag and tossed it into the outdoor trash can on her way to the car.

Not that she knew where she was going, but she couldn't be in that house one more second. Not until she got her head on straight. Who would have broken into the house? And why?

And why did she have to be pregnant?

Still trembling, she climbed into the car, locked the doors and started it up.

She jammed it into reverse... but didn't hit the gas.

Screw that. She wasn't running. She'd had enough of that as a kid.

But she wasn't taking any chances, and she kept the engine running and an eye on her surroundings as she dialed the phone, tried to keep her voice as calm as possible as she spoke. "Kevin, it's Jamie."

"What's wrong?" Her foster father's voice held worry immediately. She'd had to get used to calling him Kevin rather than Dad when she joined the Bureau—very few people knew of her relationship with the U.S. marshal who worked in close conjunction with the FBI, and she wanted to keep it that way.

"Someone's been inside my house. I'd call the police—"

"Don't. I'll be there in five minutes."

"Okay." She closed her phone and pocketed it. Outside, a breeze blew through the trees, making shadows move, and though she felt a little silly looking for the bogeyman inside them, she kept watch, the radio humming softly in the background. Before she'd met Chris, she'd never used the radio for anything more than news and traffic reports. Now she listened to music all the time, found it soothed her.

Her hand involuntarily went to her belly again—she hadn't had time to fully process this news, but God, Chris had been right.

Damn him.

Several times over the course of her job, she'd helped a marshal herd a new family off to witness protection—her job ended once they reached the new location. She'd never see them again, and they'd never be themselves again either—some of them cried about that, the way she had, others were silent with shock and some argued. Bargained. Begged.

In the end, there was no choice—they'd leave the comfort of the car and head into the small building that was no more than a prison with a kitchen and a bedroom, a place that would be their lives for the next three to four weeks, until new identities were created.

It had taken Jamie a long time to stop referring to herself as Ana. Longer still to stop calling Sophie "PJ"—and even today, hearing her sister refer to herself by that long-lost name tore at Jamie's heart.

Who would they have been had they never been found? It was a question Jamie didn't often like to revisit and one that she couldn't help thinking about during times like this, when the walls seemed to be closing in on her.

She'd sworn she'd never do that to a child. Mike hadn't wanted children either, hadn't argued or cajoled like the boyfriend she'd had before.

Mike hadn't known much about her at all. She'd liked it that way, liked being the woman with the made-up past given to her like a checklist—her real childhood blotted out to form a more generic, happy one. Mike didn't know she was adopted, thought Kevin Morgan and his wife were her and PJ's biological parents.

She didn't even know where her own parents had been buried.

Chris opened the shower curtain quickly and without warning. "Knocking. Have you heard of it, Jules?"

She hadn't meant to sneak up on him—or attempt to

anyway—but when she'd climbed up the familiar stairs to the top floor and found the bathroom door open and heard the shower running, she'd walked in, seeing him the only thing on her mind. "Sorry. The door was open and I just..."

He looked big—bigger and more powerful than he'd looked even a year earlier.

Without her heels, she stood five foot eight and still she had to strain to look up at him and found she couldn't tear her eyes away.

"Can I help you with something?" He sounded angry at her, which, truth be told, happened nearly all the time since Maggie had died and he'd gone out of control and Jules hadn't known how to help.

They'd been so young. And she still didn't have a clue as to what Chris needed. "The people you rescued—the woman, Natalie, she's my friend."

"Your friend should've stayed in the States, making movies." Chris put both hands on the shower rod and leaned against it as he waited.

"You look good, Chris. Really good."

"So do you, Jules. But that was never the problem between us." Without warning, his hands moved; he worked the ring off her left hand—the product of her faked-for-the-press engagement to a fellow actor—and flung it across the bathroom and then he picked her up and brought her, fully dressed, into the shower with him.

She didn't protest, not when he pulled her shirt up or when he pushed her leather skirt down; she didn't care about ruined makeup or clothing or anything when she was in Chris's arms.

He'd been so right—this was never, ever the problem. It was just so complicated between them, always so off balance.

This time didn't feel any different and she wondered why she'd come here at all.

Jules was beautiful, always had been, always turned him the fuck on to the point of no return.

It would be so easy to do, to spend time in her arms, in bed, the shower, the floor—just in her. They played this game well together, but beyond the sex, Chris knew what he'd be left feeling.

Nostalgia. Love, for sure, but not the kind that he could live with for the rest of his life.

Jules wasn't the woman he wanted pressed against him; he was kissing her and picturing Jamie and that wasn't fair to either of them.

The thing of it was, he was pretty damned sure Jules was picturing someone else when she kissed him too. It was just so familiar and comfortable. But it had to stop.

The shower was too damned small for a foursome. "Jules, I can't."

"Are you hurt?" When she'd first come in, she'd stared at him like she was seeing him for the first time. She always did that after she found out about one of his near-death experiences, which thankfully didn't happen all that often. Now there was a regret in her eyes that matched the way he felt.

With her makeup washed off, she looked so much like the sixteen-year-old he'd fallen for, could still remember the astonished look she'd given him when she'd discovered him in the school's parking lot, preparing to hot-wire her classic Mustang convertible, two weeks after first catching sight of him in the cafeteria.

"What are you doing? Are you actually trying to steal my car?" Long-limbed, tan, every high school boy's dream, Jules should've been far out of his reach. She was a junior to his freshman; she barely even looked at the senior boys but Chris knew he'd try anything to be with her, as surely as he knew he had to take her car for a spin.

"Won't be stealing if you give me the keys," he drawled calmly, seconds from pulling the wires out from under the dashboard. The car smelled like her—a combination of sugar and suntan lotion and wild times.

Her neon blue eyes blazed with anger . . . and with something else too. "I'm not—"

"I just want a ride. Give me the keys."

She'd handed them over, but had scrambled into the passenger side next to him. "Do you even have a license?"

"No. Never needed one where I grew up."

"Where's that?"

He'd turned to her and grinned. "I'll tell you after I kiss you."

"There's someone else, isn't there?" Jules was asking now.

"Yeah, there's someone else."

Jules simply nodded—she pulled away from him and he got out of the shower and helped her out as well.

"I'll grab you some clothes," he told her before he gave her the only towel and left the bathroom, shutting the door behind him.

Shit.

It was already well past seven at night. He'd slept for most of the day, woke to Nick making him dinner. He'd eaten, even though he wasn't hungry, and then he headed up the stairs, to his own shower and his own room. Everything just the way he'd left it, except it wasn't the same.

He grabbed another towel from the hall closet, just as Jake bounded up the stairs.

"Hey, have you seen—?"

Chris pointed toward the door.

"Ah." Jake looked between the door and Chris, his eyebrows raised. "I'll just leave you two alone, then."

Obviously, Jake hadn't sent Jules up here—but Jules being Jules refused to listen to anyone but herself. It was one of her most endearing qualities, since he and his brothers had pretty much the same philosophy. But in this situation, Chris wished she'd have listened to reason.

Still, he was going to make sure that one woman listened to reason tonight, no matter how hard Jamie protested.

Less than an hour later, Jamie found herself back inside her house, Kevin at her side. His face remained tight as Jamie spoke with him, his eyes perusing the mess in the bedroom.

"Wanda has a key?" he asked finally.

"Yes. For years. She knows I work for the FBI—she wouldn't do something like this."

"Give me her number anyway."

"Fine." She'd be less one housekeeper for sure after this.

Maybe that was for the best—she'd never liked that Mike had given an outsider a key to their home. Then again, Mike hadn't ever realized just how much of an outsider to her life he actually was. "My sister's back."

Kevin glanced up from where he was dusting for prints. "She came to see me yesterday. I told her you were out of town. I thought maybe she'd stay here once you returned."

Jamie didn't respond and he didn't press. Instead, he bagged up the fingerprinting he'd done. "I'll have my guy run this tonight. Why don't you come and stay with me?"

God, she wanted to say no, that she could take care of herself. That she had a weapon. But convincing Kevin to take no for an answer wouldn't be an easy task and she couldn't blame him. There were too many variables.

"It's late. I've got protection." They both knew that was code for *Grace won't appreciate it*. Kevin's wife had reluctantly taken in the girls, and while they easily thought of Kevin as a father, Grace had always remained Grace, a woman who regarded them with equal amounts of displeasure and fear.

Although Jamie had never understood what had attracted Kevin to Grace in the first place, she now understood that love—or lust—led you to strange, dark places.

"It could be Alek." She spoke the name of the man who'd hunted her family for years—their reason for going into witness protection—and tasted the bitterness on her tongue.

"Could be," Kevin agreed. "But that's highly unlikely. You know as well as I do that being stalked is not uncommon for an agent. Current cases?"

"No one who'd do this," she muttered.

"That's what they all say, but you're not in the business of making the people you arrest or their families happy. I want you to write up a list of your cases from the last year—flag anyone you're worried about...or should be. I'm assigning a team."

"You're overreacting."

Kevin slid his coat off. "If you're not leaving, I'm staying here tonight."

"I don't need a team, Kevin."

"You do. At least for a little while." He motioned for her to sit and that seasick sway feeling took over again. Stubbornly, she remained upright, refusing to even grab the back of the couch to support her.

"Tell me what you're so worried about," she insisted.

"Gary Handler's escaped."

Mike's killer. The man who shot her. "When?"

"Two nights ago, when they were transferring him," he admitted. "You were still out of the country. Lou called me—we decided not to worry you unnecessarily. We have our best men on it. We assumed he'd be trying to get out of the country. But once you told me what happened..."

"Shit." She did sit finally, crossed her legs in front of her in a perfect yoga pose that her instructors had told her would relax her but still felt more stressed than ever. "You should have told me immediately. I'm not a child."

"I know that. I also know he's got no reason to come after you. You have enough pressure, Jamie. Enough worries. This shouldn't be one of them."

If Kevin only knew. "Somehow, I don't see Handler as the type to rearrange my furniture."

"No, he definitely doesn't fit that pattern. And for him

to get your address . . ." Kevin trailed off. "Give me your list of suspects and I'll run them by the profiler."

"I don't want Lou to know anything about Alek."

"He won't," Kevin promised. He'd kept every promise he'd ever made to her, and she had no reason to believe he'd break one now.

CHAPTER

6

After an hour, Kevin had been called in to handle a problem with a witness, and since she'd once been one such emergency, Jamie had urged him out the door.

"I'm capable, Kevin," she'd told him, showed her gun and her badge to remind him. "Gary Handler will not get to me a second time."

She knew Kevin as well as he knew her—he was remaining calm for her. Agreeing with her that after all these years, this could not be the nightmare he'd hoped was behind her and PJ for good. Agreeing that Handler, actually the lesser of two evils, was a real threat.

"Kevin, it could've also just been someone messing

with me—kids pulling a prank. Nothing was stolen," she reasoned.

"It spooked you enough to call me."

"I always call you—it's in the rules."

"Yes, you and your sister follow the rules so well," Kevin had muttered, his hand still on his phone, ready to call in and tell them he couldn't take the job that night.

"Look, it's weird, yes. But let's both try not to make more of it than it is—that would help me," she'd told him, and reluctantly he had agreed.

And in his absence had stationed two undercover marshals outside her house. They nodded to her when Kevin introduced them to her and then went back to their post, no questions asked. She was sure they owed her foster father favors and equally sure Kevin had told them only the bare bones of her situation.

As much as she hated needing the protection, she was grateful that she didn't have to be on full alert, not when the migraine that had been threatening since last night had gotten a full hold on her.

She'd taken Tylenol earlier in the vain hope it would help—a futile way to try to gain control over the pain. But with the pregnancy test showing positive, until she decided what to do, anything stronger was out.

Instead of putting her clothes back into the drawers, she decided to wash all of them—didn't like the idea of an intruder touching her things. So she put in loads of laundry and she wiped down her dressers and inside the drawers and put the mirror back in place . . . all while trying not to think about Chris.

Yet he weighed on her mind more heavily than PJ or Gary or anything else.

Finally, the comforter for the bed was dried. She planned on spending the rest of the evening in bed with her gun and an ice pack. But before she could head toward the kitchen to grab the ice, she heard Chris calling out her name.

Chris.

How the hell had he gotten in here?

She hated the way she wanted to run to him. She'd never wanted to do that with anyone, never needed comforting in that way. "I'm in my room."

She heard her front door shut, and then, "What's going on? Why are there men guarding your house?" he called out as she turned and walked to the living room, to catch him before he barreled into her bedroom. He wore a green bandanna tied around his head, jeans, a T-shirt and on his right side a gun stuffed into his pants. He looked good. And worried.

"This has nothing to do with the case." She grabbed the couch tightly, hoped he couldn't see her death grip on it, even as the throbbing pain on the side of her head intensified.

"Is this about PJ?" He obviously wasn't going anywhere until she told him what was happening—and then he *definitely* wouldn't leave. Her own personal wall of security.

"It's nothing; my house was broken into. My foster father's overreacting."

Chris's eyes blazed. "Dammit, Jamie, just because you carry a gun doesn't mean you should stay here like a sitting duck. Especially not now." He muttered something to himself, sounded like he was speaking a foreign language—French, maybe.

"I'm not being driven out of my home by what could just be a break-in."

He cocked his head to the side, not buying it at all. "If you're staying, I'm staying."

"No way."

"I'll camp out in the backyard if I have to." He stood stubbornly in front of her, feet planted, towering over her, daring her to challenge him.

It was a magnificent sight really, and had this been any other situation, she would've stopped to admire him. But staying on her feet was becoming impossible, something Chris noticed before she did, because in seconds she was in his arms and being carried toward her bedroom.

Protesting further was suddenly far too much work. All she wanted to do was stay cradled in Chris's strong arms, lying on her bed with him as his hands worked their magic. The pain eased marginally, enough for her to talk.

"You were right. About me being pregnant," she told him as his hands massaged her neck. "I hate it that you were right, that you knew before I did."

"I know."

"Right, psychic. Forgot," she mumbled.

"Nothing to do with that. I'll be back in a second."

He eased away from her and then she heard the water running in the bathroom. He was back quickly with a damp washcloth that he placed on her forehead. "This has some rubbing alcohol on it—it should help."

"That feels good," she mumbled.

"Hold it there," he instructed. She did, remained up-right at his request as he took a spot behind her, began to massage her shoulders and her neck again. "You're still tense as hell."

"Pain does that to a person."

"I thought you were going to blame me, so I'll take that answer." He paused. "Those men aren't FBI—I'm not get-ting you in trouble by being here."

"They're not FBI," she agreed. But the trouble part . . . he had no idea. "You have good hands."

"You've mentioned that before. In Africa, the first time." He paused. "And the second time too."

She tried to hold back a small, snorted laugh but couldn't. The throb had receded to a dull ache but the pain still threatened to come back as bad as it had been. His thumbs dug into the soft, slightly tender flesh by her neck and it hurt, but she let him do it, knowing that by easing that tension, she would feel better.

She wasn't sure how long he worked on her, but at some point she realized his hands were up under her shirt, palms on her bare skin.

"Better for the energy this way," he'd murmured, not trying anything beyond the massage. And as the tension in her neck and shoulders was relieved, the pain became bear-able. "How long have you had migraines?"

"As long as I can remember. They're not from stress," she added quickly. "People always think they are, but they're not."

He didn't say anything to that. She pulled the washcloth away from her face and he took it from her and put it across the back of her neck. The damp fabric was still cool enough, the alcohol made her skin tight and tingly.

"I'm sorry for last night. I didn't mean to slam in here and lay all that crap on you," he said, his voice rough with leftover emotion.

"It wasn't crap," she said softly.

The bed dipped with his weight, and she turned to look at him. Propped on one elbow, he stretched across the mattress like a big cat taking in the sun. Relaxed, almost lazy; yet Jamie knew there was nothing lazy about him. "The pain is better. You need to leave."

"You can't stay alone. Who's going to take care of you?"

"Never needed anyone to do that. I suspect you never have either."

"That's true. But I like being taken care of," he said. "You took care of me in Africa. And I liked it."

"You were hurt." She stared at him. "You still are."

"Little bit."

"Most men don't like women fawning over them."

"Jamie, you don't exactly fawn. You're just capable as anything."

"Yeah, only a headache can bring me down. God, these suck." She put the washcloth onto the night table and shifted to lean up against the headboard. "You shouldn't be here."

"I know that, you keep telling me that. But I do a lot of things I shouldn't, and stopping now doesn't seem all that appealing to me. So shut up and try to relax; you look like hell."

"You sure know how to compliment a girl."

He smiled—not his typical wide grin but close enough

to make her want to reach across the space between them and stroke his cheek. Just being near him was helping her pain—she wasn't sure why or how, but she wouldn't knock it.

"We've finally got a bed and I can't make good use of it." His voice was husky, low and sexy—and half-joking too, but not really.

Disappointment coursed through her, because yes, between the headache and the men planted outside the house, coupled with the investigation, it was all impossible.

Six feet nearly seven inches of impossible lying close enough for his hand to reach out and rest on hers.

There was so much between them—time spent together in Africa, that first trip that bonded them more quickly than she'd ever have thought and the investigation now that threatened to tear them apart as fast.

She should be telling him again to get out of her house, that she was in danger in so many different ways—that she *was* danger—but she didn't say a word beyond his name, a whisper she wasn't sure he heard.

He did, moved close to her, and she cupped his neck to bring his mouth to hers.

The kiss was soft but threatened to go to maximum implode within seconds. And one small tilt of her head was enough for her to feel a warning throb of pain return.

He sensed it, pulled away and murmured, "I can give you some more relief, baby—for a few minutes, at least."

She'd take anything at this point, especially if he could continue to simply touch her... but she never expected what he did next.

He climbed behind her so his back was against the

headboard and eased her against his chest with her body between his legs. She immediately felt his arousal and she wondered how it was possible for her to feel so crappy and so turned on at the same time.

"In Africa, on the plane, you looked so goddamned sexy, with your shirt all hiked up and your hair down..."

His hands traveled along her T-shirt as he spoke; he pushed the soft cotton up around her breasts, baring her still flat belly, and then one hand continued downward, slipping under the waistband of her shorts and between the juncture of her thighs. "And then, when I held your hands over your head and got you naked, and you tried to tell me you hated me..."

"I was lying."

"I know."

She licked her lips, which were suddenly very dry. "We connected then, you know that."

"Yeah."

Her brain screamed, *Stop him, stop this,* but her body had turned traitor and it wasn't going back. She held her breath for a second as his fingers moved to the cleft between her legs, began to stroke the warm, wet flesh with a persistent pressure that threatened to make her forget everything. She let a small moan escape, the one that had been drumming up in her throat since his hands began their exploration of her body.

He heard it too, pressed a kiss to the side of her neck, and for several blissful minutes she was pain-free. Her skin was warm and damp and while his fingers touched her, she imagined he was naked next to her, skin to skin, and nothing else was in their way—not the headache or the investigation or her past.

"So pretty, Jamie...you look so pretty right now," he murmured as his free hand danced over her nipples, which felt ripe and taut under his caresses. The combination of pain and pleasure nearly proved to be too much and she screwed her eyes shut and tried to jerk out of his grasp.

"Give it a minute, baby—I promise, this will help," he told her, his fingers working her toward the ultimate pleasure. Her belly tightened, her thighs attempted to close on his hand and finally...finally her orgasm washed over her, taking the pain and worry with it as Chris pushed her further still.

"Chris—please...oh..." His fingers still worked her sex, and she pressed her hips up to meet his hands as the wave of her climax hit a second time and she felt like they were the only two people in the world.

"Let it go," he said, and she did, shuddered through a long series of contractions.

She was still quaking from the aftershocks when he whispered for her to "Sleep now."

It came more easily than she'd thought, lying spread, with his hands on her, content.

When she woke, he was still behind her and it was still dark out and her pain was a dull ache instead of unbearable. "How long did I sleep?"

"About an hour. Here, drink this water."

She did so, noted that his palm was splayed over the bare skin of her belly, where her shirt had remained pulled up. She tried to imagine her belly big with child and a life with Chris that didn't include worrying about witness protection, but she couldn't.

"We don't have to talk about this now," he said when she pulled her hand away with a quick jerk, and she hated that she was so transparent to him. "But your headaches will be worse for a little while—the hormones."

"Great." She pushed away from him, sat up and hugged her legs to her chest. "How did you know that would help?" she asked, well aware that her cheeks flushed as she spoke.

"It's cute that you blush." He ran a finger down one side of her face. "I read up on migraines."

"Because of me?"

"Yeah, because of you. You had them in Africa and I figured now you wouldn't be able to take meds. The orgasm thing—it's just a theory, but it sounded like the most fun to try out."

She bit her bottom lip lightly and then, "Someone's been inside my house. That's why the men are here. It happened two days in a row, I think. He moved my things around. But there was no forced entry. My foster father set up the security." She peered up at him. "Why did they let you in?"

"I know one of the guys."

Of course he did. This world of military and secret agencies was so small. "The man who killed Mike, the man who shot me—he's escaped."

"And you think he's the one breaking into your house."

"I don't know what to think. We're just being cautious at this point. For him to come here, after me, would be pointless. I'd think he'd be better served getting out of the country and going to Colombia, where some drug lord can cover his ass."

"How long ago did that happen—with you and Mike?"

"Ten months. And I hate that he might've been in here, touching my things. But I hate it even more that something like this, something that could be considered a routine threat, a hazard of the job, needs to get my foster father up in arms because of my background."

Chris didn't say anything, just put a hand on her arm and rested his head on her shoulder. He got her and didn't try to break her out of self-pity mode. It was a good thing, because she needed to do that herself—it was far too dangerous to have to depend on someone else.

Jamie's bedroom was only slightly less stark than the main room, still with the white carpet and white walls, but there were some photographs—black-and-white stills—and the comforter was a soft shade of blue. There were books piled on the nightstand—an eclectic mix of fiction and nonfiction.

An iPod, black. Chris had thumbed through it while she'd rested and found several songs he'd sung to her back in Africa. Now he found himself humming while his forehead pressed against her back.

Her breaths were deep, although not easy. He could tell she was thinking, planning . . . deciding how much further to let him in. And he simply waited for her to continue— she would, and he was well aware that pushing her further wouldn't get him the information he wanted. Like more details about this Gary Handler bastard and how he could get his hands on him himself.

She seemed convinced it was Handler; the evidence pointed to him, but if it wasn't him, if it was someone else from her past, he'd take care of that too—knew it with a certainty that he hadn't felt in forever.

The fierce, primal urge to protect Jamie that had been there in Africa had only intensified. And now he remained as fucking close as he could possibly be to her without stripping her down and taking her, which was not an easy urge to fight.

She'd trusted him at a time when she trusted no one. She could try to tell him that she'd had to, that she hadn't had a choice when he snuck onto the plane headed for Africa and her sister, but he didn't buy that for a second.

"I'm glad you came here tonight," she whispered finally. "I almost called ... wanted to. But ..."

"Yeah, I know. Look, Jamie, I won't let you get in trouble for this, I'll take the brunt of it. But I couldn't leave things the way we did last night. I shouldn't have thrown all of this at you the way I did. Not with everything else you're dealing with."

"The timing wasn't the best—but you didn't know about the break-in."

"It freaked you out. I can see that."

"It just ... came at the wrong time."

"It's all right to be scared."

"I don't want to be. I keep telling Kevin that I'm fine, told the men watching the house that too. I think they believe me. And I'm lying to all of them."

"You know as well as I do that fear's a good thing—the

best thing that could happen to you. Fear keeps you fierce, sharp. That's how you need to be right now," he told her.

"I used to think that way, but I don't know anymore, Chris. The night Mike died, I was terrified." Her voice was low and shaky and she still didn't turn to look at him. Instead, she stared at the wall in front of her as though she could see the entire scene playing out in living color. "I thought I was prepared for anything. I mean, I'd had the best training. But the shots came so fast and I wasn't ready. I was vulnerable."

By the tone of her voice, it was obvious that was a feeling she despised. "There we were, in this desert just beyond the Texas–Mexico border, and I remember thinking, *This is it—all these months of tracking this asshole and we've finally got him.* But it wasn't over—it was a trap. Handler was waiting for us—him and another guy, who was killed on the scene."

She wiped away a stray tear with the palm of her hand and continued. "I think those first shots killed Mike instantly. I don't even remember firing my gun, but I found out later that I'd hit Handler in the back. And then I looked down at Mike and there was so much blood. He was bleeding everywhere. I grabbed him. Tried CPR. But it was too late." The tears flowed freely now that she'd gotten the story out in its entirety.

"It wasn't your fault. You did everything right."

"But I couldn't save him."

"You did your job."

"I was supposed to protect him, the way he protected me."

Chris shook his head. "You were too involved—that's

not always a good thing with a partner. It throws your game off. Makes you more vulnerable than you would be otherwise."

"You think you were more vulnerable on your last mission because you were close to Mark?"

"I'm vulnerable every time I go out with those guys—we're all close. Hell, I work with my brothers a lot of the time. The only way we get to do that is because they were never officially adopted by my parents. And yeah, it's getting harder with every mission." He hadn't wanted to admit that, hadn't even realized how much he meant it until the words spilled out.

"I never thought about that with Mike. I think...I think it was harder for him. He loved me more than I loved him." She looked over at him. "That sounds horrible, doesn't it?"

"It's the way you felt." He paused, and then, "You're bringing a hell of a lot of baggage with you to your job then and now."

"My other options were fry cook or working at a dry cleaners." She grimaced. "This was the best option for me. I could protect myself. I had a built-in wall around me with the FBI—there was no way anyone would be able to investigate my real background information."

"I'm sure Mike understood about your past—"

She cut him off. "He didn't know."

"You were with him for five years...why didn't you trust him with that information?"

"I trusted him. It wasn't like that." She stared down at her hands—he'd noted when she'd come to speak with him in the hospital in Africa that she wasn't wearing the wedding band anymore. Now she held her hand up, acknowledging what he'd noted. "I took it off a week after I got back from the DRC. It took a while for me to get used to my hand without it."

"It's always hard to lose someone special."

She laughed, a short, almost harsh sound. "Mike was planning on leaving me. I found a letter. He wrote it a few nights before he died."

"I'm sorry, Jamie."

"I failed him in so many ways. All because I was doing what I was supposed to, according to the great gods of witness protection. I told myself I was protecting him by not telling him everything, but really I was protecting myself." She rubbed the back of her neck. "He said that I was cold. And he was right—I am."

"You *were*," he corrected. "On the plane in Africa, in the hotel last week, tonight when I made you come, you were anything but cold."

"So I just needed the right man?" She sounded angry about that. He should've tread more carefully. But hell, that had never been his nature.

"Yeah, I think you needed the right man. Needed to let yourself go. It sounds like with Mike...you must not have had passion between you. He was a fool to want to let you go."

She jerked away from him. "Don't you dare say anything bad about him. He loved me. I know that. I'm not the easiest person in the world to live with, to love, and he did it for years."

"I'm not, Jamie."

"We had to hide the fact that we were together from everyone. Sometimes, I think that was a mistake—if I'd told my supervisor, gotten another partner, even quit and found something else to do..." She shook her head. "We hid what we had—that was a big part of the problem."

"That's bullshit and you know it, Jamie. Because anyone who sees us with each other, whether we're sitting across a table in a lawyer's office or walking side by side in the grocery store, would know we were together—it's not something we could hide for years from friends or colleagues."

"You didn't tell your CO, did you?" she demanded.

"I haven't told him anything, but he's not stupid. We're not going to be able to hide things between us for much longer."

"Get out." She pulled herself from his embrace, as things quickly went from fire to ice.

Yeah, he had that effect with his honesty. "I'm leaving this room, this house, but I'm not leaving you here alone."

"I'm not alone. And I already told you, I've had a hell of a lot of practice keeping myself safe."

"There are all different kinds of safe, Jamie—all different ways to fake it too." He stuffed his hands into his pockets, turned and ducked his head slightly on his way out the door, the habit of a man whose height trained him to do so.

But she wasn't letting it go—she was still so angry, at the entire situation, at him especially, and he'd been prepared to bear the brunt of that anger. Still, he hadn't realized how much it would fucking hurt.

"This isn't your job, Chris."

"Anything that involves you possibly being hurt is my job. I don't give a damn if you don't get that right now."

"You're going to get me fired."

"The FBI doesn't know I'm here." He paused and then let some of his own anger loose. "You think I like screwing myself and Cam? That it's fun watching my career go down the drain because I can't remember, point by point, what the fuck happened during that riot?" he demanded, and then lowered his voice. "Just let me do what I need to do."

"What you need to do is stop trying to control this situation. You have your own to deal with."

"You are my situation. Don't you get that? Ever since I first kissed you . . . And I'm not going to let something happen to you just because there are circumstances keeping us apart."

"There's more to this than the investigation."

"I know that. But right now, I'm dealing with one thing at a time." He moved to leave and then stopped. "You're so tough, Jamie, so strong. But you don't have to always be that way around me. You know that, right?"

"Yes, I know that. I've let my guard down for you—I've let you in."

"Letting me into your house isn't the same as letting me in," he said evenly. "You've kept me on the outside of your life. Even in Africa, when we were looking for PJ and Nick, you told me things, like your witness protection status, and still managed to stay inside your glass house."

"You haven't let your guard down for me either, not really," she shot back.

"Maybe not."

"What happens when the walls do come down, for both of us?"

"I don't know. Are you willing to find out?"

"I've come further with you than I ever have with anyone, Chris. I'm willing. Probably since the first day I met you. There's just so much to deal with, so much to talk about."

Chris didn't say anything for a long moment, and then, "My mom died when I was fourteen—and I knew before it happened, because of my gift, the same way I knew about Mark."

"Oh, Chris." When he'd told her last night about his gift, she hadn't taken into consideration how it might affect his entire life.

"It happens with anyone I'm close to. So . . . there's my fucking wall." He sounded half-angry even to his own ears and he wasn't exactly sure where that anger was directed— at himself or at her. "You can let me know when you're ready for yours to come down."

"I don't know if it will. If it can."

"So you're never going to tell me what happened to you when you were little, then? Why you're in witness protection?"

"I'm not supposed to. Ever. To anyone."

"I'm not just anyone. Not anymore, not ever, no matter how hard you're trying to fight me."

"You don't know everything. And once I tell you, you're involved. I can't take it back. And once you're involved, you're a target."

"So what, better that I don't know, like Mike?"

"Drop it."

"I'm sorry, Jamie, but no matter what, unless you stay completely unattached to anyone or anything, there's danger."

"I can't give you what you want."

"You can, you just won't. I'm in this. *We're* in this. And it's not just us anymore, so we've got some major shit to figure out here."

She hugged her arms around herself. "The more people who know, the harder it is to control. The more people you get close to, the more you put them in danger. Don't you see, if we get involved, it's not only you and me and the baby. You've got a family. Things will get complicated."

"I don't mind brick walls. I won't keep running into them, but I'll sure as hell find another way around it. If I can't do that, I'll blow it the fuck up, but rest assured, I will get through." He paused, and then, "I know your name used to be Ana."

Her mouth opened but she didn't say anything.

"It's what you named the baby I delivered in Africa," he explained, and yes, that had been her reasoning. It had felt good to say that name again out loud, even though it wasn't hers any longer.

She'd practiced and practiced in order to get rid of Ana—to stop responding to the name, to stop writing it on her school papers. As an eight-year-old, the concept of being reborn couldn't be explained the way it can to an adult. It was hard and confusing, and for a long time she hated her new name, the one given to her when Kevin took her and PJ in.

Follow the rules and you won't get harmed. It really was that simple. Except following the rules, especially the strict ones necessitated by witness protection, wasn't easy. "It's hard for people to follow the rules, because they have to leave everyone behind. No one wants to do that, no matter how much they're told that they need to look at it as a fresh start, a new opportunity. It's so much easier said than done. This is so much further than I've ever gone before, than I've ever wanted to go." She reached down until her hand found his, laced her fingers through his. His grip was firm but he didn't relax his stance. "People around me die, Chris."

"Nothing to do with the fact that you surround yourself with danger, right?" he challenged. "Mike was in a dangerous job. Your parents—your mom, she put herself on the line. Jesus, Jamie, you've got to understand that people make their own choices. Including you."

With that, he turned away from her and left the house, leaving the door partially open between then.

CHAPTER
7

J amie saw the marshal—the one Kevin had posted on her front porch—nod to Chris as he walked past, across her lawn, and disappeared into the woods.

Whether or not Chris was planning on camping out there was none of her concern. Or it shouldn't have been, even though the tug in her gut told her otherwise.

"It's been quiet," the marshal named Sam told Jamie now.

"Good. That's good."

"Get some sleep. I'm moving inside in about ten minutes. Ollie and I will be here all night," he continued, mentioning the man who was currently settled in on the screened-in porch off the kitchen.

"That's fine. I'll be in the bedroom. And, um, that guy, he might stay out there tonight."

"Yeah, he told me. Fucking snipers are always crazy," Sam said, although a small smile played on his lips.

"Yeah, crazy," she muttered as she went inside, closing and locking the door behind her. She was still so angry at Chris for making assumptions about her relationship with Mike.

You're angry with him because he hit on the truth in about three seconds flat.

Mike had been her first partner when she joined the Bureau. She'd been so excited to be in the field finally, after all the training and the studying and the intensity of everything, to move into a new kind of on-the-job pressure was something she'd been looking forward to.

Mike, not as much. He hadn't been thrilled to be partnered up with a brand-new field agent, never mind a much younger one—and a woman, at that. And he'd let her know it from day one.

But he'd actually been a big softie, helping her along through procedures, letting her take the leads in some of the collars they first did together. They'd made a damned fine team—he'd often commented on how she was much more skilled than most new agents.

Of course, he didn't know the kind of background, the on-the-job training she'd had.

Mike was fourteen years older than she'd been. Although he hadn't looked or acted it. She supposed the combination of constant togetherness plus the close quarters they'd shared bonded them—at first because she'd needed a place to stay after her roommate had gotten them evicted from their apartment. She'd refused to go back to Kevin, and as soon as Mike found out she was planning on staying in a cheap motel by the thruway, he'd told her he had a spare room.

In so many ways, they'd never been anything more than roommates. She'd started out in the spare room and somehow, after the first few months, they'd gradually moved into a sexual relationship.

Mike hadn't questioned her—didn't ask about her past or what she wanted to do in the future. He let her live in the moment, which had most likely been their downfall.

By the end, they'd been back to living in their separate bedrooms. Jamie had been looking for apartments on her own and wondering how they could actually stay partners on the job once their personal relationship ended.

Of course, she hadn't been given the chance to find out. And then she'd discovered that Mike had left her the house in his will. A punch in the gut, to be sure, but she hadn't been able to bring herself to sell the place yet.

Speaking of guts, hers rumbled, and she realized she hadn't eaten since breakfast. Not good.

Her hands wandered to her abdomen. She might be able to hide it for another four months maybe, if she was lucky. Most female agents went on desk duty for the majority of their pregnancy. Too much risk and liability for everyone involved.

Few women returned after maternity leave, even though they left saying they'd be back. She wondered which camp she'd fall into and then pulled her shirt back down over her belly and grabbed some crackers and fruit and brought them into her room.

She wondered where PJ was, if she'd come back...if they'd make up as if nothing happened, the way they always did. Still, the invisible wall would be there between them, holding back the things they could never—and would never—talk about with each other.

Jamie would call her tomorrow and make things right somehow.

For now, she stretched on the bed, smelled Chris on her pillow and sighed as she bit into a fresh peach.

At least your head feels better.

Her cheeks went hot and she wondered if a cold bath was in her future.

PJ was watching him.

At first, Saint thought she was part of his dream-slash-nightmare, her concerned face appearing in his line of vision through the sliding glass door as Mark's bruised face faded from his sights. But when he woke fully, he realized she was really there, like some beautiful, capable fallen angel.

He didn't acknowledge her. Instead, he turned onto his back in the dark—his comforter was on the floor, along with the top sheet, and he'd lost track of the pillows too.

She hadn't been there when he'd gotten home—he'd checked for her casually, even though he told himself that he was crazy to let a random woman sleep on his deck, to offer her the key to his house.

Yeah, crazy—he was more than halfway there.

She'd been in the house while he was gone—she'd used

towels and she'd washed them and piled them neatly on top of the dryer.

When he'd first climbed into bed, he'd thought about her, sleeping on the deck below, heard the light rain drumming along the wood and the windows and reached down to fist his cock.

This had happened last night too. He needed the relief. Everything hurt, a soreness borne mainly from grief and helplessness, and no matter how long he ran or how much weight he lifted, no matter how far out he swam in the surf and let the current batter his body, he was still unable to sleep. The second his eyes closed and his mind drifted off toward elusive REM, he heard the screams, Mark's screams—even though he'd been a million miles away from Africa when Mark was killed, he knew he'd never stop hearing them.

After the initial shock of the nightmare wore off last night, his thoughts had turned to PJ and he'd stroked himself to completion in the shower.

Tonight, he didn't bother to get up, laid with one arm over his head and the other hand moving up and down his rock-hard erection.

Even without looking, he knew she was there in the dark, watching. It was hot and dirty and he wanted her to do more than watch, wished she'd push her way into the room and into his bed, the way she'd pushed herself unwittingly into his life, just when he'd needed someone the most.

He gritted his teeth as he continued to stroke his heavy cock, his body tensing with the impending orgasm—his hand-job would typically be quick but since she watched, he drew it out, enjoyed the ache in his balls.

With his eyes closed, he could picture PJ on him, riding him . . . and it took everything he had not to stop and head out onto the deck to take her there.

The deck outside Saint's house had two levels. Sometime after midnight, PJ had pulled herself up to the higher floor just to prove to herself that she could again watch over a sleeping John St. James, the way she had the night before.

Tonight, things were taking a decidedly different turn. He was naked, completely stripped down, and after the nightmare that made his covers twist and turn and fall to the floor, he'd lain there and reached for his cock.

Her own mouth had dropped when he'd done that, spread his legs and played with himself for a few minutes before he began to masturbate in earnest.

His body was beautiful—she'd noted that last night, but now, seeing it splayed naked, his hip bones jutting out under his eight pack and hard pecs and large hand that moved along his hard cock . . . She realized she was actually holding her breath.

He'd thrown one arm over his head, his eyes appeared closed, as if he was lost in thought and pleasure as his hand worked his shaft—and she should not be here, watching this. Watching him.

It was foolish to think she could be the one to keep away his bad dreams, like some kind of living, breathing dream catcher. And still, even now as she watched him doing something intensely private, she knew that if she could keep away the bad dreams by her presence, she'd stay here all night.

God, he looked good. Despite the cool air, a thin trickle of sweat ran between her breasts. She could do this with him, slide her hand between her own legs, match his rhythm.

She'd forgotten how long it had been for her—before her time with GOST last year, she'd had an active, if not varied, sex life. She'd behaved more like a guy, not wanting to get tied to any one person. For the past year, she'd pushed her needs far underground, never giving them release.

Tonight, as she watched Saint pleasure himself, she wanted nothing more than to give herself permission to help him. Ever since she'd lain on him the other night, she'd felt the hard contours of his body against hers.

She swore she could hear his long, drawn out moan through the glass doors as his back arched, and still she couldn't tear herself away, watched him come all over his hand and abdomen and chest and felt the tight wetness between her own thighs.

After, he looked content, eyes closed, head tilted toward her.

Did he know she was there? Had he been thinking about her?

One thing was for sure, he wasn't asleep yet. His hand reached for a discarded T-shirt, used it to wipe his chest down, and she took that opportunity to back away into the shadows.

With her hands fisted at her sides, she watched him throw the shirt to the ground and turn on his side to face her, his sex still heavy between his legs, his eyes open and staring toward her.

Or at her.

She swallowed hard, her throat tight and dry, the nervous feeling in her stomach like wild butterflies threatening to make her act on impulse, the way she'd always done. She could strip here, in front of him, bare herself on the deck and pad barefoot toward him. He would see her scars—the outward ones . . . but then, she was pretty sure he could already see through her to her internal wounds as well. And that made her stomach jump around even more as his gaze held hers.

There was no way he could see her clearly, yet somehow he had her locked in. She couldn't move until he closed his eyes or turned back over. Or got up from the bed and walked toward her.

It would be incredibly easy for her to step inside, into his bedroom, his bed. His life.

She didn't deserve that. Too many amends to make first. And so she remained standing on the deck until he finally closed his eyes.

He slept until the dawn and once the light came up behind the ocean, she went back down to the lower deck and made the call to Africa she'd been thinking about all night.

Dave answered on the first ring. "What do you need?"

She smiled into the phone. "I need you to track down a body for me."

She'd met Dave Fredricks—a mercenary working in Africa—after GOST disbanded. GOST, short for Government Operatives Specialty Team, had been a secret, government-organized group of mercenaries who'd been culled against their will from places like Witness Security. Their lives were already threatened, and the masterminds behind GOST took advantage of that, went further threatening their families, a very effective way to keep them in line.

And she'd been a part of that. Yanked from CIA training after a stint in the Air Force, she'd been told that Jamie would be brought into GOST if PJ didn't cooperate. And so, for eight torturous months, she had.

She'd been a shell when it was all over, hadn't been ready, willing or able to go back to the States, and so she'd hooked up with Dave. He'd offered her jobs—mainly, she'd done security, had refused to take on anything that was too similar to what she'd had to do for GOST—and he'd given her a place to live, hadn't judged her on anything she'd done. He'd simply listened. He'd also given her some semblance of safety, and she'd be forever grateful to him for that because, in doing so, she'd found herself ready to come back home and face her life again.

Now she gave him all the details she knew about Mark Kendall and his last known position. And when she hung up the phone, the first sense of peace she'd had in a long time settled over her.

When the sun came up and men arrived for the second shift, Chris left Jamie's backyard and headed for home.

This Handler guy could hurt her just as easily during the day, of course, but men like that counted on the night. They were cowards—and cowards didn't change their patterns. Besides, he didn't want Jamie to get into trouble, and from what the marshal had told him, the FBI would no doubt be getting involved if Handler wasn't caught soon—they wouldn't let one of their own hang in the wind without protection, whether Jamie agreed to it or not.

Chris certainly didn't need the FBI to see him guarding the agent investigating him, and besides, he was meeting Cam at 0600. His house was empty, so he showered quickly and headed to the diner near the JAG office to talk with Cam. Cam's own meeting with Jamie and his lawyer was at 0900; Chris's, a couple hours later.

Cam was waiting for him, coffee poured, newspaper spread out on the table, which he quickly folded up. The man looked as tired as Chris felt.

"How are things?" Cam asked. He sounded concerned, and yeah, Chris must've looked more like shit than he'd thought.

Cam was ten years older than Chris, had been Army from nineteen—went from Ranger to Delta and had seen a hell of a lot of action with both groups. And, as he'd told Chris on the phone, this mission had rocked the shit out of him.

Not an easy thing to do.

"Not bad." Chris said in response to Cam's question, and slid into the booth and ordered his own coffee.

"You've got to eat."

Chris didn't bother arguing, added a breakfast special to his order and waited until the waitress left before saying anything else. And then, "You ready for your meeting?"

Cam shrugged. "Not much to get ready. Agent Michaels has all my notes and she's done everything but scan my brain for a memory chip. Besides, it's not me they're after. I don't know what else I can bring to the table to help you out, bro, but I sure wish there was something."

Here, in the relative quiet of the diner, the men could go over that last night, point by point. But the fact remained that, because of the circumstances, there hadn't been a hell of a lot of talking going on the night Mark was killed—it was all reaction.

"There was a locked door inside the embassy—it had to be stocked with C4. The explosion was well planned."

"We were compromised from the second we landed," Cam agreed.

Chris ran his hands through his hair, pushing it off his face for the millionth time. It was much too long, as was Cam's—the way he and his team were supposed to wear it so they wouldn't get tagged as military. In many places in the world, the U.S. military was not a welcome sight.

He'd tie it back before he dressed in uniform for the meeting with Jamie and the lawyer.

"I'm sorry I can't help more with anything," Cam said.

"Tell the truth—that's all the FBI is looking for."

"If you believe that, I've got a fucking bridge to sell you," Cam told him fiercely. "You watch your goddamned back, all right? Don't trust the FBI farther than you can throw them."

Chris nodded slowly, and Cam muttered, "Shit, sorry. Look, it's just that I'm used to leading men, not losing them," Cam noted grimly, pushed the coffee cup away from him.

The Joint Task Force had been born long before 9/11, but this had been the first time either man had been a part of one. Chris was pretty damned sure he didn't ever want to be part of one again—Cam's feeling appeared to be mutual. But Chris knew there was more to it than that—the look in Cam's eyes was that of a trapped man, and it had nothing to do with their failed mission.

"I leave in the morning. Training for a new Op begins in forty-eight hours. My men are waiting for me. I finally got the okay to call in and speak to them last night. Fucking Delta has more rules than the Pentagon," Cam muttered.

"I haven't been to the range since this happened," Chris admitted. "I can't even see myself moving out again."

Cam nodded slowly. His expression seemed to make it okay for Chris to continue, to tell Cam what he couldn't say to his brothers or to Saint.

"When everything's said and done, I don't know..." Chris faltered. Felt completely disloyal, as the brothers had promised one another long ago that they would all remain in the military and retire together. The plans for what they would do afterward had always been sketchy—none of the men had ever liked looking very far into the future, and a life outside the SEALs wasn't something any of them had been ready to consider.

Until now.

Cam was watching him carefully. For Chris, finishing the sentence would make it real.

"I don't know if I want to stay in," he said. Firmly. Because it was the truth.

Cam nodded. "So you'd finish up this tour and then...?"

And then. "I don't know. I don't even know if they'd accept my not re-upping now."

"But if they did," Cam said. "You'd get out."

"I think so. But this could all be a reaction to Mark. A temporary one." He buried his face in his hands. "Fuck, I don't know," he said, his voice muffled. "I don't know what I want. I do a lot of good, I know that. But death is hitting too damned close these days. I used to think that people were brought into your life for different reasons—to teach you lessons, to help you through the hard times..."

"Sometimes people come into your life for good things," Cam said, and yeah, that was a surprising revelation, something Chris hadn't exactly thought about. "One thing I'm sure as shit about is that this life isn't for the weak." He finished his coffee, and grimaced as he looked at his watch. "Fuck, I'm going to be late."

Cam stood—his sleeves were pushed up, and for the first time Chris noted the mark of a tattoo that had been lasered off on his left forearm.

"What about you? You ever want out?" Chris asked.

Cam paused, stared out the window for so long Chris thought there was someone out there waiting for him. But when Chris glanced outside himself, he saw nothing but an empty parking lot.

Finally, Cam turned back to Chris. "Do I want out? Every fucking day of my life," he muttered, and then walked out without looking back.

CHAPTER

8

After leaving Cam, Chris stopped on base to fill out some necessary paperwork for his medical leave and he met with the doc, who told him he was healing well but not to push it.

That was, of course, not going to happen, but Chris gave the doc credit for saying it with a straight face. "You can do light PT. Better yet, go to the range and blow up some shit. That should keep you happy for a while."

"Yeah, sounds good," he muttered, because his gut clenched when Doc mentioned the range. Typically, it was his favorite place to be, and he knew he needed to force himself to head there immediately, to push himself over the initial hump.

This had been the longest he'd ever been away from firing a weapon since he'd entered the Navy ten years earlier.

He kept most of his rifles under lock and key in the training room. Now he opened the metal bin and surveyed his choices.

In the field, he used the match grade M25, but today, his first impulse was to grab his favorite, a worn Parker Hale M85 from the U.K. Mark had given it to him years earlier, when it became apparent Chris would overshadow the senior chief as a sniper. Mark gracefully handed over that position for the good of the team and worked on being Chris's spotter.

Now Chris ran a hand over the long, worn barrel, his fingers instinctively rubbing the old notches, the deep scars of the metal. The rifle had been used, and used well, a gift to Mark from an SAS operative he'd worked with in his early days as a SEAL.

Sentimental value—today, he needed that to be enough as he walked to the open range set up toward the west end of the base.

The Marine in charge checked his ID again and his weapon. Said he was sorry to hear about Mark, and Chris nodded, but couldn't get past the gate fast enough.

It was loud and crowded because it was a perfect day for shooting—high visibility, low wind. Chris put his iPod ear buds in, rather than the standard earplugs, to drown out the constant, sharp sounds of bullets hitting their targets.

Belly down. Adjust scope. Try to forget his spotter wasn't there.

He brushed it off, because he had to do this. Time to get back on the motherfucking horse and stay there.

He turned the music to blasting in a futile attempt to keep his mind from running away from him while he concentrated on the target—a trick Mark had taught him when Chris found himself distracted...

Fuck.

Come on Chris, pull your shit together.

Target locked.

The first time his skills had been used in a combat situation, he'd destroyed three compounds full of illegal weaponry. He'd done so easily—it had involved no loss of life.

Most of the time, a sniper's biggest contribution was the art of surveillance, which meant watching and listening, without the benefit of actually hearing what the enemy said. Instead, it was about sensing. Checking hand movements. Gut instincts. And sometimes, plain old-fashioned luck.

Time to rock.

But his finger didn't move, not when Mark's face, bloodied and battered, flashed in front of him.

He pulled away from the scope fast, realized he was breathing hard and drenched in sweat.

He turned over in the dirt and lay, faceup, staring at the clouds, attempting to convince himself that he hadn't just had a panic attack, that his heart wasn't beating hard enough to come through his fucking chest. Told himself that his nerves were jangled from the investigation, from seeing Jamie.

Told himself that somehow it would be all right.

He knew he wasn't supposed to feel better immediately about what happened, or anytime soon, but the pain was still a hot, fresh jab he didn't want anyone to see.

Mark was gone and Chris couldn't help Jamie. There

was no one he could fucking help right now and that just about killed him. It was never more than at times like this, when his gift haunted him relentlessly, that he hated it.

His parents seemed to deal with their gifts effortlessly. Chris had never been able to integrate it as well and so he tried to tamp it down as much as possible. Even so, the universe's rhythms always seemed to affect him more than other people—it was why he chose to spend time alone, as too much of the world at a time could wear him down quickly.

Music was okay. Large crowds, not so much. He felt too much push-pull, too frenzied, and so anytime he could take a mike and sing, he would. It calmed his nerves. Centered him.

Jake would roll his eyes when he talked like that but Chris knew both his brothers got it.

He broke down the rifle and got the hell off the range. Halfway to his car, his phone began to vibrate in his hand. He hadn't even realized he'd fished it out of his pocket minutes earlier and was just holding it, waiting for the call to come in.

He flipped it open as he stuck his keys in the ignition. "I knew. I knew, and I let him go anyway."

"Would it have mattered? You saw what you saw." His dad's voice was calm and quiet, as if he knew saying the wrong thing now could cause Chris to hang up the phone.

"It might have."

His dad didn't say anything then and Chris sighed as he pulled off base and headed toward the lawyer's office.

"I don't know if I believe that destiny's set in stone," he continued.

"You don't want to believe it. You're still thinking in

terms of good and bad, not what is." His father was patient, always so fucking patient with this issue.

"Maybe it should've been me."

"No."

"How can you say that? You weren't there." Chris tapped the edge of his fist lightly against the steering wheel.

"I can say it because if it had been your turn, it would've happened. You can't control everything, Christopher, no matter how hard you try." Dad paused. "You think you're at a career crossroads, but you're not—you're at a life cross-roads . . . but you've known that for a while now. Stop try-ing to walk around this one; you're going to have to travel straight through the fire."

Fuck. "I can't talk about this anymore."

"I'm just glad you finally picked up the phone," Dad said quietly.

Chris couldn't say the same, especially not the way his gut churned and his throat tightened. "Later."

He clicked the phone shut and held on to it tightly, in case Jamie called. Which, of course, she hadn't, because she was still pissed off.

He tried to picture her with Mike—with any man be-sides him—and he couldn't; somehow, the only way he saw Jamie was with him at her side.

There was so much he knew about her—and so much more he needed to know, about what happened to her when she was little. The whole story. Maybe because he just couldn't shake the very real feeling that the break-in at her house wasn't about Gary Handler, no matter how many in-dicators pointed to the man.

He'd be back there tonight, unless she needed him sooner.

B y morning, Jamie's head felt better even though she hadn't gotten much sleep after Chris had left.

He left because you threw him out.

"He shouldn't have been here anyway," she muttered, even as her face flushed remembering what his hands had done to her. Between her legs ached with that sweet soreness that only came from being touched well; the rest of her night had been fueled by hot, sweaty dreams of Chris that left her sheets a twisted mess and her ever-so-slightly cranky.

"You're still talking to yourself." It was more of a comment than a question from Kevin, who'd arrived an hour earlier and insisted on making her breakfast. He leaned in to pour her a mug of coffee and she put her hand out. "No thanks."

"No coffee?"

"I'm trying to cut back. I'm doing the tea thing now. Decaf."

Kevin didn't say anything and she wondered when—how—to tell him about her situation.

"My men said you had a visitor last night," Kevin said finally, after taking a long slug of his own coffee.

"A friend stopped by."

"Until three in the morning."

"I didn't know I wasn't allowed to have boys over after midnight. Besides, he's not a suspect." Not in this case anyway.

She had a meeting at JAG later with Chris and his

lawyer that she wasn't looking forward to, especially not after the horrible way they'd left things last night.

Kevin shook his head. "Right now, everyone is. How do you know him?"

"He's military, a SEAL." She checked her watch as she steeped her tea—she had two hours to continue stewing over the mess. Her supervisor had already called her twice that morning about the Gary Handler situation and she wondered how long it would be before the FBI decided she needed protection.

"Name," Kevin insisted.

"Chris Waldron."

"I met him in Africa. He saved a man's life." PJ's voice floated across the kitchen.

When Jamie turned toward her, PJ held up her hand and gave a small wave. She didn't smile until Jamie did and then she moved forward and sat down at the table.

Kevin slipped the surveillance monitor he'd set up last night into one of the kitchen drawers before he turned back to PJ.

"Plenty of food here," he told PJ, gave her a wide smile. Both had agreed earlier not to tell her anything about Handler or the break-in for right now. The men who'd watched Jamie's house through the night had left about ten minutes earlier, so PJ would have no reason to be suspicious. And luckily, PJ seemed to only catch the very last part of their conversation, which was Kevin asking about Chris.

"I'll take some eggs," PJ agreed, but refused Kevin's offer of coffee and ignored his mumblings of something not being right with the world when people stopped drinking coffee in the morning. Instead, she went to Jamie's fridge and pulled out a Diet Coke, and for a few minutes things were normal.

If Kevin knew what had happened to PJ in Africa with GOST, he wasn't letting on, treated her exactly the same as he always did—joking with her, telling her she needed to eat more.

God, it was nice, so much so that Jamie was nearly able to forget that Gary Handler could be gunning for her. The feeling of dread balled in her stomach and she sipped some of her tea in hopes it would quell the feelings.

PJ was eating eggs and sitting across from her, and Jamie realized how lucky her sister was to be alive. But PJ had always been lucky, a cat with nine lives, even though she never saw her good fortune as luck. And so they talked about everything but their jobs and their pasts.

"How's Grace?" PJ asked finally.

Kevin's face tightened for a second and then, "I don't know if we'll be together for much longer."

"I'm surprised you lasted this long."

"PJ, Jesus." Jamie fought the urge to kick her sister in the shin under the table for good measure.

"What? It's the truth."

"It is the truth." Kevin took another slug of his coffee and grimaced. "Christ, I make shitty coffee."

Jamie wasn't sure what to say next, wondered if the heavy cloak of guilt for all the lives around her that got messed up ever got any lighter. But Kevin's phone rang, saving them from any further awkward conversation.

When he stepped out of the kitchen to answer his call, PJ conspiratorially leaned forward, her elbows on the table.

"Why's Kevin asking about that Chris guy? Are you dating him or something?"

"Yeah, something," Jamie muttered.

"He seemed good for you."

"You met him for five seconds."

"Longer than that. And you like him."

Jamie rolled her eyes. "As if you know what I like."

"As much as you know me. That's why we fight." PJ made it sound so incredibly simple, and maybe it was—at least that part of it was. But everything else was all mashed together in a large ball of complication that was impossible to pick apart at this point.

No, much easier to shove it into the closet and pretend it didn't exist. But Jamie was tired of doing things the easy way. "No, PJ. I don't know you anymore. I don't know what happened to you in Africa when you were part of that group."

"I'm not ready to talk about that. I might never be." PJ shrugged, took a long drink from the can of soda before putting it back down on the table and staring at it like it held all the world's secrets.

"Where have you been staying?"

"With a friend." She paused. "He lives on the beach. He's military. A SEAL, like Chris. John St. James."

Great. Just great. Jamie shot her a look. "You used to avoid Special Forces men like the plague."

Her sister smiled. "I'm not marrying him or sleeping with him—or planning on staying with him. I'm just camping out on his deck. And stop trying to change the subject about Chris."

Deflecting the topic away from herself was definitely PJ's

modus operandi, but still, something in her tone didn't convince Jamie at all. Maybe it was the way PJ had avoided looking at her when she'd spoken, or the fact that she was busying herself buttering toast, when Jamie knew she didn't like butter, but it was enough to tell her that something was up.

She wanted to tell PJ that Saint was Chris's CO, that the men were friends, but she didn't. She wouldn't mention the investigation either—couldn't, really. But it would be nice being able to talk about Chris with someone. "Chris and I had a fight. About Mike. Or something."

She pulled apart the toast with her fingers and shoved a piece in her mouth so her stomach wouldn't be completely empty for the meeting.

PJ pressed her lips together before she spoke again. "You loved Mike . . . but you weren't in love with him."

"You weren't there all that much. You have no idea what Mike and I had."

"He was a father figure. A friend. You were living like roommates, not lovers."

Jamie wanted to tell her to go screw herself, that she was completely and utterly wrong. Instead, she blurted out, "I'm pregnant. And it's Chris's."

"Pregnant," PJ repeated, stared Jamie up and down as if looking for physical evidence. "You're sure?"

The test could be wrong. No, she couldn't lie to herself any more than she could lie to her sister. "Yes. And Kevin doesn't know," she added quickly with a glance over her shoulder, out the opened doorway of the kitchen, to where the man stood on her front porch.

"You've got to tell him. You might need more protection with a baby. It makes you more vulnerable. You have to know that." She turned back at PJ's words to see her sister gripping the back of the kitchen chair tightly, her hand nearly white from the pressure.

Jamie almost told her about Gary Handler but felt as if she'd already revealed far too much. She didn't want PJ here, gun in hand, protecting her. It was too soon to hit her sister with another potential danger; until Jamie knew what PJ had gone through as a forced mercenary—eight long months of bondage—she was prepared to keep her problems to herself.

Well, most of them. The pregnancy was just too big to ignore—too much for her to sort through alone. And she certainly wasn't ready to discuss it with Chris.

"I don't need any more protection."

"You told Chris—he knows, doesn't he?"

"I had to. You know Nick was involved in what happened in Africa, that Chris traveled with me. He only knows we were in witness protection, though—he doesn't know who we really are or what happened."

"You've got to deal with this immediately, Jamie. How the hell could you let this happen?" PJ demanded. "Bad enough that you nearly got married."

"There's no law that says I can't get close to someone. That's your rule—the one that keeps you from anyone who tries to care about you."

"You're not turning this around on me." PJ's voice shook. It was probably the most upset Jamie had ever seen her. "I can't be here."

"What are you talking about?"

"I have to stay away from you. If that fucking psychopath Alek follows me and finds you, the baby...I'll never forgive myself."

"You never have forgiven yourself—that's part of the problem."

"That's what some therapist told you, right?"

A sudden sharp sound came from the front of the house—probably just the guards coming back, maybe scraping outdoor chairs around, but it put PJ into full alert mode.

To be fair, Jamie had jumped at the sound too, had put her hand to the weapon that was holstered over her plain black T-shirt. All the fear of seeing the bedroom ransacked came flashing back and she knew there was panic in her eyes.

PJ reacted to that, immediately began to check that the windows and the sliding glass doors that led to the back patio were locked before she shut the shades, drew them tight so the sunlight was gone. And then she grabbed the kitchen table and prepared to flip it onto its side so it would provide cover for some of the glass—provide cover for some invisible enemy who, in PJ's mind, was already shooting at them.

"PJ, you're acting cr—"

PJ whirled around on her, gun drawn but pointed to the ground. "Crazy? Maybe I am, Jamie, but you're waiting here like a sitting duck—you've always done that. Don't you know that he could come get you at any time?"

Jamie took her hand off her own gun. "I can't think about it that way. I'd lose my mind!"

"What the hell is going on here?" Kevin stood in the middle of the kitchen, looking between the two women. Jamie was breathing hard, the tears rising, and she cursed

PJ and Chris and her hormones, was ready to hunt Gary Handler down single-handedly at this point.

"Ask Jamie—ask her about the baby, about how she's going to keep a child safe." PJ looked around as if realizing what she'd done.

"What baby? What is she talking about, Jamie?" Kevin asked.

Jamie didn't bother to try to sidestep the question—he had every right to know what was going on. "I'm pregnant, Kevin. It's Chris's baby—the man who was here last night."

"Is he marrying you?" Kevin demanded. He'd always been old-fashioned, so much so that neither PJ nor Jamie had even tried dating when they lived at home with him. A big man who carried a weapon for a living put a real kink in the old social life.

"Kevin, we're not even dating . . . I mean, I don't know what we're doing." She glared at PJ and then continued.

"I want to speak with Chris," Kevin told her.

"I don't think that's such a good idea," Jamie said.

Kevin looked torn—as if he wanted to hug Jamie and yet part of him was squarely on PJ's side. But his softer side won out and he reached over to embrace her.

She allowed the hug, buried her face against his shoulder the way she had that very first night she'd met him, all those years ago when she'd been young and scared and had no idea what the future held.

Not much had changed at all.

"I wish you'd told me—with everything else happening, it would've been a good idea," Kevin told her.

"I just found out. I'm still trying to process it," she admitted.

"What else aren't the two of you telling me?" PJ demanded, and no, there was no keeping anything from her now. She was deeply in mission-mode, her gun still grasped tightly in her hand, her eyes watching the environment around them instead of focusing on Jamie and Kevin.

That was actually the correct way to do a watch, something a lot of people didn't realize. If you watched the person who was in trouble, you weren't actually watching the trouble.

Kevin remained silent as Jamie took a step toward her sister. "Gary Handler—the man who shot me—escaped. I think he's been here."

PJ didn't say anything, but her chin raised as if in response to a threat. "I'm staying with you."

"I don't want you here. You're too volatile right now," Jamie told her, despite the fact that it broke her heart to do so. "You shouldn't even be carrying a weapon. You know that."

PJ slid the magazine out of the gun and laid both on the counter next to the coffeepot before she brushed past them and out the front door.

Neither Jamie nor Kevin stopped PJ from leaving. But Jamie started when the door slammed shut, and then she began to pick up the table on her own, until Kevin stopped her. "PJ is right to be upset."

"No, PJ is overreacting. I'm not letting Alek rule my entire life anymore. I stopped looking over my shoulder the past couple of months. I took back control. It felt good." It was because of Chris, but she didn't want to bring him up again now. Kevin was upset enough, blanching at her words.

"You're never going to have the security you want until Alek is caught. And now, with the baby coming, the possibility of starting a family, you'll have to keep your guard up."

"The trail's been cold for a long time."

"You need to think ahead, to the *what if.*"

"I've always thought about that. But suppose I want to live in the right now?" It was her turn to demand, to get angry—to ask the hard questions.

Kevin had been doing this for a long time—dealing with people who were forced to lead different lives, people who were scared and angry and upset. He wasn't backing down. "For someone in your position, that's not possible."

"Why is it possible for PJ, then? She seems free as anything."

"Physically, she might be. But here"—he tapped his head—"she's even more trapped than you feel."

Jamie knew that.

Kevin continued, "I know you resent hearing all of this. I don't blame you."

"My parents followed all the rules and they still died." She heard the mix of resentment and grief in her own voice, hated that it was all so raw whenever the subject came up.

"They died because your mother screwed up," Kevin said evenly... revealing a truth Jamie had never known. "She called her best friend from home—started that about two months before she was killed. She called her the same time once a week to talk. And that's how Alek found your house in Minnesota. Your mother broke the cardinal rule of witness protection."

And now she was following in her mother's footsteps. She put a hand over her mouth, even though she wanted to shout to Kevin that it wasn't the same thing, not at all. But she couldn't, because the pain of her mother's betrayal stung. "Why would she do that? I don't understand..."

"She was lonely. She planned to...she was going to leave your dad, Jamie. Leave all of you behind and start a new life somewhere else."

"I can't believe it." Didn't want to believe it.

"Your mom's best friend was found dead twelve hours before your parents' murder."

Jamie opened her mouth and then closed it. She grabbed the table for support as what Kevin told her began to sink in. "PJ...she knows all this?"

He nodded. "Jamie, I'm sorry—I shouldn't have told you like this. Shouldn't have told you at all."

"I guess I'm just like my mother. Giving away the position to a stranger."

"I never wanted you to know any of that. I wish to hell I hadn't told you."

"And I wish you'd told me earlier. Don't you see, we were safe until she stopped following the rules. If you'd told me..." She faltered, because she knew that even if she'd known, she'd have told Chris about her past in order to save her sister. "I can trust Chris. I know that. It felt good to admit it to someone. He understands—"

"He can't understand, Jamie. He might say he does, but is he willing to follow you if you have to go into hiding again? Will he give up his family for you and not resent it?"

"I know my father resented my mother for putting all of

us in danger, I know that in the end he hated her," she spat at him. "I'm not stupid, Kevin. I heard all their fights."

Her mother had disappointed her in so many ways—the fights, the way she'd been there in body but not in spirit, when Jamie needed her so desperately. But Jamie had never, ever expected to hear that her mother was the reason they'd been found. Her mother was supposed to be a fierce protector, and instead, she'd betrayed them all.

And now Jamie was doing the same thing, ready to put a child—one that shouldn't have been conceived at all—in danger.

"I need to be alone," she said finally, her voice sounding flat and wooden to her own ears. "You need to all just leave me alone."

"You know we can't do that," he said, even as his beeper sounded. His job reaching out to him. Another family needing him. She could see it in his eyes as he looked from the numbers on the display to her.

"Go," she told him. "You help someone else follow the rules, Kevin. Go help people keep their goddamned secrets to themselves."

Something was wrong. Chris could tell from the second Jamie pushed through the doors of the JAG office and faced him.

Yeah, she'd been pissed at him last night, but the look on her face, the one she was trying so hard to cover right now as she sat across from him at the long table, was well beyond what had happened between them.

She was all alone on her side, while he sat next to Saint

and his lawyer, and Chris wanted to get up and sit next to her.

Mark would've damned well understood it.

Saint, not so much, as evidenced by the hardness in his face when Chris had admitted to him that he'd seen Jamie since his most recent return from Africa.

You're digging your grave, Saint told him as they drove to the JAG offices. *Tuck your fucking testosterone into your pants and check the fuck up. Now.*

A good plan. And based on the way Saint had reacted, Chris figured keeping secret the fact that Jamie was pregnant was best for all concerned.

If the investigation didn't wrap up soon, though, Jamie would have to walk away from the case—and as much as Chris hated seeing doubt in her eyes when she asked him about Josiah, he didn't want her job compromised because of him.

"Let's get started." His lawyer sifted through various folders on the large, rectangular oak table in front of them. It was quiet in here, cool and dark and stately.

It made Chris want to play loud music to break the energy up. Made him want to reach across the table for Jamie's hand . . . and fuck, he wasn't usually this much of a sap.

He was being careful not to acknowledge their connection, except to give her the once-over to make sure she was feeling better. That things with the man stalking her were under control. But still, he hadn't been lying to her when he told her that their attraction was hard to hide.

"Chris, keep it together," Saint muttered when he saw Chris's hands begin to tap the table. Chris put them out flat and tried to keep his feet steady on the floor as he concentrated on Jamie.

"I've spoken with Captain Cameron Moore," she began, directing the statement to him, and okay, so that's the way they were going to play this one. "According to him, none of your team members were happy to have Josiah running point for the mission."

"How is that relevant, Agent Michaels?" his lawyer asked. Chris didn't tear his eyes from Jamie, because he knew what she was getting at.

"Do I have to spell it out? From the start, the team didn't like Josiah's plan. If Chris and the others conspired to get him out of the way—"

"Why the fuck would I conspire against my team? These were men I trusted to watch my back." Chris heard the anger in his own voice when he interrupted her.

"But you don't think Josiah Miller should've been in charge?"

"He had the least amount of combat experience. Besides, there was nothing to negotiate once we got in there."

"So you don't think Mark stepped over the line?"

"Of course he did." Chris stood fast, the Styrofoam cup of coffee Saint had poured him earlier jolted and sloshed onto the table. "He stepped over a line we straddle every damned time we go out. But he saved lives."

"You don't know that for sure. If he'd stayed put, you might've come back with your entire team."

"I didn't realize they taught twenty-twenty hindsight at the Bureau," he spat at her, realized his hands were shaking from anger.

"Josiah sent notes to his supervisor. He said that his team wasn't allowing him to take command effectively."

"They overrode a decision he made—they didn't have to hurt him to do that," his lawyer pointed out.

"Then all your client needs to do is to tell me about Josiah's final moments." She sounded strong, looked strong, but Chris could see she wasn't enjoying this at all. And she was overcompensating out of fear that the other men could tell there was something between them.

She cared. She could love him—he was sure of that, and it helped to ease some of the pain the past days had wrought.

"I've told you what I remember. I can go over it with you again," Chris offered, but she was shaking her head and closing her small leather notebook.

"I need more, Chris. You've got to understand that. The FBI isn't backing down on this."

It was her first breach of professionalism, and she caught herself for a moment. But then she continued, looking at Saint and the lawyer. "I've closed the case against Cameron Moore. I don't want *this* case to go any further. Find a reason for me to close it. Please."

With that, she left the room.

His lawyer looked at Chris. "Do you know her outside of this proceeding? Because she shouldn't be working this case if you do."

"Yeah, let's kick off the agent who wants to help Chris and bring in a brand-new, impartial fed who wants his head on a stick." Saint stood. "We'll take our chances with Agent Michaels, understood?"

Saint waited until the lawyer nodded and then told him, "I need a minute alone with Chris."

"That's fine. Call me when you're done. I just need a few more minutes with you both."

Saint waited until the door closed, leaving them alone, before asking, "You want to share a little more with me about what's going on between you and Agent Michaels?"

The words came out before he could think. Or stop himself. "I'm in love with her."

"Oh, fuck, Chris."

"Yeah, that's pretty much what Jake said." Chris paused. "Nick already knew."

Saint continued muttering to himself in Cajun French, a language Chris also knew intimately.

"And she's pregnant," Chris added, which made Saint stop the muttering. Now his CO simply stared at him in disbelief.

"Mark knew... knew that I loved her," he continued. "We talked about it while we were reconning for four days straight on this last mission. I feel like maybe if he hadn't known about my feelings for Jamie, he wouldn't have chosen to go into that embassy alone, he would've taken me with him. Maybe he would've organized a way for the four of us to get some order over the chaos and still save the family."

They'd been belly-down in the jungle for twelve hours overnight. The only move either of them had made in that time had been to close their eyes, one man at a time, to stay fresh and rested.

When dawn had hit, he and Mark shifted back for more cover. Twenty-seven hours into the mission and already they'd lost a man.

"Do you love her?"

"*I could.*" The words came out faster than he'd intended, which told him that there was a powerful truth to his admission. "*Everything between us happened so fucking fast—there wasn't time to think about anything or analyze it, it just was.*"

Mark was cleaning his rifle as they spoke. "*So what's the problem?*"

"*Baggage.*"

"*Hers or yours?*"

"*Both.*"

Mark paused in cleaning his weapon. "*You're going to let that shit stand in your way? All that bullshit doesn't matter. Call her when you get home.*"

"Mark did what he wanted when he wanted. Especially after his second time being captured—he really just fucking went for it." Saint shook his head. "I'm not surprised that he was the first one to tell you not to let anything hold you back from Jamie, if she's who you really want."

"She is."

Saint nodded. "Looks like she wants you too. So she'll investigate. And there's nothing for her to find, right?"

Mark's final words to Chris from that night echoed inside his head and he could swear he smelled the burning fire as if it was right in front of him, could feel the heat on his face . . . could see the serious look in Mark's eyes that forced the promise from Chris.

I'm asking, Chris . . . I need you to do this for me . . .

Chris had done it. "No, there's nothing for her to find."

CHAPTER
9

She'd been as unprofessional as shit.

Jamie wanted to bang her head against the wall but went with calm and cool, as if she'd totally meant to tell them to find a way to clear Chris. She'd shut her notebook and stood as regally as possible and exited without a look back at the men who'd been seated across from her.

Chris had been right about what he'd said last night—there was no real way to hide the attraction between them, and she wondered how she could be so incredibly angry at someone and still want him so much.

She should've brought a lawyer from the Bureau with her to the meeting. Maybe that would've kept her on a short leash. Or, at the very least, gotten her released from this case.

Her supervisor had given her this job as a way to redeem herself, and so far she'd done everything possible to insure that wouldn't happen. Based on today's performance, she needed off this case. Or a miracle to show that Chris hadn't done a thing wrong during the mission.

Now, against her better judgment once again, she waited in the outer office area to have a talk with Saint. He remained behind closed doors with Chris and the lawyer for a good fifteen minutes more before he emerged, alone. Thank goodness—she wasn't ready to face Chris again just yet.

She really wasn't ready to face the broad, handsome CO either, but she had no choice if she wanted to find out about her sister. Looking to a near-stranger for information about PJ should've been familiar to her by now, but it still hurt.

She'd always known so little about her sister's love life. Maybe because there wasn't much to know—at least on PJ's end. Every man she'd been with had fallen a little bit—or a lot—in love with her. But PJ had never felt the same.

However, something about the way PJ looked when she spoke of Saint had made Jamie realize there was more going on there than even PJ realized.

Saint was handing in his visitor's badge at the front desk. She stepped up next to him and did the same, and he acknowledged her with a curt nod before attempting to turn away.

But she caught his arm and said, "Saint..." and then hesitated briefly, as she couldn't judge the look in his eyes.

Perhaps the flare there had something to do with the fact that she still held his arm—not a good idea at all, and she quickly released it. "I need to speak with you, in private."

"I'm not authorized to speak with you concerning Chris's case. You know that as well as I do." His look was pointed, but not unkind.

"It's about PJ."

"PJ? How do you know her?" His eyes narrowed slightly, his voice took on a protective tone, and yes, her instincts had been right on the money.

"She's my sister."

Saint looked surprised and then motioned for her to walk with him. He waited until they exited the building and were in the open air of the parking lot before he spoke. "She told me she had a sister—she never mentioned you by name, though."

"Yes, well, she wouldn't. She came to see me this morning, and she said she's staying with you."

He kept his eyes forward and continued walking. "She's living on my deck."

She raised her eyebrows. "On your deck," she repeated.

He shrugged. "She's got a sleeping bag and a tent."

"Can't you invite her in?"

"Have you met your sister?"

"Okay, yes, point taken. She's stubborn."

"Beyond stubborn," he muttered.

"What's your address? I'll come get her."

"Seems to me she's not looking to be rescued."

She stopped in front of him, blocking him from walking any farther, her frustrations of not being able to control anything in her life spilling over onto him. "You met her less than two days ago. You don't understand—she's..."

"Fucked up. She's fucked up," Saint finished for her as he stepped around her and moved toward a large, black SUV. She caught up with him as he opened the driver's-side door and finished, "Who isn't?"

She had no answer for that one, because certainly, at this moment, she fit into that category. "I'll come get her," she repeated.

"Leave her. She's fine." Saint's voice was gruff. "She'll come inside, or back to you, when she's good and ready. Not before. Pushing her will only make things worse."

"She's not going to stick around. She never does."

"And you're telling me this, why? To warn me?" Saint was obviously through listening to her, was inside the car and closing the door as he told her, "Time's up, Agent Michaels."

She didn't bother to argue—there was a firm set to his jaw. He'd gotten the message. She stepped back and stood there as he drove out of the parking lot.

If she really needed to, she could get Saint's address, go to his house and grab PJ. But what then? After this morning's episode, it was all too clear that PJ hadn't dealt with anything that had happened to her in Africa with GOST.

No, maybe PJ was at the right place with the right person. Saint seemed as if he could handle anything. Whether or not he could handle her sister remained to be seen, but it appeared that he'd already taken up that gauntlet.

As Saint's car exited the lot with a resounding screech, Jamie's cell phone vibrated in her bag. She fished it out as she began to walk to her own car, flipped it open, and said hello without checking the caller screen.

"Just because you've got men watching you and your house doesn't mean I can't get to you, Jamie. You can't keep yourself safe forever." The voice was deep and angry, and there was no mistaking it was Gary Handler's. Months of surveillance, listening in to his conversations had embedded it deep within her brain. "I just had the pleasure of killing one of your agent friends—Heather Linn. She had no idea what hit her."

She circled around, phone to ear, gun drawn from its holster, and let her gaze sweep the bustling parking lot. There were plenty of hiding places around, although she couldn't imagine Handler would have followed her here.

He must've found her cell number on something inside the house. "You're going down, Handler. You might as well turn yourself in."

"I've got nothing left to lose, Jamie. I'm not going back to prison. At least not before I finish what I started the night I killed your partner."

"I'm ready for you, Handler. I always have been."

Gary laughed, a harsh boom in her ears. "You put up such a good front... it's going to be a pleasure watching you die."

"You bastard," she started, but he hung up quickly—so the call would be too short to trace, no doubt. If Gary had learned his lesson, he'd be using a disposable cell phone anyway.

Heart pounding, she moved quickly, boots clicking on the pavement as she hurried toward the relative safety of the building. She pushed open the heavy doors that led to the lobby.

She scanned the area, looking for a familiar face, someone in disguise, anything. There was security at the gates—she would check with them once she called in backup.

She needed to get the heck away from the glass doors, although they were double reinforced, and so she moved toward a small waiting area.

Phone in hand, she began to dial her supervisor, as Chris came out of his lawyer's office.

Her focus shifted toward him . . . and she jumped as her phone rang. Speak of the devil. It was Lou.

"Gary Handler killed one of our agents last night," he told her without any preface as soon as she answered. "He left your picture on top of Heather Linn's body. A picture of you outside our offices, dated the day you left for Africa. Handler's fingerprints are all over it."

Jamie hadn't known Heather well, but that didn't matter. She was a fine agent and a nice woman. Damn, she'd gotten married recently. "Handler called me—just now. He told me he killed Heather."

"Where are you?"

"At the JAG office. I just finished interviewing Chris Waldron."

Chris, who'd walked through the lobby like a heat-seeking missile headed full force toward her and currently stood by her side, taking in every word.

She stared down at the pinpoints in the otherwise all gray carpet, in order to collect herself so she didn't have to look into Chris's eyes. "Where was Agent Linn killed?"

"Outside the train station—apparently, she got a tip that's where Handler would be."

The tipster was most likely Gary Handler himself, or someone he paid a quick buck to make the call for him.

"As a precaution, I've sent an agent to sweep your house and wire the outside with infrared and cameras. Bugged the phone lines. Kevin told me there were no prints, no forced entrance. We'll get the bastard, but until we do, I'm putting some agents on your tail—Lyle Marcus and Paul Winston," Lou continued.

She knew there was no way out of that one. And now, with even more proof positive that Gary Handler was gunning for her, this wasn't the time for her to refuse. "Stay inside. I'll send Lyle and Paul for you now. You'll know more when they get there," Lou said, and clicked off.

Chris was standing in front of her, practically body blocking her. Once she hung up, he simply said, "Tell me," without taking his relentless gaze off the lobby.

She didn't bother arguing, told him about Handler and his call. "He left me a message on the agent's body. A photograph of me, outside my office. A recent one."

Chris's eyes finally met hers as he took her hand in his. "We've got to get you out of here."

"Agents are coming to escort me home. My house is being swept. It's under control."

"It's not under control at all. And if you think I'm letting you go back home alone, you're out of your fucking mind, Jamie." He led her to a chair, and yes, sitting was good. "Did you eat today?"

She rolled her eyes at him but nodded yes.

"Where are your car keys?" he asked. She reached into

her pocket and handed them to him, watched as he gently eased off the back portion, where the battery for the automatic lock was. Then he clipped the wires and she looked at him in surprise.

"You think there's a bomb in my car?"

"I don't know what the hell to think, but I'm not taking any chances," he said, pulled out his phone and made a call. After a quick conversation, of which she only caught a few words, he told her, "Nick's coming. Explosives are his specialty. I'd rather he check out your car first, then the FBI can have a go at it when they get here."

Yes, there would be no harm in that. Especially if there was an explosive planted that could hurt innocent people in the parking lot.

She was so glad Chris was here. Glad she wasn't alone. Her stomach grumbled and Chris gave her a look.

"You don't need to worry about me constantly."

"Don't tell me what I need to do, Jamie. I'm always here for you. You know that. You might not see me, but if you need anything, you just call my name."

His voice became a low growl as he spoke. It sent a jolt from her belly straight to her groin and she swore that if he said one more thing, she was going to kiss him right here, in the middle of the JAG lobby.

How he could take all concerns away in seconds like that, make her feel there were no problems to worry about, even as he stood completely on guard.

Nobody was getting past him. It was the most comforting thought she'd had in forever.

———

Saint opened the sliding glass door and motioned for her to come inside. PJ had been pacing the deck angrily since leaving Jamie's house, refusing to return any of Kevin's phone calls, but she smelled food now and she couldn't refuse that.

She'd gotten as far as the kitchen table when Saint turned toward her. "Where did you come from before this?"

She paused, not wanting to answer.

"Is it classified?" he continued.

"No. Not anymore."

"If you don't want to tell me, just say so. You haven't had a problem telling me anything else so far, though." Saint shoved a large plastic cup from a local fast food place in front of her, plus a bagful of actual food. "Here—unless you were planning to catch lunch with your bare hands."

"I'd use a net. Asshole," she muttered. He'd turned his back to look through some mail on the counter, but raised his hand to acknowledge that he'd heard her comment. She tore into the food, letting the grease satiate her the way she hadn't been able to let Saint do last night.

"I met your sister," he said finally, his back still to her.

"You what?"

"She's investigating one of my men. She asked me about you."

"What did you tell her?"

"To leave you alone."

She could've seriously kissed him for that, almost walked over and did so, until he came to her and sat down across the table. "You're a spook, aren't you? Maybe black-listed."

She snorted and took a long sip of chocolate shake through the thick plastic straw. "You've watched too much TV. And how did you know what flavor milkshake I'd like?"

"I guessed. This isn't my first rodeo, PJ. I've been in the military for eighteen years, sixteen of those in the SEALs. I've been around more than my share of feds and spies, most of whom have been trying to recruit me."

"I suppose you have." She threw the empty containers in the garbage pail. "Thanks for the food."

"You can't go back out there—it's pouring."

Indeed, the storm that had promised to come all day had reared its head. Rain hit the doors at an angle and the ocean roared in all its powerful beauty. "I can't stay in here."

"Because you don't trust yourself around me?"

She gave him a long look, and yes, he'd absolutely known she'd been watching him last night. "You hit the nail right on the head, Captain. I don't trust myself at all. I haven't for a long time and I don't think I can start now."

Her words hung between them, but before he could ask any more questions, her phone rang. She glanced at the screen and saw that it was Dave, the man she'd called late last night after she'd witnessed Saint's nightmare and its aftermath.

When she answered the phone, Saint continued to watch her as she listened to Dave telling her, "PJ, we found him, called the Marines to collect the body. It's being transported to the States as we speak."

"Are you sure it was him?"

"The Marines confirmed it according to the information they had," Dave said.

This wouldn't be easy for Saint to hear, no matter how badly he'd wanted Mark found. And she wasn't sure how he would react to what she'd done, but she couldn't worry about that now.

"Okay, hang on a second. I have his CO here." She moved the phone away from her ear and looked into Saint's intense blue eyes. "My friends in Africa, they found Mark's body. They turned him over to the Marines searching the area."

Saint simply stared at her for a moment, as if not comprehending. "You did that for Mark?"

"For Mark. For you." She felt her throat tighten with a sudden rush of emotion.

"I can't believe..." He swallowed hard. "For me..."

She actually had to press the phone into his hand and then, finally, he raised it to his ear and spoke to Dave, confirming some identifying marks. Hearing what he didn't want to hear—that Mark was actually dead, not recovering in some remote African village and ready to come home, injured but alive.

When he hung up, he handed her the phone. Instead of thanking her, he simply sat heavily in one of the kitchen chairs, a fresh grief etched into his handsome face.

Ignoring all her instincts to just leave, she closed the gap between them and sat next to him, touched his forearm. "I'm sorry you couldn't have been the one to find him. But at least he's found. He'll be buried in peace. That has to mean something."

His eyes were wet. "It means everything—you have no

idea. I just can't get past the fact that it should've been me on that mission, not him."

"You should know that you can't think like that."

"No, I mean it was supposed to be me on the mission. Up until two days before, I was on the mission docket." He slid his hands along the table for a second, palms down, and then he scratched it unconsciously with his short fingernails. "Mark filled in for me at the last minute. I had a family emergency—my mom was sick and needed surgery. Mark insisted I go be with her. He was big on family, since he didn't have any. He considered us his family, especially Jake and Chris and Nick—he watched them come up through BUD/S. Christ."

"I believe that when it's your time, you go. Doesn't matter, because at that moment, you're where you're supposed to be," PJ told him as she put her hands over his. "I don't know much, but I don't think Mark would want you to do this to yourself."

He opened his mouth to say something and then thought better of it. Instead, he muttered something to himself and then asked, "Who the hell are you, PJ?"

She couldn't answer that question any better now than she could two nights ago or two hours ago, felt that familiar fight-or-flight urge hit, the way it had earlier at Jamie's house. Thankfully, she stopped herself from overturning the table and drawing her gun. No, instead, she stood and backed away from Saint. "You have no idea who I am, what I've done."

"Then tell me."

"No."

He was on his feet now, moving toward her. "You've killed people."

She had. And if she'd still been in the military, there would've been less guilt waking her up at night in a cold sweat. But the things she'd been forced to do in order to keep Jamie safe, the times she'd thought she wasn't returning from Africa in anything but a body bag, if at all ... She thought about the men she'd left behind, the ones who hadn't gotten out with their lives, and she wanted to get the hell out of Saint's house.

She'd broken her own rule—she'd let him in, enough for him to think he could break down her barriers.

Which, if given enough time and the right circumstances, he could. "Don't come closer, Saint. Please."

"I've let you into my home. My life. My feelings. You've watched me make myself come ... and you wanted to be in that bed with me," Saint said fiercely. "Tell me what you've done. Tell me who you are. I know you were in the military."

The military—yes, she could tell him about that. Maybe that would be enough. "I was in the Air Force. I was a pilot."

Whenever she thought about flying, she felt the familiar tightening in her stomach. Nerves. She knew her CAG would've told her that the best pilots felt them, that it was better to have some fear than none at all.

She ached for the days when she'd felt none, even though that lack of fear had probably contributed to the accident two years earlier, the crash that happened when she was still in the Air Force. The reason she'd resigned her commission. "I was flying a C-130 over Africa when the engine failed."

She'd tried without success to rectify the engine failure. She'd kept some of the team on board too long, trying to fly while the controls systematically shut down, along with the wind. "There were six Rangers on board with me and my co-pilot—we were taking them to their LZ. We'd gone in more quickly than usual for an emergency extraction and didn't have the extra supplies that might possibly have saved us all."

One rig for eight people. Even if they doubled, men would've been left behind and they refused.

She'd been the only woman on board. "I remember them shoving me out of the hatch. I went up with the wind, and the plane...it pitched toward the ocean and there was nothing I could do but watch it happen." If it had just nosedived, the men on board might've had a chance, but the explosion had taken care of that.

"I'm sorry, PJ."

"Yeah, you're sorry, I'm sorry, everyone's sorry." But she wasn't done yet—if Saint wanted it all, he'd get it. And then she could walk away. Mark's body had been found, her work was done. "They wouldn't let me fly anymore—I didn't want to anyway. I got an honorable discharge and the CIA recruited me. And I was in their training program until I was recruited for another position. For a group called GOST."

"GOST," Saint repeated. Yes, he knew who they were—Government Operative Specialty Team. Mercenaries at the government's command, and its mercy.

There had been an entire series of articles on the now-disbanded group, by journalist K. Darcy. The president had convened a cabinet to investigate how and why the group was formed, as well as how and why all the members of the group were dead—except for two.

And now one of them was standing in front of him.

Yeah, she was fucked up, but she had a damned good reason to be. And suddenly, he knew he didn't want her to leave. "Jamie said you won't stay."

"What do you want me to say, Saint? That she's wrong?"

"Yeah. That's exactly what I want you to say. I want you to tell me what you felt when you watched me jack off last night. Were you wet for me?"

Her mouth dropped—she hadn't expected this.

"Yeah, I think you were. I think you were so close to touching yourself, getting yourself off...but you don't want to admit it."

PJ was like a feral cat. She'd attack if rubbed the wrong way, but right now, he didn't have the patience or the heart for a gentle lure. Instead, he grabbed her, probably a mistake, and yet even though she dug her fingernails hard into his shoulders, she kissed him back with a ferocious need that was almost overwhelming. He could feel the strength pulsating off her slight frame even as she resisted with her body.

When she jerked away from him, he let her. She put the back of her hand against her mouth, stared at him, stunned, before she began to circle him, half-crouched. He took the same position, because she knew how to fight—and how to fight well. He had known that from the second she'd pulled the knife on him on the beach.

"You had no right to do that."

"You liked it," he told her. "You have a right to feel."

"Don't you dare attempt to analyze me when you've known me all of two days."

"Why not? You've been handling me since the night we met, treating me like I'm going to fall apart any fucking second." He was as angry as she was now. He moved to her again, got a good hold on her, wrapping his arms around her upper body and holding her immobile with her hands down at her sides.

He wondered why she wasn't struggling more. Why she was half smiling at him.

In about three seconds, he knew the exact reason. She literally had him by the balls. He froze, his life in her hands—and of course, his dick didn't care about anything but her touch. "I'm going to back off." He spoke quietly, put his hands in the air.

"Tell you what," she murmured. "I'm not."

His body tensed expectantly, but the only thing she did was stroke him through his BDUs as she watched for his reaction. Which was, of course, to grow rock hard under her touch and allow her to unbutton and unzip his pants.

His breath came in short gasps as she discovered there was nothing between his skin and the BDUs. Her hand cupped his balls first—and Holy Mother of God, he needed her now.

Right now. "PJ, please—"

She cut him off with a kiss, a long, lingering, gentle kiss that ended with her sucking his bottom lip for a second while her fingers played along his cock.

He groaned. "I'm taking you to bed. Now."

"No, not in your bed. Outside."

"You're kidding." He stared at the rain sheeting the deck.

"I thought you said you could handle the weather."

"I'll show you what I can handle, *bebe*." He lifted her, carried her out the door. His foot still ached from the stitches, but his body ached in other, more important places, and that made any other concerns diminish considerably.

They were soaked from the second they crossed the threshold to the deck. He set her down on the lounge chair rather than put her inside the tent, to see how serious she was about getting naked in the rain.

In a show of faith, he tore his T-shirt off over his head and tossed it onto the deck.

Her clothes clung to her thin, finely muscled frame, and fuck, it was better than any kind of wet T-shirt contest he'd ever seen.

Slowly, appreciating his gaze on her, she pulled the shirt off and leaned back, palms braced, head back, mouth opened to catch the rain. And then she worked her pants off until she lay on his lounge chair in a pair of tiny black underwear.

She was thin and fit and tan and she was waiting for him. Inviting him. Her breasts were perfect, nipples taut, and he was on her quickly, mouthing one with an insistent suck. He heard her cry out softly, as if she hadn't expected that and she tried to move away, to free herself, to tell him no.

Her words were lost in the sounds of the crashing surf.

The rain intensified and he moved down her body, practically ripping the thong from her.

The small triangle between her legs beckoned—he dragged a kiss down her belly, until a sharp yank at his hair made him stop. He looked up at her as she held his head tightly—she was shaking her head, and God, all he wanted to do was bury his face in her pussy and make her feel, wanted to taste and tease and fuck her with his tongue, but something in her eyes stopped him from pushing the issue.

Whatever the reason, he'd get to the bottom of it eventually.

For now, his dick was begging him to move the hell on and he rose from his knees and stood in front of her.

She tugged at his already undone pants, her hands digging into his ass before he could kick them off his ankles, her legs spread for him.

With his hands cradling her ass, she rotated her hips against his sex, hands in his hair. The moans that drummed up from the back of her throat drove him wild, filled him with the uncontrollable urge to play king of the castle and make her his queen.

She was nearly beyond control herself. "Don't make me wait. I want to . . . need to . . . have to . . ."

"I don't have anything."

"I don't care . . . please. I'm on the pill. Hurry."

There was no arguing—her body took him in after an initial resistance, and she wasn't letting go until she'd taken her fill. Her ankles held him so hard he knew he'd see bruises by morning—and he so didn't give a shit. He went faster, deeper, as she yelled his name into the wind.

Rain whipped their bodies. They were both slippery

and slick and it took a hell of a lot of balance for them to hang on to the chair as their pace grew more frenzied. And she took him as much as he took her, in full view of anyone crazy enough to be out on that darkened afternoon in the middle of a thunderstorm.

One of the best parts of Nick Devane's job was demolition. When he was on the wiring end.

Dealing with a bomb someone else might've planted? He'd definitely rather get laid. But since that wasn't an option in any way, shape or form for at least twenty-four more hours, since his girlfriend was on the other side of the fucking planet, he found himself under Jamie Michaels's car in the pouring rain, looking for an explosive device that, if touched the wrong way, could blow him sky high.

Jake, who lived for this shit, was next to him, whistling as he flashed the penlight along the undercarriage.

Dumb-ass. "You're supposed to be checking the interior."

"I already did. It's clean."

"So is this." Nick sighed as the relief coursed through him, the way it always did at the end of a job like this.

"What the fuck is going on here, Nick? I mean, I'd rather be the one to do this so Chris doesn't get blown to shit, but what the fuck? He's not talking to us—he's really inside his own head."

Nick shrugged, the gravel digging into his skull as he did so. "He's always there."

"This is different. Much different. It was the way he was after Mom died." Jake frowned as he mentioned Maggie, almost as if he'd borne too much grief already and wasn't ready to add more. Mentioning her name could, more often than not, bring a smile to the brothers' faces. But sometimes it hit like a sucker punch and left them momentarily reeling.

"Maggie would've known what to do for him."

"We do too," Jake said firmly.

Nick wanted to grin at the bravado in his brother's voice—it had been there since the men were boys and met when they were eight years old. And really, Jake had no idea what to do for Chris right now. "Jamie . . . she's good for him."

Jake snorted. "Jamie's trying to put him in fucking jail for doing his job. How the hell is that good?"

"I asked him if he was with her last night, if she was taking herself off the investigation," Nick told him.

"What did he say?"

"That he didn't realize he had to check in every five minutes. And then he told me—and you—to keep the fuck out of his bedroom."

It was Jake's turn to sigh—his typical wounded sigh—and Nick knew if given the opportunity, his brother would do no such thing. Which was why Chris put the call in to Nick and not Jake.

"I'll call him, tell him it's clear," Nick said, but Jake had already flipped his phone open and was dialing. "Stay off his six, Jake."

"I'm not an idiot, Nick. I can handle things with tact, you know," Jake told him and then started speaking into the phone. "Oh, yeah, hey, Chris—car's clean." Jake was quiet as he listened. "Yeah, I'm sure." He paused. "So what, you're going to make sure Jamie's safe and she's going to keep investigating you and possibly destroy your career and send you to jail?"

Way to stay off his six, Jake.

"He fucking hung up on me."

"Big surprise there." Nick slid out from under the car and Jake followed. They'd wait here until the FBI came to make sure no one could tamper with the car, and then they'd figure out how to help their brother, who didn't seem to want their help at all.

CHAPTER

10

Jake wasn't happy with her. And even though she'd never met him, Jamie could feel the chill through the phone as Chris spoke in a low, growling voice, his shoulders set in a tense stance as he'd turned his back to her.

She held tight to her emotions, kept them wrapped up so she didn't think about anything but getting through this situation.

Think of it like a case—distance yourself. Profile Handler. Figure out what the hell he wants from you.

If Gary Handler had wanted her dead, he no doubt had been close enough to take a shot when he'd taken that picture outside the FBI offices. Could've waited inside her house and surprised her then, when she was completely off guard. So this was about torturing her, making her pay for ruining his gravy train. The drug lord he ran for in Mexico had a hit out on him, thanks to the FBI floating a rumor that Handler had turned evidence.

"Car's clear," Chris said, breaking her reverie. "And your backup's arrived."

He didn't mention his conversation with his brother, but she noted the tension around his eyes. She was sure hers looked similar. Even though it had only been an hour since she'd gotten the call, it felt like time had moved in slow motion.

There was only one thing she was sure of—she didn't want Chris to leave her side. And as she stood to greet her fellow agents, she put a hand on Chris's arm.

"Don't worry, I wasn't planning on going anywhere," he told her with just a hint of a smile.

"Let's get you out of here, Jamie," Lyle was saying, forgoing the usual pleasantries. It was all business, and Paul was right behind Lyle, nodding in agreement and asking Chris who the hell he was.

"He's a friend. He's Navy, a SEAL," she heard herself say. "He'll take me home. You guys can follow." Whether or not the fact that she was taking the man she was supposed to be investigating with her on a personal matter was something the agents would tell Lou, she couldn't be sure. She only knew that she needed Chris with her now.

Lyle's next words proved her instincts correct.

"Jamie, there's something at your house we need you to see, something the agents found when they swept it," Lyle said quietly, his eyes flicking to Chris's briefly.

Still, she stood firm. "I'll drive with Chris back to my house. He's aware of the situation."

Lyle looked at her like he didn't want to say yes, but Chris was already pushing her past them. Together, the four of them walked quickly to the two cars, parked right next to each other.

Just as Nick and Jake had seemed to materialize out of nowhere, they'd also disappeared before she and Chris approached the car. And still, she had no doubt that they were watching until the second she got in.

Within moments, both cars were on the road. She took a deep breath, kept her gun drawn, eyes darting to her side-view mirror.

"Do you want me to call your sister?" Chris asked.

"No." She paused. "PJ is staying with Saint."

He didn't say anything, simply raised his eyebrows as he threw her a quick glance. Obviously, Saint hadn't mentioned that development to him.

"I told her that I didn't want her with me. That she was too volatile. That she was dangerous to me," she continued. "It was a horrible thing to say. I went all that way to bring her back, and then when she finally does show up, when she wants to help me, I tell her to leave."

"If she's unstable, she doesn't belong near you."

"She's not. I mean, she's a little overzealous when it comes to protecting me, but I overreacted."

"Maybe a little space between sisters isn't a bad thing—she can have her space, you have yours, right?"

"Says the man who lives with his brothers."

"Yeah, well, that's different. Mainly because we're all

loose cannons, but typically not at the same time. Not anymore."

She glanced over at him. "Jake seemed pretty protective of you."

He snorted. "Jake's always protective. And you need to be more protective of yourself."

"In case you've forgotten, I am an FBI agent."

"Yeah, I know that, but under these circumstances—"

"Don't you get it? I refuse to be helpless. I'm not giving in to this asshole. I'm not giving in to anyone."

Chris's jaw tightened. He didn't say anything for the rest of the ride, not until they pulled into her driveway. Only then did he turn to her, his voice low and fierce. "I want to tell you that you shouldn't be walking around by yourself, out in the open. I want to lock you in a room and guard the damned door so nothing and no one can ever hurt you. But hell, I know I can't do that, I know you can't lock yourself away because you've been threatened. And I'm proud of you for not backing down."

She didn't know what to say, so she simply took his hand in hers for a long moment. Squeezed it.

He squeezed back. Then, "Anything look out of place to you?"

She'd automatically checked as they'd pulled up; there were no signs of change on her front porch or the yard.

There was another car already in her driveway—the agents who'd been through her house, the ones who'd found something.

"Are you ready?" Chris asked her as Lyle and Paul approached her car.

"Yes. Let's get this over with." She got out of the car and

the four of them walked through the front door together, and were promptly greeted by a female agent Jamie didn't recognize.

"Agent Michaels?" she asked, and Jamie nodded. "We didn't find anyone inside your house, but there's something on the screened-in porch you should see."

"Show me."

The agent hesitated for a brief second, enough for Jamie to know she needed to steel herself for this one.

She never locked the small screen door, figuring anyone who wanted in could easily tear the screen, and she'd rather that didn't happen. The door beyond it, leading to the kitchen, was steel reinforced and that was what mattered.

But today, right now, she wished she'd locked it. Not that it would've stopped Handler—he would've left his present for her on her doorstep then.

Chris put a hand on her back as she stopped and stared at the glass-topped table.

The pregnancy test, the one she'd thrown into the garbage can, was laid out carefully, next to the box it came in, the two pink lines still stark in the small white square.

Handler had gone through her garbage—knew she was pregnant.

She could feel all the agents' eyes on her, waiting for her to confirm that she recognized the evidence.

Breathe. Just breathe, Jamie, she commanded herself so she wouldn't freeze up.

She forced herself not to touch anything, not to grab the personal items and bring them back inside and lock them up.

"Why is he doing this? It doesn't make any sense. I

mean, if Handler's free, he should be escaping to Central or South America, not hunting me down. It's just not his style."

Chris didn't answer that, telling her instead, "I don't want you standing out here." And yes, he was right. Handler could still be close, could've been here setting this up when he called her.

Chris was angry—she could see the fierce look in his eyes as he stared between her and the test. She stiffened her spine and held it together, for both of their sakes.

I'm not giving in to anyone.

She moved away from the table and went back into the house, the evidence of her most recent past—and her future—etched finely into her memory, prompting a determination she hadn't felt in a long time.

P$_J$ and Saint moved into the tent when she began to shiver. He'd dried her off with a towel from her bag and then had gone inside briefly to retrieve his cell phone. When he climbed back into the tent with her, he'd called Chris and told him about finding Mark. And then he'd called the admiral and asked if he could view the body when it came in.

After that, she'd held him and let him lose it in her arms, the way he never would in front of his team. Or maybe not in front of anyone. He didn't cry or anything like that, he remained silent—so silent—in her arms, held on to her tightly, as if protecting them both from some unknown force outside.

And then, when his grip loosened slightly, she'd pulled

him back down onto her, liking the weight of his body on hers. Liking the way he made her feel.

Now, hours later, they remained inside the tent in the rain-darkened late afternoon. The rain had long subsided and they remained pressed together. Resting. Breathing.

"Are you going to stay with Jamie from now on?" he asked. "She wanted to come and pick you up, but I wouldn't give her my address."

She swelled with pride at his protectiveness, but that quickly gave way to the feeling of sadness when she thought about Jamie, about the way she'd completely and utterly flipped out that morning in front of her and Kevin. "My sister doesn't want to see me right now."

She turned away from Saint, not bothering to get dressed. He'd opened the flaps of the tent so they could get the cool night's breeze and look at the ocean without fear of being seen. Not that he'd been worried about that at all before—thankfully, the beach had been deserted and his deck was high enough that someone would need binoculars to see what they'd been doing.

She ached between her legs, a soreness borne from pure pleasure—she'd forgotten the sensation completely and now her body reveled in it.

"She seemed worried about you, not angry."

"No, she can never stay angry at me for very long. It might be better for her if she could."

"I like that you're staying here," he said finally. "I'd like it better if you came inside, though."

"I've come in as far as I can for right now. Can you understand that?"

"I can." He paused. "Do you want to be alone or can I

stay out here with you and try to catch some shut-eye? Otherwise, you're just going to climb up to the top deck and watch me sleep."

She smiled. "You can stay, Saint."

He ran a hand over her bare hip. "Thanks." He paused. "I'm going to see Mark later."

The plane carrying Mark's body would land in Virginia sometime this evening, according to Dave's calculations. From what he'd mentioned, Mark's body was in bad shape. "Maybe you're better off with your memories," PJ said.

"No. I have to see him, or else I'll never believe he's gone," Saint responded firmly. "I mean, this morning... I called him. I called Mark."

His voice sounded dark, far away, as he stared up at the nylon blue ceiling of the tent.

Her heart clenched for him, because she knew what that felt like. After her parents were killed, she'd found herself calling out *Mom* or *Dad* several times before remembering that there was no mom or dad around her any longer. "It takes time."

"The phone rang and I thought, *Mark always picks up on the first ring.* But then I remembered, and I hung up. My hands were shaking. I had a meeting with the admiral, and I kept thinking, *I'm not going to make it through this day.* If I'd waited to hear his voice mail message, I wouldn't have."

Normally she would remind him that he did make it through the day—but he hadn't, not really. Today had been too much of a pileup, culminating in Mark's body being found. It crushed any lingering hope Saint and his men might've had, and maybe that was even harder than knowing immediately that their friend had been killed. Instead of saying anything, she turned in to him again, and then there didn't have to be any words.

It was time for Jamie to call Lou. Beyond time. A call that he no doubt expected, based on the findings at her house.

What it wasn't time for was to talk about the baby with Chris—too much, too complicated. Her head was already throbbing a bit and she sipped on the tea Chris had made for her and tried to forget that there was still so much distance between them, so much ground to cover.

She was simply grateful that he was here.

And so she dialed Lou's number, started right in once she was put through to him—she didn't let him speak, afraid she'd never be able to get it all out. "In light of what's happening, it's best that you take me off Josiah's case. I'm pregnant. Chris Waldron's the father. It happened long before this case opened, but still..."

"So the test Gary left you wasn't a guess. He knows about your condition."

"Yes. He went through my garbage." She closed her eyes for a long second. When she opened them, she noted that Chris hadn't moved from his position by the window, but she had no doubt he'd heard every word.

On the other end of the phone, Lou remained silent for a long moment, and then, "Give your most recent reports to Agent Cooper. Take all the time you need. And don't you dare try to argue with me about surrounding you with protection now."

"I won't. Thank you, Lou."

"Kendall's on his way home."

She glanced toward Chris, clarified, "They found Mark's body?"

Chris stood a little straighter then, set his shoulders. She stared at his back as Lou spoke in her ear. "No autopsy yet, but they sent the preliminary findings." He rattled them off and she noted that the coroner's initial assessment was consistent with what Chris insisted he saw, the damage that had been inflicted through torture.

"Thanks, Lou. And I'd like to insist that Josiah have a second autopsy, with a brain scan."

"That's not SOP."

"I don't really care. Until I hand it to Coop, it's still my case."

Lou grumbled, "I don't want anyone to hang for this if it's unwarranted. Just take care of yourself, Jamie. If you're not comfortable staying at home, there's a safe house—"

"I'm staying," she said.

"I figured you'd say that." Lou clicked off and Jamie put her phone down.

"It's done. I'm off the investigation," she said, and finally Chris turned from the window and faced her.

"Ah, Jamie, I wish you hadn't done that—for your own sake."

She stood, moved toward him. "I can't lie about this anymore. You and I both know that, especially after what happened today at the meeting."

"All you're doing is looking for the truth about Josiah's death—there's no harm that can come out of that," he said, and still, her hands fisted by her sides as if prepared for a battle. There was always a battle happening when she was with Chris—inside, her emotions fighting with logic, and she knew which one she wanted to win.

She nodded, because what else was there to say? They'd gone through the facts so many times, and she kept turning Chris's story over and over in her head, mixing it with Cam's version and trying to come up with something plausible. But even though she knew how memory grew hazy when life and death were involved, had told him as much last night when he'd held her, she knew there was something more bothering her about his case. "Josiah's autopsy didn't clear you. And I know you're holding something back—I don't know why, but you are. I won't be the one who hurts you, Chris, any more than you've already been."

He looked at her with an expression she didn't recognize. "We've got a lot to talk about."

"We do. But—"

"Not now." He was rubbing the fingers on his left hand together as he finished for her. "I won't be the one who hurts you either, Jamie."

With Chris restlessly prowling the house, rifle in hand, while the FBI agents remained outside, stationed at the front and back deck doors, Jamie was slowly going insane.

She got it—a man's protective instincts went into overdrive when a female was around. She'd dealt with it from her earliest days at the Bureau.

Shake it off, Michaels.

"Everything's covered." Chris popped his head into the kitchen. "Why don't you lie down and get some rest?"

"Because I'm not five and I don't need a nap," she snapped.

He nodded and wisely backed away from the kitchen.

"Agent Michaels, Handler's call to you looks to have come from a disposable cell phone," Lyle called to her from the screened-in back porch. She'd figured as much.

She placed her gun on the kitchen counter and realized she needed to do something. Anything. And so she gathered bowls and flour and pre-heated the oven and began to prepare things for baking. Bread was good; bread required lots of kneading to take up the nervous energy in her hands.

She hadn't done this in a while, not since Mike's death. At first, she felt awkward, like she didn't remember how to do it, thought about looking up the recipe to make sure she had it right. And then she realized that *right* was a relative term and it wouldn't matter anyway.

Hands in the dough, she was immediately transported to childhood, for better or worse. She remembered her mom baking, remembered lazy days spent helping her in the kitchen.

She couldn't practice law, and resented having to take a lower-level position in another field to stay under the radar. So in a few months her mom had quit her job at the post office. After that, she'd devoted her time to keeping house and raising the girls, did it with the same vim and vigor she'd given in the courtroom.

Even now, as Jamie stuck her hands in the dough to fold in the last of the flour, she flashed back easily to that kitchen, small but well kept, with bright yellow Formica counters and maple cabinets.

No one can get to you during a Minnesota winter. And

that was true—no one had. No, Alek had waited for a hot summer night, when the windows were shut, the A/C blaring noisily. No one had heard the intruder.

A crack of thunder that sounded too close brought her back to her own kitchen. She'd nearly overworked the dough because she'd gotten lost in thought.

Maybe she'd make dinner for the agents. And for Chris too. She was rusty, but anything was better than takeout again.

After Mike's death, she'd found herself surrounded by food she'd made, more than she could possibly eat. But even when he was alive, it had been too much—she'd been cooking for a table-full of people, just the way Mom had always cooked too much for two adults and two small girls.

So much waste, her father used to say. Mom would get upset and dinner ended up with PJ eating calmly, Jamie with a stomachache, as her parents shouted at each other in another room.

Just like Mom, trying to prove I'm good enough—trying to prove I can do it all.

She tried to resist the strong urge to throw the bowl across the room. Her hands tightened into aching fists—she wasn't sure how long she held that posture, but it was long enough to make every muscle in her upper body clench.

Before she could stop herself, she'd swept the bowl off the counter, knocking it to the ground, and enjoyed the satisfying crash it made. Then she was looking for other things to break, the way she felt broken inside, but Chris's arms went around her, stopping her.

"You're going to hurt yourself."

"I don't care."

"But I fucking do. Do you understand? I care."

Still, she struggled against his grip, tried to pry his arms off her—but his chest was like iron against her back and there was no way she was getting away from him. "I don't want you to. You shouldn't."

"Tough shit," he growled, and then his voice softened. "Tell me what's really going on with you. Please, Jamie."

This time, she couldn't stop herself. "I'm repeating what my mother did—putting this baby in danger." She tried to keep the anger out of her tone, but she tasted the residue of the bitterness anyway. "I didn't know until this morning when Kevin told me . . . she called her best friend. She'd been doing it once a week and no one knew. Again, her choice. Her selfish, goddamned choice. She was supposed to protect us. It was her fault we were in witness protection to begin with and then she was the one who screwed it all up. A mother's not supposed to do that to her kids."

Her voice shook as she continued. "She was going to leave us, was planning to run away somewhere with her friend and just leave me and PJ and our dad behind. She said she felt trapped. And I don't know how I'm supposed to feel about that."

"How *do* you feel?"

"Angry. So goddamned angry, I could scream. How could she do that to us?"

Chris didn't answer.

"God, I've hated her and loved her for so long, and now . . . now I just hate her for what she did." She heard someone crying and realized that someone was her. Finally, Chris's grip loosened, enough for her to turn in to him, bury her face in his chest and bawl her brains out. Crying until she couldn't breathe, until she was sobbing with no tears. Until she was raw and exposed and exhausted.

"Damned hormones," she muttered roughly, pushing away from him and wiping her cheeks with her palms.

"Yeah." His hand went around her waist and then moved over her belly. "They look good on you, though."

She couldn't help but smile a little at his words. "I shouldn't have told you."

"You didn't tell me anything that could compromise your life, Jamie."

"Before Alek came and killed my parents, he went and killed my mother's friend first," she told him. "I'm not worried about just me anymore. I don't want anything to happen to you because you're with me. I couldn't live with that."

"You didn't force me on the plane to the DRC. I went willingly because I was worried about my brother. I got involved. I made my choice." He released his grip on her. "Do you get that? I made my choice."

"I get that."

She realized now that Chris had put music on—it wasn't loud, just loud enough so she could hear the backnotes, the rhythm. She turned to the sink and ran the water so she could rid her hands of the dough and flour still stuck to them. He remained behind her, his face dropping to her neck.

"I know how capable you are. I do get it, Jamie. Always have when it comes to you." His breath was warm on her ear, his hands caressed her hips and then began to travel upward, over her shirt but still headed in a very distinct direction.

"Chris, now's not the time."

But he wasn't listening at all as his hands moved along her breasts—she shut the water off, her hands still wet. And she wanted, oh, how she'd *been* wanting, unable to shake the way her orgasm at his hands the night before had made her feel. She'd tried to re-create it herself, but it wasn't the same.

His hands . . . hands that held a sniper rifle steady, and delivered babies, hands that could make a woman lose all semblance of control.

Maybe she'd been wrong all along, maybe it was the best time for this. For Chris. She'd been attempting to push him away since they'd first met and he'd been pulling her to him just as hard. Even when he'd walked away from her, he'd still left the line extended for her to follow. "I never expected you," she whispered.

"I never expected you either, Jamie. Never expected any of this. I wasn't looking—and maybe the not expecting is what's made it so damned good." He deftly undid the buttons on her shirt, exposing her bra. The shades were long pulled down, the agent on the back screened-in porch hidden from view.

His hands wandered over her breasts, still covered by the simple, sensible white bra—she felt anything but sensible as his thumbs brushed the taut peaks through the fabric, before sliding inside. He rolled her nipples between his thumb and forefinger, and she groaned and turned to him.

He lifted her gently onto the counter so they were nearly face-to-face. He was still taller, his fingers working her nipples until they were swollen and sensitive, and God, she wanted his warm, wet mouth on them.

"I want to make you forget, Jamie," he murmured. "When I'm with you like this, I want to make you forget anything but me."

His mouth covered hers first, a long, hot kiss that left her trembling with need, and then he dragged his kisses along her neck and down the front of her opened shirt until he caught a nipple in his mouth. She sucked in a breath and wound her hands in his hair, half holding him there, and wished they were alone, really alone, so she could let go, call out his name.

She settled for silent pleasure, especially when his hand moved between her legs.

"I bet I could make you come like this," he told her, pressed his hand against the fabric of her pants. "Fully clothed and not able to stop yourself."

She didn't argue, not when his mouth sought her other nipple and tongued it before sucking it between his teeth. Now her hands gripped his shoulders as she felt herself moving against the pressure of his hand, seeking the relief he offered. She bent her head, buried her face in his hair and let out a soft moan as she realized how close she was— and then she stopped trying to hold back and came, hard, clutching at him and whimpering softly.

He held her, stroked her back, murmured, "This is nice. It's always so hot and fast. I like taking my time... like watching you break apart, little by little."

"I want more."

He pulled back to look at her. In case he didn't get the message, she let her hand wander between his legs. He was rock hard and she wanted him naked and in her bed. "I want to send the agents away. Or have you take me away."

"Yeah, you have no idea how badly I want that. But it's not going to happen right now."

"Why's that?"

He moved gently out of her grasp, straightening his pants. "Kevin just drove up."

Shit. "Shit." She buttoned her shirt in seconds flat and turned away from Chris to collect herself.

Palms flat on the counter, she got her breathing under control. There was nothing she could do about the flush she was sure had spread across her face.

Chris was good at making her forget her troubles, her mind...everything.

"I'll go out and meet him," he was saying.

"Chris, no—that's not a good idea."

"Why not?"

"Kevin is...he's tough. Overprotective."

"You mean he'll have no problem threatening to cut my balls off, right?"

"Pretty much." She paused. "He knows about the baby. And you."

Chris nodded slowly. "All the more reason for me to go introduce myself."

He was gone from the kitchen before she could stop him.

CHAPTER
11

Chris Waldron was a fighter. Kevin knew that the second he looked into the younger man's eyes.

Kevin recognized the same intensity he himself had once had, when he was young and in love and had something to prove to the world.

He still had a hell of a lot to prove.

When he'd roamed the streets of Brighton Beach in Brooklyn, he was a poor kid with a chip on his shoulder. His dad deserted the family when Kevin was born, and his mom worked long hours, so Kevin was always in charge of himself. He ran wild through the streets, making friends... making connections.

Hiding Jamie and PJ's parents from the Russian crime

syndicate was easy for Kevin—he knew the ins and outs, knew what that particular group was like, knew their foibles. He'd grown up with them.

From street thug to cop, he'd worked his way up the ranks to detective quickly. And he'd gone undercover, pretended not to be above taking bribes from his old friends in order to get information on higher-ranking members of the Russian crime syndicate.

Once he'd gotten the information, his life had been in danger. That's when the U.S. Marshals came after him with an offer, based on his experience.

As a young marshal, he'd so far avoided being the one who counseled the families during their three-week-or-less phase of learning *I'm not who I was anymore.*

But that ended when Patricia Jane and Ana were ushered into his life, huddled in blankets they'd been given from the musty trunk of a patrol car. Fourteen-year-old PJ had blood on her hands. Ana was eight, still a baby in so many ways.

There was no way he could have put them into foster care—there wasn't a system of checks and balances for them there. It would've been too great a compromise to their safety. He knew what the Russian crime syndicate was capable of, knew that keeping Ana and PJ close was of the utmost importance for their well-being.

He'd been married to Grace for three years at that point. They'd dated in high school and all through his time with the NYPD—she'd been hoping that his job as a marshal would be safer.

She'd been cold and unforgiving, even then, and Kevin blamed himself. A detective's wife dealt with a lot. When he'd gone undercover, their relationship suffered. High-school-sweetheart love was far different than grown-up reality. Her attitude only grew worse after they'd taken the girls in. There was nothing else he could've done at that point. He felt responsible, was responsible, because he'd looked into their mom's eyes when she'd first won the case against the head of the Russian crime syndicate and promised her that nothing would ever happen to her children. And while bringing them into his home had brightened his life in more ways than he could count, in Grace's eyes, it had done irreparable damage to his marriage.

When all was said and done, the only thing he had left to console himself with was the knowledge that he had done the right thing—the only thing, under the circumstances. If it meant keeping the girls safe, he'd do it again in a heartbeat.

With that, he took one last look at the newspaper clipping—the obituary of Alek's father—before stuffing it back into his pocket. Jamie didn't need to know about this now, not when it had been confirmed that Gary Handler was the one stalking her.

Even so, that information still sat uneasily in his gut.

Maybe this is a good thing . . . Kevin can meet Chris . . . like him . . .

But the loud, angry voices in the hallway squashed that fairy tale, made Jamie move quickly to sweep up the dough and broken bowl. By the time she got to the living room, she found her foster father and Chris eyeing each other hostilely.

"Kevin, this is Chris—" she began, but Kevin held a hand up.

"He's already introduced himself. And you still haven't said what you're doing here," Kevin said to Chris, his tone leaving no doubt as to his anger. Chris stood his ground, even as Kevin went toe to toe with him.

Chris was much, much taller, but Kevin was stocky and broad—the two would most likely be an even match in a brawl, although Jamie did not want it to come to that.

"I'm here for Jamie," Chris said.

"Yeah, I figured as much."

Chris's phone rang then, saving her from actually stepping in between the two of them. "It's my CO—I've got to answer," he said, and stepped away to take the call.

She turned to Kevin. "You've got to calm down."

"And you need to start using the common sense I know you have."

"Chris knows. He has a right to be here. And I will not be treated like a child. I won't hide from this man. Handler's gone from being stalked to being the stalker, and he's probably reveling in it. He can't be allowed to turn the tables like this."

"You shouldn't stay here, Jamie."

"Where else can I go, Kevin? He knows where you live too," she argued, as Chris returned, snapping his phone shut. "Is everything all right?"

Chris nodded. "I've got to take off for a little while. That was Saint—we're going to see Mark. If it was anything else, I wouldn't leave you now," he told her, and then asked Kevin, "Are you staying here with her?"

"Yeah, I'm staying with her."

"Do you have any leads on Handler?" Chris asked, and Kevin was in his face.

"This isn't your business."

"She's my business. Don't doubt that for a second, sir," he told Kevin before turning to Jamie. "If you need me, call. Immediately."

He didn't wait for an answer to his command before he left the house, closing the door heavily behind him.

She turned back to Kevin, "Chris has been watching me—"

"I know that—my men let me know this morning." Kevin shook his head in disapproval. "That's not his job."

"Suppose you had to choose between your job and the person you thought you might love?" she asked him.

Kevin smiled, but his eyes didn't light up at all. "I did, Jamie. I chose the job. I chose you and PJ, and I'll never regret that."

She wasn't used to sleeping next to anyone. After an hour of watching Saint actually doze, PJ decided to slip inside and make him dinner. He hadn't eaten that she'd seen since she'd arrived, and although she hadn't been with him twenty-four seven, she suspected food had been the last thing on his mind. Grief did that to a person—she noted that fact from her own too-thin frame and felt her own stomach rumble in response to the scents of cooking food quickly filling up the kitchen.

The glass door slid open and she glanced at the clock. Three hours.

"Three hours. A goddamned miracle." Saint ran a hand

through his hair, ruffling it—it already stood out in all directions and he didn't seem to care. He'd pulled on a pair of shorts, but her face heated as she stared at his chest.

It's the heat from the stove.

She turned back to what she was doing. "I was hungry. But I'll never eat all of this. You have to help me finish it."

He gave a grunt in reply—he was still groggy, she supposed. And then she heard the scrape of his chair, a small acquiescence, and she smiled.

"I told you before, I'm well aware that you're handling me," he said finally, once she put a glass of water in front of him.

"Then you're also well aware that you're allowing yourself to be handled."

"Because you're not a member of my team or my mother. You, I can handle."

"Now, that's not an innocent choice of words." She turned the gas off under the rice and continued to stir it.

"Nothing that comes out of my mouth is innocent, Patricia—I thought you knew that already."

Patricia. She hadn't been called that in forever, liked the way it sounded with his drawl. He'd asked her earlier what PJ stood for, and now she remembered him whispering her name in her ear while he was inside of her, and felt the shiver go up her spine.

She was in deep.

God, she didn't like the way she felt around him—a spinning tire, out of control, a ride on a fast-moving Ferris wheel, her belly out of whack in a way it never was, even in the planes she'd flown.

And just like all the other times she'd felt out of control, she was waiting for the inevitable crash to happen—real or emotional.

Yes, short, meaningless affairs were easiest, ones that satisfied her physical needs and let her walk away without looking back. Without caring.

When she looked at Saint, she knew she cared.

Quickly, she put the rice and chicken on a plate for him. It was close to six but it felt much later. The rain had started in again and brought a cloud covering that blanketed the house in darkness.

Saint had flipped on the main lights in the kitchen before he'd sat down—she'd been working with only the ones above the stove.

After he'd eaten his fill, he sat back with his water in hand and checked the messages on his phone. After a few minutes, he closed his eyes and shook his head, like *I don't need this shit right now*. And at one point, he outright groaned.

"Everything all right?" she asked.

He sighed heavily and put the phone down. "My mom's coming into town tomorrow."

"Oh." She'd been pushing the rice around on her plate, not really eating much of anything. "I'll make sure I clear out of here by then."

"You don't have to do that. She's not staying here. I'll meet her at her hotel for a quick meal. It's only one night, on her way to New York to do some shopping." He shook his head. "You're welcome to come along."

"Yeah, sure. 'Hi, Mom, this is the woman I'm currently fucking.'"

Saint finished his water in a long swig, and she admired

the way his neck flexed as he drank. Then he put his glass down and said, "Fuck you, PJ. Or Sophie. Or whoever the hell you want to be. I know what you're trying to do. It's not working."

"What are you talking about?"

"You play a nice head game. Try to push everyone out of your way so you can be the one in control, the one to come running back in and fix things. But guess what, honey, I'm not running. So what the hell are you going to do with someone who doesn't run away?"

She didn't know, had never had that happen before. "You'll run. They all do."

He laughed, the sound echoing through the room. "Yeah, we're all the same, right?"

"I never said that."

"Maybe you should listen to what you say a little more closely, then. Besides, I heard that you're the one who leaves. Maybe you force the men out of your life so you can say they left. Handy excuse, right?" He pushed his chair back abruptly. "I'm out of here."

She hadn't meant to do that, to shoot her mouth off about meeting his mom when he was about to identify the body of his best friend. And she couldn't find her voice to apologize, didn't stop him as he brushed past, simply sat at the table and stared out at the rain.

She hated that Jamie had told him that she would leave, hated that Saint was right—completely, utterly right. She lived on auto-pilot most of the time, trying not to think too hard or feel too much or give anything away to anyone. She was danger—TNT—to herself and to Jamie . . . and to any man who got too close.

The body. Saint couldn't bring himself to think of it as Mark's body—not until he saw it. Sure, the Marines mentioned the tattoo Mark had, and two long scars on his thigh, but Saint still could not rest until he saw that Mark was here. At home. At peace.

Chris had insisted on coming with him. His SEAL sat in the front seat of the truck, tapping his fingers on the door handle, and normally Saint would've bitched at that. Tonight, he didn't. And when Chris began to sing, Saint didn't say a word either, just let Chris's voice carry him to the parking lot of the morgue where Mark's body was being prepared.

The memorial had been moved up to tomorrow— *Better that way,* the admiral had said. *These boys need closure.*

"Ready?" Saint asked. He was out of the car and heading toward the building without waiting for an answer, and somehow Chris was right on his six.

Both men were in uniform for this—jungle BDUs, just the way they'd both last seen Mark. The halls were quiet and cold . . . and fucking creepy as shit.

Saint had already seen a copy of Mark's last will and testament. Mark wanted to be cremated, his ashes spread across the Florida wetlands, his favorite place to fly over.

Saint would see that it was done.

"It's not pretty," the coroner warned them as he led them to the room where the body rested. "He's been badly burned."

"Post-mortem?" Saint asked. *And please fucking God let that be true.*

"It appears so. He's also got several bullet wounds—

most likely that's what he died from. We're doing an autopsy. The FBI requested it. But based on the reports, it's pretty clear how he died." The coroner's face was set in sympathetic lines.

Saint turned to Chris. "You're sure you still want to do this?"

"I'm sure," Chris said, his face tight. The nervous energy had gone, though, replaced by a calm Saint saw him use when sniping. But still, Chris lagged behind Saint when the door opened and they saw a sheet-covered body lying on a metal table in the cold room.

Saint walked in first, right up to the body. When he nodded, the coroner pulled the sheet down, slightly past Mark's shoulders. Saint forced himself to keep breathing, to remain calm—for himself, for Chris and for Mark.

Especially for Mark.

Chris stood at the door while Saint walked in, walked right up to Mark's body and talked to his friend in a low voice.

He couldn't hear what was being said, only heard a small break in Saint's voice and fought the urge to run.

Move forward, his dad always told him and his brothers. But even so, Nick and Jake had both been forced to look back on their own pasts in order to find some semblance of peace. Chris knew he'd be no exception.

Seeing Mark's body was moving forward. And so he walked over to his teammate's body, and he nearly flashed back to the night Mark died.

Don't go there... do not go there, he told himself over and over, until his mind listened and he was here, in the present, with Saint's hand on his shoulder and Mark's body in front of him.

He'd been burned badly—nearly beyond recognition, facially. But somehow, the scars on his leg and the tattoo on his chest were still visible. A miracle in the middle of all the hell.

Chris's gaze traveled down to Mark's hands, to stare at the missing fingers and then back up his body.

Saint stepped away, to give him some privacy. And Chris whispered to Mark, "I did what you asked. I did everything you asked me to do," before he turned away.

He opened his mouth to tell Saint that he needed out, when the door opened and Nick and Jake were both there.

Nick had told Chris an hour earlier that he wasn't sure about doing this, and Chris could tell that Nick was still uneasy in his decision to accompany Jake here.

Both had seen their share of dead and still neither moved from the door to Mark's body. Jake's hand was still on the door frame, as if he was ready to make a quick escape at any minute.

Neither brother's eyes had left Mark's body, though. And then finally, Jake moved forward with Nick behind him, and the three of them stood together and said their good-byes to Mark.

The rest of the team would have the opportunity as well, before the public memorial.

"You and Mark were both heroes that day, Chris. No matter what the hell happened out there," Jake told him quietly. "You just remember that, all right?"

He could only nod, afraid he wouldn't be able to get any words out. Nick's hand clamped his shoulder in support.

And when the men exited the building a few minutes later, the four of them stood there for a while, just breathing.

"I need a damn drink," Jake said finally, and yeah, they all did.

"We'll meet you there," Saint told Jake and Nick, who nodded and went to their car while Saint and Chris walked to Saint's.

But once Jake's Blazer pulled out of the parking lot, on two wheels at top speed, Saint's phone rang—he grabbed it and answered with an abrupt, "St. John," and then he simply listened for a few seconds. "That's great news. He's right here. I'll tell him."

Chris knew what the news was before Saint clicked his phone closed and said, "You're clear. The autopsy on Josiah revealed no shots from an M25."

Chris nodded, leaned against the car door as a partial relief washed through him as Saint continued, "I guess Jamie Michaels meant what she said."

Chris shook his head. "Jamie took herself off the case— she didn't want to hurt me."

He didn't ask about Mark's autopsy, wondered if that would still be necessary.

Tell him. Saint would understand what happened out there. Of course he would, would've done what Mark had asked. But to add that burden to Saint's shoulders was something Chris wasn't planning to do.

Saint was solidly career military, smart as shit and could easily make admiral.

Chris wanted Saint to do so with a clear conscience.

There was no one for Chris to tell. Hell, he didn't even want to think about what happened, had refused to let it dwell in his own psyche.

It'll come out eventually.

Yes, eventually. But he'd make damned sure it wasn't tonight.

Chris and Saint were only fifteen minutes behind Jake and Nick, but both men were already well ahead of the curve.

Chris waited for Saint to lecture them, but instead, his CO said nothing, just nursed a glass of JD and sat at the bar, as if waiting for the inevitable trouble.

Still smarting from Kevin telling him that he'd fucked up Jamie's life enough and to get the hell out, Chris downed a second shot and then pushed the glass away. It wasn't going to help—it never did.

Loud music, drinking and brawling, the usual way the three brothers processed grief, the way they'd done so after Maggie's death. Except now they limited their destructiveness, knew how to pull themselves back from the brink.

That didn't mean, however, that they wouldn't go as close to the edge as possible.

Because the rest of his team was there too—and Jules, of course. He didn't see Cam, but that didn't mean he wasn't hiding out in a corner somewhere.

His mind wandered back to Kevin. The man was built like a bull and had a serious history to back it up. Chris could tell almost immediately that Kevin had grown up tough. For him to accept Chris, one of them would have to roll over and play dead.

Chris wasn't willing to be the one.

"Come on, man, get your ass up here!" The lead singer of the local band was motioning for Chris to take the stage with them.

He decided *Why not,* ditched his drink—threw himself into the music instead, because he could lose himself there just as easily, maybe more so. People were screaming and yelling and he was performing under the hot lights, and yeah, it was a rush, a fucking great rush, but it would never be a career for him.

Could've been, but he'd made the decision to stay away from that life a long time ago. He'd grown up watching hot stars become has-beens—that change happened so fast it could make your head spin. It was a hell of a business and it wasn't something he'd ever wanted to be a part of.

He'd never been all that sure of what he wanted to do with his life. Medicine was an obvious interest, as was delivering babies—but he didn't know too many male midwives.

So yeah, he wasn't sure which way to turn. But this, the singing onstage, right now this helped.

Typically, he noticed the women in the audience, yelling, flashing their tits, dancing like hell, but tonight, he was up there for the pure screaming pleasure of sound—the loudest, hardest bass line the band could deliver, the pulse of the drums beating a rhythm into his head until his skin shone with sweat and he couldn't feel anything anymore but the delightful numbness of performing.

He was still sore, still hurt, but he played hard. *Live*

hard, play hard. The brothers had always carefully ignored the *die well* part of that statement, for so many reasons, the least of which was that none of them had been very sure they'd live to see their eighteenth birthday and saw no reason to tempt fate further.

His eyes barely focused on the crowd, because the woman he wanted wasn't there—no, she was stuck at home, and the only reason he wasn't with her was he'd earlier promised the agents at her door he wouldn't show until midnight, and yeah, he wasn't in the mood to get the men looking out for Jamie's life in trouble or distracted.

And he wasn't sure how long he'd been up there—the band was hot, the crowd more so, and it was definitely a night for losing yourself.

Even Jules was dancing like she didn't have a care in the world. No one bothered her here—there wasn't a camera or paparazzo in sight, just a lot of off-duty military men, and people they'd gone to high school with. Many were one and the same.

It felt like weeks had passed since he'd been at the range, but really, it was only hours that filled the spaces. He was exhausted mentally—physically, he was charged enough to run or swim or blow something up for the hell of it.

He got off the stage, still shirtless, and grabbed a water. Nick and Jake were doing shots and Saint was just sitting there, monitoring them. Jules was suddenly by Chris's side.

"Hey."

"Hey, Jules. I heard the press has lost track of you."

She shrugged. "They'll find me soon enough."

They walked out back—it was dark enough for semi-privacy—and ended up sitting on the stone wall, the way they had so many times in the past. And suddenly, Chris wanted to break away, shift out of this place and head straight to Jamie's house.

He checked his watch. Still too early. The last thing he wanted was to be spotted by her. Because, at the very least, she'd think he was crazy—and he *was* crazy, but not because he was trying to keep her safe. So he'd stay here for now, with his brothers and with Jules, and he'd show up at midnight, which was when he'd told the FBI he'd be there.

If Jamie wanted him there now, she'd have called him herself. She'd know by now he'd been cleared of Josiah's death.

"This is like old times," Jules mused.

"It's not old times," he said, heard his own harsh tone and cursed himself silently.

"I know that, Chris. I really do. But sometimes, it's just nice to be back with the people who used to know you best." She hugged her jean-clad legs to her chest and lit a cigarette she'd pulled from behind her ear. After she took a long drag, she offered it to him and he accepted it.

"Used to, huh?"

"Yeah, used to." She took the cigarette back from him, held it between her long, graceful fingers. Only Jules could make smoking look that good. Part of her charm—something she didn't even have to try. "This other woman... where is she?"

"She's...ah...She was actually supposed to be staying away from me as part of her job." Except that was no longer the case.

"So how's the relationship supposed to work?"

"Haven't figured that one out yet," he admitted, and for

a few minutes they sat in comfortable silence. He took the cigarette back from her, pulling a few long drags.

"If it's that difficult, why try?" Jules asked finally.

"I think I love her."

Jules was silent for far too long. Chris steeled himself for tears or yelling or something. But he got none of that. Instead, she asked, "Then why don't you go get her?"

"It's complicated."

"You've never let that stand in your way before," she told him. "Why start now?"

He leaned over and he hugged her, hard. Buried his face in her neck, the way he had when she helped him mourn his momma, and he remembered how good of a friend she'd been to him.

In past years, they hadn't been very good to each other, not the way they should've been. Her arms went around him and he lifted his head.

And then Jules tried to kiss him, and shit, he'd fucked this up again.

He pulled back and so did she, hopping off the wall and looking away from him. "Jules, please, I'm sorry—I didn't mean to give you the wrong impression."

"Bullshit." Now she was looking at him, eyes blazing. "You know, I've been accused of not wanting you but at the same time not wanting anyone else to have you—I think you're just as guilty of that."

Maybe he was. The thought of Jules with someone else—really with someone else—made his gut churn.

He didn't love her—correction, he wasn't in love with her. He knew that with a certainty, because he'd left his heart with Jamie and she still hadn't fucking given it back to him. "Jules, you need to move on. Away from me. Please."

Jules opened her mouth and then closed it. Turning, she walked away from him, slamming into the bar, and he stood outside for a few more minutes, finishing the cigarette before following her inside.

Jake and Nick were still pounding back drinks, their pace not promising to slow anytime soon. A couple of tables down was a nice group of Marines, sitting close enough to hear Jake make a comment about the Marine Corps, and those in it, despite Saint's attempts to shut him up.

And then Chris looked up and saw Izzy at the door of the bar. Next to her stood Kaylee. The two women waited, and watched Jake and Nick, a mix of love and concern on their faces.

His brothers would each have someone to take them home, to pull them back from the fire.

Tonight, Chris was responsible for pulling his own self back. He was sweating and strangely content as he slid out the rear door of the bar again, leaving behind the mass confusion and walking the few miles toward home.

Chris had left for the morgue an hour before Coop called Jamie. Hesitantly, she answered and was greeted by his cheery, booming voice.

"Josiah's autopsy showed he was killed by an M88 .50 caliber sniper rifle, not an M25, which is what Waldron uses," he said, and her heart surged with relief.

It was over.

Coop continued, "As you know, the initial assessment

showed the bullet passed through Josiah's skull—the entrance and exit wounds were consistent with that of an M25."

She did. The edges matched, but without a bullet, they'd been forced to rely on testimony alone.

"But your instincts were dead-on—with the scan, the coroner found a fragment in his brain. When they compared it to the slugs they found in his chest, they were able to determine it came from the same gun—not an M25. Not a Sig either. Waldron's damned lucky the coroner found that fragment—without it, we'd have to decide whether or not to proceed with a court-martial."

"Luck was on Chris's side, for sure."

"Yeah, well, the guy's innocent. There's no solid evidence that Chris Waldron killed Josiah. Beyond their disagreement, the group worked well together, based on all Josiah's reports."

"What reports?" she asked.

"They just came through—the Marines recovered his computer in the wreckage. He never sent them through, obviously, but he kept up with his daily notes," Cooper explained, and she felt herself sag with relief. "Oh, and the shot between his eyes was done at closer range than the ones to his chest. That's consistent with Waldron's story that Josiah was running toward the rebels who had Mark Kendall in their possession. The autopsy on Mark Kendall is also complete. It showed several bullet wounds, including one between the eyes and one directly to the heart. The coroner says it's tough to tell if it was post- or ante-mortem, because all Kendall's injuries happened so close together. The shots might've killed him, but he was already well on his way to dying."

"Did either of those shots match Josiah's weapon?"

"No slugs—passed right through the body. Could've been an M25, but more likely it was an M88 . . . those rifles are common with the rebels in that area of Africa. I'm just not sure why they'd shoot him in the face before they threw him in the fire," Coop said. "Who the hell knows—maybe the rebels have some humanity after all."

Jamie sat up straight in her chair, a chill running through her. Because no, the rebel soldiers didn't have any humanity, but suddenly she knew exactly who did—her pillows still bore his scent of crisp cypress and soap and man.

Whatever happened out there had absolutely nothing to do with Josiah and everything to do with Chris and Mark. "Does Chris know?"

"Yes. I spoke to his lawyer before I called you," Coop said. "Hey, are you doing okay?"

"Hanging in there. It's not easy being on this side of things." She frowned a little as she glanced at her own gun, sitting on the table, next to her water bottle and crackers.

"I'd imagine not," Coop said. "I'm glad Waldron was cleared. That mission was FUBAR."

Coop was a former Marine. Like Lou, his loyalties had been tested with this investigation.

"Thanks for letting me know, Coop, and for getting this done so quickly."

"You did all the legwork," he said. "All I did was get to make the call."

CHAPTER
12

Chris was damned comfortable out here, in the dark woods in front of Jamie's house. He wanted to be inside with her, but he knew watching her from afar like this was more effective.

He'd put on his face paint, more out of habit than true necessity. But then, he had no idea what this Handler asshole learned in prison or from the drug lord he'd worked for.

His eyes scanned the area tirelessly—left to right, his periphery open to any movements. One agent remained inside the front door, just behind the closed blind. Every once in a while, Chris saw the man's shadow when he shifted.

He didn't see anyone else passing the other front windows, which meant Jamie and Kevin were in the middle of the house, the kitchen. A good spot for them. Safe. Nearly untouchable unless a bullet got lucky.

Two hours had passed since he'd arrived, one hundred and twenty minutes of him lying on the small stone retaining wall, staring at the house.

Mark had always been his point man on missions—had been a damned fine sniper in his own right, one who had no problem letting Chris take the majority of the shots. Mark kept him lined up, made him focus, especially in the early days when patience and practice went hand in hand. Now it had become a part of him, a religion, something he couldn't turn off even when he wanted to.

He held his rifle steady, the stark realization that he might not be able to fire drumming through every nerve ending.

If you have to take a shot, you can. You will.

He knew that much was true.

His mind kept flashing back to Mark—Mark in the morgue, Mark on the mission...

Fucking son of a bitch. Chris shook his head and then looked through the scope of his rifle.

The only thing he could see was what happened on that night at the embassy—the events he hadn't been able to tell anyone about, the ones that had been keeping him from firing his rifle.

The screams had turned to wails—inhuman-sounding noises that ran right down Chris's spine as if someone was walking on his grave.

Mark put a hand on his shoulder to steady him. "Keep your eye on the prize, Chris."

Chris was already belly-down on the wall outside the embassy, which was lit up like the Fourth of July. Except this was no celebration and the smell of blood, fresh and metallic, clung to the humid air around him.

There would be no good end to this mission—every one of them knew it was a failure. And even though that was no fault of theirs, it still wasn't sitting easily. Especially not when the ambassador's children began calling out the embassy windows for help.

"I'm going in there—I don't give a shit about Josiah's orders," Mark told him suddenly. The men had been told to pull back, to get the hell out of Dodge before it was too late for them. And although Josiah had given the orders for all of them to stand down, Mark and Chris hadn't been able to back away from what was happening around them.

Josiah was as horrified by the sight as the rest of them were.

Chris didn't hesitate once Mark made his announcement. "I'm going with you."

"Not this time." Mark's eyes were so serious—there wasn't the usual glint behind them. His mouth was set, his rifle held loosely in his hands. "You get the kids out. I don't care what else happens. Let Cam and Josiah deal with the parents—you get the kids."

"That's suicide."

"And I'm not taking you with me. My choice." Mark's voice was firm—the man was dead set on going, and going alone. Chris had no doubt Mark would take him down if he tried to stop him.

Mark laid out his plan, about how he'd sneak in and distract the rebels. Kill as many as he could. "Maybe I'll get lucky for a third time—what do they always say, the third time's the charm?"

"Yeah, that's what they say."

"Cover me. I need enough lead time that Josiah can't stop me."

"I can do that." *Chris felt like he wasn't exactly in his own body at that point, that none of this was really happening. Everything had simultaneously slowed down and sped up, and he couldn't catch his balance or his breath.*

"Listen." *Mark's face was set in serious lines.* "If they get me . . ."

"I'll get you back from them. I won't leave you here."

"No, I don't want that. If they capture me, they're not going to let me live for long. Don't let them kill me. I don't want to die by their hands. If I'm that far gone . . ."

Chris looked at his senior chief in the darkness. "Don't ask me this, Mark. Don't you fucking dare."

"I'm asking," *Mark said evenly, though Chris smelled the fear on the man.* "Between you and me—only you and me— I'm asking . . ." *A moment later Chris was alone in the dark, watching Mark disappear into the back door of the embassy.*

He knew it wasn't the last time he'd see Mark alive, but it would be the last time they would speak.

I'm asking . . .

Mark had known what he'd been putting on Chris. Had known Chris would have to live with what he'd been forced to do forever . . . which is why Mark hadn't waited around for the answer to his question.

I'm asking you to kill me.

Chris knew his part of the sacrifice was small as hell compared to what Mark had ultimately done. And when he'd watched the rebels carrying Mark's body away from the embassy toward the large bonfire to the south, when he'd seen Mark's left hand move with the familiar signal, Chris had pushed the children along with Cam and their parents and ignored Josiah running toward Mark. He'd centered his shot and he'd taken it, swift and clean. One shot, one kill—this time, not for a mission but for mercy.

That didn't make it weigh any less heavily on his soul. Chris suspected it never would.

The clock read 2:13 A.M.

Jamie hadn't wanted to sleep. Shortly after she'd spoken with Coop, Kevin had left and she'd paced the house restlessly, wanted nothing more than to go outside to Chris.

But now, she woke, disoriented, with Chris over her bed.

"Come on, baby—we're out of here." His voice was calm, his touch gentle as he carried her out of the bed and the room, and finally the house. Halfway across the lawn, she found her voice and started to ask what was going on, but he broke into a run at that point, stopping only when they'd gotten through the woods and onto the road—and still, when he placed her on the ground, he shielded her body with his.

She struggled for a second, saying, "Chris, please—"

Seconds later, the ground rumbled and shook and the explosion shattered the early-morning quiet. She didn't dare peek over Chris's shoulder, simply buried her face against his shirt and breathed in his scent instead of what she knew would be smoky air.

His arms covered her head, his body a shield to hers—she felt a small rain of debris come down around them and knew that her house was gone.

Chris stared at her. "I just knew. Okay?" was all he said before he moved his weight off her and helped her up from the ground.

She hadn't been aware that she was shaking until then. "What was that—what did he use to do that?"

"Your own gas lines," Chris said, his voice low so only she could hear. "Probably on a timer. Basically undetectable with a minuscule leak. With the wind shift that happened half an hour ago, though, I smelled it."

Her hand went instinctively to her belly. "The baby?"

"Everything should be okay—your windows in the bedroom were cracked. But we'll get everything checked."

"Lyle and Paul?"

"They're all right—they went out the back after I came in. I told them to go, that I had you," he told her as sirens rang in the distance. "The FBI hasn't been keeping you safe, Jamie, not to my standards. Now it's my turn."

"I need to call Kevin."

"You can do that from the road. You can't go to Kevin's house," he told her. "I'll take you to my house—or to Saint's."

She shook her head. "I won't compromise those places."

"We'll check into a motel, then—you can call Kevin and your supervisor from there."

"There's one place we always use . . ."

"Then we're going to avoid it," he said grimly. "I have an alternative."

She wanted to argue, but everything he'd said made sense.

Chris didn't have his bike tonight—instead, he had an old Chevy Blazer, which he'd parked around the corner.

He helped her in and pulled away, just before the police and ambulance arrived. She turned to watch them pull up her driveway.

For the first time ever, she was grateful that the house was in such a deserted area—no neighbors to worry about. No one was hurt.

But if Chris hadn't been there...

"Don't think about it. I was there," he said, handed her his cell phone. "Call Kevin and your supervisor."

It was only then that she realized she had nothing but the clothes on her back.

Sentimentality wasn't her strong suit. In fact, it had been carefully carved out of her life, she was more used to it than she should be.

There hadn't been time to take anything from the old house after her parents' murder. No, she and PJ had been taken out the back door, whisked away in the middle of the chaos, through the yard to a waiting marshal's car.

She'd been crying, small, sobbing gasps and PJ held her hand, stoic. Blood still on her clothing and her hands, which later Jamie remembered finding on her own. And when they'd gotten to the hotel, she'd continued crying, for her parents, her blanket, her doll collection. Everything left behind. Everything but the nightgown she wore.

She stared down at her legs, barely covered by the long

T-shirt she'd ended up in after her late-night shower, and wondered if anything would ever change.

It was after two A.M. when Saint pulled into his garage. At first, when he heard the pounding, he thought it was coming from inside his own head after spending all those hours at the bar. But the loud music was coming through the door from the living room, bellowing out of the massive speakers he rarely used. Really, he hadn't spent this much time in his house ever. He'd always been on the move, either with work or play, never stopping to sit back and enjoy, because...

Because.

The room was completely rearranged. He blinked as he stood at the opened door, because it hadn't been like that before he'd left, but suddenly, the couches, the chairs, even the coffee table was in a different place.

He continued moving through the house, dropping his bag as he entered the lit kitchen. PJ was standing at the counter, pouring sugar on a bowl of corn flakes.

She glanced up and caught his look. "What? You've got nothing with sugar in this house. I had to improvise."

"Because sugar's not good for you."

"Neither is the fast food you brought me," she commented.

"It was a hunch." Based on the Snickers bar wrappers he'd seen on his deck, plus the can of Coke. "Did you rearrange my living room?"

She shrugged. "Yes. Things were out of place."

"My couches were out of place?"

"Yes. The arrangement was bothering me."

"You're not even sleeping inside the house."

"But I have to look into this room from outside," she pointed out, and he cocked an eyebrow at her.

"I could close the shades at night."

"Trust me, this works better."

The thing was, it did work better. The living room looked...well, it looked lived in. More than it had in all four years he'd lived here. It looked like...a home. Even with the tent out on the deck.

"I can put it all back."

"No, leave it." He grabbed his bag and locked it in the closet with his weapons and then tried to figure out what to do next.

She was here. Adding more sugar to the cereal, shaking her head at him and saying, "You really eat healthy, don't you?"

"You say that like it's a bad thing."

"No cookies at all?"

He shrugged. "You didn't tell me you wanted cookies."

She put the bowl down. "Saint, look, I'm...I don't know—"

He stopped her. "Let's not worry about this. Why don't we let it play out, no matter where it leads?"

She took a bite of her cereal and chewed slowly. And then she nodded and walked back outside, to the deck.

She'd thought about packing up and leaving more than once in the hours since Saint left—stormed out, actually, muttering something about training exercises.

He was pushing her away, pushing her to make the next move. And so she did, by staying put in his house.

She hadn't realized how much she missed being in a man's arms. Relationships were a big no to her, but sex... sex was freeing. Sex always made her feel as if she was flying, each orgasm sending her higher than she'd been before.

She hugged her arms around herself for a second, the thin T-shirt not doing a great job against the night wind off the ocean.

The newspaper she'd been reading by the light above the deck was still on the outside table. It had blown open, and now she closed it. The front page held an article by K. Darcy—aka Kaylee Smith, the reporter who'd come to Africa to blow the lid off GOST.

Kaylee had lost her ex-husband to the organization.

"I know her." Saint had followed her to the deck with a bottle of water in one hand and an apple in the other, and now he looked over her shoulder.

"Me too." She ran a palm over the article as if that would help her commit it to memory. "I never spoke to her about this, about any of it. Not really."

"Then how did Kaylee get all the information?"

"You really don't know?"

He sat next to her. "I didn't ask Nick or Chris all that much. I simply threatened to kill them the next time they went off half-cocked to help a woman."

She couldn't help it—she laughed, partly because he was so serious.

"If I'd only known then..." He trailed off, not finishing his thought.

"Kaylee got her information from Clutch, a man I worked with. The only other one who survived."

"Where is he now?"

"Last I saw, somewhere in Africa, with the woman he loves." She pushed the paper away. "Are Nick and Kaylee still together?"

Saint nodded the affirmative, and that made her happy.

"What about you, PJ? Was there ever anyone for you? There must've been someone."

"Yes." She leveled her gaze at him. "There were a lot of men."

He didn't react, at least not in the way she'd wanted him to. Instead, his gaze traveled down her body and back up again, and when his eyes met hers, there was a certain satisfaction in them. "None of them ever made you come the way I did today."

She could've lied, but he'd know. "That's true. But maybe it's simply beginner's luck."

"This is the beginning, but it has nothing to do with luck."

Her body rumbled alive at his words, shuddering from the residual ache of the earlier sex. But he didn't move toward her and she noted he held his keys in his hand, felt a slight twinge of disappointment that he was leaving again.

But that was short-lived, because he said, "Come take a ride with me."

She hesitated briefly, but he wasn't giving her time to say no. He'd already started walking off the deck and toward the garage. She jumped down and landed in the soft sand, following him. "It's late. Where are we going?"

"You'll see when we get there." He clicked open the garage door and they both walked inside—he climbed into the driver's seat while she held on to the passenger-side door handle for a second and then jerked it open.

"I hate surprises," she told him.

"Yeah, me too. It's something you'll like, all right? So just get into the car."

She settled back in the big SUV, feeling lost in the black bucket seat. The windows were tinted and she liked that feeling of added protection. He backed the car down the long driveway and turned onto a road leading away from his house.

The music was playing low on the radio and he reached over to turn it up. She put a hand out and stopped him. "Are you okay?"

He glanced at her briefly. "No. But I will be. Seeing Mark was something I needed to do."

She nodded and let him blast the music.

Fifteen minutes later, he pulled off the main road, into what she recognized almost instantly as a small, private airport. As he showed ID to the man at the gate, her gaze skipped across a row of Cessnas and she realized she hadn't been behind the controls of a plane since the fateful crash in Africa, with GOST. The one she hadn't talked about with Saint . . . with anyone.

She'd told herself that there hadn't been the opportunity, which was a total lie. But the fact that she could admit it had to be a step in the right direction.

Finally, Saint pulled up near one of the planes parked against the far left gate, illuminated by the lights along the outer edges of the lot, and got out. She followed and found herself standing next to him and the Cessna.

He put a hand on the plane's door and then quickly took it away, stuffed both hands into the pockets of his jeans and stared at the sky. And then, when he took them out, he lifted his palm toward her—in the center was a black key. "Here you go."

A key, presumably to the plane they stood next to. "What's this for?"

His gaze settled directly on hers. "I thought maybe you'd take me up sometime."

"Saint—"

"It was Mark's," he said quickly. "He left it to me. Now I'm giving it to you."

"What? Wait—you fly?"

"He was teaching me. Mainly, I just liked the feeling of being up there. The plane would be wasted on me. But you . . . All the papers are inside the plane. You let me know when you're ready."

"I can't accept this." She held out the key to him but he shook his head and shoved his hands back into his pockets.

"You found him. That was what I needed. Let me do this for you."

"Why are you being so good to me?"

His chin lifted. "Because right now, it's helping me a hell of a lot."

"I told you what happened to me in the Air Force. Then in Africa, I survived an airplane explosion meant to kill me and three other men on board. The men died—men who had protected me for months. There was nothing I could do but walk away and leave them there."

"I'm sorry, PJ."

She nodded and held out the key again, but he shook his head no. "Please take it. I—"

"You know, Mark was captured twice. On top of that, he escaped certain death more times than either of us cared to count. He'd always tell me, *My luck's not going to hold out forever, but it's sure nice to have around.*" Saint rubbed the back of his neck as he pictured his friend coming off a plane after he'd been released from the hospital. "One time, they'd kept him in a hospital for three weeks, to get him back in shape after a two-week-long capture by the FARC in Colombia. Mark and two other private contractors had escaped and hid along the border until we grabbed him. He'd looked like hell, but the first thing he asked the doc was when he could fly again. Doc told him that he should stick to the water, like a good Navy boy."

She smiled.

"He never once doubted his ability to get back in there and do his job. He lived for it. For us."

"I wish I'd known him. I feel like I do, when you talk about him. He's not so different from a lot of the guys I knew in my past." Her voice had a wistful quality to it.

"I think he would've really liked you," he said. "He'd think that this was right."

"You really were his family, you and your team."

Saint nodded. "Mark's family was all kinds of fucked-up. He'd been on his own since he was seventeen. He was sitting on a huge trust fund that I don't think he touched much."

"His parents died?"

Saint looked up at the sky and then at her. "His father killed his mother and then killed himself. They were wealthy as hell, and they were so unhappy."

"That's horrible."

"He never dwelled on it. So please, stop arguing. Just accept the plane. Enjoy it."

"I don't know where I'm going after this."

"So take it with you." He paused. "Where are you thinking about going?"

"I have no idea. I never think about the future anymore. For so long, I've never let myself look more than one day ahead. Never let myself dream about tomorrow—any tomorrow." She stared down at the key in her hand. "I sound like a real downer, don't I?"

"You sound like you're lying to yourself. You've thought about the future."

She had no answer for that. She'd left so much of her life on another continent that sometimes she felt like she was walking around half-naked, with no cover. Vulnerable. Soft. Weak. Her future always seemed cloudy, like she was seeing it through fogged glass—she could make out the edges, but the middle, the most important part, remained blurred.

"I can kill someone with my bare hands," she told him quietly, even as she stared down at her own palms as though they would betray her at any second. "A woman shouldn't be able to do that. I shouldn't know the things I've learned . . . everything in my life has revolved around violence and guns and death."

She could smell death even when she wasn't close to it— its scent sticky sweet and cloying, which quickly gave way to the stench of decay. "I don't feel like a woman should."

"You feel like a woman to me," he said quietly.

She hadn't realized that he'd put his arms around her, that he was holding her close, and that she was holding him too, had wrapped her arms around his waist and pressed her cheek against his chest. She hated herself for needing.

"This is happening fast ... between us. It's happening too fast."

"I know that."

"I don't know what to do about it."

"Until you figure it out, you're free to stay on my deck or in my bed. Free to have your way with me too ... on the deck or in my bed."

She smiled. "I don't know anything about you ... except that you're kind."

He narrowed his eyes at her. "You're not going to call me sweet, are you? Because I'd really hate that."

She laughed in spite of everything—found herself doing that a lot when she was around him. "I don't know much, but sweet's not something I would call you. At least not to your face."

"Accept the gift and I'll tell you anything you want to know about me."

It was a promise she couldn't resist.

Chris didn't say much as he drove, trying to beat the dawn to get to the small hunting cabin. Instead, he listened to Jamie talking to her supervisor and to Kevin, heard the exhaustion in her voice as she repeated what she knew.

What he knew was that her house was gone, and holy fuck, it had been too close a call.

At first, he'd wondered if Lyle and Paul were in on it, or the other agent he hadn't met, the one who'd initially done the sweep, since they'd all had access to the house under the pretense of searching it. But creating a leak in the gas line and using it as a bomb was crude and easy to miss, and he cursed himself for not checking her house more thoroughly himself.

He hadn't gotten to her house until midnight—the gas leak could've been there well before that.

But he couldn't think about that now—there was too much crashing down around him, and if he let himself lose focus again, he could lose Jamie for good. Let the FBI and Kevin make their plans and hunt down Handler—Chris would hide Jamie away until they caught the asshole.

"I don't know where we're going," Jamie was saying into the phone, with a quick glance at Chris. He didn't respond, wouldn't give that information out over a cell line—no fucking way. The time for mistakes was long past.

"Kevin, you can reach me at this number," she continued—held it together until she hung up the phone and put it on the console between them. And then she shifted so he couldn't see her face, although he saw the slight shake of her shoulders.

He didn't tell her it would be okay—he would make it so, but she needed to experience this delayed reaction. All he did was reach over and grab her hand.

He held it tightly as he drove the car off-road, toward the old hunting cabin. He hadn't been there in at least a year, but he knew Nick came here often. He claimed it was for maintenance purposes, but Chris knew better. His brother enjoyed the solitude of the place, the memories.

For Chris, the memories would be overwhelming—he felt their threat as he drove farther through the backwoods. But the cabin was safe as hell. And right now, that was the only thing he could give a shit about.

They'd only been driving for an hour when he pulled up

the long, private dirt road and parked around back of the cabin, under the hidden carport.

Jamie finally turned to him, her eyes still wet. "Thanks for this."

"You don't have to thank me. Come on, let's get you inside so you can rest." He helped her through the tall grass in the dark and onto the porch.

Jamie paused. "It's so pretty. Even in the dark—pretty and peaceful."

"Yeah. It was my mom's favorite place to hang," he said quietly. "She used to come here for the peace and quiet, to get away from all the testosterone in the house. But we'd follow her. So no peace and quiet—but a lot of good memories were made."

"Your mom probably wouldn't like me so much, not after I've brought you so much trouble."

He chuckled quietly. "She knew I never went anywhere without trouble. Come on inside."

She looked over her shoulder toward the road they'd driven in on—sunrise was still a while off but the promise of dawn was here with its soft light. "You're sure no one followed us?"

"There's one way in and out—Nick hung some cameras a while back so we could see the edge of the road. But I would've known if anyone was on our six."

It was true—they'd been the only ones on the road for the past half hour. And so she followed him inside the small cabin, which was clean but pretty damned bare. There was a small couch and a table and chairs, a kitchenette and not much else but a large, soft rug that took up the middle of the floor. "Please tell me there's a working bathroom."

"Yeah, there is—through there," he said. He locked the door and turned on a single light.

He rustled around in the front closet to find blankets and sleeping bags—there was barely enough room for her on the couch, and he wouldn't be sleeping anyway, so he piled the sleeping bags on the floor. "I'm sure my brother's got some extra clothes in the back of his car—I'll go check as soon as we get some sunlight, okay?"

She didn't answer. When he turned back, he noted she was staring at him.

"Your face," she said finally, and yeah, he'd forgotten to wipe the damned cammy paint off earlier.

"I'll take care of it."

"No," she told him, the sureness in her voice making him start. "It's my turn to take care of it."

The ache coming from Chris was suddenly palpable—and through the haze of her own recent pain, Jamie recalled what he'd been through over the past hours as well.

"There's nothing to take care of. Try to sleep," he said gruffly, as if he could feel her thoughts.

"I don't want to sleep anymore. I feel like I've been sleeping for too damned long," she told him as she began to move toward him.

It seemed to take forever to reach him across the small expanse, to drag her heart, which was slowly recovering from years of trusting no one.

When she finally did, she took his hand in hers again and led him past the kitchen and living room and into the bathroom as the cabin began to fill with a soft light.

She was surprised he allowed it.

"Sit." She pointed to the edge of the tub, and still he followed her direction without question, sat while she wet the washcloth at the sink.

He knew what she was about to do, closed his eyes when she brought it to his face, the greens and blacks and khakis smudged over his cheeks and eyelids and forehead and nose in a crazy swirl that was still somehow controlled—a definite pattern drawn with a purposeful hand.

Using the wet cloth, she continued to wipe the paint away, using firm, broad strokes. It wasn't a fast process but she didn't rush, liked seeing the clean cheekbones uncovered, then the broad forehead and full mouth. She left his eyes for last, wanted to see them open. When she did, the intensity of the two different colors watched her, waiting for her to make the next move.

This time, she would. Fueled by both will and desire, she tugged his shirt over his head, ran her hands across his shoulders, behind his neck, through his hair once she released the bandanna.

"I'm sorry. So sorry. You've lost a friend. You saw it happen. I know what that's like, Chris. And you haven't had any time to mourn."

His gaze held hers steadily. "I'm mourning in my own way."

"By throwing yourself into watching me."

"You need watching. You tend to get into trouble," he muttered. "Bad enough I couldn't be with you twenty-four seven to keep you safe. It's important that I keep you safe . . ."

"You have. You are. Chris, I understand survivor's guilt.

I've lived with it for so long. Too long." She stroked her hands through his hair.

"Now's not the time. You've been through hell."

"Now is all we have."

"You don't understand, Jamie. You don't know what I did."

She froze for a second at the look in his eyes. "Then tell me. Please."

He didn't say anything right away. Instead, he squared his shoulders even more than they'd been, and then he started.

"I followed Mark's orders. All of them. You have no idea how badly I wanted Josiah to save Mark, to get him away from the rebels. But even if he'd been able to do that..." He stopped, took a deep breath. "Mark was almost gone. He never would've made it. Even after what the rebels did, the way they tortured him...and they were going to do more. I'd told Mark I wouldn't let that happen. He made me promise to do something, and I kept that promise."

It was as she'd suspected earlier—Josiah tried to save Mark and failed, so Chris did the only humane thing he could...he followed Mark's last wishes. A sob caught in her throat for Chris, for Mark...for all of them on that horrible night.

Chris continued. "Mark knew I would know when it was time. He'd been captured before—he said, *I won't die at their hands.* And so I waited—and I didn't see Josiah anymore, and Mark gave me the signal. Twice. I ignored it the first time, told myself that it wasn't true, that he was already dead. But he wasn't and I couldn't let them kill him—not the way they were going to do it."

"And you were prepared to carry this around with you forever?"

"I still am." He looked at her. "You're the only other one who knows. It was his final wish. No one from your office would understand that. They'd think if I could kill my own teammate, I'd have no problem killing Josiah if he got in my way. And I just couldn't say any of it out loud. Because then it would be real. I could give two shits about the investigation, about what happened to me because of what I did for Mark. I just didn't want any of it to be real."

"You didn't kill Mark, Chris. You can't think of it like that. For all intents and purposes, he was already dead."

"I just couldn't watch. They were going to . . . Fuck." He drew a deep breath. "They were going to throw him into the fire, and he was still fucking alive. There was no other way I could help him. So I did what I'd want someone to do for me."

"That night, you were all heroes."

"I don't feel like one."

"Let me help you with that, then."

"You didn't want me two months ago. Even two days ago . . ."

"That's not true." She touched his cheek gently. "You might be psychic, but that doesn't always mean you see what's right in front of you. You were so busy looking into my secrets, you'd forgotten to guard yours. You don't like to let anyone inside," she said softly, even as her hands played with his hair.

"That's the way it's been for a long time," he admitted.

"Why?"

"It's easier that way."

"That's such a bullshit answer."

He snorted and stood and she let him off the hook. For now. A little. "You work totally off instinct and impulse." Her head dipped to kiss his chest and when her hand went to his pants, she heard a breath catch in his throat as his erection pressed his BDUs. "Did you ever think of trusting someone else as much as you trust your own instincts? Because I knew I wanted to trust you, to be with you, from nearly the first second we met. I knew because I let myself get distracted," she practically whispered. "I never let that happen."

"You have no idea how badly I wanted to drag you back into that car, that hotel, to make you stay in Africa with me for at least one more night. And then I figured that for you maybe it was just the adrenaline or the fear or both, and from that point on I pretended our time together meant nothing. I've been away on missions ever since I got home from that trip. I couldn't let myself think about you. I tried not to."

"Did it work?"

"Not even a little bit."

"Good." She paused. "On the ride here, I kept thinking that I'd just lost everything. But here, I'm realizing that I've got everything I need."

Losing something to find what you really need.

Chris smiled then and she realized she was, for the first time, seeing a truly happy smile, not filled with worry or pain. And she'd been able to bring that out in him, despite everything.

Her hands still remained on his shoulders as he asked, "What do you want, Jamie?"

"You," she whispered. "Can that just be enough for now?"

"Yeah, that can be enough."

She watched his face carefully. "You saved my life."

"And you're saving mine right now. Every time you touch me or say my name, you make me feel human again," he said quietly. "So go ahead, make me feel."

The words held more command in them than seduction, and yet they turned her on to the point of no return, made the ache between her legs intensify, the longing turn sharp and biting. He remained in front of her—handsome and strong and oh-so-willing to make everything but the two of them go away, if only for tonight.

He grabbed her then, pulled her body to his, and she planned on agreeing, because sex was so much easier than talking . . . than thinking . . . than anything.

With Chris, it was everything.

He carried her into the living room, setting her down gently on the floor, among the soft blankets and the sleeping bags, even as she nuzzled his neck.

He knelt in front of her, waiting. His pants hung low on his hips, emphasizing the jut of his hipbones and his impossibly ripped abs. Jamie reached out, ran a finger down the string of small scars along his left side. "What's this from?"

"Shark bite. Long story. Not now."

"Right—not now," she whispered.

She unbuttoned and unzipped his pants. They dropped easily to the ground, revealed he was naked underneath—and completely aroused. And then he was tugging her shirt over her head, unclasping her bra, sliding down her pink underwear.

She loved the way his breath hitched as he pulled back to gaze at her body.

"Beautiful," he told her, his voice nearly reverent. "So fucking pretty, Jamie."

She felt pretty, like she could conquer anything. "Lay back—let me."

He complied, propped himself up on his elbows, his face wearing that lazy, heavy-lidded look she loved, because there was nothing lazy about it. No, he was simply biding his time, waiting for her . . . waiting to see what she wanted to do.

She slid her body over his and he groaned at the contact, groaned louder as she kissed her way along his chest, her tongue flicking his nipples, turning them into hard pebbles.

"You smell so good—you always do," she murmured against his neck. "Fresh and wild."

He smelled like freedom—hers, theirs—and there was no way she could ever get enough. Her tongue licked a path down his chest to his abs, her breasts brushing his arousal. It jutted between them and she shifted back and forth, letting his hardness brush her nipples, which were so hot and tender and longing for his touch.

"You're fucking killing me," he told her, and she just smiled.

And then she knelt between his legs and took him with her mouth, her hands. He rumbled deep in his chest as her mouth circled him, pushing her to take it further, to be bolder.

"Jamie..." But his voice was lost when she continued working him. His hips arched toward her, her fingers dug into the skin of his thighs until she knew he wouldn't last long.

She released him and he shuddered—he'd been clutching the sleeping bag with his hands, his head thrown back, his hands in tight fists as he tried not to come under her caresses.

"Seriously. Fucking killing me," he muttered, lifted his head to gaze at her again as she crawled up his body. He took himself off his elbows and lay flat against the floor, his arms snaking around her waist.

"I'm going to take you," she told him, even pinned his arms above his head. She circled his wrists with one hand as best she could, holding them to the carpet while her other hand moved between his legs to stroke him.

He pulled in a hard breath through his nose.

She thought about protection for a fleeting second and then laughed out loud. "Sorry... it's just that I was about to ask about condoms."

"Yeah, that ship has sailed." His hand traced her belly, his voice so deep, eyes intense. He appeared relaxed and yet still coiled, his rock-hard arousal ready, waiting for her.

"I want to make you feel good... want to make you feel everything."

"I'm there, baby. Come on, climb on board and take me for a fucking ride," he urged.

She threw a leg over him, straddling his prone body, her sex wet and ready to accept him. She eased herself onto his erection slowly until he arched his hips up into her, pushing himself inside of her to the absolute hilt and making her suck in a breath as her body gave way to him.

The ache inside her womb was deeper than she'd ever experienced, made her entire body pulse with fever for him.

And what had started out slow and sweet turned, and Chris took control, as if he hadn't had her body in forever and needed it as much as he needed air.

He rolled her, gently, still inside her, and then he claimed her.

There was no other way to say it—he *claimed* her, with his body, as a white-hot fire spread behind her eyes. Her entire body trembled as he rocked against her, and God, she didn't want it to ever stop, wanted them joined like this, wanted to feel like this forever.

She cried out, hadn't expected the magic to overwhelm.

He wasn't stopping, telling her how he felt with every stroke.

Jamie came—hard—and holy fuck, it felt amazing as she pulsed around his dick and he nearly came too. But Chris forced himself not to—not yet. He had other plans. It was time for him to explore, to map her body, to plant his flag, stake his claim, the way he'd done in Africa.

This time, he wouldn't let her walk away from him afterward—no matter what.

He pulled out of her, groaned as he did so. His cock twitched, missing the contact as he began to kiss his way down her body.

She didn't have many signs of pregnancy—the telltale line wasn't running down from her navel yet, and her nipples had barely gone from the pink they'd been to a rosy brown. But her breasts were fuller, for sure—heavy in his hands—and she responded in a way she hadn't before when he touched them.

Her back arched toward him, pressing her breasts into his hands. "Mmm, that's nice."

"Just nice?" He brought his mouth down to a nipple, suckled it hard enough to cause her to jump and moan, and yes, that's what he wanted. Because *screw* nice.

He was through playing.

"No, not nice, not nice at all." She wound her hands into his hair, keeping his head there. She was still breathing hard from her first orgasm—it would be the first of many, if he had anything to say about it.

And dammit, he was going to say something about it. He worked his way down her body, the way she had done to his earlier, spread her thighs and ran his tongue along her slick folds.

He practically hummed. "You taste good."

He'd wanted to do this to her on the plane, in the hotel, in her kitchen, but fuck, it was worth the wait. He buried his face between her legs, heard her begging.

Her hips rose off the floor, her heels dug into the rug and then his shoulders as he licked her until she came again, crying out his name.

Suddenly, he couldn't wait any longer, climbed up and took her with a long stroke, her sex contracting around him again, hot and wet—and holy shit, he was done.

"Jamie..." He closed his eyes as his orgasm overtook him, his body shuddering with his release. He didn't move for several moments and when he finally lifted his head, he found her watching him, a small smile on her lips.

"Am I still alive?" she murmured. "Because I feel all floaty."

"You're alive. And we're not done yet."

"Good, that's good." Her hands roamed his back, and his cock hardened. "Hmmm, you are ready."

"Always for you, Jamie. Always for you."

Within minutes, he was proving it to her again.

CHAPTER
13

Saint didn't park in the garage—as he pulled into the driveway, he noted through his open window that the beach was quiet. The storms from earlier had receded along with the tide.

PJ got out of the car and automatically began walking toward the sand, as if the thought of going inside was a foreign concept. But halfway there, she turned and waited for him, cocked her head and watched him.

He hadn't spoken about his past to anyone in a hell of a long time—with another woman ever—and he wasn't quite ready to spill his guts as he'd promised.

Still, he owed her. She'd told him things, and he never went back on a promise.

But delaying, he was damned good at that.

"Let's go for a swim," he said, didn't wait for an answer before he'd stripped out of his clothes. As he suspected, she was game, followed fast behind him, her clothing flying, and then they hit the water—man, it was still goddamned cold.

He grabbed for her waist—she slipped away from him easily, dove under the dark waves. He waited for her to come up; when she didn't for a few seconds longer than he was comfortable with, he felt the catch in his throat.

Until, of course, she swept his legs out from under him, leaving him to crash backward. He sputtered as he came up for air.

She was in front of him, treading water. Smiling.

"Damned Air Force isn't supposed to teach you to swim," he said, and she laughed and swam away from him.

He caught her halfway up the beach, swung her into his arms and managed to get them both up to the deck before the crowd of partygoers walked in front of the house.

"That was close." He placed her down and shoved the hair off his face. "I've got some towels here."

He reached into the bin next to the surfboards and pulled out a towel. He'd much rather keep her naked, but she was shivering.

He'd get her dry and then make her wet. A damned good plan. And as he rubbed her shoulders with the towel, he nuzzled his face into her neck. She moved toward him, her bare body against his, and yeah, talking wasn't on his mind anymore.

She looked at him, the light from the deck casting a soft

glow over her face. "There must be so many women who want to be with you."

He didn't let go of her, even as she attempted to wrap the towel around both of them. And yeah, it was time.

He heard his accent thicken when he told her, "There was a woman once...and then, after that, there were a lot of them."

"She was someone special."

"Yes. And I did everything I could not to let her get away."

"But she did."

"She died."

PJ didn't say anything, just tugged the towel a little tighter around them in an attempt to cover his shoulders. And so he continued, the words coming out in a thick rush of emotion. "We'd been dating from high school—sophomore year. She wasn't exactly my family's first pick for me. She was pretty wild, her family was too—and fuck, it was fun."

"She was your first love."

"Yeah. My family's pretty wealthy. They had plans for me that didn't include falling in love with Emeline and enlisting in the Navy. They didn't understand me back then. Still don't, I guess."

"Tell me more about Emeline."

"You really want to know?"

"No, because I'm jealous. But yes, because she was so important to you."

Her honesty nearly killed him. "We'd been together for two years, just graduated, when we found out she had bone cancer. And so we got married. We were married for two months before she died, and I stayed with her every single second of her illness. When she passed, I enlisted, because I didn't know what the hell else to do."

"Saint, I'm sorry. I can't imagine what that must've been like."

He'd been seventeen, in love. Married. Watching the girl he loved slowly dying and not being able to do a damned thing about it.

Emeline had been so pretty, so fucking strong. When she died, he was sure he'd never find his strength again. The Navy had given him a chance to show off his physical strength—but BUD/S, that had truly been hell. He'd tried to rely solely on his body, with his mental game shot to shit, and it hadn't worked. In order to pull his ass out of the fire, he'd had to get his head back on straight.

"Was she pretty?" PJ was asking.

"Yeah, she was."

"You'd still be with her today."

"I don't know. I'd like to think that, but I sure as shit can't predict the future. I had no idea I'd end up doing what I'm doing...or sitting here with a woman who a couple days ago wanted to slit my throat."

That made her smile. "I didn't want to—you were being..."

"What?" He moved his body as close as possible to hers.

"Insolent. And I was simply trying to make sure you were all right."

"I'm not okay." He lowered his head to murmur against her neck. "You going to help me?"

She would, let him know by simply threading her fingers through his hair. "I don't know what to do with myself.

I left Africa because I couldn't figure that out—I'd hoped it would be different here. But I barely have any money in the bank. No place to live. When they took me into GOST, they cleaned out my apartment. Anything I once had is gone, except for a few weapons and some clothing. That should matter, but when I'm here with you, like this, it doesn't."

"You're starting over. And I told myself that if anyone ever came into my life who made me feel the way Emeline did, I'd fight like hell to keep her. And I'm prepared to fight, PJ—make no mistake about it."

With that, he brought his mouth down on hers in a long, hot kiss that had her dropping the towel she'd been holding, leaving both of them naked in the semi-privacy under his deck.

Saint was kissing her, a hot, demanding kiss that took her breath away and made her ache for more. Yesterday, they'd had sex multiple times, but they hadn't kissed, hadn't done more than the bare basics, which had still been amazing.

But now, with his mouth on hers, PJ lost any hope of protest. The man was too damned strong—his will could, and would, break down any last resistance within her, given time.

And apparently, he felt that moment had come.

"I want you in a bed this time," he murmured after he'd pulled back from kissing her; PJ struggled to catch her breath, and her senses. Because her knees had been pretty much knocked from underneath her, and if Saint's arms weren't around her, she'd be a puddle in the sand.

A highly contented puddle.

Although she was long dried off, the wind still brought a chill to her body, and in Saint's arms, she was cold and hot, and she buried her face against him as another group of beach walkers passed by, far enough away and so into their own rowdiness that it wasn't a problem.

Her breasts pressed his hard chest, his thighs were like iron against her and his arousal felt like velvet steel when it rubbed her belly. She moaned into his mouth, tried to remember how long it had been since she'd actually kissed someone, and couldn't.

But she knew no one else had ever kissed her like this, like they owned her. Saint had everything it took to back up that claim—and more.

It both scared and thrilled her.

"You're thinking," he murmured against her mouth. "No more. Not now."

As if to help her along, his hand dipped between her legs, fingers stroking her sex, making it wet and hot and causing her to writhe against him, toes digging into the sand as she struggled to remain upright. He certainly wasn't dragging her to a bed, but he was taking her—there was no doubt about that.

His name escaped her lips, a whisper at first and then louder as the pad of his thumb found her clit and didn't let up.

"Yeah, that's better, Patricia Jane . . . keep going."

"You . . . keep . . . going," she managed, and God, he did, first with a finger inside of her and then he added a second and a third, moved them inside of her until she thought she'd scream. And maybe she did—she lost track of everything, including her name, as the familiar tightening in her groin began. She was so wet, and he was kissing her neck, sucking lightly as though wanting to mark her.

He was making her his, and that was all it took to push her over the edge. She came, hard around his fingers, and he was whispering things to her—sweet and dirty words that made her murmur back to him, calling him *baby,* and whispering, *hold me,* and she never wanted this to end.

"Come on, let's get you inside—into that bed."

She couldn't think of any reasons to protest as he carried her up the deck stairs, slung her bag over his shoulder and brought her into the house.

It was only once they were inside the silence of the house that they heard the beeping coming from her bag.

"Your phone?" he asked.

"Shit. I keep forgetting it exists."

He lowered her to the ground and handed her the bag. She fished inside and pulled out the shiny new cell phone she'd bought two days earlier. New number, new start. But when she called her voice mail and heard Jamie's voice telling her, albeit calmly, about the explosion, she felt the familiar pangs of panic embrace her like an old friend.

"Everything all right?" Saint asked. She handed him the phone so he could listen to the message himself. He did and immediately dialed the number of the last caller. "The call was made from Chris's phone," he explained, and then, "Hey, what the hell's going on?" to Chris when he answered.

Saint listened for a few minutes, mouthed, "Jamie's okay, she's sleeping," and then said, "Do you need us to do anything?"

She moved away from him to stare outside. It had to be

close to six in the morning—she'd stopped wearing watches a long time ago—and adrenaline began to buzz through her.

Someone was threatening her baby sister again—there was no way she'd sit tight for that.

"Okay, Chris has her someplace safe," Saint said when he hung up. He handed her the cell phone and she held on to it.

They were still naked, in the semi-dark of Saint's living room, and he folded her into his arms. "She's okay, PJ. We can go see her, if you want."

"No, that's okay."

"Chris is the best person to keep her safe," he continued. "He loves your sister."

"I know." She'd seen it in Chris's eyes when they'd met in Africa, noticed the way he'd watched Jamie, for just a second too long. "She doesn't want me around, says I'm too volatile."

"Are you?" His blue eyes glinted when she turned into his arms and he stared down at her.

"Sometimes. Maybe."

"You'll get better. Hang on to the phone." Again, he picked her up and carried her up the stairs, sweeping away any imminent worries.

There was nothing she could do right now anyway— losing herself further into Saint seemed to be the best plan. And the only plan he would allow.

It had been a long time since Saint had made love to a woman. Sex, yes, and plenty of it, but this was so fucking different. So good.

He'd forgotten, been dead inside for so long and had convinced himself that wearing a hair shirt for Emeline was going to be his lot in life.

He was learning again, how to touch a woman, really please her—enjoying being with someone for longer than a single night, sometimes a single hour.

She didn't realize that she told him everything he needed to know, even when she didn't ask outright. Often, it was all in her eyes or in her hands, in the throaty cadences, and he was going to make it his mission to learn every single one...and brand some undiscovered territory as well.

Tonight's mission was all about keeping her calm and relaxed, getting her mind off her sister, even as she sank her fingers into the soft flesh between his shoulders and collarbone because she was kissing him so hard, like she couldn't get enough, her tongue teasing his, her mouth hot and fierce, and oh yeah, he wasn't stopping anytime soon.

Yesterday, she'd been relentless, demanding, almost as if trying to make sure he could keep up with her. That he wouldn't refuse her anything.

So far, he hadn't.

Now when he put her down, she sank deep into the mattress, letting his weight bury her. Her arms wrapped around his shoulders, legs around his waist, and she tried to guide him inside of her.

"I want that, honey, you know I do. But not yet."

"Saint..." Her tone was plaintive, but also held a certain amount of warning. He covered her protests with a long kiss and then he moved down her body, his tongue teasing her belly button, his fingers playing with her taut nipples, until her back arched off the bed.

"Yes . . . oh, yes," she murmured.

But he wasn't even close to his goal.

She'd told him no earlier, that it was far too intimate, that she wasn't ready for more than pure, straightforward sex. And he'd honored that request.

Now her hands twisted in his hair, a pre-emptive strike as he moved down between her legs, let his tongue trace her inner thighs, teased her until she begged him to stop.

He didn't—dipped his head farther despite the vicious tug on his hair and buried his face between her legs. He slid his tongue inside of her and she went completely still. When he moved his mouth again, he felt her open for him, as if her body was unfreezing from a long winter.

With his hands on her inner thighs, he tasted all of her. Wouldn't be able to get enough of her, her moans. He suckled the engorged nub as she writhed on the bed, halfway between loving it and hating him. And that was all right, because dammit, he wanted her to feel. Everything.

Wanted her to know that he wouldn't stop.

And so he licked and sucked and used tongue and teeth and made her come twice before he let go of her thighs.

She was furious, as he'd suspected, but not so much that she didn't roll over and mount him, taking him inside her slick center like this was some kind of sweet revenge. Her palms curled against his chest, her nails raked him, and he didn't care, rocked his hips up so he could get into her as deeply as possible.

And finally, finally, she relented, let him roll her now so

he could take her hard and fast, until her orgasm hit and she surrendered to him completely.

Jake woke and heaved a loud, disgruntled groan to the person currently trying to wake him up.

His head was pounding. He'd figured Isabelle would've been slightly more sympathetic to his plight, but he guessed that being forced to listen to one too many renditions of "Midnight Rider" had been her breaking point.

Still, he and Nick did a pretty damned good job with that song.

"You're being very loud," he muttered, and fuck, it hurt to talk.

"It's called breathing."

"Loud breathing." He buried his cheek against the soft cotton. "This is why I don't drink."

"Speaking of which, here's some juice, some toast. And Advil." She continued to nudge him until he lifted his head and grabbed at the juice and the pills.

Then he took a bite or two of the toast as Isabelle moved behind him and began to rub her palms along his back, and his body stirred to life, despite the searing pain behind his eyes.

"I guess you need this reminder every once in a while," she murmured, not a hint of anger or judgment in her voice. She got it, got him on every single fucking level— and yeah, this reminder, coupled with her hands sliding on his bare skin, was perfect.

"Are you naked?" he asked without lifting his head.

"Yes."

In one swift movement, he was up and had her firmly in his arms. And she was, indeed, naked. And beautiful. And his.

When he'd rescued her, he'd never expected to fall in love with her. But he had, probably that very night.

She'd been attacked—raped, left for dead. It had happened months earlier, but sometimes when he was making love to her, he flashed to the bruised places on her body the night he'd found her. And he'd find himself focusing on those areas, spending time kissing and touching them, rehealing them. And she knew too, would stroke his hair or murmur his name as if to reassure him that she was okay . . . strong. That she got better every single day.

But the scars of her attack had been so deeply ingrained in both of them, snuck up in ways they didn't always expect. Like when Isabelle left him for a couple of months to go back to Africa, to work with Doctors Without Borders again.

He'd lived with his heart in his throat nearly every day. And now she was back, because of another tragedy in their lives. "Thanks for coming to get me last night at the bar."

"You can make it up to me all day."

"I don't want to wait," he told her.

"I'm naked—there's no wait."

He grinned, ran a hand along the curve of her bare hip as she settled against his lap. "I'm not talking about sex. I'm talking about the wedding. I don't want to wait another nine months to marry you."

"Jake, you promised my mother she could do this wedding the way she wants to. My God, you've got to see the bridesmaid dresses she's picked out." Isabelle shuddered visibly.

"You don't have any women friends, except for Kaylee—how are you going to have bridesmaids?"

She rolled her eyes. "I don't know. Cousins, maybe."

"Cousins?" His head began to throb more at the thought of meeting her family, and he got back to the topic at hand. "Look, your mom can keep planning—we'll do that whole big stupid wedding thing. But when I say my vows to you for the first time, I don't want to do it in front of nine million people."

Her voice grew soft. "You want to have a ceremony before the ceremony?"

"Yeah. Just us. My brothers. Dad. Your mom would never have to know." He kissed her shoulder before he spoke again. "I want to fucking marry you—right now if I could. I've never been a patient man, and after everything that's happened over the past week ... Jesus Christ, I don't want to wait."

Isabelle watched him carefully, her eyes wide and clear, and she nodded. "I like that idea."

"Good. Then we'll do it at the end of the week—Friday."

"And what will we do until then?"

He flipped her swiftly so her body was pinned beneath his. "I'll keep you busy, don't you worry about that."

———

Jamie slept peacefully, curled against the pillows and blankets that were in disarray on the floor. Considering how many times they'd made love, Chris was surprised he hadn't passed out himself.

It was pure adrenaline that kept him up and moving, as if waiting for the other shoe to drop.

He checked the monitors—no movement in the driveway. Thought about calling Nick or Jake . . . but knew there was someone else he needed to speak to first.

He jumped off the porch and moved around the cabin, looking to see if anything seemed out of place.

Thought about how everything was about to change, how much things already had. And then he pulled out his phone and dialed, sat on the edge of the porch in the lazy haze of the morning.

"Hey, sorry—I know it's early there," he said when his father answered.

"I'm always glad to hear from you—I don't give a damn about the time," Dad said, his voice groggy from sleep. "What's going on?"

"Nothing. Everything." He paused. "I'm sorry."

"I am too, Chris."

"I've, uh, got a lot of things going on," he said, waited for his father to say he knew. But this time, Dad didn't say anything like that. Chris ran his hands through his hair as emotion flooded him. He'd been to hell and then heaven and back again in the space of hours, and he almost felt dizzy.

"What can I do to help you? Say the word."

Chris paused and then blurted out, "I'm going to be a father."

There was dead silence on the other end of the line, and Chris wondered how he'd managed to surprise Dad with that one. The man knew everything, knew when Chris was just thinking about getting into trouble—how could he miss a baby?

"You know it's a boy," his father said quietly, and by his tone Chris knew the man hadn't missed a damned thing.

He rubbed the center of his forehead with his fingers, tried to picture himself as a father and couldn't. "So he'll have it, right? The sight?"

"He'll have it."

Chris closed his eyes, phone still pressed to his ear. "I've got to go."

"Sometimes I hate it too," Dad told him, then he told Chris he loved him and hung up.

Chris stayed where he was for a while, just breathing, thinking . . . planning.

Nick couldn't have kids of his own, and hadn't wanted any. Neither had Jake. But now that his brothers had women in their lives, things would be different. He'd already seen both men change—for the better, and they were damned good men to begin with.

But with him . . . a kid . . .

He thought about how he and Jamie were about to drag a baby—kicking and screaming—into a world where he'd have to deal with his parents' pasts. Wondered if he was strong enough.

Jamie had already told him that she could handle things, handle him.

Handle the two of them together.

But it wasn't going to be just the two of them. And whether or not he was ready for that was the big question he wasn't able to answer yet.

He looked down and saw he was rubbing the fingers on his left hand together and immediately put his palm flat on his thigh.

CHAPTER
14

Jamie slept until early afternoon. When Chris heard her stirring inside, he came in from the porch.

Her hair was tousled, eyes sleepy, and fuck, she looked pretty. It took everything he had not to crawl under the blanket with her.

But last night, as good as it was, had made him too vulnerable. Watching her now would be a full-time job—no time to let his guard down. "I'll make you some breakfast. Or lunch."

She yawned and nodded and he began to rifle through the cabinets.

"MREs or soup—your choice." He glanced over his shoulder as she rolled her eyes. "Soup it is."

She came up behind him, rubbed her cheek against his shoulder. "You don't happen to have any decaf tea, do you?"

"Yes, right next to the muffins and pies."

She gave a soft snort in reply.

"There's some Parmalat milk—that's good for you," he said, pulled the cardboard container out of the cabinet. "There are some crackers here too. They should be fresh— Nick comes up here every couple of months to check on the place."

He dumped a can of soup into a pot and put it on the stove, then grabbed glasses and bowls and silverware and put them on the table in front of her. She'd hugged her knees to her chest, her bare heels balanced on the edge of the wood chair. Her palms were flat on her knees, the Navy T-shirt he'd brought in from the car long enough to cover her to mid-thigh.

"Are you feeling okay?"

"Tired. Stressed. Typical day in the life of an FBI agent who's being hunted down." She went for the joke but ended up pressing her lips together in a grim line.

He noted that her gun was right next to her on the table. A good sign, despite her words. She was up and alert. He poured the milk into two glasses and pushed one toward her.

"Did Kevin call?" she asked. "He was going to check on the insurance."

Yeah, that had been a fun fucking conversation—more like a growling match than anything, even though both men wanted exactly the same thing: Jamie's safety. "He did. Wouldn't tell me anything. He's pretty pissed I won't give him your location."

"I'm sure he understands," she said quietly.

"I gave him Nick's number, told him I won't give him the location over the phone but that Nick would know. Saint called too—for PJ," he told her. "She's upset. I told them you were okay but that I didn't want to wake you."

She nodded. "And if she wants to come here..."

"She can. Saint knows where this place is," he reassured her, took the cell phone out of his pocket and slid it across the table to her. "You should also check in with your boss, see if there are any new developments."

She didn't pick up the phone. "God, this is weird. I've got a psycho drug runner after me and I keep thinking, *Where am I going to live?*"

"It's called survival instinct." He ladled the soup into the bowls, then put the pan back on the stove and sat across from her. "I'd worry if you weren't thinking about that."

She leaned back in her seat. "I guess."

"You can stay with me," he offered.

"And your brothers?"

"And their girlfriends," he added.

"Sounds crowded."

"In a good way."

She didn't answer, was too busy staring at his left hand. He'd been rubbing his fingers together again, and shit, he grabbed the glass of milk.

"You do that sometimes, with your fingers," she said.

"Sometimes," he agreed, downed the glass of milk and kept his hand wrapped around it.

"So I'm guessing it's something you don't want to talk about."

He didn't, no, not now—really, not ever. "It's part of my

gift. Half the time I don't realize I'm doing it or what I'm sensing." He sighed, pushed the glass away and locked his hands together.

"What's it like? Your gift?"

"It just happens. I get a feeling or I know something. Like intuition, but stronger. But look, everyone's got feelings like that some of the time—most people choose to ignore it. But people who are close, really close, sometimes claim they can feel when the other person is upset or in pain."

"That's true. Because I knew, going to Africa, that PJ was alive. Knew it in my heart." She watched him. "You know things like that all the time."

"I seem to know what people need," he agreed. "Sometimes it sucks because it doesn't coincide with what I need or want. And you need to go to the doctor. Today. I should've taken you last night."

"Everything's fine. I would know," she told him. "More importantly, you would."

Fuck, she was right. But he was done discussing his gift for now. "There's a clinic about a half hour from here. They have an ultrasound machine."

"Okay. If it will make you feel better, we'll do that."

Jamie lay on the exam table with a sheet covering the lower half of her body, belly exposed. Chris was pacing as if she was readying to give birth at any second.

The doctor—Dr. Evelyn James—glanced over at Chris and then confided to Jamie, "Fathers are always nervous."

Jamie didn't have the heart to tell her that Chris was

about ready to shove her to the side and begin the exam himself. Thank goodness, he refrained. Instead, he muttered to himself as the doctor put the cold gel on Jamie's stomach and began to move the probe around.

That's when Chris really began to hover, his head practically blocking the screen.

"I'm going to need some room, sir, unless you'd like to do the exam." It was an attempted joke on the doctor's part, until Chris made a move to take the probe from her.

"Chris, please. Let her look."

He backed away and then pointed at the screen. "Heartbeat."

The doctor smiled, although her patience seemed to be wearing thin. "Yes, there's a heartbeat. Everything looks great."

"There was a small gas leak at my house. Thankfully, I was sleeping with the windows open, but..." Jamie said, forgoing the whole *and my house exploded* part of the explanation. Better to let the doctor think they were some random couple vacationing in the area.

"We can do a blood test to check your CO_2 levels," the doctor assured her. "I'd also like to do a quick pelvic exam. Just to double-check the baby's size and position."

"That's fine."

"Do you have any idea when you conceived?"

Jamie gave her an estimated date and the doctor turned the wheel of a paper chart. "You're due sometime in late December. Right now, that's the most exact I can be. I know most women like to have a specific date, but it's rare to have a baby deliver on time. But you'll know more when you have your next ultrasound and we take some measurements."

Chris was staring out the window through the half-opened blinds. If he'd heard the doctor, he didn't react. "I'll give you some privacy for the exam," was all he said, and stepped outside the room.

Dr. James was quick—the exam was completed in under five minutes and Jamie was sitting up as the doctor snapped off the gloves and threw them in the trash. "You need regular checkups, starting next month. Find a doctor, and a hospital where you'd like to give birth."

"I'm thinking of trying a midwife instead," Jamie said as she wiped the gel from her belly with the towelette Dr. James handed her.

"If you need some recommendations, I've got them," the doctor offered on her way out of the room.

Jamie shook her head. "Thanks, but I've already got someone in mind."

Chris remained quiet on the drive home from the clinic, didn't argue when Jamie told him he needed to rest—he'd done nothing but take power naps for the last twenty-four hours, so yeah, he should get some sleep.

"I'll only need a couple of hours of rack time," he mumbled, was asleep before his head hit the pillow, his body stretched on the floor on top of the sleeping bags.

When he woke, he checked his watch and groaned. "Why the hell didn't you wake me?"

Jamie had been sitting at the table, gun in front of her. "You looked too cute to wake."

He frowned. "I'm not cute, Jamie. Christ." He lumbered into the bathroom and washed up with a quick shower. When he returned, he headed straight for the fridge.

Soda in one hand, gun in the other, he scanned the windows before he opened the front door and stepped out onto the porch. "Want some fresh air?"

She did, and so she stepped out next to him, sat in the old swing. "Are you ever going to tell me what's bothering you?"

"What's happening in your life isn't enough?" he asked. "Shit, sorry. I know you're worried."

"I like that you know me."

"I know every inch of you. We may not have spent much time together, but I know. You have three freckles in a triangle formation right here." His finger stroked her left shoulder. "Your scars, your bruises. Small scar on your belly button from an operation. Laparoscopic—appendix."

She nodded, her attention rapt, lips slightly parted. "I know you too."

"Oh yeah?"

"You've got that interesting scar along your chest and back. And here . . . and here and here." Her fingers traveled from chest to back over the soft cotton of his T-shirt. She noticed things that most women didn't. Had from the first.

It made him want to pull back. To run, because he wasn't used to someone knowing him.

His brothers didn't count—they didn't spend time analyzing him, pushing, prodding, pressing.

Jamie would, had already, albeit in the most subtle manner ever, which made it the most disconcerting as well.

He needed to call home, check in. His only consolation

was that Izzy and Kaylee were with his brothers now, and holy hell, that was a first.

All three of them attached. In love.

Just like Momma had predicted.

You'll fall like dominoes.

Rapid succession.

No stopping it once the chain starts.

"That's beautiful," Jamie said. She'd been watching the red sky, breathing in the fact that another night had passed safely.

"I've never brought anyone here."

"Why?"

"Never found the right person."

She smiled at that but quickly turned pensive. "Do you want this baby?" she asked finally. "I mean, we haven't talked about what this means for us, not really. We've put it off."

They had—suddenly, it was in the forefront, of paramount importance. When he'd seen the pregnancy test sitting on her back table, he'd forced himself not to react, to assess the situation as if it had nothing to do with him.

He had to do that to keep back the anger at knowing that some psychopath was gunning for the woman he loved and their child. "I never planned on having kids, I didn't want them. Partly because of what I've told you— that I know when people are going to die. And partly because I don't want to pass this psychic Cajun bullshit on to anyone."

She nodded, and he continued, "I know I sound bitter. Look, my momma and my dad handled their gifts much more gracefully than I have. I blame my dad sometimes for mine. Logically, I know it's not his fault."

"It's hard to think logically when it comes to parents."

"I guess so. At first, with the gift, I didn't know any better. It was just always there. Same for my parents and most of the relatives I grew up with. People came to see us because of our abilities." When he thought back on those days, everything was bright. "It was only after I moved to New York that I noticed I was really different."

When Jake was hurt—really hurt—Chris felt it like a punch to the gut. He'd never forget that sensation of sucking air like a fish out of water, knowing something was desperately wrong but being unable to do anything about it.

His momma's gift was different. She hadn't needed to touch, could tell a woman was pregnant long before the woman knew herself. Maggie also predicted the sex of all the babies she'd delivered, and refused to touch the women she knew needed the hospital instead of a midwife and a home birth.

Your life will revolve around birth and death—you'll have a hand in each was all she'd told him before she'd died, that fucking horrible Christmas Eve turning into Christmas Day, ensuring that none of them ever celebrated those holidays again. It hadn't mattered that Maggie would've been angry with them for mourning her for so long in such a joyless way—wouldn't have mattered that she also would've understood completely.

"How did she die?" Jamie asked.

"Cancer. Ovarian. It was quick. At the time, they didn't have the treatments they have now. You would've loved her.

She just had this way of making everyone want to hang
around."

"Like your brothers."

"Yeah, well, they didn't have much of a choice. Once she
wanted you to do something, once she made up her mind,
there was no stopping her."

"Ah, an inherited trait." She paused and then, "Were
you mad at your mom when she died?"

"As stupid as it sounds, yeah, for a while. But I guess
bringing Jake and Nick into our family—it was meant to
soften the edges of the grief. We all got a hell of a lot closer
after that."

"I'm so sorry, Chris—about your mom. And Mark. And
the way you know things. But I keep thinking..." She
paused and then she looked at him, really looked at him,
and he felt a chill go through him, hoping she wouldn't ask.
"Do you... I mean, do you feel that I'm going to...?"

"Do I see you dying over the next few days?" he
snapped, and immediately she turned apologetic.

"I'm sorry. I can't believe I asked that."

He stared up at the sky. "Yeah, me either. Please... you
can't fucking ask me that again. Ever."

"I won't."

He started to turn away from her, then realized there
was no place to go.

Chris couldn't look at her for a long time, but he didn't
move from the swing. Still, she didn't push him to talk, so
he stared at the stars and thought about his momma...as

Jamie's partially unspoken words continued to echo in his ears.

Do you see me dying soon?

Finally he looked at her. Her hands were shaking, her eyes were wet and he wanted to tell her it was okay. But it wasn't—not by a fucking long shot.

"That's why you stayed away from me, isn't it?" she whispered. "You were worried that you loved me, and that you'd know if I . . ."

"I do love you, Jamie. Tried to deny it for a while, and when that didn't work, I convinced myself that you could never bring yourself to trust me, never mind love me back." His voice held steady, but he felt anything but. "I know it's not exactly the best time to tell you that."

"It's the right time, Chris." She reached out a hand to him and he took it. "For me, safety was key. It was all about logic. Discipline. Control. But now, that's all gone. I realize that I never had any control to begin with. It was a huge illusion."

He swallowed hard. "I wish I could tell you everything would work out, but that's not the way my gift rolls."

"I'm thinking about what it must be like. Thinking that because you've fallen in love with me, I can hurt you without lifting a finger or saying a harsh word."

"None of this is your fault. It's not like you put a spell on me to make me love you."

"You're not happy about it. If you fall out of love with me, forget about me, then I won't be responsible for hurting you, the way you're hurting now."

"That's not going to happen. Once I've loved you, that's all it takes. And let's just say that I'm not falling out of love with you. I know that. Look, with my mom, she knew she was sick. She told us pretty quickly once it was confirmed," he started, took himself back to that horrible time when he was fourteen, going on fifteen, with two new brothers and a dad who was in shock from the news.

"But you already knew."

"Yes." They'd been in the car, on the way home from dinner. She'd turned around to tell them something and he'd seen it, the flash, and then it was as if she was outlined in a white light. "At first I thought we were going to be in a car accident. I made my father pull the car over. Had a panic attack in the backseat."

He recalled how freaked Nick and Jake had been for him. They'd just been getting used to Maggie and Kenny's ways—and Chris's, since he hadn't completely let them in yet. That had only truly happened after Maggie's death.

"After a few minutes, my mom took me aside and she said, *I know, Nicolas Christopher. It's not a car accident. Let's get home and we'll talk.*"

He leaned his head back to stare up at the rapidly darkening sky. "And so we went home and she and Dad told us about the cancer. About how she wasn't going to have the treatment. And I didn't argue with her; Jake and Nick wanted me to. But I knew that no matter what, treatment wouldn't help." He brought his gaze down, looked at the ground. "She died two months later. On Christmas Day. My birthday. I haven't celebrated either since."

She didn't know what else to do but grab his hand and hold it tight. "It must be so hard... But Chris, I need you to know, just meeting you changed me. So I'd take a week or a month or a year with you, if it was between that and never having met you at all."

"That sounds like something my momma would've said."

"She was a smart woman," she said. "Don't focus on what could happen. I've spent my life up until now focusing on that. Let's focus on what we've got."

"I'm not letting you put yourself in danger."

"But I'm supposed to let you do so for me?"

"Yes. Absolutely yes." He managed a small smile. "You never said how you feel about the baby," he said, and no, she hadn't, hadn't really processed any of it until this minute.

"I never thought I'd be in a place to have a baby," she said, her brow furrowed. "It's like PJ said to me, that it's hard enough trying to account for ourselves, but bringing a child into it adds a whole new sense of danger. But then . . . then I think about you, and all the worries kind of fall away."

He nodded. "We can do this. But please, for Christ's sake, don't ever ask me what you wanted to before, not ever. Don't ever ask me." As he reiterated, his voice grew tighter.

"No. I promise, Chris. Never."

That seemed to satisfy him, and so she leaned into him further, took his face in her hands and drew him to her for a kiss.

He tasted good, sweet like soda, and it made her deepen the kiss, her hands winding in his hair to keep him close. And then she was in his lap, the rifle and everything else forgotten as she straddled him on the swing, her breath coming faster as the kisses became more frantic, a dance and a duel at once. Their bodies struggling against the constraints of the swing and clothing until he pulled back, rested his forehead against hers.

His breath was as fast as hers and there was no hiding his arousal. She wanted him naked, on the chair or the ground or on the hood of his car—it didn't matter. She needed skin on skin, the feeling of weightlessness that came from making love with him.

"Please, Chris, don't stop. I want more."

"Right here?"

"Right here," she agreed.

He responded with a kiss, one that threatened to have them naked in under a minute and going nowhere fast. And that's what she wanted.

He picked her up and walked a couple of feet to lay her on the sweet grass next to the cabin, under the willow tree in the warm night air. The lovemaking was slow and hot, the tension that held her body in a vise grip melted with her orgasm.

Everything was quiet and private. Everything was all right as long as they stayed here.

As he paused near the ruins of Jamie Michaels's house, looking like just another concerned neighbor passing by, wearing a baseball cap and a sweatshirt, he mentally checked this item off his list. Lists were important—they signaled a beginning, a middle and an end.

On his list, they'd finally reached the middle. There

were still many unchecked items to go, and his fists tightened briefly as he thought of the end.

But he was getting ahead of himself... there were still more steps. More ways to make sure Jamie panicked until his entire plan was in place.

Yes, patience was a virtue. It was at the top of his list.

In Saint's arms, in his bed, PJ found the comfort she'd been seeking her entire life. She didn't know why or how, but she'd learned a long time ago not to question.

Whatever force had brought her to the beach the other night had guided her in a direction she'd needed.

It was time to explain.

"I want to tell you about me—about what happened to me when I was younger." She allowed herself to snuggle against him, that small luxury enough to find her rubbing her feet together. A sign that she was content. Short-lived, as always, but still something to be grateful for, that she hadn't lost the ability completely.

Saint didn't say anything. Instead, he took a long lazy drag on the cigarette he'd lit after they'd made love for the third time, and blew fat smoke rings that rose slowly toward the ceiling.

She didn't wait for him to respond before she continued. The only other people she'd told the story to were the men from GOST. They'd each shared their stories with one another, one lonely, bourbon-filled night in Africa.

But telling Saint—that was breaching her personal comfort level. It was putting him in unnecessary danger... but it was the only way she could possibly explain to him why it would never, ever work for her to stay in one place for very long.

She realized that by telling him, she was doing exactly what she'd been so angry at her sister for doing when Jamie let Chris in. But this—it couldn't be helped.

"My mom was a DA in New York. There was a huge case—Russian Mafia—and she refused to back down, even when the threats started coming in. The man on trial was named Borya Frolov. A high-ranking member of the Russian crime syndicate. He worked out of Brighton Beach in Brooklyn. And my mom, this was her biggest case. Jamie and my dad and me, we went into a safe house for protection before the case was even done," she told him. "Once my mom won, it was supposed to be different—we'd been told it would be over. But it wasn't; it was worse. My mom joined us and the marshals hid us. Official witness protection. And we were all right for a while—for two years. As soon as Borya was convicted, his son, Alek, made no secret of the fact that he was out for revenge. He was in his early twenties at the time, and with the power of the syndicate behind him, the marshals weren't comfortable with anything less than new identities for all of us."

"You don't have to do this. Not now . . . not ever."

"Don't you want to know why I'm so screwed up?"

"I want what you can give me—nothing more, nothing less," he said, and those words gave her what she needed to continue.

And so she told him about Alek finding them, about her mom's breach of security, how Alek tracked them down through her mom's best friend—about that awful night when she'd found Alek standing over her parents. When she closed her eyes, she could see it all so clearly—Jamie coming down the stairs to see her . . . could remember guiding an eight-year-old Jamie to the closet in her room and telling her to stay there until the police came.

She remembered shutting the closet door on her sister's scared face and knowing that nothing would ever be the same again.

"They caught him—I called in time for them to pick him up two neighborhoods down, hiding in someone's car."

She'd realized Saint had locked his legs around her own as if to protect her. It made her feel better, not weak, as she would've imagined it would.

"So I saw it—I saw him and I picked him out of a lineup. And I was going to have to testify in closed court. And he would be there, and I would have to tell the jury what I saw, in front of him."

His eyes shone and there was a fierce kindness to his words. "Jesus, PJ, you were just a kid—a baby, really."

"I was fourteen," she said, as if that made all the difference.

"Even then, you were so fucking brave. I can picture you."

She'd seen several photographs of herself from that day—but what stood out in her mind the most was a sketch from the courthouse artist. It had been done in color, had captured her dark hair and sad eyes and the yellow dress she'd worn. A happy color. "I was wearing a stupid dress—it was scratchy and I hated it."

Her hair had been in a ponytail and the marshal who was escorting her held her hand much too tightly. Everything about the courthouse that day had been too much—

too loud, too bright. The smells of coffee and body odor had nearly overpowered her. She hadn't been able to eat that morning and by the time she'd gotten to the courthouse, she'd already been sick to her stomach.

"Then the marshal who was with me got a call. And I knew something was wrong, because he got me out of there quickly." They'd gone out the back door, into a waiting van, where she'd huddled in the backseat and wondered if she'd done something wrong. "No one told me anything until we got to the safe house. And then they finally admitted that Alek, the man who killed my parents, had escaped from police custody before I had a chance to testify." She paused. "The death threats to me and Jamie started a few days later."

"Son of a bitch." His words were tight as a fist.

"The protection loosened somewhat once we were of age, we could choose what we wanted to do. We kept ourselves under the umbrella of witness protection, kept our new identities and checked in regularly with Kevin. Jamie went to traditional college. I joined the Air Force when I was eighteen. I would've stayed in forever if I could've. But after the accident, when they wouldn't clear me to fly again for the military...it felt like I was choking. Then the CIA had offered me a job, since they needed pilots with my kind of combat training, and it seemed perfect."

"And then GOST."

"And then GOST."

"Do you think...with everything coming out about what happened in Africa, you're more at risk?"

She shook her head. "Our names—our real names— were never circulated. My identity's still safe. And I'm back in the marshal's database, as is Jamie, even though we're technically not in hiding. We can take care of ourselves now. And Kevin still watches over things for us as well. They've never been able to catch Alek. I'm still the only thing standing between him and jail."

"The murders were nearly twenty years ago—would you still recognize him?"

"He's disfigured. Unless he's received a miracle, I'd know him anywhere." The monster who haunted her dreams, who followed her no matter what continent, what safe house . . . what deep sleep. "If I'd only done something then—well, things would be so different."

"Like what? What could you have done?"

"I knew where my parents kept their guns. I knew how to use one—I'd watched the marshals show my father, I went with him to the shooting range. I could've done it, but I froze."

"You were fourteen fucking years old. You've got to let go of the guilt."

She stared at him coolly. "You first."

She'd taken the cigarette from Saint's hand, treated herself to a long tug that rushed through her system, made her feel heady. Warm.

Saint stubbed out the cigarette after taking it back from her. "Pity party stops tomorrow. For both of us."

"You know what I want to do?"

"What?"

"I want to go flying. First thing in the morning. Okay?"

"Do I get to be your co-pilot?"

She smiled into the dark. "Yes, I guess you do."

"Then we'll go flying."

CHAPTER
15

P J spent part of the late morning talking with Kevin as she picked at the food Saint fixed her.

Healthy food. A good, big, healthy breakfast—and while admittedly she'd been hungry on waking, she'd instantly remembered what was going on with her sister and the weight of that numbed her.

"There are a lot of agents on this," Kevin had told her. "Jamie will be okay."

Saint had offered to change his plans so she could go see for herself that Jamie was indeed safe, but she'd refused that. He'd gone to meet his mom—reluctantly, after PJ swore to him she'd be fine. They'd agreed to meet at the plane later that day; she'd planned on looking at cars to buy, but ended up renting one instead—easier, faster, and that would give her some time alone on the plane before Saint got there. She didn't want to have a panic attack right in front of him.

She also had time to do some shopping for Jamie, a chore she never paid much mind to for herself.

But she was pretty certain Jamie wouldn't be out buying herself clothing to wear for a little while now. Not with her being threatened, and her house exploding.

She'd picked simple things: jeans and shirts, and the basic bras and underwear. A light sweater. A couple of pairs of shoes and a pair of running sneakers.

With that accomplished, it was time to do some more proving to herself.

She wove the car around the small metal birds until she got to Mark's . . . hers. Her heart beat a little faster—it felt almost illegal being here, like she shouldn't be allowing herself to even think about doing this, taking the plane up.

She got out of the car slowly, walked to the plane and used the key to unlock the door.

Stepping inside was like going home. In the Air Force, she'd always liked piloting the smaller jets—felt somehow protected, even though there wasn't much more between her and the sky than thin sheets of highly constructed steel.

According to the written report the maintenance crew had left inside, the plane was well-maintained.

"She's all ready to go," the man named Jason had told her at the gate. "Just let us know your flight plan and when you want to take off."

Just getting inside the plane will be a major step, she

wanted to tell him, but instead, she'd said thanks and went on her way.

Now she got into the main pilot's seat. Hands on the controls, she felt the familiar thrill inside her belly. She slid her fingers over them, lightly tapping each one as she went through a simulated pre-flight checklist in her head, mouthing each direction softly.

And then she sat back and stared out into the bright sunlight through the front window.

She owned this plane outright. No strings attached. She could fly anywhere she liked, could open her own business.

She could do anything she wanted, which was nothing more than to remain here. There was no reason to leave for longer than a short flight.

Danger always happens around you, the little voice in her head insisted. *One of these days, your luck will run out.*

But not today.

There was a knock on the passenger's-side door and before she could say anything, Saint was inside the plane with her, as promised. He looked slightly distracted and he didn't say anything once he sat down in the co-pilot's seat.

"Tough lunch?" she asked after a few minutes.

He shrugged, stared out the window. "She wants me to quit. That's the only reason she stopped in Virginia at all. I knew I shouldn't have told her about Mark. But he'd come home with me for holidays when we were around."

"I've been thinking about how many chances we're given—how I've probably had way more than my share, and why that is," she said, and he turned to look at her.

"Have you come up with any answers?"

"Not a single one." She paused. "People around me

die. I live through unimaginable things that other people can't . . . or don't."

"Which is why you took jobs that don't let you stay near Jamie for long periods of time."

"Yes. I wanted her to be safe. In my world, safe and happy are mutually exclusive."

"Mine too. But I'd much rather be happy. Because who the hell is ever really safe?"

She stared down at her hands, so capable when she was piloting, so helpless when it came to things like love and affection. But when she looked up, Saint's gaze told her differently. "I could love you, Saint. I know I could really love you."

He reached over and squeezed her hand tightly in response, and yes, he could love her too. "So, are we going to sit around all afternoon or are we going to fly?"

She nodded. With her hand on the controls, she hoped her luck would hold out just a little while longer.

"Let's stay in the air for a nice long time. I'll take over if you have any problems," he told her.

She looked at him as she turned the key, and the plane rumbled to life. "I'm not going to have any problems. Why don't you just sit back and take a nap?"

He laughed and held up his hands in surrender. "Best offer I've had all day. But trust me, Patricia Jane, when you're around, the last thing I want to do is sleep."

She grinned as she let the plane roll toward the runway.

Chris's phone rang sometime after two A.M. He answered it with a curt, "Hello," and then, "She's right here, Agent Carter."

Once again, after Jamie herself had fallen asleep, he hadn't—he'd been sitting up against the couch, rifle by his side, while she'd rested with her head on his lap.

They'd made love enough times to pass away the evening after Jamie's clinic visit. Things had been mercifully quiet and there was a peace in her heart she wanted to remain there forever.

Now she took the cell from him, propped up on an elbow. "Lou, it's Jamie."

"Gary's been found," Lou said curtly. "He's dead."

"Dead?" she repeated dumbly as she sat all the way up. "What happened?"

"When our agents found him, he was already murdered. We got another anonymous tip."

"I want to see the body."

Lou paused, and then, "Alone?"

"Chris Waldron is with me—he won't let me go alone."

"Can't say I blame him." Lou rattled off an address; it was a school maybe ten miles from her house. Or where her house used to be. "Get there quickly, Jamie—we want to clean up the scene fast."

She clicked the phone closed, told Chris, "I think... I think it's over. Handler's dead. I'm supposed to go to the crime scene. Actually, I want to go."

Chris nodded slowly. "Okay. We'll look at the body. I'm just glad they got the bastard."

"The FBI didn't kill Gary Handler. They found him murdered."

He stared at her, knew exactly what she was thinking. Because she'd told him everything after they'd made love, told him about her parents and Alek, her voice halting. And he'd held her and let her talk everything through and then he'd made love to her again.

With both their hair still damp from quick showers, they were on the road within fifteen minutes of Lou's call, her wearing Chris's T-shirt and sweats, both impossibly big on her, but there wasn't an alternative. Chris sped along the nearly deserted highway, singing quietly to the songs on the radio and she let that soothe her, until they arrived at the school.

"Lou said they wanted to wrap this up quickly—it's a school day," she murmured as Chris pulled up behind an FBI agent's unmarked car and rolled down his window as a female agent approached them.

It was only then Jamie realized she didn't have any identification on her.

"Can I help you?" the agent asked.

"This is Agent Jamie Michaels," Chris told the woman, and Jamie added, "You can call Lou Carter to verify—"

The agent held up her hand. "He already called, said you wouldn't have your ID. I'm Beth Miller. Come with me, I'll show you the scene."

After a quick, reassuring squeeze of Chris's hand on her thigh, she was out of the car, the night air slightly humid and sticky, the smell of death permeating the grassy area that would be filled with high school kids mere hours from now.

As an FBI agent, she'd studied many different specialties, including profiling. That was a specialty unto itself, and now she called on all the skills she'd learned as she approached the body of Gary Handler.

The ME was next to the body; he shined his flashlight on it so Jamie could get her view.

Gary Handler was splayed on his back, arms pointing right, legs awkwardly to the left. His throat had been slit, the ground muddy with blood.

"Time of death is between eleven and midnight. Whoever called this in had to be the killer. The call came in just after eleven," Beth told her. "And there's something else—a woman's name is written in blood on his chest." She motioned for the ME to open the shirt.

When he did, Jamie felt her mouth drop. Her world spun for that single instant and then she pulled it together. She could do this. Neither Beth Miller nor the ME knew what the name meant. No one in the FBI would either.

Chris would, but he was hanging back with the other agent, no doubt so he could get a better look at the surrounding area.

And Kevin would know too, would see the name *Deanna* written with blood across Handler's chest.

What the hell it all meant was something Jamie couldn't think about here, not in front of total strangers. She wouldn't tip her hand to the FBI, no matter how shaken she was.

"Could it be a drug hit?" Beth asked.

Jamie shook her head. "He never turned on the men he worked for."

"That doesn't mean anything. Our deliberate leaks made them think he did, right? Enough to have them put a contract out on him."

"This doesn't feel like a hit. But it's not random. The

body looks posed," Jamie continued. "Whoever did this is most definitely sending a message."

She snapped a couple of pictures with Chris's cell phone. "Was there anything else of note?"

Beth handed her a piece of paper that had been bagged. "It was in the guy's hand."

A birth certificate with the name Peter Romanov. She wanted nothing more than to stuff it into her pocket, but she couldn't. It was evidence—bagged and tagged—and so she took a couple of pictures of it instead, telling Beth, "I know someone who can look into this."

And then she turned toward Chris, who led her away from the scene and toward the car. She didn't look back. Couldn't.

"Talk to me," Chris said once they were safely inside the car.

She told him about the woman's name written on Handler's chest. "My mother's," she confirmed as she stared down at the picture she'd taken of the birth certificate, as though it could reveal the mysteries of the world.

"Oh, fuck."

"Yeah, that sums it up." She paused. "I've got to call Kevin. He's going to want to put me and PJ under stricter protection again."

"And what is it you want?"

"Not that. Not anymore. I meant what I said—I'm done hiding." She looked over at him. "I'm going to need your help. I can't do much, because . . ."

Because of the baby.

"You think Alek killed Gary?"

"Or someone working for Alek. I don't want to jump to

conclusions, but that's the only place my mind will go right now." She showed him the picture of the birth certificate.

"Russian name—do you recognize it?"

"No. Alek's family name is Frolov. I'll have to check with Kevin—he's the expert. I mean, the Russian mob has some big ties to Mexican drug running—they could've met..." She trailed off.

This was not good. The sick feeling in her stomach grew as she scanned the area. She saw cops and other agents, the coroner and various other necessary personnel. No one out of the ordinary.

At least not anyone in plain sight. "We need to get out of here."

Chris didn't hesitate, saw her hand on her gun as if readying herself for anything and pulled out of the school parking lot. "There's got to be a link between Gary and Alek. Whatever it is, that's what we need to explore. Call Kevin—we'll go see him."

"I need to get away from here. Let's go back to the cabin. Please."

"Jamie, look—"

"Please. Just for a few hours. I need the quiet, the peace. I need to think, and I'm not going to be able to do that anywhere else," she said plaintively. "I can deal with all of this in a couple of hours. But not now."

"We need to run that birth certificate," he said quietly. "But the FBI's not going to know the significance behind all this unless you tell them."

"I know. I need to talk to Lou about it. He deserves to know first," she said. "Can you ask Nick to run the birth certificate for me? He seems to have access to things he shouldn't. The only place he won't be able to get into is the Marshal's database."

He glanced at her. "You don't know Nick all that well, do you?"

"Just . . . can you wait to call him, until we're back at the cabin?" she asked. Because once she was back at what, in such a short time, she'd come to think of as a sanctuary, she could finally breathe again.

From the woods, he watched the police arrive—a risky move but a necessary one. Staring down his own fears was important now.

Earlier, he'd found the list in Gary's pocket, all his assignments checked off neatly as he'd been asked to do. Gary thought he was coming here to get his freedom for a job well done.

Gary had been dead wrong.

He'd stood over Gary and smiled. The positioning of the body was perfect and the plan couldn't have been going any better.

When he'd gotten Gary out of jail, he'd promised the man his freedom after doing these favors, and when the prisoner had learned that he'd be stalking and menacing Jamie Michaels, the agent responsible for his arrest, he'd been more than happy to agree to the deal.

Gary hadn't realized the world didn't work like that— the fucker was too trusting for a criminal.

And now he was dead.

"Weak. Worthless," he'd whispered to the body.

"Weak. Worthless." His father spat the words at him with

fury, in full presence of the prison guards, twenty years ago when Alek had been captured after killing Ana and Patricia Jane's parents. Father and son would be serving jail time together now, or so it seemed. And even though his father was fully protected in prison, thanks to his status in the Russian Mafia, he'd told the guards to take his son away, to put him in the general population.

His throat tightened at the memory—the thought of being in that cell forever had nearly killed him. If he'd been there any longer, he would've hung himself.

But he'd escaped, with help from his connections in the underworld—escaped and hid and then, when he'd lost all hope, he'd found them—Patricia and Ana.

Patricia and Ana would never be that lucky again. He'd known that sussing Ana out with Gary would enable him to find Patricia more easily—she'd been the one hidden from him for over a year, the one he wanted most.

With that thought, he walked through the woods and toward his car, ready to make sure of that now.

CHAPTER
16

Chris paused before he pulled off the long dirt road leading to the cabin. He got out of the car and walked a few feet, checking the extra set of tire marks.

And then he got back in the car. "Everything's okay," he told Jamie. "My brothers are here."

"You didn't call them," Jamie said in obvious confusion as they drove up to the cabin, and found Jake and Nick waiting on the porch.

"No, I didn't."

"I guess they're psychic too." There was a gratefulness to her tone, as if comfortable with the fact they'd already revetted the cabin's safety and wore rifles around their necks.

"My father must've called them," he said, rolled the window down as he pulled close. Nick approached the car, while Jake remained on the porch, watching.

"Hey, you guys all right?" Nick asked, looked to Jamie first, who nodded, and then to Chris.

"Rough night," was all he trusted himself to say.

Jake came up to the car then, helped Jamie out while Nick climbed into the passenger's seat and told Chris to park around back.

"It's okay, we've checked inside," Jake reassured Jamie as she let him lead her safely inside the cabin.

Chris drove the car the short distance around to the back of the cabin, where he'd parked earlier.

"What's going on?" Nick demanded quietly, his voice rougher than normal as they sat together inside the car. "Dad called. He sounded worried. I haven't heard him sound that worried in a hell of a long time."

"Gary Handler was killed tonight. From the looks of it, it's someone from Jamie's past." His own voice was a hoarse croak—it was the first time since all of this began that he'd had a moment to let down.

"Something to do with why she's in witness protection, right?"

He told Nick as much as he knew about Jamie's past, what she'd told him about her mother's case and Alek Frolov, and watched his brother's face turn intense.

"Will she go back into hiding, disappear if it turns out this has to do with witness protection?" Nick asked.

"Fuck, Nick, why are you going there now? This could just be—"

"A coincidence?" Nick interrupted. "Get your head out

of the sand—Jamie knows what's going on, I can see it in her face."

Chris turned away from his brother, his hands still gripping the steering wheel tightly.

"If she's got to go back into hiding, would you go with her? Relocate?" Nick persisted.

"Would you go with Kaylee? Because when you ran off half-cocked to Africa with her there wasn't a damned thing anyone could do to try to stop you."

"You tried to stop me," Nick pointed out.

"I love her, Nick. I'd do whatever it took to keep her safe."

"I know that, man. It's just that . . . Look, Jake's getting married."

"Yeah, I know."

"No. He's getting married at the end of the week."

What the fuck? "I thought he'd agreed to wait until next year."

"He says he's tired of waiting." And yeah, Chris had been surprised he'd been this patient, waiting for Izzy's mom to plan the perfect wedding. Apparently, shit like that took years. "They're doing a small thing on Friday. Just us. No one else will even know it happened."

"I wouldn't miss it. You know that," he said when he found his voice, and even then, it was tight with emotion.

His words were greeted with silence at first and then, "All right, one thing at a time. What can we do to help Jamie and PJ?" Nick's voice was calm and reassuring, the way he always got in a crisis.

"I don't know, Nick. I don't know what the hell else to do but hunt this bastard down myself," Chris admitted.

"And I don't want to bring the danger to you or Jake, to Izzy and Kaylee."

"You won't. You aren't," Nick assured him. "It's going to get better—it always does."

Chris wanted to believe that, but this time, he wasn't so sure.

Jake Hansen had a wild streak barely contained under his calm demeanor. Unlike Chris, who moved constantly, Jake was still, and yet there was an impatience that lit the air around him with a fierce energy.

This was the first time she'd met Chris's other brother—she'd never even seen a picture, but knew, just looking at him, that none would've ever done him justice.

Nick was classically handsome; Jake, on the other hand, bore the rugged good looks of a warrior—gray eyes held a hint of mischief under their concern as he led her directly to the couch. "You look pale, Jamie. I'm going to grab you some water."

"Thanks."

"When was the last time you ate anything?" he called over his shoulder, and God, she didn't know—wanted to say, *the last time your brother let me up for air,* but didn't dare make a joke now.

Thinking about the way things had been just hours before made her heart ache. "I'm not really hungry."

"I know. But you should eat something." Jake crouched in front of her, handed her an opened bottle of water and a sleeve of crackers.

She took both, drinking some water and nibbling a

cracker under his watchful gaze. Mainly because she knew he wouldn't give up until she did so.

"Listen, I've got some clothes for you. My fiancée is about your size. She gave me some jeans and stuff for you." He continued, "She also gave me these."

He held out a bottle of prenatal vitamins. "She's a doctor," he explained, and yes, she guessed Chris had told his brothers everything. "She figured that with what happened to your house, you hadn't had time to replace these."

He trailed off, his eyes on her as she took the bottle and stared at it. She hadn't even had a chance to buy them yet, had planned to do so two days earlier after the meetings at the JAG building.

Her eyes filled. "Thank you. I figured, with all this trouble I'm making for Chris, you guys wouldn't . . . that you'd . . ."

"We'll handle whatever it is, Jamie. You make my brother happy. And you've got my nephew in there," he told her bluntly.

It would be that simple to join Chris's family. Because he loved her, they would. They were that close, that fierce in their loyalty, that quick to circle their wagons. "I think the man who killed my parents is after me again."

There, she'd said it out loud—easier to say it to a near stranger than to admit it to Chris.

Jake nodded. "Can you confirm that?"

"He hasn't contacted me directly," she said, which she still found odd. And then thought about her phone. "My phone was destroyed, but I can still call my voice mail."

"Put it on speaker," Jake told her as she dialed from Chris's phone. Normally a command like that from a man

she didn't know would make her bristle, but he was right—
and here for nothing more than to protect her life—so she
did exactly what he'd asked.

The voice that came across the line was firm and clear—
she'd never heard Alek speak before, but she had no doubt
that it was him leaving her the message.

"I knew you'd grow up to look just like your mother.
That bitch took everything from me. I can't rest until it's
done. And you'll pay, Ana. You and your sister and everyone you love. Including the father of your baby."

The threats echoed inside her head—everything was
happening too fast, the danger slamming on top of more
danger, and her world did a slow slide into panic.

Jake was still there in front of her and she was asking
him to, please, get Chris, but wasn't sure if the words were
really being spoken aloud or simply echoing inside her
mind in a silent, desperate scream.

It had almost been done twenty years ago.

The chore had hung over his head for years before that,
embarrassed him on a daily basis and especially when he'd
first visited his father in jail, right after his father's convic-
tion. He'd stopped doing that with any regularity early on,
letting his mother and sister make his excuses, living up to
his role of fuckup early on.

But finally, he'd caught his break through the bitch
Deanna's best friend...he'd been monitoring her for
months. Hell, he would've slept with her, if he thought she
wouldn't have recognized him.

She'd recognized him when he'd broken into her car to

kill her and his heart had soared because he'd known he'd finally be free. And then he'd hopped a flight to Minnesota.

Later that night, knife in hand, screams muffled with a chloroformed washcloth, the only sounds in the master bedroom had been the thump of the bodies as they'd hit the floor and then the gurgling sounds as his knife made its mark, the slash like a gaping, hideous smile along the dead couple's throats.

Alek had planned to move into the kids' rooms next, hadn't expected to hear the sirens. And, as he'd gone to leave through the window, he'd caught sight of *her*.

Patricia Jane. Watching him with fear and defiance coloring her features.

Had he ever been that young? No, and any last remnants of his youth had been stripped from him the day he'd been doused with gasoline, set on fire and left to die.

And still, he hadn't been able to finish the job, because Patricia was staring at him like he was a monster.

That hadn't ever bothered him before, not until that moment. And in that split second of pause, he'd given up his chance of completing the job. The sirens wailed in the distance and he'd attempted to run, but to no avail. He'd been captured quickly and sent to prison with no bond.

After he'd escaped, he swore he wasn't going back to that cell. Ever. The time spent awaiting trial had been the longest of his life—three months stretched to eternity. And he'd hidden ever since, stripped of his power to do the job because he'd made a promise.

The desire for revenge still ran hot and fast through his bloodline—it was what his family did. They hunted, waited patiently. And then they killed.

They did it all in the name of family, of business.

There was no room to keep promises outside of that—he'd been a fool to agree to it. And yet he'd thrown his life away because of one he'd made to his best friend and brother.

He'd been festering for so long, living between worlds. He'd been unable to face his father, since Alek's inability to finish the job had effectively lost his family their status in the Russian underground. His mother and sister had been funneling him money when they could, and Alek had comforted himself that he was doing the honorable thing, that repaying a debt like the one he owed should bring him honor, not take it all away.

After this, the shame on his father's memory would be erased.

The man Ana was with—the father of the baby—he was military. Tough, but not impossible to get to. No one was impossible for him. Alek had the training, physically and mentally. He was a soldier in a much different kind of war.

On the day of his father's death seven days earlier, the last vestige of humanity had been ripped from him. His father, on his deathbed, had publicly disowned Alek, his only son.

Finishing what he'd started was the only way to make all of this better. One person at a time.

Silently, he entered the house and prepared to exact his revenge.

Chris and Nick had come into the cabin in time to hear the tail end of the message, and Jamie's response.

Immediately, Chris was on his knees in front of Jamie, who looked pale and held the phone tightly. She continued to stare at it, even though the message had finished.

"We'll wait outside until you get her calmed down and decide what you want to do," he heard Jake say from behind him, and then Chris and Jamie were alone in the cabin.

Her fear was palpable.

He eased the phone from her hands, placed it on the table next to the couch. Immediately, she pulled her knees to her chest, wrapped her arms around them, placed her chin on her knees and rocked. She reminded him of Jake, when he was coming out of one of his nightmares, suspended between past and present and so completely vulnerable.

He remained next to her, tried to abort and deflect some of the negative energy from her, like his momma used to do when one of her boys was sick or hurting. It didn't matter if the pain was physical or emotional.

Pain is pain, Momma would say. Jamie's wouldn't go away anytime soon, but if he could help to ease it . . . He'd do anything to do so.

"You need to leave now." Her voice didn't sound like her own—it was monotone, a stranger's voice.

"I'm staying here for as long as you need me."

"Don't you understand? It's real now. The danger is so real, and I don't want you to be hurt by it." She stared at him as if really seeing him for the first time. "I couldn't bear to lose you to this man. Please, you can't do that to me. You have to listen, for your own good—pick up and go. The FBI can assign me a team."

Her last words were close to a shout, then her eyes went blank again. She began to shiver and he had to bring her out of this, had to get her back into fight mode. "The last team the FBI assigned to you didn't work out so well," he reminded her, and fuck no, she wasn't getting rid of him.

He picked her up and brought her, fully clothed, into the shower with him, turned on the water and held her under the warm spray. For a few minutes, she held him fast as the water sluiced over them, and then she pulled his face to hers and kissed him, over and over.

At least until he pulled back from her. "Don't you dare, Jamie. Don't you dare kiss me like you're saying good-bye. You can forget it. You can yell and scream and get as pissed off as you want, but don't you think you're shutting me out."

She had no answer for him, simply put her forehead against his chest for a few seconds. Her hands gripped his biceps as if holding on for dear life and she was so damned still. Pulling herself together.

She wasn't convinced she couldn't get him to leave. He knew that. But he also knew there was no way in hell he was deserting her now. He'd hunt the bastard who was after her to the ends of the earth if he had to, just to keep her safe.

She kissed him again, this time it felt more desperate—she moaned against his mouth and he got it, she wanted to get lost, to forget about what her mind didn't want her to process.

He wanted to tell her that now wasn't the time, but he couldn't, not when he wanted her. Not when he wanted to make everything better for her.

Together, they dragged their wet clothing off their bodies, letting it slop onto the bathroom floor until both were naked and she was back in his arms.

Her hands dug into his shoulders, slipped off a few times until she wound a hand in his hair and the other went between his legs, throwing him nearly off balance.

"Please...please," she murmured against his moan and he lifted her so her back went against the tile wall, the familiar dance the two of them knew so well. It was hot and quick and dirty—she practically impaled herself on him, driving him in hard with a leg wrapped around his waist, ankle digging into his ass. He gained traction any way he could—not easy in the slippery steam. She'd moved on from needy to frantic and he let her have her way until she came and slumped against him.

She wasn't convinced she couldn't get him to leave. He knew that. But he also knew there was no way in hell he was deserting her now. He'd hunt the bastard who was after her to the end of the earth if he had to, just to keep her safe.

Fifteen minutes later, Jamie dressed in the clothes Jake's fiancée had given her and sat at the small table.

Chris had changed too, wore jeans and a T-shirt, his feet bare as he fixed her more soup she would force herself to eat; had to keep herself as calm as possible. "I need to call Kevin and PJ."

"Okay. Let me get him on the line for you."

"I've done this for people, walked them through danger, I should know how to handle it—and I'm falling apart."

"Yeah, right now you are. But you'll pull it together and

we'll get through it." He slid the bowl toward her, urged her to eat.

She blew on the hot broth and took a spoonful. "How can you be so sure?"

"Because in the time I've known you, I've never seen you down for long," he told her. "We'll get PJ and Saint together, and Kevin—we'll all be in the same room. We'll figure it out."

"We don't even have access to computers here," she pointed out. "We should go to Saint's, if he'll have us."

She was in planning mode. She was better.

"I think being closer to civilization is preferable in this case," he agreed.

And then she was thinking again, picturing the scene. Going through the crime-scene photos she'd taken with his phone. "How did this happen? How the hell do they know each other?" she asked, trying to keep her voice from shaking.

"You mentioned a Mexican–Russian drug connection."

"Maybe." But she wasn't convinced, bit her bottom lip thoughtfully. "I thought if Alek was watching me, I would know. I'd be able to tell. And now he's in so much further than I want him to be."

"He's not getting in anymore. He didn't count on me." The anger in Chris's voice was unmistakable.

God, she wished Alek didn't know about the baby, or about Chris. That just magnified everything.

She knew what Kevin would want, could feel the walls of a safe house closing in on her.

Being relocated sounded so innocuous. What the marshals don't tell you is that everything's different. Everything.

That you had to be different. Except you were still you on the inside. Trapped.

Chris must've seen the wheels turning inside her head—he pulled his seat close to hers and gathered her against him. "Sometimes I get involved in cases like mine . . . I have to help bring the families in with the marshals. Stay involved with the current investigations. Once, Kevin brought me in to speak with a family who needed some help. The son had gotten involved in gang activity and he was forced to testify against high-ranking members of the gang or go to jail. His family—mom, dad and younger sister—they all had to relocate with him since he was a minor, only sixteen at the time. And I remember, they were all so angry at him. I walked into the room and realized I hadn't felt that kind of anger since . . . since my parents were alive. They were always angry with each other. I used to blame them, but now I get it."

Chris continued to watch her carefully. She remained nearly in his lap, his hands wrapped around her waist, holding her. Comforting her.

"I went into the FBI so I could get strong."

"You are strong."

She shook her head. "No, I'm not. I'm just really good at pretending."

"Whatever gets you through, Jamie. But I know strong. I've seen guys ring out of BUD/S training or wash out later because they've got no mental game. You're strong as hell."

"Kevin's going to recommend a safe house. And he's going to bring in another marshal to convince me."

"I know what Kevin's going to want you to do," he said quietly. "What I need to know is, what do you want?

Ultimately, that's what it comes down to—and whatever it is, whatever it has to be, I'll support you. If you have to relocate, I'll go with you."

"I would never ask you to leave your family behind."

"You didn't ask," he told her. "It would be hell, but they'd understand. I know they would."

"I want you," she said firmly. "You, and a house with lots of windows, and your brothers and friends. And my sister and Kevin. Everyone who'll be important in this baby's life. And I won't compromise."

He nodded and handed her his phone to make the call.

CHAPTER
17

Saint heard the crash—it slammed him out of a dead sleep and had him on his feet, eyes wide open and head clear.

He'd been about to grab his weapon, when he saw PJ in the corner of the room—she'd knocked over a tall lamp and now she stood staring into the closet.

She'd opened it, was holding on to the doorknob. Her shoulders were set, and as he approached her cautiously, slowly, he saw her eyes were wide.

But she wasn't with it—no, if he had to guess, this was sleepwalking, pure and simple. She was in the middle of a nightmare, and he had to get her back to bed without waking her up.

"It's okay, PJ," he said quietly. "Close the door and come to bed."

"I have to wait for them to come . . . the police."

"It's okay. The call's been made. Everyone's safe." He put gentle pressure on the door, helped her to close it. She was agreeable, let him bring her to the bed. She lay down and put her head on the pillow for a second and then suddenly, she was awake. And she realized what she'd done.

"Shit." She sat up, hugged her knees to her chest and stared at the corner of the room. "I broke your lamp—shit, I'm sorry. I knew I shouldn't have stayed inside."

"Is this . . . is that the reason you stay outside?" he asked.

"No closets outside," she said ruefully, although there was a small smile on her face. "I'm sure that sounds ridiculous."

"No, it doesn't."

"I tried to memorize Jamie's face, in case it was the last time I saw it. Which was stupid on so many levels—because if I was dead, I wouldn't be seeing her face anyway. But I did, burned it onto my mind like a brand. And now, when I look at Jamie, all I can see is that eight-year-old face. How do I make that go away?"

"I don't know," he said as he massaged her shoulders to ease the tension in the muscles.

She nodded, let him pull her closer so her cheek rested against his chest. "I thought I heard a phone, in my sleep."

"Your cell phone was ringing downstairs. I would've grabbed it, but then—" He stopped. "I'll get it for you."

She tried not to pace while Saint went downstairs, but something was wrong.

After they'd returned from flying, they'd had an early

dinner out, came home, made love and fallen asleep. Now, with morning sunlight beginning to filter through the half-opened blinds, the slow, peacefulness of yesterday seemed a lifetime ago.

"The missed call's from Chris's phone," he said on his way back into the bedroom.

She stared at the screen. "There's a message."

She dialed her voice mail and let the message play on speaker phone. Jamie's voice—telling her that their past had truly come back to haunt them.

"Call me as soon as you get this, PJ. Please—let me know you're safe."

"Call back now," Saint said, because PJ sat staring at the phone.

"I don't want to feel this," she said, more to herself than to him. "I can't let myself feel."

He didn't know what to say to her—he understood, for sure, but no matter how stoic she tried to be, he knew the feelings would come back to her. They would haunt her, catch her in weak moments like the middle of the night or during the day at the supermarket when she was simply picking apples from the display, and suddenly the aisle was her parents' bedroom and she was fourteen years old, looking into the eyes of a killer—a man driven by family pride and revenge.

A man who refused to stop hunting until the entire job was complete.

For the first time since Africa, the familiar stab of fear was back; the enjoyment she'd taken from being out in the open and free was gone. Now she was a sitting duck, a target again, no matter what her sister said.

Saint was closing the blinds and locking windows, setting the alarms. He left the bedroom and she heard him repeating the same steps through every room in the house.

She followed him down the stairs, watched as he pulled both a rifle and a shotgun from a locked closet and placed them on the coffee table in front of her, ammunition as well, and they sat on the couch together in the house he'd attempted to make safe for her.

When she didn't reach for the phone, he dialed Chris's number and waited to hear his teammate's voice.

Jamie picked up. "PJ?"

"It's Saint—she's here, she's fine," he said, then asked to speak with Chris. There was barely a pause, and then he said, "Come here—this asshole can't get through all of us. Wait until tonight, until it's dark, and then you and Jamie stay here." He stared at PJ as he spoke. She mouthed *Thank you,* as he finalized the plans with Chris.

"Your sister wants to talk with you," he said when he finished speaking with Chris.

She took the phone from Saint's hand. "Jamie, are you okay?"

"I am. I'll tell you everything when I get there."

"It's Alek for sure?" she asked quietly.

"Yes."

"I'll see you later, Jamie. Stay safe," she told her before she hung up the phone, and then simply murmured his name. She didn't know what else to say, but luckily, she didn't have to, because Saint's arms enfolded her, until her cheek rested against his chest.

"We'll figure it out, Patricia Jane," he murmured against the top of her head. And for once, the *we* didn't scare her.

Nick and Jake spent the remainder of that day at the cabin with Chris and Jamie and began the drive to Saint's as dusk fell.

Nick much preferred traveling in the dark, especially when they were headed back into what could be enemy territory. He'd always thought of his house, and the base, as safe. After everything that had happened over the past months, he knew for sure that no place was ever really safe, and that made him as angry as it made him melancholy.

While they'd waited for the day to pass, he'd spent some time just looking around the old cabin, feeling Maggie's presence everywhere. Jake sacked out on the floor for a nap, as did Chris at one point, while Jamie curled up on the couch, sleep her only other option beyond pacing.

At one point, Nick had gone outside to the old porch and had called Kaylee, just to hear her voice. Once he did, relief flooded him, although it made wanting her that much keener.

Now he and Jake trailed behind Jake's Blazer, which Chris was driving to Saint's house. They were in Nick's Porsche, with Jake sitting in the passenger's seat—something he hated, drumming his fingers on the inside of the door at about ninety miles an hour.

Finally, Jake said, "If this asshole Alek knows about Chris..."

"He could know about us. The house." Kaylee and Izzy.

Jake nodded and Nick knew that had weighed heavily on his brother's mind since last night. "Isabelle's visiting her mom in D.C. She'll have a lot of security. I called, told her to stay there until she heard from me."

"Did she freak out?"

"She tried not to. She's trying to accept shit like this, but it's never going to be easy for her." Jake ran his hands through his hair in frustration—not at Izzy, but shit, their lives were complicated as hell. Dangerous too. And until the day the men decided to retire, none of it would change.

Nick knew it was hard for Kaylee too—she was always weighing the benefits of questioning him further versus the conversations they'd had about the nature of his job, the things he had to do. The way her life could, at times, be at risk because of it. Then again, Kaylee's job as an undercover reporter didn't always land her in the safest of positions either. "Kaylee's already left for Bangladesh. She's flying back in late Thursday night."

"I never thought I'd say this, but she's a whole hell of a lot safer there," Jake muttered. "Are we ever going to go any faster?"

After Saint ushered Chris and Jamie into the living room, the first thing Jamie did was walk to her sister.

PJ had been leaning against the edge of the couch, waiting to see what Jamie would do.

"PJ, about the other day..." she started, but her sister stopped her.

"Do you know why I finally came home from Africa?" PJ asked, and Jamie shook her head. "I missed my family."

The sisters hugged, Jamie holding PJ tightly as she tried not to cry.

"I've got some things for you—clothes," PJ told her. Jamie saw the bags in the corner and was so incredibly grateful to her sister for thinking about her. For simply being here. And so she went upstairs to Saint's bedroom to change, to wash her face, as she'd rolled into the car straight from a dead sleep in the cabin.

When she came downstairs, everyone except for Saint was crowded into his office. She caught sight of the broad man in the kitchen and she bypassed everyone else, because she had an apology to make.

"Have you eaten recently?" he asked without turning around.

"Why does everyone keep asking me that?"

"Because they're worried about you. And you didn't answer the question." He put down a plate with a large sandwich on it on the table and pointed. "Eat. I'll get you some milk."

"Thanks." She sat at the table and took a few bites.

"You don't have to apologize."

"Was I that obvious?"

"You and your sister get the same look when you're about to say you're sorry, that's all." He grinned when he mentioned PJ, and then grew serious. "You and Chris can stay here as long as you need to. Until all of this is sorted out."

"PJ . . . she told you everything, didn't she?"

He nodded the affirmative.

"You're good for her."

"She's good for me."

"Hey, Jamie, PJ needs you in the office," Chris called. She took her sandwich and walked in that direction, Saint following her.

She found PJ staring at the computer screen where

Chris had been downloading the crime-scene photos onto Saint's computer for Jamie.

"PJ, what's wrong?"

Her sister had gone white as she stared at the screen with the picture of Handler, lying on his back, arms pointing left, legs right.

"His throat was slit. And he's lying just the way mom was...he's been positioned," PJ said quietly as Jamie and Chris looked at each other silently.

"You remember that?"

"I'm not relying on memory," PJ admitted. "About ten years ago, I made Kevin show me the entire file. Notes, pictures. Everything. I wanted to make sense of things."

Jamie never had—it would've been available to her at anytime as well, but she'd never wanted to burn something like that into her memory. Her imagination was vivid enough.

Jamie clicked through the pictures on the computer, pulling up the shot of the birth certificate. "Do you recognize this?"

"No."

"It was inside Handler's pocket."

PJ's eyes met hers. "Why now, after all this time? How the hell did he find us?"

"I think these are questions Kevin needs to answer for us," Jamie told her sister. "I called him earlier—left a message, telling him to meet us here."

"I haven't had any luck with the name Peter Romanov," Nick called from the living room, where he'd been typing furiously on his laptop. "If he really exists, he's been wiped."

"Unless he's in the Marshal database," PJ murmured. She frowned for a second and then she leaned in and typed, *Borya Frolov,* Alek's father's name, over Chris's shoulder.

Borya's obituary was the first thing Google pulled up.

"Shit," Jamie breathed as PJ clicked open the obituary. "He died while I was in Africa—he died a week ago."

"And maybe that's our reason," PJ said, right before she walked out of the room.

Kevin had gotten Jamie's messages after twenty-four hours of being locked in a safe house with a new family, drilling them on their new identities. It wasn't an easy case—the father was a criminal who would be testifying in a major mob case next year. The man was angry and arrogant and it was the kind of case Kevin hated.

It was a case so important that all cell phones had been collected at the door of the safe house. He'd been worried about Jamie the entire time. Seeing a message from Chris's phone from her gave him a huge sense of relief.

But when he'd listened to it, he'd had to literally pull his car to the side of the road. Sweat poured off his face as he rolled the window down and attempted to stave off a panic attack.

He hadn't had one of those in years, not since Jamie had first gone to college away from home. For that first week— month, really—he'd lived in abject terror that Alek would find her more easily.

But nothing happened. Nothing.

Until now.

He pulled himself together, wiped his face with his

sleeve and mentally steeled for a fight. Both Jamie and PJ would refuse a safe house—he knew that.

He would just have to work that much harder to get them into one.

Quickly, he dialed the familiar number, demanded, "How the hell could this have happened," before David could get the word *hello* out.

David, his best friend—and the man who Jamie and PJ knew to call in case of emergency—was silent on his end of the line.

"Alek had to be the one to break Gary Handler out of prison." Kevin ran a hand through his hair and then put his car in gear. He pulled onto the road and began to drive. Finally David spoke.

"The case was widely publicized. Jamie's name made the papers," David reminded him. "Of course, that would mean that the chain was compromised somewhere along the way in order for Alek to learn her new identity—it would mean he's known for months."

Kevin didn't bother to correct David—didn't tell him that, yes, of course Alek would've been following Jamie's whereabouts, and long before her case involving Gary Handler. Alek had known everything about the girls' lives from the time they'd gone to live with Kevin.

Kevin had been the one to compromise Jamie—and now he had a sick feeling they would all pay the price.

CHAPTER

18

The six of them were climbing the walls in their own way while they waited for Kevin to arrive at Saint's house. Saint was in the kitchen with PJ, where they talked in low voices.

Jake and Nick were watching the front and back doors on the computer screen. Jamie sat on the couch, away from windows and doors, a blanket pulled around her and a cup of decaf tea balanced on the arm.

And Chris . . . well, he could never sit still to begin with when he wasn't sniping. This situation was more extreme than most, and while he was quick to note that he hadn't rubbed the fingers on his left hand together since earlier, when he'd gotten the sense his brothers were at the cabin waiting for him, he couldn't sit the hell down, or stop moving, to save his life.

No one commented, though, or told him to stop. His brothers knew it was useless anyway, and he couldn't stand to see the look in Jamie's eyes—nearly defeated again.

The anger was so raw and fierce, rose up from a dark place in his heart and made his fists curl and his jaw clench so hard he was sure it would break.

He wanted to kill Alek. With his bare hands. No mercy. Kill him, leave him on the side of the road for putting Jamie through this, for threatening her and their baby... for doing so much harm to the woman he loved.

Even without speaking, he could see Saint was feeling the same. His CO had been uncharacteristically quiet, his eyes constantly checking the perimeters as if he expected someone to come in any minute, which was why PJ had dragged him into the kitchen, for distraction, Chris assumed.

They typically didn't work like this—they were the hunters. People ran from them. But this man, Alek, he was inching closer and closer and he didn't have anything at all to lose.

That made Chris the most worried of all.

He started when Jamie's hand went around the back of his neck and began to massage it with firm fingers. "Close your eyes. Try to relax," she whispered.

"I'm supposed to be telling you that."

"Yes, well, you've got the next five minutes off."

He didn't argue, put his palms against the wall and attempted to relax the muscles in his neck, which now felt as if they were made of steel. "Was all my moving around freaking you out?"

"No. I love watching you move," she admitted, and smiled a little wickedly, and suddenly he knew it would all work out. The fingers on his left hand still weren't tingling, but for once he wasn't grateful that his gift had decided to leave him alone.

Be careful what you wish for, Christopher. His momma's favorite lesson to him when he was young, because he was always wishing for things to be different, trying to change outcomes.

But he felt nothing—no tingling fingers. No flashes. Absolutely fucking nothing to tell him exactly how much danger they needed to expect. His body was a giant nerve, even under Jamie's touch, his mind going back constantly to the question she'd almost asked him earlier.

Do you see me dying anytime soon...

He shook his head to stop hearing those words, and in the process, shook her hands from him. But before she could ask anything, Jake, who'd been staring nonstop at the monitors for the driveway, called, "Car."

Chris looked over his shoulder. "It's Kevin. He's coming in."

Jamie's body was strung tightly as she waited—the entire room seemed to have stilled, and she fought for control. It seemed to take forever for Kevin to walk into Saint's house, but in reality, it was probably under a minute.

There were dark circles under her foster father's eyes. She'd seen him like that before, after brutal cases and long nights, but this... this was much different.

He looked haunted.

She wanted to give Kevin a hug, but something stopped her, and instead when she spoke, the anger in her voice was unmistakable. "We know that Borya Frolov died. I'm sure you've known since it happened—why didn't you tell us?"

Kevin grimaced. "When the stalking from Handler started, I didn't want you to be unnecessarily worried."

"We might've been able to make the connection between Gary and Alek sooner," Jamie told him. "I had a right to know."

PJ was standing next to her. "Who is Peter Romanov?"

Kevin's eyes shifted to her quickly. "How do you know that name?"

Chris handed him his phone, the one Jamie had used to snap a picture of the birth certificate at the crime scene. "His birth certificate was stuffed into Gary's shirt pocket."

Kevin stared at the phone for a long time.

"Is that Alek's real name?" Jamie prompted, but Kevin shook his head and paced, as if weighing something heavily.

Finally he stopped. "No. It's mine."

"What are you talking about?" PJ asked.

"I'm Peter Romanov."

PJ stared at Kevin as if seeing a stranger. Everything was starting to unravel, and Jamie had a sick feeling they hadn't even begun to scratch the surface.

Her voice shook when she spoke—anger, fear, grief all rising up inside of her, yet she'd never felt stronger. "You need to tell us everything. Immediately."

Everything was at stake—she'd settle for nothing less.

"Jamie—" Kevin started, but she interrupted him.

"As far as we can figure out, Gary Handler was working

for Alek. Alek killed Gary—he painted my mother's name in blood on Gary's chest. And then he called me...Alek called me."

She realized she wasn't letting Kevin speak—was stopping him because he was going to tell her something—tell all of them something—she didn't want to hear. And so she played him the message from Chris's phone and watched Kevin's face go pale.

"Why did you change your name? Are you under protection, like we were?" PJ demanded. "Have you been hiding from Alek all this time too?"

Both she and PJ knew that Kevin had met Grace when they were in high school. She'd stuck by him in his early days as an undercover detective in the NYPD. She knew that Kevin had studied the inner workings of the Russian crime syndicate. Had gone undercover. That because of his knowledge, he'd have an ear to the ground in both that community and with the undercover detectives who still worked that area.

He'd moved to the Marshals after five years of doing that. Right before he'd gotten involved in their case. And now, he stood there and Jamie wondered if they'd ever really known Kevin Morgan at all.

"I'm not under protection. Not really. After I joined the U.S. Marshal's office, they decided it was safer all around if my name was untraceable. I never thought it would be a problem because Alek and I...we had a pact."

" 'Alek and I'? *'Alek and I'*?" Jamie heard her voice rise to a near shriek as the ground seemed to tumble from under her feet. Chris's hand, strong and reassuring, clamped to her shoulder and she calmed some, but her next words sounded strangled. "You know Alek?"

Kevin took a deep breath. "I've known Alek since I was fourteen years old. I met him the day I saved his life."

We had a pact.

It sounded so stupid to anyone who hadn't grown up the way they had, who didn't understand the workings of the neighborhood brotherhood—or what loyalty to their gang meant.

It was the Russian way, the way Kevin had learned all those years ago.

"Come on, sit down," Saint was telling him, and yes, his legs felt as if they couldn't support him much longer. His body was racked with chills—guilt and conscience teaming up to overpower him—and he could barely look at Jamie and PJ, who sat across from him at the table in the kitchen, as though judge, jury and executioner.

They had every right to be that. The men—four of them standing on the periphery—looked so fucking young, and still Kevin knew they understood somewhere deep inside, understood what he'd done and why.

And so he sat there and he told his story to the women he thought of as his daughters, had protected them as fiercely as he would any blood relative.

As fiercely as he'd once protected the man who wanted them all dead.

His fingers drummed the table as he thought back to his days in high school, suspended between boy and manhood.

A place he'd felt forever trapped, thanks to what he'd done on that fateful September day so long ago.

"Alek was a tough guy, always. A year older than me and he was running half our neighborhood. A rough one. I tried to stay out of the way as much as I could, for my mother's sake." He could still see his mom at the stove, hair pulled back into a neat bun, too thin, face sallow, all the laughter gone.

Promise me, Peter . . .

I promise, Mama.

Until that day he'd happened on the fight between Alek and the rival gang of Russian boys, always vying for more of the neighborhood power between them. "At the high school, they'd gotten Alek alone somehow—his usual gang was nowhere to be found. I tried to stay out of it, hid in the stairwell . . . until one of the boys poured the gas and then threw a match."

Kevin had watched with a sickening horror as the match caught—he could still smell the burning flesh and hair, could still hear the screams. "I rushed out, put the fire out with my jacket, my hands." He stared down at them as if expecting to see the scars from the second-degree burns he'd gotten. "I waited with him until the ambulance came. He told me, *Tell them you didn't see who did it. Do that for me.* And I did that."

"He was indebted to you," PJ said, and Kevin nodded.

"Alek was born into a rich family—and a tough one. The fact that I fought the way I did to save him meant that I was one of them. He was my brother. Once we stood together like that, we were bonded for life."

He'd been made part of a family he'd later betray.

The favor . . . if you ever need anything, Alek told him.

Kevin remembered insisting he didn't want anything, but Alek remained indebted. Kevin never would have collected if the girls hadn't come into his life—that's when he finally drew on the debt.

Leave the girls alone, Alek, and we're even.

He'd been asking a lot, he knew that. Alek had already been living in hiding after his escape from prison—if he didn't finish the job of killing Sophie and Ana, his father would disown him.

Kevin knew Alek was caught between a rock and a hard place, but he hadn't come near the women in all these years.

"So because you saved his life, he spared ours." Jamie spoke softly, but the hard edge of anger still tinged her voice.

"I believed that, yes."

"So why come after us now? Because his father died?" Jamie asked.

"I'm assuming it's tied to that—I've got no other explanation," Kevin admitted, although he certainly planned on finding out.

"Grace knew about this?" PJ asked.

"Grace knew—she never trusted Alek, though."

"Does Alek know where you live?" Jamie asked.

"He's always known. He's never done anything about it. I saved his life and he gave me his word he'd let you live yours—gave me his word, swore on our brotherhood. The way we grew up, that means something. But now he wants to make sure you know who I was, what part I played. Wants you aware that he knows exactly where you've been all these years. Wants you to feel betrayed." Kevin's voice almost broke, but he held it together. "You weren't in danger as long as you were with me. You have to believe that."

"I don't know what to believe anymore," Jamie said hoarsely, while PJ simply stared at him, her eyes void of emotion.

"Have you known where Alek was all this time?" PJ asked angrily.

"Not for sure. But I knew he wouldn't come after you, knew it was better if I simply didn't search," Kevin admitted.

"And you risked our lives like that?"

"If you didn't grow up that way, you can't understand." Kevin wrapped his hand so tightly into a fist he swore he'd break his own fingers. "He promised to stay away from you. He promised me."

"So now what? Because he's broken his promise."

He stared at Jamie steadily. "Now it's time for me to break mine."

Chris waited in the background—the disbelief he felt must be nothing compared to the betrayal Jamie and PJ were feeling, and still, fuck, he felt for Kevin.

Jamie, at this moment, did not. "Get out of here, Kevin," she told him, her voice calm and firm as she pushed away from the table. "Get the hell out of here and don't come back."

"Jamie, please—"

"Everything was a lie. From the beginning. Bad enough to live a life in hiding, but this . . . My God, how could you have kept this from us? How could you trust our lives to be safe with a promise from a killer? All my mother did was put a guilty man in jail and we've all been paying the price for it." The tears rose but true to form, Jamie pushed them down, even as Kevin stood and walked toward the door, his gait unsteady.

"You should be in a safe house," he said, without turning around.

"Screw you and your safe house," Jamie choked out as she stared at his back, her arms folded tightly against her body.

PJ remained seated at the table, so fucking still, like she was made of stone.

Saint hadn't moved from the corner, the look on his face a cross between fury and compassion.

None of this was good.

"A lot of fucking drama, but he shouldn't leave," Jake was muttering under his breath as Chris moved to catch Kevin before he reached the door.

Nick and Jake joined him on the other side of the marshal. "They don't mean it, Kevin," Chris told him. "They're in shock."

"Stay here—he's not getting through us," Jake said.

But Kevin was shaking his head. "I need to take care of this now. Brother to brother."

"You need help," Chris insisted.

"He's one man. And I know how he operates."

But the brothers understood all too well how one man could rip apart a woman's life. Jake had helped Izzy put the pieces back together—he and Nick had taken care of the man who'd haunted her, at significant risk to all their lives.

Alek was one man, and he'd already done a hell of a lot of harm.

"They'll never forgive me," Kevin said gruffly. "The least I can do is stop him. I'll kill him, or I'll die trying."

"This isn't the time to work alone," Chris argued, even though he knew it wouldn't do any good. Kevin's mind was made up, and he had one foot out the door. "We need to stay together."

"You need to stay with Jamie. Promise me you won't leave her," Kevin said fiercely.

"You have my word."

Kevin shook his hand and left the house, closing the door quietly behind him.

Chris turned to his brothers. "You don't have to do this."

"In for a penny, in for a pound," Jake told him roughly, a phrase Maggie had used on a regular basis.

"I'll call Max, make sure Jake and I get the leave," Nick said, but his attention turned sharply as voices raised.

PJ was pushing Saint's hands away from her and heading to the deck.

"Let her go," Jamie told Saint sharply. "Just let her go! I told you, she always leaves. Why should this time be any different?"

Angrily, she picked up his phone and Chris wondered what the hell it would take to make any of this right.

"Jamie, listen to me—you need to sit down and think this through before you go running off to your boss, or making any kind of plans. You've got to let all of this sink in," Chris was telling her, but she ignored him in favor of dialing his phone.

He grabbed it from her hands and tossed it to Jake. Jamie headed for him, and Jake backed slowly away, his eyes locked onto Chris's with a look of *you'd better stop her*.

"Give me the phone," she insisted.

"You're in no shape to speak with anyone but us right now," Chris reiterated.

"I don't need you to tell me what to do." She turned to him then, lashing out with both fists against his chest. "Your life didn't just get turned upside down. Mine did."

She punched again and he let her. And then he turned her so her back was against his chest and he wrapped his arms around hers so she couldn't flail.

She attempted to shrug off Chris's arms, but he wasn't having it. Instead, he lifted her off the ground, carried her into Saint's office and slammed the door behind them.

It was only then he released her, and she pushed away from him, the fury blazing, ready to take out some more of her anger on him. "Keep your hands off me."

"Pull it together."

He was so calm, so infuriatingly, stone-statue calm, standing in front of her like an immovable object, and she wanted him as upset as she was. "You don't get to tell me what to do, Chris. Not about this."

"I'm not telling you how to feel. I'm telling you to cut the shit—put your emotions to bed and figure out what the hell to do next."

She stared him down, but he was winning. Anger rose higher. "He lied to me. To PJ. For years. If we'd known..."

"If you'd known, what? What the hell would you have

done?" Chris demanded. "Kevin did the best thing he knew at the time—he kept you safe for years, Jamie. You're an adult now, and you're going to have to deal with the consequences of Kevin's choice. And that's what it was, a choice."

It had been. And yes, Chris wasn't just talking about Kevin now—his eyes held that faraway look and she knew a part of him was still near that embassy in the Sudan, a part of him would always be in the chaos of that battlefield where he'd also made a decision that left no one a winner.

It didn't make him any less of a hero in her eyes.

"This situation is so different. Kevin chose to stick his head in the sand."

"Sometimes, love and denial come hand in hand. It's okay to be angry with him, Jamie. But he loves you and PJ."

"I know that." She squeezed her eyes tight, heard Chris walking over to her. When she opened them, she saw he'd dropped to his knees, was pressing his cheek against her belly.

"We'll get through it. Come on, we've been to hell and back a couple of times already. Don't give up, okay?"

She ran her hands through his hair. "I won't. Just don't leave me."

"Not a chance."

*L*et *her go.*

I told you, she always leaves.

Why should this time be any different?

But it was. So completely different PJ felt as if her soul would shatter.

Everyone around her died—but this time, she wouldn't accept that. Wouldn't accept being cornered inside the house, sequestered, when she knew she could track this monster.

Right now, she needed some freedom.

She lowered herself off the deck and onto the sand. Once there, she ran fast along the hard-packed sand, water lapping her sneakers.

There was no destination, just a fierce urge to break out and away, to let the anger she felt toward Kevin and her entire life dissipate. And after twenty minutes of running alone on that darkened beach, something inside of her snapped, and then everything lifted, the heavy cloak of grief and guilt and fear, and suddenly as she pushed forward, she was finally, truly alive inside.

She needed to remember this feeling, this freedom, when things around her threatened to grow oppressive. And so she stopped running, simply stopped in her tracks, out of breath but not out of steam, and fighting an urge to let out a deep, primal scream.

She had no other choice but to turn and go back to Saint's. Wouldn't have wanted any other option. When she did so, she saw a man's shadow about ten feet behind her— a big, strong, beautiful man who waited for her. Who'd run behind her the entire time.

A man who would let her run from herself, but who would never let her run alone. *Saint.*

"Saint!"

She ran toward him at top speed, jumped into his arms, nearly knocking him to the sand. He stumbled back but held steady as she wrapped around him, arms around his shoulders, legs around his waist, her face buried against his neck.

Nearly breathless, she still managed to whisper, "I was coming back. I wasn't leaving. I wasn't leaving you."

"I know, PJ," he told her as he held her as tightly as she held him. "I know."

He did. Had from the first day she'd stumbled on him. Nothing had changed with Kevin's confession—she was still a work in progress, still healing.

"I should've checked on Alek's father. I used to—every day I used to check, and then it was every week. If I'd known..."

But Saint wouldn't let her feel the guilt. "We'll get him, PJ. I'll kill that bastard with my bare fucking hands to keep you safe."

She pulled back, stared into his eyes, lit only by the soft moonlight reflecting off the water. "I'd do the same for you."

"I know that too."

She thought he'd take her back to the house then, but he didn't. Instead, he lowered her to the sand—it was cold against her back, but his body covering hers was so warm.

"I want you, want to make you feel better, Patricia. And it's too crowded back at the damned house." Protected by the darkness, his fingers found her core, and she forgot about everything else except him.

She wondered how, after only knowing her for less than a week, he could know her so intimately, know where she liked to be touched and what would set her off so that his name would be ripped from her throat, even if she hadn't meant to call it out. Wondered how his hands felt so right as they roamed her body, finding ways to awaken places she didn't know could even be erogenous.

After she came twice, he carried her the entire way back to his house.

Kevin drove home blindly. Numb.

His only comfort was that Jamie and PJ were surrounded by men who would defend them with their own lives, if necessary.

Kevin was going to make sure that wouldn't have to happen. First, he'd get Grace to a safe place—she deserved that.

But she wasn't home. That wasn't unusual these days—if she wasn't with her shrink, she was with her friends, and he could see the dissolution of their marriage happening right before his eyes.

Kevin could let it go easily enough, he thought. It couldn't be any lonelier than being married to her was. The best part of their union had occurred, for him, when they'd taken the girls in. There had been laughter in the house. Love. Warmth.

Now it was cold as hell.

He threw his keys down and headed toward the kitchen, to see if she'd left a note, didn't hear the man come up behind him.

He felt the sharp sting of darts in his back, stumbled forward as the tranquilizer did its job. His feet went out from under him; he didn't even feel his body hit the carpet.

Somehow, he shifted onto his back, found himself looking up into a face that was familiar even as it swam in his vision. "You said . . . you'd stay away. You took their parents. That was good enough. You promised," he croaked, his breath coming unnaturally fast.

"My word is only good to my family."

"At one time, I was your family."

"At one time, you were my brother," Alek agreed. "But it turns out blood is thicker than water."

"Leave them alone, Alek."

"I can't anymore, Peter."

Peter. It had been a long time since he'd been called that. "I saved your life. I thought that meant something."

"I wish you'd let me die," Alek practically spat.

"What are you talking about?"

"This." Alek pointed to his scarred face. "I loved you, Peter, but I also hated you. Because if it wasn't for you—for this debt, for my honor—I wouldn't have been cut off from my family for twenty years. I would've been welcomed back by the Russian underground, hidden by them. Instead, I kept my promise to you, and I've lost everything."

"I had no choice," Kevin told him.

"You had a choice—you chose those girls over me, your brother."

It was the truth, Kevin had. "I looked the other way for so many things, Alek—those years I worked undercover, I never let anything happen to you."

He'd been so torn then . . . as torn as Alek seemed now. "I collected my debt, Alek—you've kept your honor all these years, don't do this now." Kevin breathed the words, fighting unconsciousness as Alek nodded.

"My father died hating me, thinking I was a coward. I put you above my family. I've lost everything. If I finish the job, and I kill a U.S. Marshal, the underground might gain some respect for me—I won't die an outcast. I'll bring some honor back to my blood family."

"We were family," Kevin insisted, saw in Alek's eyes how much all of this had cost him, how the years in hiding had taken everything and given Alek a sense of desperation he'd never had as a boy or a young man.

Kevin had forced his hand—he was as responsible as anyone for this. "Where is Grace?" he croaked.

"I've got her. Soon, it will all be over. First, we need to go back to where it all began." Alek began to drag Kevin's body out of the house, hoisted him into the trunk of the car, next to Grace's unconscious body.

In Kevin's mind, there were quick flashes of him and Alek running wild through their neighborhood, of him sitting at Alek's family's table...of him learning what it meant to be someone's brother, to be brought into a family.

And then there was the start of the darkness, bleeding into the pictures in his mind.

Yes, blood was thicker than water. He wondered why he hadn't figured that out sooner.

CHAPTER
19

Kevin wasn't answering his phone—not his cell or the landline. Jamie had been trying every five seconds, until PJ finally pulled the phone from her hand and suggested they call David Yager, their emergency contact.

In the meantime, Nick and Jake offered to go to Kevin's house, but Chris refused that request, even though Jamie jumped at that chance. "We stay together," he said.

An hour later, Jake announced another car coming up the driveway.

Chris moved past Jamie and toward the screen. "Not Kevin's."

"It's probably David," Jamie said.

Jake had already pulled his gun and was headed toward

the door. "We're not taking any chances. Jamie and PJ, go upstairs."

Chris saw Jamie was ready to argue. All he could say was, "Please," and suddenly PJ was taking Jamie's hand and tugging her up the stairs.

He waited until he heard the bedroom door close before he went out into the garage and let the door open slowly. The man, who'd gotten out of his car and was walking toward the front door, immediately stopped short and waited.

"Hands up," Chris ordered, his rifle trained between the man's eyes.

The way the guy complied instantly, showing his palms, made the tension in Chris's body ease. Whoever this was, he wasn't the threat. "I'm a U.S. Marshal—David Yager. I work with Kevin. PJ gave me this address."

"Tell PJ to come down and ID him," Chris told Jake.

Moments later, PJ was at his side, her hand on Chris's arm to lower the rifle. "He's okay. David, come inside."

David nodded, lowered his hands and walked quickly into the garage. Chris stuck his hand out. "Sorry about that."

"You did the right thing," David said.

"Did you find Kevin?" PJ interrupted, and David looked pained.

"He's missing. So is Grace."

Jamie, standing on the other side of the half-opened garage door, heard what David said.

Instinctively, Saint held her arm, led her over to the couch, and yes, sitting was a good idea.

She watched the door, a thousand things running through her mind—calling Lou chief among them, but she sat on her hands so she wouldn't dial the phone prematurely.

She'd hear David out, but she had little doubt as to what his theory would be. Alek was definitely back in their lives, and if he had Kevin and Grace...

My God.

Gary wasn't an innocent man, but he'd simply been a pawn, if her theory was correct. Kevin and Grace had done nothing but protect her and PJ all these years—and now what Grace had most likely always been fearful would happen had.

Even though David was the man she and PJ were supposed to call if something went wrong and Kevin wasn't available, that had never, ever happened before, not in twenty years. And now he was coming to them with news she didn't want to hear.

She rubbed her fists along her thighs as PJ sat on one side of her, and Chris, the other. Bolstered by the dual support, she finally leveled her gaze at David.

He looked wiped. "I went to the house. The front door was open and there was some blood. Neither are answering their cell phones. No calls from Alek or anyone claiming responsibility, but in light of what PJ told me on the phone..."

"How much blood?" PJ asked quietly.

"Not much—they were probably alive when they were taken," David said. "CSI are at the house now—they'll test the blood to determine more. But I want you two in a safe house tonight. Let us handle this. You know that's what Kevin would want."

"No," PJ said flatly. "We're not going anywhere."

Chris's cell phone rang, preempting the argument that was sure to follow. At first, Jamie simply stared at it. The incoming number was Kevin's, but she knew who would be on the other end of the line.

"Where are you, Alek? Tell me now and save yourself some time," she said, forgoing saying hello to the bastard.

"I know where you are. That's the important thing," Alek said. "There's no safe place for you—there never really was."

She was frozen, anger and grief boiling at the surface, hand on her gun as if Alek could get to her through the phone. "What do you want from us?"

"I've already started with Peter and Grace. Oh, don't worry, they're alive. For now. There's so much more that I want. Make no mistake, we're back to where we started, and this time, I'll take it all."

The words came out before she could stop them: "Not if I get to you first, you bastard."

Alek chuckled. "Well, now it's finally getting interesting. I'm almost glad I waited for you to grow up. It'll be much more satisfying."

He hung up and she listened to the dead air for a few seconds and then clicked Chris's phone shut. The anger, pure and fierce, overtook everything else, and she knew, beyond a shadow of a doubt, that she would never again live her life hiding from Alek.

An hour later, Jamie and PJ entered the house they'd lived in with Kevin and Grace, ducking under the yellow police tape, with Chris and Saint following close behind.

The place was crawling with FBI and marshals. The house had been swept for explosives. None were detected, but Alek's fingerprints had been found everywhere—he hadn't bothered to wipe anything down or cover his tracks.

Jamie looked down the small hallway leading toward the kitchen. The white-tiled floor was smeared with blood—brown, dried. It made her stomach lurch. To her immediate left was an empty syringe, tagged.

"Tranquilizer," PJ said. "Let's go upstairs."

Jamie let her older sister take the lead up the stairs. The house wasn't big by any means, and Kevin had given up his office so she and PJ could each have their own rooms. He'd simply turned a once-open alcove into a small office, and never said a word about it.

PJ disappeared into her old room. As Jamie passed her own old room on the way to the office, she noted that it was now converted into some kind of workout space for Grace, complete with a treadmill and a wide, flat-screen TV. So different, and still it was like stepping back in time.

Hesitantly, Jamie opened the closet—for a long time, she'd refused to use it, remembered having to hide in one until the police came.

And even though this wasn't the same house or the same closet, she still stepped back from it, leaving the door open as she backed out of the room and headed for Kevin's office.

In the unmistakably male-oriented office of her foster father, Jamie felt the tears rise. She pushed them back brusquely, told herself that she had a job to do. That Kevin wouldn't want her to cry.

There was a small floor safe. Jamie stared down at it for a second, and then, on a hunch, tried the date that she and PJ came to live here.

No luck.

She tried birthdays. Anniversaries. Again, nothing.

PJ came in. "What's up?"

"I need to get this open."

"I can do it," PJ said. Jamie moved out of the way and watched PJ crack the small safe like a pro. "Don't ask."

"Don't worry, I won't."

She pulled out a folder and handed it to Jamie. "That's all there is."

Jamie flipped through it quickly. "These are our birth certificates—the new ones, not the originals. Kevin's and Grace's too. That's all."

PJ sat on the floor and sighed.

"I've got to talk to Lou before I do anything else—he's got to hear about all of this from me," Jamie said. On the car ride over, she'd told David about Kevin's connection to Alek, and his shocked expression made it clear he hadn't known anything about Kevin's past either.

"You're going to tell him that you're in witness protection?"

"Yes. Even if he already suspects, I have to be the one who tells him—I owe him that much. And then we'll go look for Kevin."

PJ threw her hands up. "Where do we start, Jamie?" Alek had made no further contact—Jamie had been checking the messages on Chris's phone obsessively, and nothing. "Where would Alek take them? I mean, he wants us to follow—wants us dead too—so why isn't he leaving us some clues?"

Jamie paused for a second and then she dug in her pocket for the printout of his father's obituary. "Maybe he has without us realizing it. There's an address here—his father's house. He said something about going back to where it all began."

"And we're going to knock on the door and ask to see Alek?" PJ asked.

"No, we're going to knock on the door and get leverage." Her voice didn't sound like her own. She'd thought revenge wasn't in her blood, thought she'd let that go. But if hurting Alek's mother and sister was what it took to get Kevin and Grace back...

"I know exactly where the house is. I've been there. Years ago, I stood in front of the house for about an hour, waiting for someone to come out. Waiting for the courage to knock on the door."

"What were you going to do?"

"I wasn't sure. But now I am." PJ's eyes glittered as she helped Jamie off the floor so they could head downstairs.

"David won't let you do this," Chris said when he heard their plan. He, Saint and the two sisters stood alone in the small kitchen, voices lowered as they discussed their next steps. "He wants you both in a safe house."

"David doesn't have to know anything except that we're going to New York," Jamie said.

"Fuck David, *I* won't let you do this," Chris told her. "What makes you think Alek took Kevin and Grace to New York?"

"It's a hunch. Intuition."

"Chris and I can go to Alek's mother's house," Saint interjected.

But PJ shook her head. "We have a plan."

"What the hell are you going to do? Hold the women hostage?"

"If that's what it takes to get Alek to release Kevin, yes," PJ said calmly.

"This isn't the wild west. Or Africa," Saint told her pointedly. "Suppose Alek is inside that house, waiting for you?"

"Let the four of us take care of this," Chris said, referring to Saint and Nick and Jake and him.

But Jamie shook her head. "We need to be there—we're the ones Alek wants."

"I'm not using you two as leverage," Saint insisted.

"Alek has no more credibility with the men his father ran with," Chris reasoned. "Kevin told me as much. Alek's working alone. Which means he's got nothing to lose. He's been planning this. Studying you and Kevin and Grace for a long time."

Jamie started to pace, something having triggered in her mind. "So far, Alek hasn't done anything without purpose. Using Gary. Killing Gary. The positioning of Gary's body. And he could've killed him anywhere, but he chose a school."

"Kevin saved Alek at school," PJ said. "What high school did Alek attend?"

"I don't know, but I'm sure it won't be hard to find out," Jamie said. "Look, I'll speak with Lou, tell him we need some manpower in New York."

"How are we going?" Chris asked.

"Flying," Saint said.

"Then I'll call Glen," he said, but Saint held up a hand to stop him.

"PJ will get us there."

Chris gave a small smile—part melancholy, part approval. "Mark's plane."

"It's PJ's now," Saint said quietly, and Chris nodded.

"We'll get supplies together and a safe house secured for New York, just in case," Chris said. "We'll meet you back here and all head to the airport together."

Jamie nodded. "Okay. That will give me time to speak with my boss."

Jamie had wanted to tell Lou face-to-face, but David insisted that she was already taking chances with the trip to New York.

Chris had agreed, and so Jamie sat in an interior room of Kevin's house, with Chris at the doorway, and used his cell phone to make the call she'd hoped she'd never have to make.

Breathe, she silently instructed herself, repeated the word—and the action—as the phone rang.

Working within the closely guarded community of the FBI had been a relief for her, one of the few places she truly felt safe. Of course, she'd always lived with the uneasy notion that her background could be found out by any number of the agents who worked in the building—most of them had access to the U.S. Marshals' database when they needed it. Even though she'd been carefully hidden, her past life layered with both truth and falsehoods, she'd often wondered what Lou would say if he knew who she really was.

In about five seconds, she wouldn't have to wonder any longer.

His secretary put her right through; it felt as if years had passed since the last time she'd spoken with him.

"I know about Kevin. We're cooperating with the marshals in any way we can," Lou said when he picked up the phone. "David filled me in on Kevin's connection to this Alek Frolov character."

"And mine as well, I'm assuming."

"I should have been informed from the moment you were assigned to me, Michaels. You're not the first of my agents on witness protection. I'm always told, dammit."

He was angry. She was making all the men in her life angry today. "No one knew—only Kevin and a few other marshals. They made the decision, not me." She attempted to keep the edge out of her voice, stared at Chris's back and the way his hands tightened against the doorjamb as if ready to come to her defense at any moment. "It wasn't easy for me, but I never thought—we never thought—"

"No one ever thinks it will happen," Lou interrupted.

"I'm not going to a safe house or leaving town or changing my name. I won't do that again. If that means having to leave the Bureau, then consider it done. But first, I'm going to make sure Kevin and Grace are all right."

Lou sighed and she pictured him in the familiar pose she knew so well, with two fingers pressed to the bridge of his nose. For what seemed like forever, she waited, suspended in time, not sure how much trouble she was in.

But finally he said, "Now that I know, tell me what I can do to help you find this bastard."

It was the invitation she'd been hoping for.

CHAPTER
20

PJ flew, with Saint as her co-pilot. They landed at a small, private airport in New Jersey and rented a van big enough to fit all six of them and the rifles the men had collected.

Lou had offered Jamie a ride with the other agents, but she'd refused. She needed to be with Chris and with her sister. So he'd given her a new badge and ID and let her go.

When they landed, Jamie had a message from Lou that there were reports of suspicious activity at the high school Kevin and Alek had once attended. She was gratified to know her instincts were on target.

Jamie sat next to Chris, who drove them into Brooklyn—he was tense, she was more so.

When they got to the high school, it was close to midnight and the FBI was there along with a SWAT team and the local police. Jamie showed her badge and was let through, with Chris and PJ and the others trailing behind her.

The first familiar face she spotted was Coop. "I got your call about the school being a possible hiding place right after the SWAT team called me to this," he said. "Shots were fired from inside and the neighbors called. The records for the rental car in the lot say it's Kevin's—Alek must've used his ID to rent it."

"Have you made contact?"

"Lester's talking to Alek—trying to anyway. But all Alek wants is you and your sister." He looked past her to PJ. "I assume you're Patricia. You need a vest."

"I don't need anything but five minutes alone with Alek," she told him, her voice rising above the din.

"Let us talk to Alek. That's what he wants—us, scared." Jamie stood next to Lester, one of the best negotiators the FBI had. But she knew Alek wouldn't be happy with anyone but her on the other end of that line. "He's not planning on letting them out of there alive. We both know that."

Lester reluctantly addressed both women. "I'll walk you through this. Jamie, you take point. Remember, this guy doesn't care if he dies. Get him nervous. Throw him off his game. Once we get a bead on where he is in the building, we'll send in a SWAT team, position snipers."

She noted there were already snipers on the roof of the building. "Lester, Chris Waldron is here with me—he's a Navy SEAL, and a sniper. One of the best. If it comes down to it, I'd trust him with my life. The FBI and CIA have both been trying to recruit him for years." She pointed toward him—Chris was speaking with members of the SWAT team.

"I'll keep it in mind. But it's going to be a tough shot— I don't think this will end that easily." Lester dialed and then handed her the phone.

After three rings, it was picked up, Alek's voice calm as he said, "Hello." She took a deep breath and spoke. "Alek, it's Jamie."

"Took you long enough, Ana. I thought the FBI would have trained you better."

Jamie bristled a bit at being referred to as Ana, and put the phone on speaker before asking, "Do you need anything, Alek? Food? Water? Medical attention for either Kevin or Grace?" Keep it personal—keep using his name. Be his friend.

God, she hated him. Her fist curled around the phone as he answered her.

"Are you going to deliver everything personally? You and your sister? Is she here?"

"I'm here, Alek," PJ said evenly when Lester nodded.

"Alek, how is Kevin?" Jamie asked. "Can I speak to him, as a show of good faith?"

"Peter. His name is Peter. And he's not able to speak with you now. But if you come inside, you can have a nice chat."

He sounded cool, calm. Collected. Like ice ran through his veins. She, on the other hand, was sweating and angry. And no matter how he sounded, she suddenly realized, Alek was too.

She thought for a few seconds about the story Kevin told them earlier. Alek came from a tough family that valued loyalty. A lot of pressure for a young boy—even more for a young man who'd been forced to carry out a family vendetta. He wouldn't have been the first one to buckle under parental pressure, and this was well beyond the norm. She could use that. "You must be so angry, Alek, with your father liking Peter better than he liked you. Peter saved you, but you were scarred. Ugly. You've spent the past nineteen years in hiding, shaming your father because you couldn't close the deal and kill us."

"You don't know anything about my life."

"I know this can't end well. Your mother and sister need you alive."

"You don't know what my mother and sister need."

Lester put up a hand, mouthed, *Tone it down.*

Her instincts told her the opposite, but before she could speak, PJ was saying, "Alek, I'll tell you what, we'll trade—my family for yours. We've got your sister and mother. We'll give you them if you release Kevin and Grace. Do we have a deal?"

Her answer was the sound of a shot that echoed over the line and out from inside.

"Shot fired in the building. I repeat, shot fired," Coop was saying over the line. "Hold your fire."

Jamie stifled a sob as Alek spoke again. "I've killed Kevin—go ahead, PJ, you can have one of my family now. But I don't think you can do it—I know you don't have it in you to kill innocent people. Not like I do."

He was right—she damned him for calling PJ's bluff. "I need to speak with Kevin."

"I told you, Kevin's dead," he said. "Don't worry, I'll make it fast for you and PJ."

"Why? Why are you doing this?"

"You wouldn't understand. Couldn't."

She suddenly knew he was lying. He wouldn't kill Kevin until she and PJ were in the room with him, could see it happen. "Let me speak to Kevin."

There was a pause. Then, "First send Patricia Jane in. Let's see if she's still as brave as she once was."

PJ was already walking toward the door, shoving off Coop and Saint, who tried to hold her back.

Quickly, Jamie covered the mouthpiece of the phone. "You're not doing this. He doesn't get to make the rules."

PJ stopped, looked at her. "He already has, Jamie. You and I both know that. I'm not letting you go inside, but one of us has to. And if I can't kill Alek myself, I can line him up so Chris can take a shot. Either way, Alek's not leaving the school alive."

"We can send in a decoy, an agent," Coop was saying, but PJ shook her head.

"He'll know. Agent Cooper, with all due respect, I'm the only one who can do this." PJ stood toe to toe with Coop.

"It's suicide," Coop asserted. "And we do not send civilians to negotiate hostage situations."

"You can't watch me the entire time. I'm going inside at some point—with or without your consent. I'd much rather you were on my side, though, able to track me."

"Can you handle firearms?" Coop asked.

"Former Air Force. And CIA," PJ said.

Which just served to remind Jamie of everything at stake. "Alek, isn't there another way we can work this out?

Send Kevin and Grace out unharmed and we'll figure something out."

"I want to see PJ. I know they're not going to let you in, because of the baby," Alek answered. "And I'm getting impatient. The next shot you hear might not be as innocuous as the last."

"I'll trade—me for Grace," PJ said, loudly enough for him to hear her. "Grace has nothing to do with this. You let her go and you can have me. I'm far more important than Jamie is anyway—I'm the one who was ready to send your ass to jail."

There was a dead silence on the other end of the line, and for a moment Jamie wondered if her sister had pushed it too far. But then she heard him.

"Grace is wearing a vest of explosives. You'll meet her in the hallway. Trade the vest and I'll let Grace walk out of the building. You'll have four minutes to make the exchange—after that I'll blow the device."

The line clicked off and the sisters stared at each other.

"How do we know he won't detonate that vest the second you put it on?" Jamie asked.

PJ stared at her, unblinking. "We don't. But that's not going to stop me."

P J stripped herself of her weapons—the gun and the knives she had hidden in various pockets—while standing on the grass, about ten feet from the building. She barely listened to the instructions Lester gave her, thought about keeping one of the knives, hidden well, then glanced down at her hands instead.

She didn't need a gun to kill Alek—not at all.

As she stood there, staring at the top of her hands, large, strong ones covered them. Saint's, not Lester's.

She didn't—couldn't—look up for a few moments. When she finally did, her breath caught at the sight of him, staring at her, his eyes wet.

"You told me you wouldn't leave," he reminded her.

"I won't, not for long."

He nodded, looked like he wanted to say something else, but he didn't.

"I know you think I'm doing this to make up for what I couldn't do when I was fourteen," she said. "You might be right. But if I don't do this...Kevin put his life on the line for us. Despite her objections, so did Grace. And as angry as I want to be at him, I understand."

"Just remember, I'm not ready to let you go, Patricia. Not by a long shot," he managed, giving her hands a final squeeze. "You fight with everything you've fucking got, understand? No prisoners."

"No, no prisoners," she repeated.

He walked away first and she was glad, because she wouldn't have been able to turn her back on him. A part of her still wanted to run, to leave all of this chaos, stick her head in the sand and pretend that she was still the damaged girl, the fucked-up woman who no one could count on... who could trust no one.

But that girl had disappeared amid the events of the past days...months, maybe even years. And with that resolve, she began to walk toward the building, without looking back.

She heard Jamie call her name softly, a plea, a prayer...

an apology. She saw the ghost of Jamie's young face peering out at her from the closet and forced herself to turn, to see the face of the woman instead.

With that picture now firmly embedded in her mind, she steeled herself and walked inside the building, not at all sure what she'd find. A strange sense of calm numbed her body when the door closed behind her, and she continued to move forward, her sneakers barely making noise on the highly polished linoleum.

The school smelled like chalk and ammonia, and it was warm, so warm, as she breathed the humid air. Her shirt stuck to her back and she glanced down at her hands again.

I can kill with my bare hands.

Just then, she heard a muffled sob. She looked up to see Grace standing in an open doorway a couple of feet from her.

"Grace, it's okay." PJ tried to reassure her, but Grace turned even more pale, which made the bruises on her face stand out in stark contrast. There were traces of blood along her mouth, and yes, the woman was in shock. She wasn't moving, and so PJ walked to her swiftly.

"Grace, it's me, PJ. You're going to be fine. I'm going to get you out of here."

No response from Grace other than another whimper. The woman was small and blond and curvy—once had been considered beautiful.

PJ's palms were sweating. She wiped them on her jeans so she could unfasten the wires in the time Alek had allotted.

Four minutes and she was sure he wouldn't give them a second longer.

The clock was ticking. Hurriedly, she undid the ties on the vest, fingers shaking at the amount of C4 wired to it.

As she worked, she spoke rapidly. "Grace, when I take this off, you'll need to walk, and keep walking, straight out the double red doors. Jamie's out there—so is the FBI. And David. Walk and don't look back. I'm going to get Kevin."

Grace stared at her. "I always knew this would happen. I never wanted you or your sister. I knew this would happen."

PJ had known it too. Finally, the vest was off and she told Grace, "Go," pushed her toward the door, hard as she could. Grace stumbled, and that seemed to break her catatonic state. She began to run, slamming her fists against the door until it opened.

PJ slid the vest on, affixing the Velcro straps and the wires as she stared out, until light from the police cars momentarily blinded her.

She turned and began to walk down the hallway, felt the rush of air at her back and then nothing as the door slammed shut, sealed like the mouth of a tomb.

"Here she comes—hold your fire!" Coop shouted.

Chris watched as a woman stumbled toward them, tripped, falling to the ground. She picked herself up as an agent ran to help her.

"Grace," Jamie whispered beside him. She made a move toward her foster mother, while he looked down, realized he was rubbing his fingers together. He looked back up and saw the agent helping Grace, and Chris suddenly knew what the hell was wrong with this picture.

"She's still wired," he called out. "Get the hell down!"

Without waiting, he grabbed Jamie, ran with her as the explosion shattered the air behind them. A blast big enough to rain debris on their heads, big enough for him to smell the scorch of body and machinery and earth.

Jamie was fighting him—pushing and shoving and scratching to get out from under him. He hadn't landed hard on her and she wasn't hurt—but she was yelling, *"No!"* over and over again.

He kept her down on the ground until the rumbling stopped, until he heard the firefighters calling for backup, springing into action. Until he heard the harsh whoosh of water from the trucks, sounding like a pounding rain, and then he pushed himself off her.

She sat up—he let her do that, but he wouldn't let her stand until he checked her over. She resisted, reduced to simply whispering, "No," now.

Finally, she looked at him and the fog cleared, enough for her to ask, "PJ?"

"I don't know."

"Grace?" she asked, even though she knew. Chris shook his head.

"Grace. My God, she didn't deserve that." Jamie stared at him. "PJ was supposed to take off the vest."

"Grace wasn't wearing a vest when she came out. Alek probably planted another bomb on her. PJ only had minutes to make the exchange." Chris surveyed the damage.

It had definitely been some C4—not a lot, or all of them plus the school building would've been blown sky high. No, this bomb was about making a statement.

The two police cars closest to the building had been

destroyed, as was the back of the building, where Grace had come from. The gaping opening was nothing but charred brick, allowing them to see into the building, straight through to a second set of doors.

"PJ—my God, PJ!" Jamie screamed when she followed his gaze, saw what a hit the building had taken. The corridor where PJ and Grace had swapped the vest was now a melted mess.

"We need a phone—get me a line!" Lester was calling out, and was quickly handed a cell phone, which he immediately dialed and then placed on speaker. The line rang and rang, Jamie nearly hyperventilating.

There were no immediate signs of another body—of PJ—but knowing the condition the bodies of both Grace and the agent who'd run to help her were in right now, Chris didn't take that as a reliable indicator.

He said his own version of a silent prayer, even though he was pretty damned rusty in that department.

Fuck, don't fucking let this happen to PJ—to both PJ and Jamie. They were so close to reconnecting.

"You both okay?" Nick knelt down by Jamie and Chris.

"Yeah, we're all right. You?"

"I was on the other side of the building when I heard the explosion, doing some recon," he said as he helped Chris up. Chris's ears rung, but otherwise he was fine. Both men picked Jamie off the ground, held her steady as she stared at Nick.

"Tell me it didn't explode inside the building."

"The other side of the building's fine," Nick said. "That's where he's holding them."

"How do you know that?" Chris asked.

Nick pointed to the house nestled behind the school. "I went on their roof, looked in. Saw shadows moving in the upper stairwell. It's pretty well blocked off, according to the building plans. There's a small window, but that's about it. It's a tough shot, but unless the SWAT team's going to barrel-ass in there, it's all we've got."

Jamie nodded. "Did you tell Coop or Lester?"

"Lester knows. Coop's unconscious," Nick said. "Jake's with him." He pointed to where Coop lay on the grass. Immediately, Jamie rushed over to him, Chris and Nick following.

"He's okay—a definite concussion," Jake told her, "but otherwise okay." Jake, who was also bleeding from somewhere—it had soaked through his T-shirt, but he waved off the medical attention when it arrived, telling them to *fucking take care of the head injury.*

"It's a circus," Jamie said, looking around. "This is exactly what Alek wants. Besides PJ and me inside with him."

As Chris peered at her he realized the expression on Jamie's face wasn't terror. It was anger. Determination. All fear was gone.

"That's not happening. Under no circumstances," Chris barked at her.

She grimaced and moved to walk away from him. But he was done letting her call the shots with this. He didn't care how caveman he had to get.

He hadn't been able to stop Mark, couldn't save him— and perhaps there was no saving PJ, but there was no way he was letting Jamie sacrifice herself on his watch. No fucking way.

Chris remained stoic, shaking his head, holding her wrist, not breaking his grip no matter how hard she tried to pull away. "Remember the plan, Jamie. That hasn't changed."

"Everything's changed. If my sister dies, I'll never forgive myself."

"I know," he said evenly. "I'll do everything in my power not to let that happen. You have to trust me on that."

Two SWAT snipers were walking toward them. Earlier, she'd heard Coop tell Lester that Chris was the best sniper for this job, bar none. That the CIA and the FBI regularly tried to recruit him.

That a rifle was magic in his hands.

Now they were going to take him up on it.

She watched as the men spoke with Chris. Within a few minutes, they were handing him a match grade rifle and a SWAT vest.

Chris stood in front of her, worked with his rifle and the scope. He put his headset on; she didn't know if he was talking to his brothers or the FBI or the marshals, and she didn't care. Instead, she kept trying to feel PJ, to channel her sister . . . to pray.

Chris's face remained tight, his mouth drawn into a thin, grim line, and she realized, with a sudden, aching clarity, exactly what the problem was. "This is the first time . . . since Mark."

He didn't answer, stared through the scope and then brought it down again. "If I miss, you'll never forgive me."

"That's not true." She grabbed his chin, forced him to look at her. "That is *not* true. But I know you can do this."

He nodded, twisted his head free from her grasp. He didn't believe her.

"I want to go with you," she said.

"No," she heard Nick say, and she turned. She realized that Jake, Nick and Saint were right behind her.

"You two," Jake said as he pointed at both Jamie and Saint. "No fucking way. You're too close to this. So is Chris, but he's the best person for the job—we all know that."

Saint began to argue, but Chris stepped forward to calm him. She took that opportunity to approach Jake.

"Jake, listen . . . Chris hasn't been able to shoot his rifle, not since Africa," she whispered, yet there was no mistaking the urgency in her voice.

He watched her carefully, his smoke-gray eyes giving nothing away. And then, "Yeah, we know. We've got his back, Jamie. He can do this."

Chris was already walking away from their small group.

"We'll get him," Jake told her before he and Nick followed Chris.

She watched the trio's backs as they jogged across the field, toward the closest neighboring house. The FBI had already cleared the family out, and now Chris and his brothers began their ascent to the roof, in order to line up the best possible shot.

"He's the best," Saint told her, just as Lester called out, "Jamie, we've got Alek on the line—he wants to talk to you."

She took off at a dead run for Lester, with Saint right on her tail.

PJ felt the explosion to her core, threw herself down on the floor when the building rumbled around her, came to with a pounding headache.

Her wrists had been tied together behind her back, but her legs remained free. With her forehead against the dirty floor, she pushed her body up and got herself into a standing position. She'd been moved from the hallway into a large stairwell, which was partially lit by a sputtering, overhead florescent light that cast an eerie glow over everything.

Or maybe that was just her perception, thanks to the pain in her head. She blinked a few times and noted the shadowed men in front of her.

Alek.

Kevin.

Alek held a knife to Kevin's throat and her blood ran hot with revenge and hatred, the way it had for so many years.

Alek was a big man—bigger than PJ remembered. He wore a black T-shirt and black pants and there were several tattoos along his forearms. PJ didn't remember them being there before. "Nice moves, Patricia. But not nice enough for Grace. I guess you didn't get all the wires," he said with a slow shake of his head. "I'd have thought the military would've taught you better."

"You bastard."

She hadn't thought to check farther than the vest. He'd most likely wired Grace's legs, had known Grace would be too shaken up to tell PJ.

Grace was gone, but Kevin was still alive. His eyes drooped—he'd obviously been drugged and he was on his knees.

Alek's face was as scarred as she'd remembered. Something inside her surged when she saw what he'd done to Kevin, tying his wrists together, and to the closet door for good measure.

She swayed, the vest hanging heavily on her frame. "Get the hell away from my father."

Alek held his knife steady, the blade gleaming under the overhead lighting. "I'm afraid I can't do that. But that's sweet of you to call Peter your father. Something for him to cherish when he's dying."

Alek's knife was curved, with a particularly vicious-looking blade. PJ knew that members of the Russian Mafia used similar knives as their weapon of choice, liked to slit their victim's throats . . . the way Alek had slit her mother's and father's.

She didn't want to be here, reliving this, but Alek seemed determined to have it happen that way, to make her watch Kevin bleed to death. And this time if she tried to run, she would die instantly.

But if she didn't run, she was going to die anyway.

"Let's call Ana. If she won't come to the party, then we'll bring the party to her. She can hide in the closet, the way you told her to do last time."

He dialed the phone with one hand, the other still holding the knife to Kevin's throat. Someone answered the phone, but before they could speak, Alek said, "I'll only speak with Ana."

There was a long pause—Alek had put the phone on speaker, and she heard people calling for her sister. Moments later, she heard Jamie's breathless voice.

"PJ, are you okay?"

"I'm okay," she said, not giving a shit if Alek wanted her to respond or not. He shot her a warning look and shoved the tip of the knife into Kevin's skin so it drew blood. PJ pressed her lips together in a silent show of surrender... even though she had no intention of doing so.

"Patricia Jane and Kevin are all right for now. So sorry about Grace," Alek said.

"You've been after us a long time," Jamie said. "It must've been hard for you, being on the outs with your family, being the disappointment."

"Don't try to out-psych me, Ana. It can't be done," Alek promised her.

"He's right, Jamie—he's waited a long time for this moment. We shouldn't ruin it for him," PJ said, then turned her attention back to Alek. "Was killing your best friend part of your father's wishes?"

"Let's leave my father out of this."

"Why? Our mother didn't. She was the one who ruined your family, took it down. And you've never been able to get over it," PJ said, egging him on.

"It couldn't have been easy, hiding yourself, with your face like that," Jamie broke in. "Not truly being able to live. You were in the same hell we were, Alek."

He touched the roughness of his cheek, his fingers lingering over the scarred flesh. "I know Peter told you he saved my life."

It was only then that PJ saw the can of gasoline and the matches that were next to Alek on the floor.

"And you're not going to return the favor," she spat, struggled against the bonds around her wrists.

"No," he agreed. "Time is up, PJ."

"You were his best friend."

"And that's what kept you girls alive for so long," Alek said absently, staring down at Kevin's face.

"You still have time to make things right, Alek. To stop this."

"That time is gone."

"Snipers are in place—I repeat, snipers are in place."

The announcement hadn't come from Jamie, but Alek heard it in the background, over the open phone line, just the same. "Snipers in place? Wonderful."

He moved toward PJ with the grace of a seasoned predator. She immediately crouched low, tried to circle him—but her balance was off, with both her hands tied behind her back. She kicked him viciously, a nice blow, but it was as if the man didn't feel pain. As if he didn't feel anything at all.

Within seconds, he flipped her to the ground, held her by the throat as she struggled, kicking her legs and bucking her upper body off the floor.

"My, my, you do know how to fight, little one," he murmured against her ear. She turned her face away, and he simply laughed. "We might have to have some fun before you die."

"Let go of her, Alek," Kevin said, shocking both of them, as his voice was firm and strong. But Alek quickly pushed that aside, dragging PJ to her feet and over to the window, using her body as a shield, ducking behind her.

"Let's see how good that sniper really is," Alek said, and PJ closed her eyes and thought of Saint.

I won't leave you—I'll be back.

She would be, had to be.

CHAPTER
21

Nick flanked Chris's right side, Jake, his left, each man staring through the scope of their own rifle in order to set Chris up for the shot.

Chris could see shadows moving through the shadeless window. It was slightly tinted to keep sunlight out when school was in session, which made it hard to see through in the dark as well, but with the infrared goggles, he could easily differentiate a man's figure. "That could be Kevin."

Suddenly, the man was gone and all three of the brothers had a clear view inside the hallway—one man in a kneeling position on the floor, had to be Kevin . . . and Alek and PJ, circling each other.

"Fuck—stop fucking moving, PJ," Chris whispered urgently, as if she could hear him.

"What? Speak up," Jake was saying into his mike. "He knows," Jake said to Chris now. "*Shit*, Alek knows snipers are posted."

They watched helplessly as Alek dragged PJ toward the window, facing them, using her body to block his.

"Motherfucking cowardly piece of shit," Nick muttered, his eye never moving from the scope.

Chris stared through the infrared for a few seconds before he realized his fingers were rubbing together around the trigger of the rifle. There was never a flash of light when he was going to take someone's life—but now he pulled the goggles off and threw them to the side.

"Enough of this shit," he said, stared through his scope as the figures blurred with an image of Mark's face for just a second . . . and then he saw the two shadows.

"You've got a millimeter—you're going to be close as hell," Nick told him.

The only part of Alek he could see was half his face, staring out at them from behind PJ's head. "Close is okay," he told his brother.

"You can do this," Nick told him. "I've seen you make tighter shots with less prep."

Chris nodded, felt the trickle of sweat run down his back. Nick wiped Chris's brow, the way Mark would have, and fuck, Mark's face was in front of him.

Chris pulled back from the scope and forced himself to breathe.

"I don't know what happened out there with Mark,"

Nick said, "but I know that whatever you did, it was the right thing."

Chris had been stupid to think that his brothers wouldn't suspect what he'd had to do. They'd never ask, though, and he'd never, ever have to tell them.

"It's just another job," Jake told him. "That's the way you need to look at it. Now's not the time to fuck up your perfect record. Take the motherfucking shot so I can go home and get married."

Chris closed his eyes tight at Jake's demand as a small, harsh laugh came from his throat. It was just the release he'd needed.

And then, it was as if Mark was somehow guiding him, moving his hand to adjust the scope first and then leading it to the trigger. It felt at once completely unfamiliar and yet as comfortable as it ever had.

Nothing's changed. Nothing—and everything.

"Two shots fired from inside," Jake reported as he was fed the intel through the mike earpiece he wore.

It was time to take the shot—Alek shifted slightly, PJ moved right, and yes, there, right fucking there.

The shot sailed cleanly through the window—Chris held his breath as he watched Alek slump to the ground, taking PJ with him.

When the window shattered, PJ wasn't sure she hadn't been hit. It took her a minute before she realized she could crawl out from Alek's heavy body—remembered how, just minutes before, Alek had the upper hand, had her by the throat, and she'd been powerless to stop him.

Now she grabbed that knife and clumsily cut the bonds so her hands were free.

Kevin. Oh, my God. She crawled to him, her hands and knees cut by the broken glass, forgetting she still wore the explosive vest. Her main concern was Kevin, and he was bleeding out.

Alek, don't do this—you don't want to do this, she'd heard Kevin cry out, moments before Alek shot him.

"Stay with me," she told Kevin now as she attempted to stanch the bleeding from his stomach with her hands. "Jamie . . . Saint . . . someone—help us, please!"

Saint rushed in with Jamie and Lester, behind the SWAT team.

"Suspect is dead—repeat, suspect is dead. We need a bus. One of the hostages is down."

Saint's heart lurched when he heard that. He pushed forward, saw PJ holding Kevin's head in her lap.

She hadn't even taken off the vest of C4.

He grabbed one of the SWAT team. "She's still wearing the vest—where's the detonator?"

"We'll find it," the man assured Saint.

Jamie was next to PJ, on her knees. She'd taken off her sweater and was pressing the fabric to Kevin's stomach as PJ attempted to take off the vest.

But her hands were smeared with blood.

Immediately, Saint was in front of her. Mass confusion surged around them, but he was calm as he told her "I've got this."

"I don't know where the detonator is, it could blow at any second—I've got to get out of here."

He agreed, helped her to her feet. She paused to look at Jamie.

"I'll stay with him," Jamie insisted. "Get that thing off you."

"Do you know if it's on a timer?" Saint asked as they hurried outside, ushered by two FBI agents.

"I don't think so, but I can't be sure."

"Bomb squad's coming in," one of the agents told her, but Saint had already knelt in front of her—because bomb squad, his ass.

Nick might be the expert in demolitions, but that's because Saint had taught him every fucking thing he knew.

In seconds, he'd clipped the wires, PJ standing stock-still. Her hands were fisted at her sides, she stared straight ahead and every fiber of her being screamed for him to get the damned vest off her.

"I'm trying, baby—I'll get it," he told her as he fingered three wires, took a breath and cut the white one. "Done."

Then he cut straight up the front of the Velcro on the vest and stood to push it off her shoulders, handing it to one of the agents as PJ collapsed against his chest. "It's over, Patricia. It's all over."

Jamie rode in the ambulance with Kevin as it bounced over potholes.

"Kevin, please, just stay with us, okay? I didn't mean what I said. Please—you can't die on me before I apologize."

Nothing. She grabbed his hand and squeezed it. It was so cold—he was so pale, and the EMT was working furiously, and she felt dizzy with grief, exhausted and running on adrenaline at the same time.

She hadn't seen Chris before she'd left the scene. Those final moments were a part of a hazy memory, where time had stood still and she willed him to take the shot.

"He's coding!" the EMT called to the driver, and then he began CPR.

"We're here," the driver called back as the bus jolted to a stop.

"Agent Michaels, you're going to have to let go and step aside," the EMT instructed as the doors opened and the stretcher holding Kevin was pulled away from her.

She waited until the path was clear and went to jump down herself, but a cramp hit, low, pelvic—not good. She took a deep breath. *Cramping under stress is normal,* she reminded herself, but it took hold of her again and then she felt the bleeding.

"Ma'am, are you okay?" One of the doctors grabbed her arm.

"No. I'm pregnant. I don't feel well. Cramping."

"Get another stretcher over here," he yelled. "Take some breaths—we'll get you on a monitor, check things."

"My father—"

"They're working on him," he promised as he eased her onto the stretcher and wheeled her through the ER. "Ma'am, I'm going to give you something to stop the cramping. Nothing that will hurt the baby. It's just going to make you sleepy."

"Okay." She felt the IV needle prick her skin, watched the doctor work fast to set up the fluid, and then everything was blissful.

She woke with Chris next to her in the hospital bed, his face also on her pillow. He looked exhausted, but not sad.

"The baby?"

"Fine. It's fine. Mild cramping. Some spotting. Not unusual, given your recent exertion. They did an ultrasound," he assured her.

She nodded, closed her eyes as grateful tears spilled from them.

"However, the doctor wants you on bed rest if you can't control yourself in the future."

She laughed at that. "I'm sure you told him you'd take charge."

"I think you'll do a damned fine job of that on your own."

She was scared to ask, but she had to. "Kevin?"

"He made it through surgery, but he's still critical. The next couple of hours should tell us what we need to know."

She brought a hand up to his cheek. "Thank you. You saved them—saved him and PJ. Saved me. I would've forgiven you. You have to know that."

"Yeah, I know."

"I'm not used to this role—passive. Watching from the sidelines."

"You did a hell of a lot more than watch, Jamie."

"And I'm free . . . really free," she murmured, hearing the wonder in her own voice at the thought of leaving her past behind her, really and truly. "When can I get out of here? Because I'm ready to start living."

He gave her a small grin. "Stay and rest until we hear

about Kevin. Then we'll go home. Because we've got a wedding to go to—Jake's getting married on Friday."

His hand rested on her belly and she covered it with her own. "Me, I'm patient . . . but not for much longer," he told her. "I'm marrying you, Jamie."

She shifted so she could look him directly in the eyes. "That's good to know, because I already planned on it."

CHAPTER
22

Saint turned from the stove when he heard PJ come into the kitchen. He'd left her sleeping while he started dinner, gumbo and rice, and now she sauntered in wearing his shorts and sleeveless undershirt. And she looked damned fine in both. Better, of course, in nothing, but he'd make short work of them soon enough.

"Dinner won't be ready for another couple of hours," he told her. They'd all been up late the night before, waiting in the hospital until Kevin came through surgery and had been declared stable.

He'd remain in the New York hospital recovering for at least a week, and so PJ had flown them home in order to be there for Jake and Isabelle's wedding in the morning.

"I'll grab something to snack on, then." She opened one of the cabinets and stopped short. She closed it and opened another and had the same reaction

"Problem?" Saint asked.

She shook her head no, her eyes wide and innocent. Too innocent. "I just didn't know you liked sugared cereals so much."

"Well, I do. I need to start adding more sugar to my diet." Saint didn't look her in the eyes, concentrating on stirring the rice in front of him.

"That's why you have those boxes of cookies in the cabinet."

"Yes. That's exactly why." He turned back to the stove to stir the gumbo and heard her chuckle a little. He put down the spoon and turned to her again. "Don't you dare think that you have me wrapped around your little finger, Patricia Jane. I may be in love with you, but no one has ever done that to me and no one ever will." Even Emeline hadn't been able to do that. But PJ . . .

He sighed.

"I'd never think that, Saint," she said softly, her eyes shining a little with tears—and aw, fuck . . .

"Just because I bought a few of your favorite cereals—"

"Eight of my favorite cereals," she pointed out helpfully.

"—and a few boxes of cookies—"

"I counted sixteen boxes."

"—does not mean that you have me wrapped around your finger," he finished triumphantly.

"Thanks."

"For what?" he moved closer, still attempting to glower. She lowered her head to his chest. "For babying me. I can't believe you . . . I mean, you actually . . ." She swallowed hard, unable to finish.

"Are you going to baby me for the rest of my life?" she asked finally. It came out as more of a joke, but God, the way Saint looked at her took the laughter right out of her and replaced it with a longing she hadn't realized was there.

"Yeah, I think I might just do that," he drawled. "Is that a problem?"

She opened her mouth to tell him that it would be, that she'd never allowed that to happen and never would. But what came out was something unexpected—unexpected and real. "No, it's not a problem at all."

"Then it's settled," he said gruffly, and yes, it was settled, but it was certainly not over. Not by a long shot.

"Can I fucking get married now?" Jake called out over the din that was surprisingly loud for four-thirty in the morning.

Everyone stopped talking as Kenny said, "Jake, please," and cut his gaze toward the chaplain.

The chaplain, in turn, put his hand on Kenny's arm. "It's okay. I've known Jake for a long time."

Nick snorted and Jake made the *You see?* motion. Kenny simply shook his head—and next to Jamie, Chris laughed.

It was so good to hear him laugh. It made her grab his hand a bit tighter and he responded in kind.

"Yes, Jake, you can get married now," the chaplain told him. "Let's just make sure Isabelle's ready, okay?"

"She's ready," Jake muttered.

Last night, Jamie had finally met Isabelle and Kaylee. And then Kenny Waldron joined the party, and really, no one had gotten to sleep much before two that morning. Jake, who had never gone to sleep, insisted on going out to get donuts. With Isabelle.

The ceremony was to take place just before sunrise. The chaplain from the base had arrived at the house just after four, and Chris woke Jamie, who'd rubbed the sleep from her eyes and pulled on the dress she'd borrowed from Kaylee.

All three of the brothers and she and Kaylee and Isabelle stayed in the house last night, as well as Chris's father.

Saint and PJ arrived just after the chaplain. Jamie couldn't ever remember seeing her sister that happy. Then again, she couldn't remember being this happy herself.

Kevin would make a full recovery. They had some repairing of their relationship—and Kevin had to face his supervisor regarding their case—but they'd get through it. They always did.

"Izzy's ready," Kaylee said, coming into the living room.

"Then let's begin. Everyone, please, take your places," the chaplain requested as Isabelle came around the corner and into the living room.

Jake wore a suit, not his uniform—Isabelle's request, Jamie knew—while Isabelle wore a simple white column dress, hair loose, feet bare.

Perfect. It was simply perfect.

Jake—loud, wild Jake—the second he saw Isabelle, he completely melted right before their eyes. Jamie swore there was a collective sigh, and suddenly there wasn't a dry eye in the room.

All the danger, the fear, the pain . . . in this room, none of that mattered. It was only about Jake and Isabelle and their love—their commitment affirmed in this simple ceremony— and it was the most beautiful thing Jamie had ever seen.

"They're so beautiful together," she whispered to Chris as Jake and Isabelle spoke their vows quietly to each other, as if they were the only two people on earth.

Right now, she supposed they were.

"They've been to hell and back together—it's only made them stronger." His hand rested on her belly. From across the way, Chris's father winked at her, and yes, it had all been worth it.

No matter what happened now, she and PJ had a new family they were a part of—they had brand-new lives.

"You may now kiss the bride," the chaplain said.

And Jake did, in a sweeping, heart-stopping gesture that was as romantic as it was primal.

Jamie was the first one to clap, and then the others joined in as the newly married couple broke apart, smiling.

And then Jake opened the sliding glass door that led out onto the back deck of the house and they all trailed outside, stared out toward the woods as the sun began to rise over the trees.

Jamie felt the lump form in her throat as she thought about why they were having the ceremony this early. Chris told her about Jake and this tradition of watching the sunrise, how Jake did it every single morning as a child so he could know he'd survived another day. How all three brothers—and their father—now did it every single morning too, no matter where in the world they were.

A tradition she would now be a part of as well, because standing here in the soft glow of dawn, she knew for sure that they were all survivors. And with Chris's hands on her belly, she knew that whatever she might've lost in the past was nothing compared to the family she'd just gained.

Want more of Stephanie Tyler's
dangerously sexy suspense?
Read on for a sneak peek inside her
hot new novel

LIE
WITH
ME

Coming soon from Dell

CHAPTER
1

The sleek, dark bitch tailing him over the crest of the mountain was definitely not standard Army issue.

Cameron Moore ignored both the snow swirling furiously around his Harley and the classified stealth helo on his six as he began his ascent up the thin, curved ridge ringed by stone that would lead him to his destination.

The hairs on the back of his neck had risen half a mile earlier when he'd heard the familiar thump of the quiet bird over the roar of his bike. Now his gut tightened in tandem with the heavy whir of the rotors and *fuck*, he'd thought this was over and done with.

He'd had nearly five months of freedom, having been assured that his debt was paid in full, which meant there would be no more black ops jobs involving the CIA and this fucking helo from hell following him. But he'd been down this road before—after five years—eight years—ten years. The promise of release had never been kept, eleven years and counting.

It'll never be fully paid. You knew that . . . you just didn't want to believe it.

And still he pushed on, trying to ignore the past that wouldn't let him forget.

He'd only been back from a mission with Delta Force for forty-eight hours, on leave for the past twenty and headed to visit Dylan Scott—a man he'd met through Delta and his best friend—in the Catskills when he'd been tracked.

One of these days, Gabriel Creighton—CIA chameleon extraordinaire—wouldn't be able to find Cam anymore. The chip that had once been implanted in Cam's right forearm was only as big as a postage stamp and as slim as one too—and was long gone. He'd convinced himself that Gabriel couldn't track him without it.

Obviously, Cam had been way fucking wrong.

He didn't have to wonder what his life would be like if he'd never met the man—he'd still be in jail, serving two consecutive life sentences. And he despised Gabriel more than his father, which was really damned hard to do, considering his father had framed him for the murders and left him to rot in a maximum-security cell.

For eleven years, Gabriel had been both mentor and taskmaster. Cam had never asked Gabriel for anything, not a single goddamned favor.

The favors Gabriel insisted Cam provide for him were

always dangerous and usually above the law. Jobs that necessitated a non-CIA operator with insider information, which Cam indeed was, hiding in the job of a Delta Force operator.

If Cam's immediate supes knew what the jobs he did for Creighton really entailed, they'd never let on. And so Cam lived and worked, waiting for the magic number—the time limit Gabriel had imposed on him when Cam had been nineteen and willing to do anything to get out of that cell. A limit that only Gabriel knew.

Now he stared down at the mark on the inside of his left forearm—the result of a tattoo that had been lasered off. It wasn't completely erased, was still as much of a reminder as it would've been.

That was the thing about pasts: You could never fully eradicate them, and fuck it all, he'd tried to more than once.

Finally, he stopped the bike on the edge of one of the small cliffs and pulled as close to it as he possibly could. The wind whipped him, making it hard to hold on to his footing, never mind the heavy metal between his legs.

The stealth hovered, unable to land, but more than willing to block him. And as he stared down at the dark, cavernous chasm ahead of him, he knew his choices were limited. Going down would be the coward's way out—and he was anything but.

He'd never let go of the idea of vengeance; he tasted it like a fine wine on his tongue—it ran heated through his blood, slamming his veins with a barely concealed fury.

In all his years of military service, he'd saved a lot of people, killed more, and prayed for salvation daily.

In so many ways, he'd never left the ten-by-ten cell where he'd lived for twenty-three months, four days, and ten hours. At the time, he'd been wary of his rescuer, but he'd assumed things couldn't have gotten worse.

He'd been so fucking young—fear and bravado mixed together in a heady combination. He'd been a punk, a fighter, willing to do anything to stay alive. He had kept his pride during those years; he'd refused to let prison take that from him, the way his freedom had been ripped from him.

It had been all he had.

He finally turned around on the mountain, as he had eleven years earlier when the police chased him between a rock and a hard place. That night, the police had impounded his bike.

Cam knew that a good operative never left anything behind. He revved his bike and let it ride over the edge without him, listened as it screeched and crashed against the mountain walls below.

And then he walked to the helo and used the ropes they'd lowered to climb aboard.

Two years of max security had taught him many things: that life wasn't fair, that typically the bigger you were, the more shit you talked and the harder you went down. That this life wasn't for the weak. His time in the Rangers and Delta Force had refined those teachings until his mind functioned like that of the elite warrior he was, but make no mistake, he was still that same damned punk—and he wouldn't take Gabriel Creighton's shit anymore.

This time, he would shoot the messenger Gabriel always sent, no matter what the job entailed, and then he would walk away and deal with the consequences—any and all, because the yoke around his neck had finally tightened to where he could no longer breathe.

As it turned out, the messenger wanted to shoot him as well.

Cam noted the gun in the suit's hands as he hauled his ass into the helo, and then his gaze moved quickly to the ankle cuffs on the bench and he snapped to attention. Instead of waiting for the man to aim the Glock directly at him, Cam lunged, using the shaky motion of the struggling helo to propel himself into the man's chest even as the man barked at him to sit down.

He was too far into fight-or-flight mode to do anything else; he could smell the setup as surely as helo fuel. He'd done this dance too many times and it had never, ever looked like this before.

They went down hard, sliding into the co-pilot's seat. The gun clattered from the suit's hands and Cam stared into his eyes. It was the same man—always the same man, although he never spoke to Cam, had always pointed to the phone or the laptop where Cam would get his orders.

Cam wondered what this guy had done in his life to become Gabriel's minion.

"We...talk..." the suit croaked while Cam kept his forearm across his throat. He wondered what his story would be—if he'd gain anything by letting the man speak his piece.

But the ache in his gut was swift and sudden as he remembered that he didn't trust most people, especially strangers.

"I don't talk to people who want to kill me." As quickly and cleanly as possible, Cam shifted and put his hands on either side of the man's head. A sharp twist to the right and the suit was gone, his eyes open, his stare as dead as he was.

But the fight wasn't over yet.

Cam wouldn't let the pilots take off with him inside, would rather free-fall out than be carried off, and they knew that—Cam had seen it in the brace of the co-pilot's back the second he'd climbed on board—and as the man lunged, Cam was ready, even as the obviously well-trained man threw a nice left hook that caught Cam square on the jaw. The helo banked a hard left and Cam lost his footing for a second, hitting his head on a sharp piece of metal used to hold the hooks for the parachutes. The co-pilot also fell, and Cam was the quicker one up and at the ready, slamming his boot into the guy's chest.

The man struggled, his hands around Cam's ankle, but Cam's footing was too strong. The co-pilot knew Cam was leaving alive and didn't care who he took out in his wake.

"Who the hell sent you?" he asked, but neither man answered. "Where are you supposed to bring me?"

Again, nothing.

Cam didn't know friends from enemies anymore in this game, the wilderness of mirrors that spooks and spies dealt with on a daily—and lifetime—basis. And as he stared between the man under his boot and the pilot, who held a gun in a shaky hand while he tried to wrestle the helo with the other, Cam told him, "My fight's not with you."

The man's eyes held him for a second. Cam wondered if he'd been pressed into service as well or if he was flying this bastard bird of his own free will.

It didn't matter—he didn't have time to play savior now, not when he'd just committed suicide himself. "I'm out of here."

He took his foot off the man's chest, turned, and didn't look back, wondered for a fleeting second if he'd get shot in the back, and then dropped out of the helo and onto the hard ground with a vicious slam. He curled in a ball as the bird rose, the wind buffeting him with a harsh hand as the stealth left him behind and headed back to report the incident to Gabriel.

As he stared after the helo, well after its lights disappeared, he wondered why they hell they hadn't simply killed him on the ground when they'd had the chance—or while he was climbing up into the helo. When he was vulnerable.

What the hell did he know that made him worth something? What did Gabriel want from him?

After he'd wiped the blood off his hands and his face with snow, Cam hitched a ride with a trucker, got dropped off halfway up the mountain to Dylan's house, and then ran the rest of the way, his bag slapping against his back, wind whipping his face—his heart beating so fast from stress and fear he was pretty damned sure it would rip from his chest.

Dylan opened the door as Cam pounded on it. He didn't ask any questions, not even when Cam shoved him aside and slammed the door behind him to peer out the window.

He hadn't been followed. He wouldn't be—not tonight. Probably not tomorrow, but when he reported back into work, there could be consequences.

You've lived with the consequences for years—how much fucking worse could it be?

He felt empowered and freaked all at once.

"Did you crash?" Dylan asked finally.

Cam turned and spoke after he'd caught his breath. His hands were shaking. He'd never been like this on a mission before but this . . . this was personal. His life.

The words spilled out. "Gabriel sent a stealth bird—same kind, same suit waiting for me. He had a gun—there were restraints. I killed him and the helo took off with the dead guy and the pilots."

"Breathe, man, breathe." Dylan handed him a brandy; Cam gulped it down and then took another hit before he took the towel from him.

He stared at his friend. "They wanted intel from me—or else they could've killed me a thousand times over before I got on board. I'm done, Dylan. No way out."

His friend didn't say anything for a long moment, and then he got up and walked to a bookshelf. He pulled out a hardcover book and handed it to Cam. "Open to the back—the author."

Cam did as Dylan asked, stared at the picture of a beautiful young woman named Skylar Slavin at the back of the thriller. "Are you setting me up with her? Because I don't think I'm really dating material right now."

"She's Gabriel Creighton's daughter, Cam. His only child. The only thing he cares about in this fucking world. Skylar Slavin's the key to your future."

Cam didn't say anything, continuing to stare at the picture as the woman with the clear green eyes stared back at him. She wasn't smiling; in fact, he'd have to say she looked slightly haunted.

But still, the woman had to have had a better life than

him—had to have been loved and protected by her father. She was probably just like him, cold and cunning with a heart of steel.

"How long have you known about her?" Cam demanded. Dylan simply shrugged, that noncommittal kind he typically reserved for authority figures. Which was why he hadn't lasted long in the military at all, but had somehow managed to get out with an honorable discharge and several medals of honor.

Fucking bastard

"How long?" he asked again, this time with enough of an edge to his voice for Dylan to know this wasn't the time to fuck around.

"Five months."

"Five months? Five motherfucking months?" Nearly blind from rage, Cam leapt at his best friend in the world, ready to kill him as soon as he could wrap his hands around the man's neck.

Dylan readied for him, but Cam was like a charging bull and knocked him to the ground hard. Dylan grunted as he attempted to roll Cam off him; when he couldn't, he swung and punched Cam in the face a couple of times, opening the gash above his eye again.

"Fucking asshole," Cam said through clenched teeth, the blood dripping into his eye and onto Dylan's shirt. "You had something on Gabriel and you didn't tell me?"

"Because you weren't ready to hear it—to use it," Dylan shouted, his breath coming in quick gasps because Cam was sitting on his chest, punching him anywhere he could.

He and Dylan were evenly matched, but not when Cam's temper was riled with anything involving Gabriel

Creighton. Then he ran on pure adrenaline, an anger machine.

"I found out after your last mission. It wouldn't have changed the outcome. You always said . . . it was your fight. That I needed to . . . stay out of it. And . . . I did. For the most part. Jesus Christ, Cam—Gabriel was leaving you alone—and I didn't want you to bring trouble on yourself you didn't need." Dylan took a stuttered breath while holding his rib cage. "I'm going to kill you if you broke my ribs."

Cam leaned back on his elbows and tried to ignore the blood running from Dylan's nose. It was running from Cam's own mouth as well.

"Look, tonight, you made the move. There's no turning back. If I told you about Gabriel's kid earlier . . . I didn't want you to do anything else that could weigh on your conscience. Didn't want to give you a choice like that, didn't want you to run off half-cocked and do something that really would land your ass in jail, for good this time." Dylan fell back on the carpet heavily. "You weren't ready until tonight. I know you, Cam. Now you've got no choice but to move forward out of hell."

Cam let his head fall back and stared up at the high-beamed ceiling. Of course, Dylan was right, not that Cam would admit that to the man's face, or in writing. Ever. Dylan liked to say that Cam had been born with an extra dose of conscience, while Dylan himself had skipped that line entirely when they were handing them out. Probably off getting laid somewhere, Dylan would say.

Dylan—the man who would never betray him, the one who knew him better than anyone.

"I'm sorry, man," Cam breathed, his gaze still level with

the ceiling instead of his friend's face until he heard a crack and a small whimper—Dylan setting his own nose back in place. His friend would have two black eyes by morning. "So you want me to fuck with his family?"

"He fucked with yours, didn't he?" Dylan's eyes blazed. His friend was a fierce warrior and just as fiercely loyal when it came to Cam.

"I don't have proof." Cam's jaw hurt from keeping it clenched, and both he and his friend knew that he had no way of getting any.

Gabriel Creighton had a lot of ways to kill a man. Cam's father, just as many. But that Gabriel would kill Howie didn't make sense. Pretending to help in the search for what happened to Howie kept Cam on the line just as effectively.

And still, the questions always lingered. He stared down at the photo on the book and Skylar stared back at him. "What the hell do I do, man—hold her hostage?"

"Yeah, for starters. Gabriel's obviously kept her existence a secret for a reason, so tell him you'll expose her as his daughter. Kidnap her. Seduce her and make her fall in love with you. Tell him you'll kill her. And then be prepared to do that if it's necessary."

Cam stared at his friend. "Why the hell would I need to kill her?"

"If it comes down to you or her, it needs to be you. You have to be prepared to make any and every choice to take this all the way. Whatever gets the job done."

Jesus, that made the already splitting pain starting in his head worsen. "What's to stop him from throwing my ass in jail—or killing me?"

"He can't, if he knows you and another person know

about his daughter. Tell Gabriel that someone else knows who Skylar is. I'm your backup, your safety. Gabriel doesn't know about me—he'll only know that if you die, Skylar will never be safe. The two of you will come to a mutual agreement to live and let live."

Dylan had been straddling the line for far too long, and yet Cam knew his friend was absolutely right. "I need a better plan. I need time."

"You don't have that. Once you threaten to expose her, it's over. Besides, she's kind of famous."

Kind of, yes. He stared at her picture at the back of the book again and his stomach turned.

Like father, like daughter.

It was finally time. "How did you find out about this?"

Dylan sighed before he answered. Then: "I slept with someone. Broke into her files. And then she shot me, so I figured it was pretty damned important information."

Jesus. Dylan cut it closer to the edge than ever. Never went by the same name twice; Cam wasn't even sure what his real name was anymore. He'd met the man as Dylan Scott five years earlier—they'd served together in Delta for mere months before Dylan retired—and that's the only name Cam would call him. Except *asshole,* and yeah, he'd called his friend that many times.

Dylan rattled off the name and address. "She's on vacation for a week." He paused. "Why don't you let me take care of all this?"

It would be too easy to let Dylan do it, to take himself off the hook. He'd been passive in this situation for far too long, fighting to keep the street kid inside of him dead and buried, and his friend knew that better than anyone.

And still, Dylan was a good enough friend to make that offer.

"Thanks. But this is my fight. Always has been." He despised Gabriel—would have no problem putting his hands around the man's neck and squeezing tight, but slowly, so he could watch his struggle, the way Gabriel had been watching Cam struggle for years.

Payback would be fucking fantastic, to crush that bastard under his shoe, to watch everything he'd worked for crumble, like the soul-sucking little bitch he really was.

It was easy for Gabriel to sit back and fire orders, to have the ultimate power over Cam. Cam knew the man was nothing more than an empty, pathetic shell who took out his misery on other people. The world was full of sad little people like that, who reveled in what little power they had to make others feel as shitty as they did—but most people could only dream of getting revenge on their bosses.

Cam's was a reality, and she was staring at him from the photograph.

Gabriel would always tell him, *You don't get something for nothing.* Gabriel would finally learn the truth of those words at Cam's hands.

And if the man didn't comply, didn't care enough about his flesh and blood, Cam would have to decide what he'd do next.

You don't get something for nothing.

"You do this and then you let it go," Dylan said quietly, and Cam realized he was holding the book so tightly he'd bent the hard covers.

Did he even know how to let it go? He'd lived with it for so long, it was like a well-worn fabric. An excuse. Something to fall back on when things were shitty. Woven into the texture of his life.

Could he really do this?

You have no fucking choice, unless you want to spend the rest of your life hiding.

He finally had collateral. Leverage. He'd use it to his full advantage and had to be prepared to do anything it took to grab hold of his freedom.